SWORN IN DECEIT

Victoria Lum

Sworn in Deceit

By Victoria Lum

Published by Eternal Hearts Publishing

Editing by Theresa Leigh and Amy Briggs

Proofreading by Virginia Tesi Carey

ISBN (Paperback): 978-1-969859-01-4

ISBN (E-Book): 978-1-969859-00-7

Author's Note

This is a dark romance featuring antiheroes doing bad things to villains. Your mental health is paramount to me. For a list of potential areas of sensitive content, please visit:

https://www.victorialum.com/sensitive-content-information

Dedication

To my ladies who don't see color when looking at red flags, I hope you love the king of the underworld, Elias Kent.

Playlist

"Für Elise (Epic Trailer Version)" – Hidden Citizens
"The Phoenix" – Fall Out Boy
"Will I Make It Out Alive" – Tommee Profitt (feat. Jessie Early)
"Dangerous" – Sleep Token
"Moon" – Mandrazo & Mangusx
"Paint it Black (Epic Trailer Version)" – Hidden Citizens (feat. Rånya)
"Cravin'" – Stileto & Kendyle Paige
"Every Breath You Take" – Chase Holfelder

The Syndicate Codex

For the vow. No mercy. Our ruin for their fall.

Rule One: Look them in the eye before you pull the trigger.
Rule Two: Tell them their sins.
Rule Three: No innocent women or children.

Everything else is fair game.

—Unofficial Excerpt, *The Antihero Syndicate Charter*

Prologue: THE DEVIL'S LAIR

THE FBI AGENT

Saints Hollow Neighborhood in Chicago, Illinois

So this is what the devil's lair looks like.

Across the street, a well-fortified complex of dark marble or limestone exteriors looms among the decaying historic neighborhood. Towering walls and hedges protect it from the public eye.

I keep the engine off. No heat. No radio. No movement that might give away how I've been here for fourteen days, watching the compound from across the street, hoping to spot something that'll tell me what Elias Kent's role is in The Association.

Guards. At least four I can spot. All armed and alert.

Snow drifts down, but everything's silent—like a graveyard.

The first time I heard of The Association was in a redacted agency email mistakenly sent to me. The email vanished while I was reading it, like someone had deleted it permanently from the servers.

IT called it a technical hiccup.

It wasn't.

In their world, The Association is above the law. Evidence doesn't disappear. It gets corrected.

A wise person would look away. But I didn't.

My curiosity cost me.

An ache settles over my lungs as I reach into my suit pocket and pull out my wallet.

I stare at the picture, the edges marred with dried blood. I trace the nose, the lips I remember as if it were yesterday. Then I flip it over to the message scrawled on the back.

Stop looking. Erase The Association from your memory. This is your final warning.

Fury churns up my spine and I snap my wallet shut.

Drop it, Tristan. It's above your pay grade.

As if evil has a pay grade.

A movement on the second-floor window catches my eye. I pull out my binoculars and adjust the focus.

A woman stands behind the glass like an antique doll kept in a case.

Long brown hair, her gray eyes stare forlornly out into the street. Her hand clutches something on her chest...a necklace?

Lana Anderson doesn't look like a bride in love.

I pick up the fragment of The Antihero Syndicate charter I found a few months ago.

Rule Three: no innocent women or children.

"Do you count as innocent, Lana Anderson?" I murmur. "Or is your husband using Rule Three to protect you?"

I blow out a breath, my exhale a ghostly vapor writhing through the air.

Then I open a new document—official letterhead, sterile wording. If I don't survive this, at least there's a paper record.

I will figure out what Elias Kent is hiding.

Then, I will take down The Association.

FEDERAL BUREAU OF INVESTIGATION

Criminal Investigation Division—Internal Memorandum
From: Special Agent Tristan Clarke
To: Director of Organized Crime Division
Subject: Preliminary Findings—Anderson/Kent Investigation

Subject #1 Under Surveillance: *Kent, Elias.* Aliases: **Rook**, king of the underworld, dealer in secrets. Multiple links to underground syndicates. Formerly associated with the old-money Anderson family.

Subject #2 Under Surveillance: *Anderson, Lana.* Heiress to Fleur Entertainment. Entered a suspicious marriage with Kent approximately three months ago. Circumstances remain unclear.

Observed Anomalies:

- Frosty relationship between Anderson and Kent.
- Kent demonstrates protective behavior toward spouse while maintaining ties to criminals.
- New business dealings between the Andersons and The Association have surfaced.

Assessment: Unclear if Lana Anderson is a victim or a collaborator. May be a viable asset. Recommend a direct interview for clarity.

Known Associates (The Antihero Syndicate):
Queen—Sofia Kent
Bishop—Sebastian McEntyre
Knight—Ren (last name unknown)

King—Rafael Mancini
Pawn—Aleksei Morozov

Target Network (The Association Council; Ruling Families Known as The Six):

Berishas, Carusos, Kongs, Ivanovs, Alvarezes, and O'Callaghans

Chapter 1: BLACK VENOM

ELIAS

Lower East Side, Manhattan, New York City, Three Months Prior

Obsession is a disease. It writhes through the body like black venom, insidious and corrupting. Devotion curdles into fixation.

Until one day, it all ends in destruction.

"Boss, it'll rain soon. If we don't start—"

I lift a hand, and John immediately shuts up. He's been my driver for the past five years. He should know better.

No one interrupts me as I watch *her* from the dark sedan, keeping my distance.

My poisonous obsession. The woman I hate.

Except for twenty-eight minutes a day when I let myself forget.

The Anderson princess graced a tiny Albanian café with her presence this dreary September New York morning. She clearly got fooled by the cozy exterior—red bricks, faded awnings, blue shutters—and completely missed the graffiti tagging the dumpsters and the questionable men idling in cars nearby.

I'm here because I finally got a name—and I'm going to collect.

But of course my *zemër* chooses this morning to drink her morning roast inside a front for the Albanian mob.

Lana laughs at something the waitress says. The girl is skittish, too young, too frightened, and unease flickers in my gut. I've seen these tells on my sister's face before, and I'm hit with an urge to protect this woman from whatever she's dealing with.

But then Lana gestures wildly, her face animated as she responds to the girl.

The stress melts off the waitress's face, and she smiles.

I grip the book on my lap—Lana's favorite book, a rendition of Hades and Persephone's love story—wishing I could hear her laugh up close.

That's what Lana Anderson does to you. She blazes into your life, all warmth, sunshine, and fucking roses, and you have no choice but to be mesmerized by her. I want to bottle her brightness, inject the essence into my veins, and let it wash over me.

An antidote to my obsession. Or the fatal dose.

But no, I can't die yet. My one certainty is revenge. Everything else is an indulgence I've rationed to twenty-eight minutes each day.

She brings her cup to her lips, her pinkie finger sticking out like she's having tea with royalty.

Close your eyes. Smell the coffee.

Lana's eyes flutter shut, her lush lashes fanning across her ivory cheeks. A small smile tips her lips as she inhales. I can almost hear her audible sigh of contentment.

One small sip. Lick your lips. Then go in for a fuller taste.

My breathing quickens.

Her thick brown hair cascades down her back in silky waves as she takes the tiniest sip, her eyes brightening with delight, then goes back for another taste with gusto, downing the rest of her drink in one gulp.

My lips twitch into a smile. This is my favorite part, because it reminds me of the past I lost. But I don't think about that, because right now, that past is still within grasp.

Nothing else matters.

Lana bites her full lip, her face flushing. I know what she's thinking, because she told me almost twenty years ago.

"Kian! Stop laughing." She stuffs the rest of the chocolates into her mouth, cheeks bulging.

She looks like a cute little chipmunk.

"How embarrassing," she manages once she swallows, eyes sparkling. "Mom would roll over in her grave."

"Why?" I grin, love-drunk on her.

"Ladies don't eat like cavemen."

"You'll never be a caveman, Elise."

Her sweet laughter echoes in my head. I still remember how my heart stuttered when she leaned in and kissed my cheek.

Kian and Elise belong in another lifetime. A time when we went by different names and were completely different people.

The echo fades. The present snaps back into focus.

The waitress jerks, her head whipping toward the back. I frown, the earlier unease churning once more.

Lana cocks her head. Her sharp mind knows something's off with the girl.

She says something to the server, and the girl shakes her head, eyes frantic. Lana's frown deepens. She tucks a curl behind her ear.

My fingers twitch. I imagine that silkiness wrapped around my fingers, skimming my face—*if* I went to her.

I won't.

But in another life, she'd trail her fingers up my chest, a teasing smile on her lips.

She'd recognize me.

Not as the mobster she's wary of, but as a boy from the past who went by another name. A boy without the ugly scar on his face and blood on his hands.

My jaw tics as I catalog her—her tan dress straining over her sensual curves, the faintest hint of cleavage playing peekaboo, her fiddling with a small puzzle box she still hasn't managed to open yet. We're on the third week with this one, a record for her.

It never seems enough—these twenty-eight minutes representing a number that's haunted my darkest and happiest moments. There are always details I miss, and I absorb them like a starving man.

Ping.

Twenty minutes.

Fuck. I'm running out of time.

A memory drifts into my mind. A beautiful girl who smelled like roses. Her luminous gray eyes sparkled with mischief as she plopped down beside me in the rundown park near my home, looking completely out of place in a seedy Chicago neighborhood controlled by the Albanian mob.

After pulling my silver lighter from my pocket, I click it on and off. It belonged to my father and was the only thing that survived the night my world ended. The sound takes the edge off, but useless memories still hum beneath the surface.

A lanky man with tats on his face and a leather jacket swaggers into view, his lips curled into a sneer. My hackles rise. Lana stiffens. The server flinches when he leans down and mutters into her ear.

Then he does the unforgivable.

He touches Lana. Drags his filthy, disgusting finger over her unsullied skin.

Skin even I don't deserve to touch because I'm dirty, depraved, and not worthy.

A growl rumbles in my chest. John clears his throat. His eyes catch mine in the rearview mirror.

"Should I—" he begins.

"No." My voice is quiet. Cold.

I will handle him.

Lana balls her fists and stands, getting in his face. Her untouched water sloshes onto the table. She points to the girl, then at him, her mouth moving at breakneck speed, clearly giving him a piece of her mind.

Blistering heat rushes up my spine. My *zemër* is brave—that quality's never changed.

God, she still doesn't know how dangerous the world is out there.

How tempting it is for predators to break her.

Men like him.

Or me.

The lecherous asshole grins and pats her cheek like she's a petulant child, not a thirty-four-year-old woman.

He just signed his death warrant.

I imagine removing his hand from his body. I'm not the type to build gruesome shrines, but maybe today's the day.

Or I can feed it to the rats—God knows there are too many of them in the city.

My blood boils, but I force myself to remain still because Elias Kent is anything but impulsive. I'm patient. Calculating.

Senators quake in my presence because I can end their careers with one call. The mafia, the Bratva, the Irish mob? I can destroy their supply routes because I control the very people who make them available.

Beneath a veneer of civility, these powerful men have an unhealthy penchant for young girls and questionable funds hidden in offshore accounts. Bribery. Trafficking. Drugs. Every dark flavor of hell.

But I'm a dealer in secrets. I know them all.

The asshole leaves the table, and the waitress crumbles, tears sliding down her face. She scurries away. I fist my lighter and remember how helpless my sister was—how helpless this server girl looks.

Helpless no more, not if I can help it.

Huffing out a breath, Lana sits back down and writes on a piece of paper, her lips pursed with determination.

Despite the murderous rage coursing through me, I bite back a smile. She's doing her thing again—writing kind notes to waitstaff to cheer them up in addition to leaving a hefty tip. She rummages through her purse, pulls out something small and metallic, and sets it on the table. She then leaves the café, only to come to an abrupt halt outside the door.

A calico cat wanders across her path.

She squeals, the bright smile making her even more ethereal. Clearly not caring about the gawking bystanders, she crouches and pats the cat, who twines its lithe body around her. She's won over the cat too.

Lana murmurs to the feline, pointing to the café. The cat grazes her ankles and nuzzles Lana's palm.

Damn cat. I can almost feel her gentle touch against my face.

You're out of your fucking mind, Elias, being jealous of a cat.

After letting out a sigh, Lana says something to the feline. I can make out the words this time. *"I wish I could take you home."*

A muscle spasms in the cavernous hole where my heart once was, and a ghostly whisper crosses my mind. A beautiful girl who once told me if it weren't for her family being allergic to cats, she'd get one.

Lightning sears across the bloated sky, followed by the crash of thunder. Lana jolts, opens the café door, and ushers the cat inside.

She smiles and darts into a town car idling at the curb. She's running late for work at Fleur Entertainment Holdings, her family's company.

I grip the car door handle, my muscles aching from restraint, desperate to rush over, pull her from her car, and whisk her away.

But I stay put because my obsession is poison—an eternal addiction.

Her car peels off, and I force myself to release a deep exhale.

Ping.

Time's up.

I shove my obsession into a small compartment where my deepest grief lives and open the other box containing the darkest day of my life. I see that day in snapshots—our sofa aflame, my parents sobbing, begging for mercy, Sofia whimpering as she's hauled away, and baby Beatrice crying.

Then, there's nothing but the haunted, sickening silence.

Rage surges through me, and I let myself fill with hate and violence.

The scar on my cheek throbs, and I labor an inhale before releasing it, because hatred is strength. It's fuel for my day. It's what feeds The Antihero Syndicate—also called The Syndicate—and our vow to eliminate The Association, the perpetrators of my family's massacre.

The vilest men in expensive suits.

I clench my lighter, its sharp edges jabbing my skin. Another box closed.

"It's time," I tell John.

"Do you want me to—"

"No, keep the car running." My voice is flat. This should be quick. Exact revenge and get the kill ledger. Two things that have eluded me for decades.

Quietly, I step out of the car, coat collar up, and pull on my black leather gloves.

Never leave prints behind.

Raucous laughter reaches my ears. The café door opens. The asshole from earlier and a few of his buddies spill out.

The men freeze when they spot me, their faces paling as recognition dawns in their eyes.

Too late, motherfucker.

A slow grin splits my lips, and I advance toward them, a different obsession—revenge—teeming inside me.

I crack my knuckles. The harsh sound ricochets through the air.

Good men don't get obsessed.

But too bad for them. I'm not a good man.

And in a few moments, they'll learn what that really means.

Chapter 2: GRAY IS A COLOR

LANA

I SIT IN THE back of the car, watching the dark clouds hang low, a heavy weight pressing on my chest. The city seems off, like it's holding its breath.

Hurricane season. Stormy weather.

Everything's fine.

But a chill lingers in my bones, the same restlessness shadowing me for the last few months.

At first, I blamed it on my looming thirty-fifth birthday, and while my siblings were all paired off, I was still alone.

I told myself I was missing a passion to spark me from the inside.

But deep down, I knew that wasn't it.

About three months ago, I got the sense I was being watched.

I thought I was paranoid because every time I'd look around, everything appeared normal.

No strange flowers or voodoo dolls delivered to my doorstep. No shadowy figures lurking about. I still had our security team double-check the cameras and sweep my building.

They found nothing, but the wrongness in my gut wouldn't leave me.

I shake myself and sip from my water bottle, still tasting the lingering chocolate from the coffee at the café.

The cozy Albanian place—part of my "try a new café each morning" routine—felt out of place in the gritty Lower East Side. But the coffee was excellent and the rich chocolate was divine.

I might break my rule and go back for a second visit—until the image of the douchebag owner threatening Leanne, the server, sours the thought. I hope she'll text me if she runs into problems. Women have to stick together.

So, probably not a second visit unless someone comes with me.

I scroll through my calendar and review my schedule—three press releases to draft, a meeting with my brother Rex about the upcoming boutique hotel launch, investor calls. Dinner tonight with Chicago Memorial Hospital's PR team who just flew in—they want to organize a joint press tour to thank us for our one billion dollar donation funding their research wing. In other words, business as usual for my chief of public relations role.

Always busy, never complete.

My phone buzzes, and I smile when I see the caller ID.

Belle.

But instead of her, a toothy grin fills the screen—two front teeth, one tiny bottom tooth, part of a nose, and chubby cheeks.

I know exactly who it is.

"Little Levi! Did you take your mommy's phone?"

"Nana!" Levi grins and waves, still showing me mostly his mouth.

"Lana. Say it with me, La-Na." My chest warms. I adore kids, especially my nephew. Now that my siblings are all having babies, there are plenty of little ones for me to love.

Even if I don't end up having my own.

At thirty-four, according to books and doctors, if I want biological kids of my own, I should find a man and get on with it.

If only it were that easy.

Being an Anderson means people want me for my last name, my money, or my connections. And having four intimidating older brothers definitely doesn't help.

I shove the thoughts away.

"Give the phone back to Mommy." Belle laughs.

She appears on the screen—paint smudge on her cheek, a pencil tucked behind her ear. Classic fashion designer uniform.

"I'm reminding you about girls' night. I know Lexy's traveling and Millie's abroad, but the rest of us can still make it. It's been way too long."

A grin tugs at my lips. I miss my sisters-in-law, my best girlfriends.

"Well, you know me. Single and ready to mingle. My calendar's open."

She grimaces. "I really hope this little guy doesn't get sick again. Seems like he catches something every month. But I'm really looking forward to it."

Levi waves a sheet of paper in the background, clearly eager for attention.

"Whatcha got there, Levi?" I ask.

Belle hoists him onto her lap. They show me his masterpiece—a crayon drawing of a dinosaur holding a small gray box.

"What's the T-Rex holding? A present for Nana? It's not Christmas yet." I point to myself, grinning. It's never too early to celebrate my favorite holiday, though.

"No." Levi shakes his head. "Uncle E."

I freeze at the devil's nickname.

Now, that's a man who definitely would *not* celebrate Christmas, a day of magic and joy.

Elias Kent, known to the public as the king of the underworld, is feared by everyone—from the rich to the unsavory. I can see why. The man moves like a ghost. He's always dressed to the nines, like some gentleman gangster from another era.

But I'd never mistake him for a gentleman.

He works with my family yet makes it his purpose to ignore me or worse, speak to me only in clipped sentences dripping with cold detachment.

"Hi Elias, I love the suit."

A twitch of his lips.

"Why are you so grumpy?"

He arches a brow. "I'm not. I have no time for small talk."

The cycle repeats.

The man intrigues and offends me in equal measure. And yet, butterflies stir low in my gut whenever he's near.

There's a viciousness in his green eyes, a lethal calmness when he stands still. But there's also something familiar about him I can't place.

Either way, he's bad news. I should stay away.

But that's like telling someone to ignore the lava bursting out of a volcano.

Impossible.

"Lana?" Belle's voice cuts in. "You've got that frown again. Everything okay?"

"Oh—sorry. Zoned out. A packed schedule."

"Levi and I are heading to The Orchid later to meet Maxwell." Belle smiles, her eyes going dreamy-like whenever she mentions her husband, my oldest brother. I'd gag if it weren't so sweet.

"He's meeting Elias there." She purses her lips in contemplation. "I think the mobster's lonely. I'm inviting him to our next family dinner."

"You and your savior complex." I snort. "You just feel that way because he saved your life a few years back."

"He's done way more than that!"

I nod begrudgingly. The infuriating man has rescued my siblings from dangerous situations more than once, and for that I'm forever grateful.

Maybe that's why I have butterflies.

Misplaced gratefulness.

"Elias could use some love and warmth," Belle says, then gasps. "Levi, put that down! Got to go. Toddler with scissors. Can't wait for girls' night!"

She hangs up, and I laugh under my breath.

Soon, the car comes to a stop by my office. The looming skyscraper is my family's pride and joy.

I step out, thankful the rain hasn't started yet.

But then something stops me.

The feeling.

Hairs prickle at the back of my neck. Goosebumps bead along my arms.

The distinct sensation of being watched.

I spin around, scanning the crowds of pedestrians on Fifth Avenue, yellow cabs zooming by, horns blaring. Everything looks normal, yet unease claws its talons deeper into my chest. My jittery fingers find the emerald pendant at my throat and graze the random grooves on the back, imperfections in the handcrafted piece.

Growing up, we were taught awareness and self-defense. Being from one of the wealthiest families in the country makes you a target.

As I head for the entrance, I text Emerson Clarke, my private investigator. I've asked him to dig into my suspicions.

Lana

Any updates, Emerson? Same feeling again. Something's off.

I wait a minute. No reply.

The doorman opens the door. I plaster on a fake smile, my hands still clammy.

Before I step inside, instinct makes me look back. My feet come to a stuttering halt.

A black SUV idles at the curb. A man in sunglasses, cap pulled low, smirks.

Tires screech as the car speeds off, leaving my pulse thundering as the first raindrops descend.

Chapter 3: KILL TO BURN

ELIAS

THE ASSHOLE FROM THE Albanian café blanches when I approach him.

"E-Elias Kent. What are you doing here?" he sputters on the sidewalk outside the building as his friends scatter.

Sniveling idiots.

Not answering him, I twirl the lighter around my fingers, feeling its heavy, familiar weight, and step inside.

"Where's your father?" I ask. He's my target, the man I've been searching for.

All activity grinds to a halt.

Old men arguing in Albanian over backgammon stare at us. Dice clatter. Chairs scrape against cracked tiles as folks toss bills onto their tables and promptly exit.

"B-Back room. Why are you—we don't owe you any favors."

I snort. "You aren't worthy to lick my shoes clean."

"Atë!" he shouts, his feet tripping over themselves as he scurries to the back.

Yes, go run to your daddy.

My pristine Italian leather oxfords barely make a sound as I cross the room to *her* table and survey the scraps she left behind. This is just curiosity—keeping tabs on the enemy. Not part of my twenty-eight minutes.

The white ceramic cup is mostly empty. Deep-red lipstick marks the rim, beckoning me like a beacon in a storm.

I lift the cup, placing my lips over the red imprint, and take a sip. In a past life, this would've been a kiss between two lovers.

Useless dreams. There's no time for sentimentality.

I focus on the taste instead.

Earthy. Bitter. Strong. A good cup of Balkan coffee with lingering chocolate aroma.

Of course. She loves chocolate.

Next, I flip the folio on the table. A hundred-dollar bill and her familiar handwriting stare back at me.

Life is full of surprises. Today's storm may be tomorrow's rainbow. Hang in there. If you ever need help, call this number.

I stare at the string of digits, wondering how the intelligent head of public relations can be so naïve sometimes—leaving strangers her phone number.

My *zemër*'s weakness is her kind heart.

"What's the meaning of this? Why scare off our customers, Mr. Kent?" Vasil Çela waddles out, beady-eyed, cigarette perched at the corner of his mouth, with his asshole son in tow. My temper brightens, a sadistic pleasure curling through me.

Not answering him, I pick up Lana's receipt and carefully slide it into my suit pocket. Her kind notes—her little scraps of sunshine.

My scraps of sunshine.

"That's ours. Why are you taking—"

Brow arched, I hurl a seething glare his way, and he shuts up.

Then I take the gold-wrapped square she left for the waitress. A small piece of chocolate.

Curious, I unwrap and plop the morsel into my mouth. The nauseating sweetness registers first, always reminding me of that dark day.

But I force myself to savor it because she loves it. The unexpected spice fans the flames of anger inside me. Paprika, cardamom, and dark chocolate. Interesting.

"Where were you on February twenty-eighth? Twenty years ago," I murmur.

Slowly, I face the father and son duo.

Sweat beads on the older man's forehead, the blood leaching out of his face. "I-I don't know what you're talking about."

My veins turn to ice at his denial.

Leaning in, I watch him shrink before me. "Wrong answer. Allow me to remind you. A hardworking couple. Their three children. The youngest only three months old."

Click. The flame blossoms from my lighter. I shut it. *Click.* Again.

"Took out the mom first because you wanted to inflict pain. Then, the baby because she was..." the words hiss through my gritted teeth, "too loud. Ring any bells?"

"What?" he whispers, his eyes wide with fear. A pungent stench reaches my nostrils, and I look down, finding his pants drenched.

Revulsion churns inside me. *Pathetic coward.*

"B-But how? You're Elias Kent. You aren't Albanian. H-How—"

"You thought there were no survivors. But that's the thing with evil deeds...someone always lives to tell the tale."

A tapping sound draws my attention to the window. A man darts away in a blur of black, leaving behind a scrap of paper with a drawing of a chess piece—a black knight—fluttering against the wind. Gasoline sloshes in under the door.

I smile. Ren works fast. The men in The Syndicate are the only ones I trust now.

"Who sent you that day?" There were two masked men. One tall and muscular, the other thick and short like the older Çela quivering in front of me.

The son grabs his sleeve. "Dad, what is he talk—"

"I-It was an extirpation, m-my Rite."

My hand curls into a tight fist. The Association and its unhinged rituals and depraved violence.

"Who gave the order?"

"I-I don't know."

"Then where's the kill ledger? You at least know that, right?" I snarl. The Association keeps records of their kills; that much I do know.

The old man shakes. "Pl-Please. I don't know anything. But the Berishas have the ledgers. The Six all have copies. That's all I know."

The ruling Albanian family. They're part of The Six, the council ruling The Association. There are rumors of unrest within the family. They're the weakest link.

My silk tie cinches my neck, making it hard for me to breathe. Because I know what I need to do next—I've avoided this last step for as long as I could.

I need to infiltrate The Association; join the very people I despise.

But I'll get answers.

I'll find the murderer who ordered my family's execution, the man who shattered Sofia's life and mine.

I'll find the answer to my question: Why? Why target my small, lower-class family?

With my expression nonchalant, I pull out a metal flask and unscrew the cap.

"Congratulations." I offer it to the man who trembles like I'm offering him poison. "The finest whiskey. Go on. Drink it. A reward for the right answer."

Vasil Çela swallows, his hands shaking as he takes the canister from me. He takes a tentative sip, his eyes widening when he realizes I wasn't lying.

But when he lowers it down, I lash out, my grip firm as I douse his face and shirt with the rest of the alcohol.

He chokes and wheezes, "W-Why does this matter to you?"

Someone whimpers in the background. It's the damn waitress loitering by the back door.

"Go. Get out of here." She's not smart, but she's innocent.

She shrieks and flees, the back door banging behind her.

"Looks like you just lost one of your women." One of the thousands they traffic for the Albanian mob. Anger burns through me.

My soul is black and heart nonexistent, but there's a special hell reserved for men who prey on women.

I face the petrified older man again. "I never answered you before. Elias Kent isn't my real name."

Rule one: Look them in the eye. The Antihero Syndicate has rules to govern the monsters living within us.

I fist his collar and lift him off the ground until he's at eye level.

Rule two: Tell them their sins.

"It was *my* family."

His eyes blow wide. Sneakers squeak, a terrified gasp, and his son flees, finally registering they won't make it out alive.

I draw my gun and fire a round into the younger Çela's back. A wretched scream tears out of his throat.

Rule three: No innocent women or children. The third and final rule.

Everything else is fair game.

The sniveling son groans on the floor, red spreading on his shirt. I remember the server girl shrinking in his presence—classic battered woman syndrome—and how he disrespected Lana.

Not innocent. If I weren't pressed for time, I'd chop off his hand and choke him with it to teach him a lesson on consent.

The older Çela claws at my wrist, kicking, thrashing as I restrict his airway. He reeks of whiskey and sweat, the most unpleasant combination. It'll be a fucker to get out of my clothes later.

I drop him, and he scrambles toward his son, the two trying to escape. Pathetic.

Leaning down, I grab a cigarette from the old man's pocket and thumb the lighter.

A small flame leaps, writhing a seductive and destructive dance in the air.

"No! Please," the old man babbles. "W-We'll do anything. Tell you anything. You can have all my money—"

I punch him across the face. Blood and spittle fly from his mouth.

Money? I have enough wealth to rival any billionaire. Can money turn back time? Can money bring back everything I've lost?

"*Mirupafshim*, asshole."

Goodbye.

The cigarette flares, its tip glowing orange. I'm riveted by how something so tiny can cause so much destruction.

Like *her*, if I let myself think it. But I don't.

Caustic smoke reaches my nostrils as I hold the cigarette over him.

"See you in hell."

I smile and drop it, watching the flames catch on his whiskey-soaked clothes, engulfing him in seconds.

Screams of terror fill the room as I calmly walk out the front door.

But then I fucking hear it.

"Meow."

My feet freeze, and I look down, finding the calico cat staring at me, its back arched up, fangs showing.

Vicious little creature. Images of Lana smiling at the cat play behind my eyelids.

"I wish I could keep you."

The spot beneath my rib cage throbs, and without thinking, I scoop up the cat.

"Your lucky day," I murmur, and walk out the door, ignoring the cries behind me.

The cat claws my neck and draws blood. Smart, this little one.

Ren, dressed in his usual all-leather attire, hasn't taken off his motorcycle helmet. He cocks his head and snaps up his visor, incredulity in his dark eyes when he spots the cat. Up close, he looks paler than usual. There's a fleeting pinch in his forehead—gone in a split second—I'd miss it if I didn't know him so well.

"Do I even want to know?" He points to the cat and signs with his free hand. The assassin of The Syndicate smirks.

"Shut up."

"I don't speak," he taunts back and shakes his head, amusement in his eyes. Then he strikes a match and lights the Molotov cocktail in his grip.

"Ready? The pawn took care of the cameras. He says you can't do shit without him."

I roll my eyes at his mention of Aleksei Morozov, the hacker genius of The Syndicate. If it weren't for his usefulness, I'd kick him out of the group so I wouldn't have to hear him gloat.

"I already zapped them." Impatient, I show Ren the debugger in my pocket.

Ren grins, the flaming bottle in his hand, and faces the building. *"For the vow."*

I answer, "No mercy."

My jaw tics and I chain the front door shut. Knowing Ren, he's already locked the back.

"Let it burn."

The bottle smashes against the wall. Flames engulf the building, and I walk away.

The cat's heart hammers against my ribs.

Mine doesn't.

Chapter 4: A MEMORY OF RAIN

ELIAS

THE SLEEK SKYSCRAPER OF glass and chrome dominates Fifth Avenue even as storm clouds and drizzle render the world a muted gray. I'm meeting Maxwell and Rex Anderson, two of Lana's four older brothers, at The Orchid, Fleur Entertainment's crown jewel. Here, all dreams can come true—from the best restaurants to the specialty sex and strip clubs on its Rose floors.

But for me? It's a playground. Plenty of secrets to go around in those darkened halls.

Years ago, I couldn't have stepped through its doors. But I rose from the ashes and engineered my way in.

Bishop Seb

It's done, I presume. Don't need to bail you out, do I?

My lips hitch up in a half-smile at Sebastian McEntyre's text message. The Syndicate's resident psychopath never wastes time.

Rook Elias

I'm surprised you care.

Bishop Seb

I don't. Emotions are meaningless. But if you were caught, it'd make my job difficult.

Rook Elias

Right. What's an Irish mob lawyer without leverage? I thought you were a one-man show.

Bishop Seb

Professor *and* lawyer. Only the stupid rely on himself and not use the people around him. Remember what happened in Sri Lanka?

I arch a brow. We never talk about Sri Lanka.

Bishop Seb

You're alive. That's all I need. Talk when you're in Chicago.

John guides the town car to the curb. I peel off my coat, unfortunately ruined by whiskey and blood spatter from the café mishap half an hour ago. The local news reports it as an explosion stemming from a gas leak. A quick call to the FDNY fire chief took care of that. After all, I saved his kid from a kidnapping two years ago. A favor for a favor.

Calmly, I fix my hair, taming the dark strands and lock away the monster.

"Mr. Kent, welcome back to The Orchid." The doorman bows when I exit the car.

I flick off lingering ash from my suit jacket. Then I notice a crimson stain on my white, invisibly hemmed shirtsleeve.

Fucking Çelas, nuisances alive and dead. Another suit I'll have to burn tonight—a waste that makes the boy I used to be wince.

The drizzle comes down harder.

Footsteps pound the pavement as New Yorkers escape the sky's wrath, the rain quickly becoming a deluge.

"Here you go, sir." Someone hands me an umbrella, and I look up.

It's red.

A singular spot of color in the world of gray, just like another day long ago.

Rocks bite into my knees. Rain cuts into my eyes. My short, sixteen-year-old frame shivers from the cold.

Hunger carves a relentless hole in my stomach.

Then a red umbrella—vibrant and unforgettable—just like the girl holding it.

The beautiful girl from worlds away who smells of roses.

The only person to stand between me and the storm.

The sudden crack of thunder jolts me back to the present. I straighten to my full six-foot-three height and thank the footman. Puberty caught up, along with scars, blood, and everything else.

These memories? They escaped their damn box again.

Useless scraps of my past. I need to work on reining them in.

Twenty-eight minutes. They're only allowed to roam free for twenty-fucking-eight minutes a day.

No more, no less.

Chapter 5: WHISPERS OF FEAR

LANA

MY FINGERS SHAKE AS I reread the email. I fiddle with the emerald pendant nestled on my chest, grazing the tiny notches again.

> Ms. Anderson,
>
> Apologies for the delayed response. Per your request, I shadowed you for two weeks. No unusual persons noted, but this SUV with Illinois plates appeared within a hundred feet of you on three separate occasions, which could be coincidental.
>
> Regardless, I'd advise caution.
>
> Emerson Clarke

I flip through the photos of a black SUV with tinted windows. Lingering outside Fleur. Near the Italian deli I frequent. A block from my Upper West Side apartment. It looks similar to the one outside the office this morning, but I can't be sure.

Chill curdles inside my gut as I cross my office on the forty-ninth floor to the large window overlooking Fifth Avenue.

Rain hammers the glass panes, the wind howling a mournful wail. Fog mists over the city, an endless swath of murkiness. How I wish it were spring—sunshine, flowers in bloom.

Normally, I'd curl up on my oversized lavender armchair at home and read. But worries swarm my mind instead. Why would anyone follow me? For money? For photos? Something worse?

My chest tightens.

I stare at the black puzzle box on top of my desk.

Could it be my mysterious admirer?

No, it can't be.

These puzzle boxes started showing up randomly years ago. When they first appeared, our family was on high alert. I had a bodyguard tailing my every move, expecting a stalker to escalate. But the gifter covered up his or her tracks well.

And nothing ever happened. Just the occasional puzzle box.

Eventually, I shed the bodyguard, eager to get some semblance of normalcy.

Over time, the puzzles became a treat I'd look forward to...a strange comfort. Whoever this person was knew I'd enjoy them.

I rub my arms. It's toasty in here, but I'm still so darn cold.

Unsettled, I flip on the flat screen, hoping some background noise will cheer me up.

"—reporting from what used to be Café Aroma. Officials say the fire was contained to the building—"

My mouth drops as I stare at the wreckage of the quaint coffee shop I visited this morning. Charred walls, blackened floors, melted plastic. Nothing recognizable.

What the hell? Everything was fine a few hours ago. What about the other customers? Or Leanne, the waitress with sad eyes?

"Two men, believed to be the owner and his son, were found deceased."

Two men. So, not Leanne. Relief sweeps through me, followed by a pinch of guilt. Two people died today. That's still sad. *Even if it was the asshole who scared Leanne.*

"Arson isn't suspected. Rumors alleged the café may be a laundering front for 'The Association.' But whether the mysterious society exists is still unproven."

My blood runs cold, and my mouth dries. The goosebumps return with a vengeance.

The Association exists, all right. The news makes them sound like an urban legend, but I know better. They're real—rich and powerful.

Unstoppable.

Unless you have someone more dangerous on your side.

His face crosses my mind—dark hair, a masculine jaw, a singular scar, and blistering emerald eyes. I shake it off.

The Association has tried for years to recruit my family. *We should be flattered,* they say. *Unlimited power will be ours.*

But when we said no, they resorted to threats and violence—embezzlement, kidnappings, and what they did to my half sister, Taylor, when she was sixteen? I shove the dark thoughts away.

Repulsed, I turn off the screen. My palms sweat as the earlier unease burgeons into fear. *There's nothing to be afraid of. I'm safe.*

I slip my pendant back into my dress, nestling it against my skin. The metal warms, and a heartbeat from the past pulls me under.

Hollow Gardens. An elm tree. A carved message on its trunk. A boy who stole my heart and whispered my name like a prayer—my first and only love—who vanished one day without a trace.

Where are you, Kian?

Enough sulking around.

Action, not reaction. I type a message to Emerson.

Lana

I'd rather play it safe too. I saw a similar SUV this morning outside my office. I'll be careful. Let me know what you find.

With renewed determination, I grab my purse and Emerson's packet, then head across the sky bridge to The Orchid.

I'll chat with my siblings or get a quick massage to settle my nerves. Then I'll tackle the pile of work waiting for me. And starting next week, I'll volunteer at the animal shelter Belle used to work at. Time to find that missing passion.

Fifteen minutes later, I stride into our family's reserved room at the club. My family is big—seven of us, not including Dad. Someone's always here.

The grand halls are quiet today, my footfalls echoing against marble. Muffled conversations take place in secluded alcoves—deals made, news disseminated. A few patrons and waitstaff nod as I pass them by.

Low chuckles reach my ears when I open the door to our room.

Maxwell, who's the CEO, sits on the leather sofa, a tumbler in his hand, and a smirk on his lips. He loosens his tie and shakes his head at whatever's being said.

Across from him, in classic reformed playboy dishevelment, is my partner-in-crime growing up, Rex, who's number three in the Anderson sibling pecking order: Maxwell, Ryland, Rex, Ethan, myself, then our half sisters Grace and Taylor.

They stand when I enter—our etiquette classes growing up clearly paid off.

"Oh, look what the cat dragged in. Ditching work, little miss E?" Rex snickers.

I narrow my eyes. "Look who's talking, *Cassius*."

Rex scowls. He hates his middle name. Our parents alphabetized ours—Maxwell Angus, Lana Elise, all the way down the line. We're the alphabet siblings.

"At least I actually get work done," I quip and launch myself into his open arms, immediately feeling more settled.

"It's all about working smart, not hard."

I snort. Classic Rex.

"Everything okay?" Maxwell asks, clearly concerned. "Not like you to stop by midday."

The man misses nothing.

"Just rattled. The café I was at this morning got burned to a crisp. The news said something about The Association. Then there's this." Releasing a sigh, I hand him the packet. "It might be nothing, but still..."

My brothers frown as they look over the papers.

The temperature of the room drops ten degrees. A muscle pulses in Rex's jaw, and Maxwell's gaze hardens. They stare at each other.

Click.

Click.

I whirl around, my mouth parting when I see the maddening devil step out of the bathroom. His fingers twirl his lighter, clicking it on and off.

Driving me crazy.

The man never smokes, but he makes his presence known by clicking that thing. I bet it's a coping mechanism for whatever ailment infects his twisted mind.

Elias Kent, with his dark, formidable looks and towering frame, sucks the oxygen and light out of every room, all without saying a word. His startling green eyes snare mine as he advances toward us, his strides slow and measured.

Danger and menace radiate from him.

His stony gaze sweeps down my body, like he's coldly assessing my value.

But then, for a split second, something shifts.

There's a flicker of heat in his eyes.

I hiccup, my skin warming. The slow, sensual drag feels like a caress.

I'm going nuts. I hardly know the man.

"The Association, you say?" His voice comes out in its usual gravelly whisper.

Grayish daylight from the windows cuts his face in harsh shadows. Were it not for that menacing scar spanning his left cheek down to his jaw, he'd be handsome—beautiful, even.

He reminds me of a panther—sleek and elegant, but one hundred percent predator.

You can never turn your back on him.

"I-I didn't know you were here. Don't you need to patrol the Rose floors or something?" I swallow, my heart sprinting in circles for no reason.

Almost a decade ago, Elias inserted himself into our business, helping us manage the personnel working on the five floors of sex and sin. Maxwell said without Elias's tight leash, chaos would happen. Rich people and vulnerable sex workers equate to problems.

Unless there's a mobster feared by all watching your every move.

"Stay the hell away from The Association," Elias snaps.

Another command. Not even a please or a hello.

A little sugar first would be nice. I clamp down on the thought. Absolutely not.

He narrows his eyes as if he senses my changing mood. "And stick to your safe little cafés here. No coffee is worth your life."

The man looks down his nose at me, contempt dripping from his voice.

Indignation sears my insides. "What's it to you? The last I checked, I already have four older brothers, and none of them break laws for a living."

His lips twitch—just barely—I swear, the man has no soul. He cocks his head as if studying me like a problem to solve. Then, a shadow crosses his eyes, and he arches his brow, clearly finding me lacking.

I don't like him at all. But the darn butterflies beat their wings in my stomach again.

"Trust me. I wouldn't want you for a sister."

"You overbearing, misogynistic—"

"Whoa." Rex tugs me back. "I'm all for fun and banter, but this stretches beyond—"

"Shut it, Rex."

"You should look into this," Maxwell murmurs, still staring at the photos. He hands them to Elias.

I snatch them back. "No way. I'm in more danger with *him*," I eye the mobster, "than a random SUV when everything could be a coincidence, anyway."

"Give them to me." Elias snaps his fingers.

"No."

His eyes turn glacial. "I won't ask twice."

"Or what?" Because I have no sense of self-preservation, I step close to him. "You'll tie me up and rip the papers out of my hands?"

Elias's eyes flare, a sharp hitch of breath to follow. He doesn't respond, but stands still, towering over me, his throat rippling as he swallows.

I struggle an inhale, my nerve endings lit up like sparklers.

He leans down.

"Don't tempt me," he whispers, so softly only I can hear.

A shudder moves through my traitorous body. *Why am I reacting this way to him?* I shove the papers at him.

“Fine. Look all you want. It’s nothing, guys. I shouldn’t have brought it up.”

Not waiting for a response, I storm out the door, eager to escape the suddenly stifling heat.

And I swear, the asshole’s dark chuckles follow me out of the room.

Chapter 6: THE STATUS QUO

ELIAS

SHE BOLTS OUT LIKE she's fleeing the apocalypse, and the smile slips off my face.

But before I face the men, I breathe her in—intoxicating roses. Sweet and unforgettable, just like that rainy day a lifetime ago when I was someone else.

One second. One small moment of indulgence. I'll deduct this from my twenty-eight-minute quota tomorrow.

"So, what do you think?" Maxwell asks, his tone sharp. "Is this SUV a credible threat? There's not much to go on."

Slowly, I turn back to the brothers who've become my good friends over the years, even if they don't know they've invited a fox into the henhouse. This friendship will end when I join The Association, the very people they hate. Invisible ropes cinch around my lungs. I shove the feeling down.

The papers rustle in my grip. I scan the letter and images. Illinois plates. Tinted windows. The SUV kept showing up where she was. My jaw tightens, red misting my vision. How did I miss this?

Coincidences don't exist in my world. If they're circling her, she's on a list, and they want something from her. And The Association's lists only end one way.

Any other assumptions will get you killed sooner.

Dread coils low in my gut.

"Illinois," I murmur. Chicago is the headquarters of The Association, but they don't know that. "Out-of-state plates. Sticking out like a sore thumb. It's—"

"A warning," Rex finishes. "They want us to know she's being tracked."

He straightens, all traces of humor gone. He, like his brothers, has experienced The Association's brutality. Last year in Monaco, their bullet almost ended him.

"They don't take 'no' for an answer." Maxwell paces in front of the fireplace. "I'm tired of being threatened. It's time to do something."

"Legally, Maxwell? Or my methods?"

The eldest Anderson levels his icy gray stare at me. His jaw tics. "Who am I to stop a certain mobster from protecting his friends? A favor for a favor, right, as you say?"

The intelligent asshole, wording his request with plausible deniability.

I stride to the wet bar and pour us a drink. Top-shelf whiskey in hand—pricier than our family's monthly grocery budget when I was a kid—I return and hand him a glass.

"You saved me in the alley ten years ago. I never forget."

A ghost of a smile curves his lips. He understands that's a yes from me. I'll look into this, exact violence, and he doesn't have to worry about a thing.

He clinks his glass with mine and takes a sip. "You're a good man and a loyal friend, Elias. We both know real criminals hide in plain sight—the very people in this club. I'm glad Ryland and I found you that day."

The hollow spot beneath my rib cage aches, but I ignore it because guilt has no place in my life. That day in the alley—they have no idea what happened.

It's all a game of chess, and I've been several moves ahead.

"Mister brooding mobster likes to think he's the big bad shit, but we see you, Eli." Rex grins, winking at me.

"Call me Eli again and I'll share photos of you with your wife. The Rose floors vintage."

"Dude, not cool. That was before I met her. And where do you think the nickname 'Rex-a-Million' came from? Had to earn those million orgasms somewhere."

I snort, turning away before a smile betrays me.

"You love us, Eli. *Eli. Eli*," Rex needles and slaps my shoulder.

"You'd think marriage and fatherhood would make you grow up." Maxwell shakes his head. Rex and Olivia gave birth to twins recently.

"And becoming boring farts like you all? No, thanks."

The brothers bicker and laugh. Such warmth and love. Things that don't belong in my life.

A weight presses down on me as I slip toward the door. Before I can leave, it suddenly swings open and in barrels Belle, Maxwell's wife, balancing their preschooler, Levi, on her hip.

"Elias!" She beams and squeezes my arm. "You're a hard man to find. Dinner next week at our place, okay? Don't be a loner."

The invisible chasm throbs behind my sternum. "I don't do family dinners, Belle. Last I checked, I'm not an Anderson."

"Nonsense. You're one of us now, especially after helping us so many times." She winks, then turns to her son, who Lana claims is her favorite nephew. The beguiling woman has stars in her eyes whenever she's around her nieces and nephews. She'd be a wonderful mother someday.

And a wife to a lucky bastard. *Never you. Of course not. You hate her.*

Belle asks, "Levi, we want Uncle Elias at the dinner, right?"

Levi gives me a toothy grin and nods.

"We shall see." A lump forms in my throat.

My phone buzzes, and I glance at it.

Bishop Seb

Case closed. Gas leak from busted pipe. You're clear. The chessboard is ready. Time for step two?

Step two—join The Association, the dark side. I bite my cheek, relishing the lash of pain, and type a response.

Rook Elias

Yes.

"Just give it up, Eli, step into the light, come to the dinner," Rex hollers.

Without answering him, I nod at Belle, barely mustering a smile. She stares at me expectantly, her gaze trusting. Levi hands me the piece of paper he has in his hand.

It's a crayon drawing of a T-Rex holding a lighter and a little boy. The words "Unkle E" are scrawled on top.

Red crayon. His favorite.

“Maxwell said he was meeting you here. Levi insisted he wanted to draw you something.” Belle kisses her son’s face.

I ruffle his hair, my chest on fire.

For a moment, I’m reminded of my childhood, my parents smiling at each other—their love steadfast and unshakable—Dad playing peekaboo with little Beatrice.

Before The Association burned it all down.

Sliding my hand into my pocket, I grip my lighter and leave the room.

I glance at my watch to see how much time has elapsed.

Twenty-eight minutes of lies. In another life, this might’ve been my future. Family. Kids. Light.

Just not this one.

Chapter 7: TERMS OF DAMNATION

ELIAS

One Week Later, Chicago, Illinois

"THE INFAMOUS ELIAS KENT graces us with his presence. To what do we owe the pleasure?"

Edon Berisha waves me into his office on top of the eyesore that is Berisha and Sons Corporation headquarters, a gaudy skyscraper in the shape of a fucking gold dildo, built smack center of Michigan Avenue.

The building is tasteless and vulgar, just like the family themselves—criminals dressed in luxury, rotten to the core.

Oh, he's prepared for me. Three men flank him like dogs at heel—his sons, heirs to his multi-billion-dollar empire.

Agron, the eldest and COO, levels a stare at me, his eyes sharp and calculating. Ilir, the middle son, lights his father's cigar with the smugness of an Ivy League lawyer. Dritan, buzz-cut and built like a soldier, has one hand inside his jacket.

I'd bet anything they're armed, ready to empty their clips into me at any second.

I scan the room. Gold everywhere—lamps, chandeliers, even the doorknobs.

Three windows, one emergency exit, two security cameras. Plenty of blunt objects to block projectiles. A circuit breaker a foot away. Pour water on it, and everything goes dark.

Boom! As Aleksei would say. *Everything's better with a boom.* The man should be an explosives specialist, not a hacker.

"Didn't expect a welcome party," I murmur and take a seat across from Edon. "I'm flattered."

"Nothing less for the person who's ruined so many of our plans." Edon smiles thinly, his eyes flat. An average person would think he's your regular billionaire—short man, thinner than he appears on camera, gray hair meticulously combed over.

But I know better.

The Berishas are the newest of The Six—the only family to have joined The Council in the past few decades. The other five are founding families of The Association. It takes ruthlessness to climb to the top. You don't step over bodies. You make them.

"It's just business. No hard feelings." I turn the lighter in my hand, feeling its reassuring weight.

"Our deals with the Andersons," a curl of smoke slithers in the air, "you've come in between us. Hard not to have any 'hard' feelings."

"They weren't going to pan out. I saved you time and energy."

When The Association threatened the Andersons in the past, I assisted my friends—whether with intel or reinforcements. Back then, I didn't realize how tightly locked down The Association's kill ledgers were.

How there was no way for me to find the man behind my family's murders unless I became one of them.

A miscalculation on my part.

The grandfather clock in the corner chimes four times. The room thickens with smoke and silence.

"Color me curious. What are you doing here, Kent? Do you need a favor from us? What is it you do again...a favor for a favor? A secret for a secret? Because the answer is no."

Edon sucks on his cigar and releases a plume in my direction, his eyes goading.

"Cutting to the chase. I like it." I click my lighter once, twice, then snap it shut. "I have a better one for you."

Swallowing the acid rushing up my throat, I lean in.

"I want in."

The sons stiffen.

Agron speaks up first. "In? Our properties, our clubs?"

"The Association." I want to spit out the words, but I rein in my disgust. Anything for revenge.

Edon arches his brow, his mouth parting to respond, but I hold up my hand.

"Do me a favor and don't pretend you aren't part of The Six. Yes, I know about it. Let's skip the denial dance and tell me your demands."

The man studies me, his gaze inscrutable. "Why the sudden interest? Your loyalties...shifting."

"A man like me doesn't have loyalties." I spin the lighter across my knuckles. "I want power. That means The Association. Word on the street, your family's losing its grip. The others in The Six aren't happy with you."

Edon's eyes flash with anger, but it disappears in an instant.

The old, sly fox.

Smirking, I lean close. "The Association doesn't like weakness. You're the newest family. I could only imagine what they'd do to you. You need me on your side. What happened with the Andersons? Just appetizers. Inconsequential. Now imagine what I could do if I were your enemy."

The men shift, the atmosphere hostile in an instant.

Dritan unbuttons his jacket, flashing me the gun at his waist. A warning.

"Easy," his father murmurs and looks at me with renewed interest. "You've got nerve. Walking in here with no backup and only threats."

"A man like me always has backup. And I'm worth more to you alive than dead."

I reach into my suit pocket.

Dritan and Ilir both draw their weapons. Two gun barrels point at my face.

"Relax. I didn't come here without gifts." I smile despite my pulse quickening.

Negotiation is a game of chicken. Let's see who blinks first.

I pull out a white envelope and slide it over the desk. "A belated birthday present, Mr. Berisha."

Amusement glitters in the old man's eyes as he examines the documents inside. His gaze snaps to mine. "How did you get this?"

"I won't bore you with the details. You want that land on the north side, but it's an Irish stronghold. Here's the deed with your name on it. I even threw in a port for free. Will come in handy with all your personnel...relocations."

Human trafficking. The fucking bastards.

Edon hums under his breath and hands the document to Ilir, who slowly lowers his weapon. As the chief legal officer, he brokers the most brutal deals, leaving his opponents with pennies to their names, if they're lucky.

Strange disappearances are more apt.

Ilir scans the pages, a frown creasing his forehead. He hands them back to his father.

"It's legit. No loopholes."

"It's a gift. No strings attached. Meaningless to me but everything to you." The phone buzzes in my pocket, warning me I've been here for twenty minutes.

Most deals are made within the first half hour. After that, I lose the advantage.

Time to move things along.

"Imagine what I could do *only* for your family. If I were part of The Association, that is." I knock my lighter on his desk.

Once. Twice. Three times.

The words are unspoken, but from the sharpness in his gaze, he knows what I'm offering. Having my black book of secrets on his side will give him unprecedented power even within The Six.

"And Agron," I glance at the oldest son, who's scrutinizing me like a pest under his shoe, "sweep your car more often. Trackers stick. Unless you want your wife to know you're fucking her brother. Not to mention all the bad press you're generating for The Association."

Agron's jaw tics. "Y-You assho—"

"Turp! Mbylle gojën!" Edon slams his fists down.

Disgrace. Shut up.

"Ilir, how remiss of us not to offer Mr. Kent refreshments. Not very hospitable. Go fetch the best *Raki*. To celebrate our new friendship."

"Wise choice," I say, sliding my lighter back into my pocket.

Ilir arches his brow and hands me a tumbler. I take a whiff—sweet. Hints of plums.

As I bring it up to my lips, Edon says, "You know the rules of the Rite? No one gets an exception, not even you."

"A crime of your choosing, documented on video." That's how they control you—indisputable proof of your wrongdoing, but power beyond your dreams.

"And?"

My gaze snaps to his. "Once you're in The Association, you can never leave."

Alive, that is.

Unless I burn it all down.

"Failure to follow the rules, betray The Association, and you and everyone related to you—your relatives, distant cousins, people you've never even met—will be hunted and executed."

My vision reddens. My parents. Little Beatrice. Their last screams.

He expects me to bow to them. To submit. To kneel. That will *never* happen.

I crush the images with a smile. "Naturally. I'd expect nothing less."

The old man grins, clearly pleased. "You know, I predicted this day might come. Someone like you can't be content lurking in the shadows, trading secrets and blackmailing people. You have hunger in your eyes, something I recognize in myself. So I've prepared. I've contacted the Scheduler in advance."

Scheduler?

There's so much I don't know about The Association, and I don't like being in the dark.

"All Rites are cleared through him. The bastard thinks he's all-powerful." He scoffs, disdain clear in his voice. "For your Rite, break into The Orchid vault and retrieve something for us. Lana Anderson's box. That's part one. Complete it on this date and time." He slides me a piece of paper.

Lana.

Something rattles behind my rib cage. She *was* on a list—it was a hunch before but now confirmed.

"Done." I swirl my drink. "What's part two? You said two parts."

"Accomplish part one first, then we'll talk. Can't expect me to reveal all my plans." Edon's eyes narrow as he lifts his drink. "You know...your relationship with the Andersons will end once they find out."

The damn knot forms in my chest again, but I keep my face impassive. "What relationship? There are only deals and games."

I down the alcohol.

He laughs. "I like you, Elias Kent."

I'll burn the world for the identity of my family's killers, even if it means I burn myself with it.

A flash of brown tresses appears in my mind. Soft laughter. Red umbrella. A gentle, untried kiss. Strains of Beethoven's "Für Elise" linger in the air.

"It's my favorite piece," she says, her eyes shining with warmth. "And next week, for my birthday, I'm getting it." She points to the mahogany music box tucked away in the darkened corner of the antique shop. "Waiting makes it more special."

I shove those images away.

No cost is too high.

Not even her.

Chapter 8: VAULT OF LIES

LANA

The Orchid, Manhattan, New York City

I STARE AT MY cryptic text message exchange last night with the asshole extraordinaire as I stand in the lobby of The Orchid vault and concierge level.

Elias

Meet me Saturday at 8:05am on the Vault floor. It's important.

Lana

What, not 8:08am or 8:03am? No please? And what could I, lowly Anderson you never even say hi to, do for you, my Shadow King of Nightmares?

I admit it wasn't my best moment. Girls' night got canceled. Taylor just found out she's pregnant, which explains why she's been looking green these days. Alexis is trekking across the Amazon with Ethan. Millie is vacationing in Europe with Ryland. Levi came down with a bug, much to Belle's dismay. The others are dealing with newborn routines.

I don't blame them for putting me last now. With their families expanding and the cutest little kids in tow, it makes sense that priorities shift. Heck, I'm lucky my best girls are my sisters or sisters-in-law, and we won't grow apart because we're a tight-knit family.

But it's lonely to be left behind.

So yes, I may have had a girls' night all by myself, three sheets to the wind when I received the asshole's text message.

Tapping my heel on the marble floor, I scroll to the rest of the messages, half of which I don't even remember typing.

Lana

Shadow King, did the devil finally come to collect you? Why are you...you? Why are you polite to everyone else but me? What have I ever done to you? Why can't you ever say *please* and *thank you*?

Elias. Whatever your middle name is. Kent. Answer me.

His response came ten minutes later.

Elias

Please.

I remember frowning at the odd message, then realizing he was asking me to show up here this morning.

Curiosity got the better of me. What does the devil need me for?

But now it's ten past eight, I haven't had my morning coffee, and the man himself is nowhere to be seen.

Ugh, Lana. Why did you show up?

Because you were intrigued by the enigmatic man whose chuckles make your panties wet and harsh commands make you want to slap him.

After he pins you against a wall and has his way with you.

My skin heats, and I groan at the unwanted image. Biological clock, dammit. I need better choices.

"Thank you for coming," a soft rasp ghosts my ears.

"Holy crap!"

My phone tumbles out of my grip. One leather glove-clad hand shoots from behind me and catches it.

"Were you a cat in your past life? How do you move without sound?" I spin around, and my mouth promptly dries.

The Shadow King is wearing all black today—a form-fitted suit, vest, tie, the works. He looks like he's aiming to be best-dressed at a funeral. I take in the well-honed muscles straining against his clothes, the drumming vein on his neck, his intense gaze drilling into me like I'm a secret he wants to unravel.

He resembles those sexy assassins I see in movies—the ones who'll cut off someone's fingers for touching his woman and smile the entire time while doing it.

My core throbs, and I curse myself. Completely inappropriate.

"Occupational hazard," he murmurs.

Elias Kent's eyes—the brilliant emerald green reminding me of a boy in my past—lighten a smidge.

That's it. I need to find a man and get laid. This is what I get for saving my first time for someone special—perpetual horniness. But conflating my sweet Kian with this murderer? I'm definitely losing it.

"You were absolutely a cat in another life," I mutter.

"But you like cats." His lips curve into a ghost of a smile.

I frown. I never told him that before.

"Come." He pivots.

My feet move automatically before I can yell at myself for obeying another one of his brusque commands.

That's when I notice he has a small entourage with him.

Four hulking men wearing earpieces, tattoos peeking above the collars of their dress shirts. But the last one, a blond with pale skin and thin lips, sneers at me, his gaze crawling down the length of my sweater dress.

Like he's undressing me with his eyes.

Disgust roils inside me. Alarm bells ring in my head.

"Eyes off her," Elias barks at the men, who stiffen and avert their gazes.

My chest constricts as I slow my strides, eyeing the small group. I don't recognize these people, and I know most of the members here. They're the rich and elite, not these...thugs.

"I'm waiting." Elias pauses and turns, his gaze steady. "Don't test my patience. *Please*, Ms. Anderson."

I stop, my gut twisting with nervousness. Elias sometimes brings staff to assist with the Rose floors.

But this isn't it.

"Who are these people?" The four men straighten. They reach for their waists. "What's going on?"

"It's for your family. That's all you need to know." Elias holds my gaze.

Then he smiles.

Every hair on my body stands at attention.

I spot an anomaly, something I almost didn't register.

The blinking red light of the security camera in the corner. It's gone. *Why are the cameras off?*

Shaking my head, I unwittingly step back. "No. I'm not moving until you tell me. This feels off. Even for you."

"Lana," he warns, his tone still cajoling, but those piercing eyes harden. "They're my bodyguards."

What? I scan the menacing men again. *No. Definitely not.*

Elias's hand curls into a fist, and his eyes flash with ire.

Danger.

Terror seizes me—ice cold and brutal—and I bolt for the nearest concierge office.

He's faster. Elias reaches me in a matter of seconds and clamps his hand over my mouth.

His arm bands around my waist, iron and unyielding, and he carries me toward the vault.

I kick and scream, jabbing my elbow into his ribs, my heels dragging on the floor.

Useless. It's like a fly swatting at a flame. I can't break his grip. I can't breathe.

I'm being kidnapped in broad daylight.

"Stop it. I'm not hurting you." His lips press against my ear. "Now listen carefully. You're going to enter your passcode to the vault. Quietly. We'll walk inside. You'll open your box. No one gets harmed."

Bastard. I knew he wasn't trustworthy. My brothers treated him as one of their own, but deep down, I just knew.

"I'm setting you down. You scream, and security will come. You scream, and they will die. Their blood will be on your hands." His breath puffs against my ear as he whispers, "Do as I say and I'll get you out. You can hate me later. Nod if you understand."

I nod, my heart pounding a mile a minute. Anything to appease the monster so he'll let go of me. If he's lying, I'll be dead. If he's telling the truth—

Get it together, Lana. Calm. Stay focused.

Then I'll think of a way out of this.

"I'm trusting you, Lana. Don't make me regret it," Elias rasps as he sets me down.

Cold air crashes between us, and I shiver.

The four men he's with have their pistols drawn. The blond one murmurs something—a foreign language—to his buddies.

"Smile, Ms. Anderson. Don't spook anyone." Elias curls his hand behind my back, not touching me, but I feel him all the same. A whiff of his cologne—vetiver and smoke—reaches my nose.

My traitorous body hums.

Stop it, Lana. Damn hormones.

"Wh-What do you need from my box?" I seethe. "My brothers trusted you. They took you in. They said you were family. How dare you—"

The maddening man tsks. "Don't know when to shut up, princess, do you? Do as I say."

He stops us in front of the thick metal doors of the vault. It's not just a simple passcode. There's a biometric component and a retinal scan.

The damn bastard must know all this, and that's why he needs me.

The weakest Anderson link.

My fingers dig into my palms as anger shoots up my spine.

Get out of this alive, Lana. Do as he says.

I force myself to even out my breaths as I enter my passcode: 2 28 11 24 3 4. My birthday, February twenty-eighth; Kian's birthday, November twenty-fourth; and March fourth, the day we met.

My pendant thumps against my sternum with every breath, the small gem feeling heavier, almost deceptive, like it's trying to tell me things aren't what they seem.

A sharp inhale puffs against my ear. I snap my gaze to the devil.

His eyes. They look haunted. Why?

"Go on," he rasps.

His men shift restlessly behind us. I hear the clicks of their safeties disengaging.

Hands trembling, I press the alarm sequence only my family knows, then hit enter.

Please let someone see the code red. Anyone but him.

The first lock flashes green. Then the palm scan shows up.

Elias places my hand gently on the scanner. Like he wasn't threatening me seconds ago.

His touch is careful, almost protective, and the twisted tenderness makes my skin crawl.

Beep. The lock disengages.

Finally, the retinal scan.

Nausea churns as I lean in, my ears perked and listening for footsteps, anything to indicate someone got my secret code red message.

Nothing.

A third beep and the door opens.

The men whisper something in the same foreign language.

The blond one says, "Hurry, woman."

"Quiet," Elias snaps at them. His lips brush my ear. "Inside. Ladies first."

Ignoring the tremors in my body, I straighten, head held high, and step into the vault.

Sterile light reflects off the rows of lockboxes. My legs shake as I approach the box in the far-right corner.

My box.

There are family jewels. Some letters.

Nothing worth betraying the Anderson family for.

Footsteps reach my ears. Help is here. My heart jolts, then deflates when a thin, unfamiliar, older man in a black suit walks inside the vault.

Not security.

"Right on time," he murmurs, checking his watch. He takes out a notebook, a fountain pen, and jots something down.

"Who are you?" Elias rasps.

The man smiles. "You can call me the Scheduler. I handle the logistics for the Rites. You passed your first test." He nods and retreats. "Continue on."

Rites? The room shrinks. I think I'm going to be sick. This isn't a robbery. It's a fucked-up ritual. And I'm standing in the middle of it.

Silence reigns for a beat after the man leaves.

"Unlock it now." Elias pushes me forward. "Quickly, Lana."

Taking a deep breath, I press my thumb against the last sensor. The box pops out. Elias grabs it and takes it to the nearby table, the thugs hovering nearby.

Sweat beads on my forehead, and my legs shake. I grip the table for support. I need to stay strong—I can't panic now.

His men fidget and pace, their eyes darting toward the exit. Their guns are steady in their hands.

I shrink behind Elias.

The Judas. The man betrayed all of us.

And yet, I still feel safer behind him than anywhere else in this room.

Elias rummages through the papers in the box.

The blond catches my stare and taps the gun barrel against his palm. He winks and mouths something I don't catch. Something vulgar.

I look away. Acid roils in my stomach. Elias retrieves an envelope—Mom's letter I'm supposed to open when I turn thirty-five. An ache flares behind my sternum. I treasure this letter. It's one of the few things Mom left me. Why does he want it?

He slides it into his pocket. "Done. Pack it up, gentlemen."

We file back into the main hall.

Will they let me live? I've seen their faces. They'll never let me walk away.

Dread punches my gut, and just when I open my mouth to ask Elias, the world stops.

"What's going on here?"

A familiar voice. The commanding tone. *No. Shit, no.* Security is supposed to come. Not him.

I look up, finding Maxwell staring at us. His gaze takes in the guns, the thugs, Elias, and me.

"Lana? Elias? What's going on?"

I can't answer him.

"Run," I mouth. *"Run."*

Maxwell stiffens. "Elias, what's the meaning of this? Let go of her."

The devil tightens his arm around my waist, tension obvious in his muscles. But his voice is casual and calm. Like we're talking about the weather.

"Lana was just showing me around. Thinking of getting a box here. She was helpful. Why don't you head to the lounge and I'll join you later."

To explain. To BS. To lie to him.

My brother eyes the guns. I can see his mind working. Calculating.

"My men were just being careful," Elias adds with a chuckle. "I have many enemies."

He tells the blond, "Put away your gun. We're in the safest place in Manhattan."

The thug slowly holsters his weapon, his gaze frigid.

Maxwell narrows his eyes, then he looks at me again.

I force my expression into calmness—the men will kill him if I do anything wrong.

"Fine," Maxwell murmurs.

Relief sags my shoulder as I watch my oldest brother walk away.

Don't turn back. Don't do anything stupid, Maxwell. Don't. You have a wife and a kid.

But I know him too well. And he knows me too.

He yanks the emergency alarm.

Loud sirens blast throughout the building. People pour out of their offices. Steel shutters drop, locking the vault. Security—finally—storms out of the stairwell doors.

"Take them out. No survivors," the blond shouts, voice gleeful.

I scream as someone plows into me, knocking me onto the floor. My knees crack against the marble. Pain flashes white behind my eyes.

Gunfire explodes and mayhem swirls around me.

People drop like boulders in a rockslide. Screams, terrifying screams, ricochet off the marble.

I curl into a ball, my hands covering my head. I'm shaking so hard my teeth clack. I don't want to die. Not like this.

Suddenly, the scent of dry vetiver and smoke wraps around me.

Elias is covering my body with his. He shoves me into a corner.

"Stay here. Don't move."

His warmth leaves me, and Maxwell shouts in the distance. "Lana, go! Fucking go."

I come to my senses and scamper to my feet.

Acid rushes up my throat as I see the bloodshed for the first time.

Bodies everywhere, streaks of red tagging the walls and the floor. My stomach lurches. The world tilts, and for a second, I think I'm going to black out.

Three of the four thugs remain standing, mad laughter ripping from their mouths.

Crimson soaks the blond's hair, his lips twisting into an unhinged smile as he shoots the guard next to him. A gut shot. Then a headshot.

Bob, the new concierge, lunges forward—only to be caught by a knife. Once. Twice. The thug doesn't blink. He exacts his violence until Bob collapses onto the floor.

I just talked to Bob last week. We had coffee together. His wife just had a baby.

My feet move before my mind catches up. Maxwell has a gun in his hand—I don't know how he got it—he's taking out soldiers who look like the thugs.

More bodies drop around me. More gunfire. Smoke invades the air.

I duck as someone screams, my body still moving toward Maxwell.

Almost there. A few more steps then I'll reach him.

A gun barrel presses against my temple.

A muscular arm pins me against a heated body.

"Call your men off, or I'll blow her brains out," Elias commands.

Maxwell freezes. He lowers his gun and yells, "Down, everyone. Stop. Weapons down."

Steel digs into my skin. I shake. My vision tunnels. All I can see is the horror in my brother's eyes.

"Shhh. You're okay," Elias murmurs, his voice soothing, like he's calming a crying child.

Crazy. This man is nuts.

"Don't do this, Elias," Maxwell tries again. "You want something from us? Just ask. I'll give it to you. All of this. Yours."

Out of the corner of my eye, I spot movement. Alfred, our head of security, charges—

Bang.

Bullet to the forehead. His body crumples, his lifeless eyes staring into nothing.

The blond laughs—the sound sharp and manic. He kicks Alfred's body and drags his boot through the blood like a child smearing paint.

He grins at me.

Then he aims his gun at Maxwell.

My mouth parts in a scream, then I—

Bang. Bang.

Two shots crack behind me.

My heart stops.

Maxwell jerks, his eyes wide, then he looks down. Rivers of crimson spread across his dress shirt. His face twists in pain, and he collapses to the ground.

"No!" I cry.

I turn around.

Smoke curls from Elias's gun.

Not the blond's.

Elias's.

He did this. This monster who stood in our home. Came to family weddings. Who pretended to be one of us.

Fury scorches through my veins. The monster has the gall to appear shell-shocked, his fingers white-knuckled around his gun. His gaze, heavy with something resembling regret, snags on Maxwell for a beat.

But the expression vanishes.

An inhuman scream rips out of me, and I launch myself at him.

Elias blocks my attempts and hefts me over his shoulder like I weigh nothing.

I kick, scratch, and bite. Anywhere I can reach. Feral with hatred.

"You shot my brother! You fucking piece of shit! Just kill me now because if I don't die, I'll make the rest of your fucking life a living hell!"

Elias ignores me, carries me into the elevator, and enters the override code.

I thrash in his hold, trying to break free.

But it's useless.

Through the ringing in my ears, I hear the blond's wild and gleeful laugh as the thugs continue their slaughter.

But I barely notice.

All I can see is Maxwell, the brother I've looked up to my entire life, lying lifeless on the white marble floor, his blood pooling around him as the elevator doors close.

My brother. My protector. My anchor.

Shot by the man he trusted.

Shot by someone I thought was, at worst, a shadow in our midst.

Shot by Elias Kent.

"I'll kill you," I scream.

Then, a sweet, sickly smell fills my lungs.
Darkness drags me under.

Chapter 9: THE LETTER

ELIAS

FUCK.

This didn't go according to plan. Lana was supposed to trust me when I told her I needed something from her box to protect her family. If pressed, I'd reveal it was related to her SUV stalker.

She'd ask more questions, but I'd have the answers. The men with me? New bodyguards.

She'd believe me. After all, I'd saved her brothers multiple times before.

I dispatched the Albanians after the chaos and hightailed to my safe house. The bastards no doubt headed straight to the Berishas, and with their body cam footage, there'd be no sugarcoating this disaster.

I told them they'd get their precious letter—still unopened in my pocket—after I settled things with the Andersons.

No way I'd hand something so important to those bloodthirsty lowlifes who are lieutenants in the Albanian mob.

Faint traffic hums through the windows in this nondescript apartment. I pace the length of the room, the city alive while the chasm inside me swallows me whole.

Strategies rattle through my mind. Possible moves on the chessboard. Ways to get out of this.

Part one of my Rite was to steal the letter. That's done. I don't even know what part two is.

Fucking shit.

My gaze snags on her.

Lana. My obsession. The woman I hate because of the role she played on the day that changed my life.

I must never forget.

She lies asleep on the king-sized bed, the chloroform still holding her under. She's clad in one of my white dress shirts. My housekeeper changed her out of her blood-soaked outfit after I carried her inside a few hours ago.

Quietly, I pull up a chair next to her bedside.

Under the afternoon light, she looks even more beautiful. Her thick lashes kiss her cheeks; her inky dark hair splayed across my white pillowcase. Her pulse flutters in her neck as she shifts on the bed, her plump lips relaxed.

A break from the nightmare she had just lived through.

She moans—the soft sound going straight to my groin. *I'm a sick motherfucker.*

I lean in, wanting to feel her breath on my skin, to let her roses cloud my senses until they wipe away the stench of death and destruction.

I haven't had my twenty-eight minutes today yet.

A reprieve. I need my twenty-eight minutes more than I need air.

Releasing an exhale, I lock up my anger, hatred, the violence coursing through my veins.

My fingers tremble as I touch a lock of her hair. So soft and silky. Innocence and perfection I shouldn't taint, but I'm a weak man.

I wrap it around my fingers, once, twice, then lift it to my nose and inhale.

Sweet, tantalizing roses.

For a moment, I'm sixteen again with Lake Michigan's breeze whispering across my face, the icy water numbing my swollen knees. I feel her gentle fingers tracing clumsy letters into my palm while humming her favorite Beethoven piece under her breath.

The girl who's never left my memories, who believed a broke, dyslexic kid could be more.

My phone buzzes.

"Kent," I whisper, not wanting to wake Lana.

"I'm packed and ready to go. This is my new number," my sister, Sofia, drawls in a smoky voice. "What's next?"

"We survive. I'll figure something out."

"You always do."

"How were things before you left?" I ask.

Sofia helped me manage a few clubs on the Rose floors. We coordinated our exits in case anything went awry with the heist, and thank God we did.

"Chaos. The FBI, counterterrorism, every acronym showed up before I left. The Andersons are freaking out."

Guilt tightens my throat. "How is he?"

Snippets flash behind my eyelids. Maxwell's cutting gaze of betrayal. The blood soaking his shirt. His fear for Lana.

It was a no-win situation. A choice between Bekim and me.

Bekim the Deranged, as the Albanian mob called him, would've gutted Maxwell if he fired first. He would've relished it.

My bullets gave him a chance.

"He's in surgery. Last I heard, there's significant blood loss. But you had good aim. Ren would be proud. Both shots missed his vital organs."

"I did what I had to do."

Life carved a monster in me. Betrayal. Terrible choices. Loss. All part of the game of chess we're playing.

"They'll never forgive you. I know what they mean to you. You gave it all up. What if this doesn't—"

"It was all a game, Sofia. You knew that." The words ring hollow. "Getting into The Orchid, gathering intel and secrets. I played them, and we're finally here. So close to finding out who killed our parents and little Beatrice. And..."

Who took you.

Sofia disappeared the day our parents died. I scoured the ends of the earth and couldn't find her.

But eventually, I did. Three years later.

She was a changed person then. I killed her handler, faked her death, but it was too little too late.

I never knew what happened to her during those three years, and she refused to talk about it.

I would slaughter every single bastard who did this to us.

"The past is in the past," Sofia replies, her voice hardening. "I'm on the next plane out. See you in Chicago."

She hangs up.

A heavy breath escapes me, and I loosen the tie around my neck. Lana whimpers, her angelic face suddenly twisting in fear and pain as a nightmare grips her in its throes.

Probably nightmares about me.

Berating myself for my inability to resist her, I brush her hair back, my breath hitching as I touch her without my gloves for the first time in decades. Gloves were my way of keeping her at a distance. But now, with her so close to me, I suddenly forget why I need to stay away.

My fingers shake as I trace her cheek. Her warmth sizzles my skin and my chest spasms.

"You're fine, Elise. You're fine," I whisper. "Everything's fine."

She thrashes, then quiets, my voice seeming to settle her.

A spark of warmth, an insidious craving, flares when she grabs my hand and snuggles it.

Just like that day on the lake when we were different people. A lost boy, beaten by life but with beautiful dreams of the future. A princess feeling suffocated by her gilded cage.

Her chest lifts and falls, drawing my attention to the pulse fluttering in her neck.

She looks good in my clothes. If I had my way, I'd have her dressed in my shirts all day long so the world knows she was mine.

I want to kiss the soft skin where her vitality beats. Inhale her light at the source. Whisper promises on her lips. Tell her who I really am. Tell her I'm not the monster she thinks I am.

One more kiss. Just one more.

Sweet kisses at sixteen weren't enough. I didn't know what I was doing then.

But I do now. Fuck I know just what to do if I had the chance.

Heat rushes to my groin. I'm a sick fuck. Incurable. I should go to Rafe for a confession when I get back to Chicago. The priest of The Syndicate is there to absolve us of our sins.

Yeah, right. My soul is so dark, no amount of bleach could cleanse it.

Biting my cheek to distract myself, I pull out the letter from my pocket—the document that sparked my point of no return.

Carefully, I unseal it. Why would The Association risk a high-profile heist in broad daylight?

I unfold the single sheet of paper and read.

My stomach drops. Fear shoots through my veins. My attention snaps back to Lana, who's unaware of the future awaiting her.

This—what just happened in the vault—is only the beginning.

They aren't done with her yet.

Whatever part two of the Rite is, I'll walk through it—fires, flames, and hell. And Lana, the woman I hate? I'll make sure she gets out alive.

Carefully, I reseal the letter and put it away.

Decision made, I pull out my phone and type a message to the Berishas.

Elias

I have the letter. Complications happened. Requesting meeting at my NYC safe house.

I glance at Lana again, who's now gripping my hand like it's her lifeline. Gently, I swipe my thumb over her skin, giving her a gentle squeeze.

Heat sears me from the simple touch, warming parts of me I thought were long dead.

She relaxes and lets out the softest sigh.

I whisper a vow I never thought I'd make.

And that organ behind my rib cage, the one I thought was burned to ashes along with my parents when I was sixteen, flickers to life.

Chapter 10: DEVIL IN DISGUISE

LANA

BLOOD EVERYWHERE. TERRIFYING SCREAMS. Heart thrashing out of my chest. Thundering gunshots. Elias's voice in my ear, low and lethal.

Maxwell lying in a pool of scarlet.

A strangled gasp tears out of me, and I bolt upright.

My vision swirls, my head woozy, like I'm seconds away from drowning. I focus on physical sensations. Cotton sheets. Soft mattress. Dark room. Only a sliver of light peeks through the closed curtains.

Where am I?

Maxwell.

The memories pummel my mind in violent snapshots. Elias at The Orchid. His entourage. The vault.

The cold press of his gun barrel against my temple.

Oh my God, Maxwell. Visions of my brother lifeless on the ground send me scrambling out of bed.

My eyes burn as I remember staring helplessly at his still body when the elevator doors closed.

Please tell me he's okay. There was so much blood. How can anyone survive losing that much?

My lips tremble, grief punching my gut. We're the Andersons. *We're strong motherfuckers,* as Rex would say. I have to have hope.

Calm down, Lana. What did your self-defense classes teach you? Assess, then react. Panic will kill you.

Escape first. Everything comes later.

Blowing out a deep breath, I take a few steps, my bare feet registering the rough carpet. Cool air hits my legs.

Hold on, I'm not in my clothes.

My hands fly over my body. I'm wearing someone else's shirt. My legs are bruised, stomach in knots, but no pain in unusual areas.

I don't think I was violated.

Hands trembling, I stumble to the window, and peel back the curtain.

Determination sharpens my senses.

Focusing on the landscape outside, I note the barren trees first, their gnarly branches stretching toward the gray skies. A wrought-iron fence encloses the park like a prison. The puddles on the ground tell me some time elapsed when I was out.

It wasn't raining this morning.

My gaze snaps to the right, taking in the familiar church spires in the distance. St. George's Episcopal. Rain-soaked brownstones stand sentry around the square. A statue looms in the center of a circular hedge.

Gramercy Park. I'm in Gramercy Park.

I examine the white dress shirt I have on. A man's shirt. High thread count, soft as silk. I recognize quality when I see it. Driven by instinct, I lift the collar and inhale.

Dried vetiver and woodsy smoke.

Elias. This is his. Why am I in his shirt? Why did he take me? And why did he need Mom's letter?

Endless questions pinball around my mind, but I shove them away. I'll have time for that later.

Quietly, I tiptoe toward the closed door, sweat beading on my neck.

"Shit," I mutter when the knob doesn't give. And it's sturdy. Unbreakable.

Ugh. Why didn't etiquette and self-defense classes include lock-picking?

My gaze sweeps around the room again—it's bare bones, clearly a temporary place. There's only a bed and a lamp on a simple nightstand. Nothing I can use. I glance toward the window. I didn't see a fire escape, but perhaps I overlooked something.

"Fuck no!" A growl reaches my ears and I flinch.

More faint sounds. Angry voices. A chair scrapes against the floor. Heavy footsteps. Conversations in a foreign language.

They're coming from the other side of the wall.

I press my ear against it. Anything I pick up may aid my escape.

"I fulfilled my end of the bargain. You got your letter," the familiar, raspy voice says. Elias. He has to be talking about Mom's letter from my safe.

"...may have overestimated you...only part one." Someone's talking to him, but the stranger's voice is too soft. I can't make out his words.

"I'll take care of them. No need to go nuclear," Elias responds.

Them? Who? Us? Me? He must be near the wall because I hear him clearly.

"The Association won't be pleased...the Rite...her."

The Association?

Heavy breaths saw out of my lungs as the levers slide into position—a complicated puzzle box that's invisible, but they're all the same.

All puzzles have answers.

Elias is part of The Association.

My chest locks tight, my hands forming fists by my side.

The bastard. He's been a mole all this time.

"We'll keep her...thirty-five..." *What?*

A few beats of silence follow.

Then Elias's voice again, as sharp as a blade.

"I'll marry her. I'll marry Lana Anderson."

"What!" I quickly clasp my hand over my mouth.

Too late.

The door crashes open, and a hulking man fists my hair and drags me out.

Chapter 11: THE IMPOSSIBLE TASK

ELIAS

AGRON SNEERS ACROSS FROM me in the makeshift office. "You failed, Kent. We overestimated you. Only part one and what a fucking mess."

He spits on the floor. "I hope you have your affairs in order because you aren't getting out of this alive. Unless..." The man smirks. "I heard a rumor. Elias Kent never kneels. How about that? Drop to your knees right now, and we'll spare you."

A flash fire hits me in the chest, but I bite my cheek, forcing myself to remain still.

The smell of charred wood and burning cloth overwhelms my senses. Then the sweetness—gasoline and flames, melted chocolates in my pocket. Desperate screams. Pebbles digging into my knees.

Figments of the past.

"I never kneel for *anyone*." The words are quiet, but Agron heard them loud and clear. "*Ever*."

He narrows his eyes and points his gun at me.

Click. The safety disengages.

"How about I end your life right now?" He aims the steel barrel against my forehead.

A bitter smile hitches my lips. I don't move, don't react.

Never let them see your desperation.

Emotions make you a loser before your first move, and I never lose.

With one leg crossed over my other knee, I adjust my cufflinks. I knock my lighter on the table.

Knock.

"What?" he growls.

"Just thinking how someone like you got your position. Daddy must be pissed. Eldest son. Should've been the family's pride and joy."

I tsk. "But fucking your brother-in-law? *Really?* Are you a top or a bottom? Never mind. I can check my pictures."

Knock.

Checkmate.

A roar bellows from his throat, and he's on top of me in a second. He jams the barrel against my temple, his arm shaking with restraint.

"Say that again."

"You really should work on that temper."

"Boys," Edon's voice commands from the laptop. "Enough."

His son shoves me back into my seat. Sweat beads on my back, but I act unbothered.

Instead, I dust off my jacket. The asshole wrinkled it. Damn. A loose seam. Will need to get that fixed later.

"Kent, The Association isn't happy. A bloodbath. A public spectacle. Your Rite is incomplete, and you kidnapped an Anderson. The Scheduler is livid. What are you going to do about her?"

My thoughts flash to Lana, who was still asleep when I left her room an hour ago for my emergency meeting with the Berishas.

She didn't want to let go of my hand. She clutched it like a drowning man would a lifeboat, like she needed me to survive.

It took every ounce of willpower to walk away.

"We can't let her go," Edon continues.

A sudden urge seizes me—to scoop her into my arms and disappear. To forget everything and turn back time to when Kian and Elise still existed.

Madness. Utter madness.

"You solve this, or you won't live to see tomorrow," he warns.

Tension thickens like a plume of poisonous gas.

"If I die, all your secrets are out. Dead man's switch. You must've expected that."

"It's a risk we'll take."

Our gazes hold, neither of us blinking nor yielding.

He's a much better chess player than his eldest. I guess the apple *does* fall far from the tree.

"I'll take care of them. No need to go nuclear," I murmur.

"You have twenty-four hours or I'll let Agron put that bullet in your head." Edon's voice hardens. "And the letter wasn't what we'd hoped.

I'm sure you've read it. We'll keep her until she turns thirty-five. Then we'll get what we need."

My lighter clatters on the desk. Agron's attention snaps to it, a flash of awareness dawning in his eyes.

Fuck. Juvenile mistake.

I force out a smile and ignore him, focusing on the father. "It'll be messy for you. Taking an Anderson hostage for six months. You sure you want to risk that?"

"We have the mob for this work."

Dread punches my lungs. The mob and gangs are foot soldiers for The Association. Bekim, the Deranged, and his manic eyes flash through my mind. The way he leered at Lana like she was a piece of meat.

Keeping my gaze steady, I reply, "I know them. The Andersons are stubborn. Relentless. They won't submit. They'll create trouble for you."

Agron chuckles from his spot across the table. A sickening smile crests his lips. "Then we'll send her back in pieces."

My knuckles tighten, white around my lighter.

Over my dead body.

He stands and leans toward me, his voice a lethal whisper.

I might have underestimated him.

"I never told you," he says, his voice filthy, "I swing both ways. And that luscious piece next door? I bet her pussy is tighter than my brother-in-law's asshole."

My ears ring. *Swoosh. Swoosh. Swoosh.* A copper tang hits my tongue.

I've bitten myself. Drawn blood.

Agron sits back, the haughty smirk back on his face, his eyes glinting with satisfaction.

I'll carve them out of his skull. Stuff them down his throat. Wipe the memory of Lana from his brain. After all this is over, I'll take my time and wrench out every morsel of pain from him.

But first, I strain a smile.

I release my grip on the lighter and force myself to calm.

Arching my brow, I shrug. "Doesn't matter. She means nothing to me. What's part two?"

"P-Part two?" Agron sputters, clearly confused at my abrupt change in topic.

"My Rite. I finished part one. What's part two?"

His father barks out a laugh and claps...a slow, mocking sound.

"The infamous Elias Kent. Unruffled even when staring death in the face."

The older man leans toward the camera. "Part two is impossible for you, I'm afraid. But since you're curious, I'll tell you. We want the Andersons to join The Association."

His words echo against the walls, and the room shrinks before me.

My nostrils flare and I inhale. I shouldn't be surprised. The Association has wanted this for years, despite every refusal. The Andersons are influential and respectable. Having the family on their side will only bolster The Association's power. But Maxwell and his siblings have too much honor to join them.

And now? With him in the ICU, the bloodshed at The Orchid, and Lana locked in her room next door?

Edon might as well ask me to turn the sky green.

"Impossible task, you see? We'll take Ms. Anderson off your hands."

Agron gets up and strides to the door. "Looks like I'm going to get my first taste of the Anderson cunt. I hear she's a virgin. Thirty-four and untouched? I'll have to find out if that's true."

I shoot up so fast, the chair crashes against the wall behind me.

"I'll marry her. I'll marry Lana Anderson." The words are out of my mouth before I can stop them. It's an impulse to stop the bastards from having her. But as my mind spins with the ramifications, I realize this might be the solution.

A feminine gasp filters through the wall.

My chest constricts. Lana's awake.

"Looks like someone wants to join the party." A sneer carves up Agron's face, and seconds later, he drags Lana inside by her hair.

She stumbles in, her face flushed with anger, wearing nothing but my shirt.

She's fucking glorious.

"Let go of me, you asshole! I'm not marrying anyone, least of all him!" She points at me.

My pulse riots, my fingers twitch, but I force myself to remain still.

Relax my shoulders. My jaw. Unclench my fingers.

A good chess player never shows his tells.

Agron tosses Lana into a chair. My *zemër* stiffens, blows the hair out of her face, and gets back up. Ignoring the fucker, she storms my way and jabs me in the chest.

"Elias Kent, if you think I'll marry you after you shot Maxwell, you're delusional!"

"And yet...you will."

Her intoxicating roses hit my nose, and my skin lights up before I exhale. I soak in every inch of her—her cheeks brightening in an alluring shade of pink, her charcoal eyes burning hot with hatred.

I bet I can make them burn for another reason.

"You're the last person I'll marry." She stabs me again with her finger. With each jab, her voluptuous tits sway underneath my shirt. The movement hardens my cock in seconds.

Fuck me.

"You don't get to decide," I rasp, my voice guttural and thick. "Not a democracy, Lana."

I sprawl in my chair, thankful the table is blocking Agron's full view.

But my princess misses nothing. Her gaze snaps to my groin. Her lips part, eyes widening when she sees my hard cock saluting her through my pants. The maddening pulse beats faster at the base of her throat.

Kill me now.

My nostrils flare, my dick lengthening with each second. I swallow a groan when the tip begins to leak.

Hatred and arousal, a razor-thin edge between them.

"If you want Maxwell to live, and little Levi to grow up with a dad, you'll marry me. This isn't a choice." Slowly, I sit up. My gaze drops to her full lips. Plump. Red. Enticing. How will they taste now? Will she bite me? Draw blood? "Trust me, I won't miss twice."

My words snap her out of her trance, and she backs up, her arms crossed over her chest.

"No. I'm *never* marrying you. I fucking hate your guts."

"It's either me or them." I jab my thumb at Agron, who's observing us like the calculating COO I saw in his father's office the first time.

"You think they'll let you live? That The Association will let your family off the hook after all this?"

My pulse jerks as I take her in—if her eyes could kill, I'd be a dead man five times over.

A masochistic streak sears through me. She hates me so much. How will it feel to tame that passion into something else? Let her burn me to a crisp?

"Marry me or bury him. You have a brain, Lana. Use it." I lean in and murmur, "Don't get any ideas. The cops, the Feds, all in my pocket or The Association's. There's nowhere you can run where we won't find you. And you should know by now, I kill without remorse."

Her face blanches. I ignore the pinch behind my rib cage and keep my focus on her. She's wavering.

One more little push. "You're strong, Lana. Only five months of marriage for your family's safety. A small price to pay."

She balls her hands into tight fists.

Checkmate.

I see the moment she realizes this is the only way out if she wants everyone to stay alive.

"You fucker," she seethes. "I. Will. Kill. You."

"Get in line." I arch my brow.

Edon clears his throat. He studies me through the computer screen.

I roll my lighter over my knuckles again.

"You said it was an impossible task. Part two. You mentioned you didn't get what you wanted with the letter. That's why you need her."

Click. A new flame bursts from the lighter. I snuff it out.

"This will solve everything. Multiple birds with one stone. I'll watch her. Keep her by my side. She'll be bound to me by marriage, and de facto, the Andersons as well. If they want her safe and happy, they'll kneel to The Association."

And I'll finally claw into the heart of The Association and find my answers.

Click. I restart the flame.

The sounds reverberate in the room, dense with silence.

"Leverage, my friends. It's all about leverage."

Edon purses his lips. "It's out of the box. I'll need to convince the Scheduler. He's strict about the Rites. Especially something so impossible."

Click. I snap the lighter shut.

"No task is impossible," I say softly, smiling at Lana even though every inch of me singes with a satisfaction I don't dare name. "Not for Elias Kent."

Chapter 12: THE CONFRONTATION

ELIAS

HOSTILITY PERMEATES THE AIR the moment we step through the double doors of the Anderson Estate that evening. Agnes, their housekeeper, hurls a withering glare at me before scurrying away, no doubt to notify the man of the house of our arrival.

It's a surprise visit. I don't want the Andersons to have time to prepare. Sources tell me Maxwell checked himself out of the hospital and only Rex is with him, the rest of the family having just left after visiting.

We have to move fast, and surprise is half the effort.

"Come on, fiancée," I murmur, linking my fingers with Lana's. A sharp current runs through me from the contact despite my leather gloves preventing our skin from touching.

I can't afford to touch her. I need my wits about me.

"Let go of me, you motherfucker," Lana grits out. She twists her arm and pulls, but I give her no quarter.

She then stabs the sharp heel of her stiletto into my shoe.

I grunt. Pain burns through me, and my eyes immediately water.

But I don't let go.

I'll never let go.

For a moment, as I struggle to catch my breath, my heart palpitating, a stray thought slips into my consciousness.

Kian finally got to have his Elise again.

"You can drop the act." Lana digs her nails through my leather glove. "No one's watching. Everyone knows the truth here. Let go of me."

Chuckling, I wipe the moisture from my eyes. "If you only knew how much your fight is turning me on."

"You sadistic sack of shit."

"And that potty mouth of yours." I graze my finger on her chin. She swats it away. "I never knew the Anderson princess could cuss up a storm."

"There's more where that's coming—"

Her breath hitches when I haul her against my body until we're a hairsbreadth apart. Our shoes squeak against the floor. We collide with the wall next to the entryway table.

"Remember what I said earlier, princess. Marry me or bury him. Your choice. I'll never take away your choice."

Lana's eyes flash with anger. She raises her hand to slap me.

I catch her wrist and pin it against her back, forcing her to arch up and look at me.

She moves again. Her free arm jerks toward the table. Metal clangs. A glint of silver flashes in my vision.

The sharp edge of a blade points at my throat. A letter opener.

My pulse roars in my ears, my senses heightened. Her gray eyes. Burning hatred. Lethal and violent.

Fucking intoxicating.

"Go on," I rasp.

Another enticing gasp tumbles out of her rosy lips. Against my willpower, or lack thereof, my body responds. Every muscle coils. Sharp need threatens to obliterate any rational thinking.

"Not there." Slowly, I move the blade closer. "Here. Under my chin. That's where the blood vessels are."

I wrap my hand around hers, feeling her tremble.

I press the tip harder. A sharp pinch. Wetness.

Her breath escapes in a hiss, her eyes snared at my throat, at the blood trickling down my neck.

"Go on," I rasp, "I started it for you. Press harder. One cut and I'll bleed out in twenty seconds."

Her hand shakes, her eyes darting from my face to my neck.

"You're nuts." Her pretty pink tongue dips out to wet her lips.

I grind out a guttural groan. The perfect Cupid's bow. The soft bottom curve. I can almost taste her sweetness.

"Are you going to do it? Or are you going to waste my time?" My throat is parched, and I swallow.

The air vibrates, each molecule incandescent. Nothing matters except for the woman in my arms.

"Let's save the foreplay for our wedding night." My voice is rough. Sandpaper.

The letter opener clatters to the floor.

"I'll *never* sleep with you." Her chest moves up and down, up and down. My blood heats, pooling in my groin as I press closer, just a tiny inch, to feel her tight body throbbing against mine.

"Never say never." I swallow another groan, my mind blurring at the edges. "Maybe you'll enjoy it. Beg me for it."

Her tongue darts out again.

Static blows out my hearing.

Just a taste, Elias. A tiny taste. She wants it. Dilated eyes. Flushed face. Those tight little nipples beading under her shirt.

She's *still* wearing my shirt. My housekeeper bought her a new sweater and leggings, but the sick, twisted monster inside me wanted to parade her around in my clothes.

Lana's eyes drop to my mouth. She doesn't notice it, but she's swaying her body against mine—gentle grazes, soft gyrations—like she needs the touch as much as I do.

She may hate my guts and want to kill me in my sleep, but her body?

It wants me.

Male satisfaction suffuses me, and before I completely lose my mind, I release her and step back.

She flinches, eyes wide with shock and arousal.

"Let's get this over with." I pivot and walk upstairs toward Maxwell's study before I change my mind.

The man himself meets us at the top of the stairs. In a wheelchair, with a gun perched on his lap, aimed at me. He looks pale, his forehead beading with sweat.

But those intense eyes—*the* Anderson gray eyes?

They're lethal and strong. They promise I won't walk out of this building alive.

Rex stands behind him, a gun in his hand.

"Maxwell," Lana gasps, flying over to her brother and throwing her arms around his neck. She scans his bandaged torso before hugging him again. "You're okay. Oh my God, you're okay."

"Lana," Maxwell murmurs, brushing his free hand down her back. "I was so worried about you."

She trembles and shakes her head. "No, *I* was worried. It's all my fault. I should've known Elias was up to no good. I shouldn't have met him alone. I should've—"

"No." His voice hardens. "If anyone's to blame, it's me. I found him in the alley, bleeding, with a knife buried in his gut."

Maxwell stares at me from beyond her shoulder. "I took pity on him. Convinced Ryland we should take him to the hospital. That we should check on him. When he recovered, I was the one to convince Dad we could use someone like him at The Orchid."

He lifts his gun, his arm unwavering. "I saved his life, and this was how he repaid me. Repaid us."

"Enough talking. Can we shoot him and get it over with?" Rex growls.

His words trigger something in Lana because she quickly untangles herself from Maxwell.

"No!" She shakes her head. "He's part of The Association!"

Her words echo against the tall ceilings. The brothers' faces are grim. Light flickers from the dimly lit sconces, casting looming shadows in the hallway.

"We figured as much," Rex says. "We never should've trusted you."

His words land like a gut punch. I force myself not to react. This is an outcome I've predicted.

But it hurts like a motherfucker.

"Once a snake, always a snake," Maxwell murmurs. He holds up his gun and cocks it. "Any last words?"

"No, we can't kill him. The Association will go after you all," Lana begs, her voice frantic. "In fact...I...we'll..." She takes a deep breath and straightens while her fingers gnarl against her shirt—*my* shirt. "We'll...I..."

She can't get the words out.

Marrying me is such a nightmare, the normally poised head of PR, someone who always has the words, can't speak.

Ignoring the sudden pain gripping my chest, I take pity on her. "We're getting married. In one hour. Here on the premises. I've made the arrangements."

A shocked silence descends on us. Even the crows have stopped crying outside.

Rex is the first to recover. "What did you just say?"

"Lana and I are getting married. That's the only way for you all to stay alive."

"Over my dead—" Maxwell shakes as he rises from the wheelchair.

"Sit down," Lana commands.

She explains the situation with the Berishas—as much as she knows—to her brothers.

"I can't risk it. The Association is brutal. We saw what they did at the vault. Levi has to grow up with a dad. And you, Rex. You have twins. The cutest little babies. And the others—we can't risk their lives." Teary-eyed, she clutches Rex and Maxwell's hands, imploring them to listen.

"This is the only way," she whispers.

"I won't have you sacrifice yourself for us," Maxwell says.

"We have billions. We can hire the best security and disappear," Rex agrees.

Ignoring the guilt twisting my gut, I stare at Maxwell. "I want a word with you. *Alone.*"

"No." Rex moves in front of his brother.

Eyes narrowed, Maxwell scans my face. I force myself to remain impassive and hold up my hands. I have no intention of hurting him.

"Give us a minute," he says to Rex.

"You sure—"

"Yes." Maxwell turns to Lana, his voice thick as he says, "We Andersons stick together. I don't care what threats are out there. We'll survive this. You don't need to sacrifice yourself."

Lana doles out a wobbly smile. "It's my choice. Think about the others. The little ones. It's my choice, Maxwell."

She pats her brother's hand and with one lingering look, she and Rex step inside the office, leaving Maxwell and me on the landing.

For a moment, neither of us speaks. I think back to the gloomy day a decade ago when they saved me. He and his twin, dressed in their fancy polo shirts and slacks, found me as I lay bleeding against the wall by the dumpsters behind Fleur.

Maxwell didn't hesitate. He didn't do what I thought he'd do—recoil in disgust or step away in horror.

He rushed up to me, shredded his shirt, pressed it against my wound, and stabilized the knife, not caring that my blood was soaking his skin. Only concern was in his eyes.

That concern is long gone now.

"Only I can protect her," I say, ignoring the jagged rock stuck in my throat. "They want to keep her. The Albanian mob. In their hands, I'm afraid—"

I can't speak. I can't describe what will happen to Lana if she doesn't marry me.

Maxwell pales as understanding dawns in his eyes. "Why, Elias? Why? We couldn't have been that wrong about you, could we?"

"I have my reasons. Reasons that don't concern you."

I turn away. An unfamiliar sensation suffocates me. Heaviness. A throbbing pain so deep, it's in the depths of my marrow.

Grief.

For ten years, aside from the twenty-eight minutes each day when I'd let myself dream, I had a family outside of Sofia. A family untainted by grief. These men claimed me as their own, despite my best intentions to stay detached by avoiding nonessential meetings, like the family dinner Belle invited me to before.

But they're relentless—the Andersons. They pull you in with their loyalty, camaraderie, and warmth, and whenever I'd step through the doors at The Orchid, I could forget about the bloodshed, about the violence in my life.

A reprieve.

But all good things must come to an end.

"All you need to know is," I stare at the antique grandfather clock at the end of the hallway, "they will kill her. But before then, they will defile her, pass her around from man to man. They will snuff out the light in her eyes."

I've seen it before—the way Dad looked at Mom's still figure as the flames took them. His eyes were dead—no will to live. The Association took everything soft from our house and burned it to ash.

My hands fist at my sides. "Do you want to risk it, Maxwell? Do you want to be on the run forever? You saw what they did to others. All the murders. The crimes."

I face him. "Play along. This game is too advanced for you. This could all go away if she marries me. I can protect her. The choice is simple. Me or them. Who do you trust more?"

Maxwell's eyes sharpen. He scans my face again.

He's considering it.

"You owe me a favor, Maxwell." I saved he and his wife's lives years ago when a madman nearly ended their love story before it could begin. "A favor for a favor. I'm calling it in now."

His throat works, those startling gray eyes of his inscrutable.

"Her choice," he rasps, "and if one hair is harmed on her person, I'll bleed you out myself."

He spins away as the grandfather clock chimes.

Just like the day I met her twenty years ago.

But unlike that day, the sound is hollow.

A somber death knell.

Chapter 13: INTERLUDE—THE RED UMBRELLA

KIAN

Past: Chicago, Twenty Years Ago

THE FIRST TIME I saw her, the rain had teeth, but I wouldn't change it for anything.

The grandfather clock inside the antique shop had chimed like it was mocking me.

"Kneel, pretty boy. That'll teach you not to steal. Be lucky that's all you're doing."

I shivered as the storm drenched me. The rain came earlier this year. Chicago was freezing in late March, especially with wet clothes sticking to my body. My fingers were sore, smelling of machine oil. The whine of sewing needles rang in my head long after my shift ended at the garment shop. Little Beatrice's milk money sat in my shoe, but I couldn't spend it. She needed it more than I did.

Mom would be mad when I got home since I'd make her late for her night shift. Instead of asking a neighbor to babysit, Mom would always wait for me to come home because our family was paranoid.

Dad had three rules: don't open the door for strangers, don't tell others details about our family, and be gone when people started asking questions.

You'd think we were spies instead of a family of five with barely enough money to keep the lights on, holed up in a tiny, crumbling apartment in the middle of mob territory.

As the wet pavement bit into my knees, I scoffed, thinking about what Dad had said before.

"We Lestes are proud people. Old, respectable lineage. Your grandfather was one of the richest men from Albania until he lost everything."

Right. Pride and lineage did diddly squat. And you'd have to hit me over the head with a baseball bat to convince me we were ever rich to begin with.

Lightning split the sky, thunder rumbling after. I snuck another glance at the pendant through the store window.

A fucking dare got me into this mess. That and hunger. Always hunger.

"Go to the antique store. Snag the emerald pendant. They don't keep it locked up," my high school bully said. My reward? Twenty extra dollars.

Easy, my ass. Shoplifting from a store owned by the mob was a stupid decision, really. The man was right; I'm lucky I'm only kneeling as punishment.

Not losing a finger or a hand.

And who was I fooling? I stuck out like a sore thumb in my tattered jeans and busted-up backpack. My bleached hair—a glaring shade of blond instead of my natural dark brown—was another poor choice. I was caught within minutes.

Lightning splintered across the sky again, and the rain drummed harder. A gust stabbed my face as I swayed on my knees.

Shit, it's cold.

The gravel dug deeper into my knees, and my stomach growled.

As I mulled over my poor life choices, the rain suddenly stopped.

I froze, then looked up, first spotting the bright red of the umbrella.

Then I saw *her*.

She didn't look real. She looked like a lone sunflower blooming among decay.

She cocked her head and stared at me with her large gray eyes. I suddenly forgot how to breathe. Her hand fiddled with a dark-brown braid, some twisty thing I'd seen my younger sister, Sofia, attempt at home.

"Why are you kneeling?"

"For fun, obviously."

Her lips twitched. She stepped closer. My heart stopped working.

My body heated from her near presence. Fuck, I was burning up. I raked in a greedy inhale—roses, she smelled like roses. She smelled like everything I was not.

"You'll get sick," she said, shifting so her umbrella covered me more than her.

"Sick, me? Please. My five-seven powerhouse frame can handle a little rain." I smirked, jittery, like I'd been electrocuted by a downed power line.

She snorted, then crouched. "How old are you?"

"Sixteen."

"Huh. You are tiny."

I rolled my eyes. "Thank you, Captain Obvious. Puberty skipped me. Would not recommend."

My gaze swept over her again—perfectly smooth skin, plump pink lips, beautiful silky hair, not a strand out of place. Her navy dress uniform was completed with knee-high socks like the ones they wore at those rich schools over in Ashbourne Heights.

"How old are you? Why are you here? Shouldn't you be warming up somewhere cozy, drinking fancy hot chocolate or something?" I asked.

The mystery girl beamed at me. "Fifteen and four days. Maybe I'm looking for adventure. Cozy cafés are overrated. Unless they serve Geraldine's Chocolates. They're to die for."

They also cost an arm and a leg. But clearly that didn't matter to her.

"Four days, huh?"

"Every bit counts."

"Well, happy belated birthday then."

She grinned. I shivered again, my heart thundering louder than the storm. This time, it wasn't because I was cold.

"I'm...Elise. On a spring break class trip from New York City. And you?"

"Elise." I tested her name on my tongue. Tasting it. Savoring it. It was sweet, just like her.

"I'm Kian. Kian Leste."

The tempest had raged that day, but I didn't feel a drop. She stood there for two hours with me, warming me with her presence, lighting a fire in my chest.

No one had ever stood between me and the weather before. And no one had ever since.

Chapter 14: BRIDE IN CHAINS

LANA

Present: Anderson Estate, New York City

MY HAND SHAKES AS I brush out my hair in the back parlor facing the rose garden.

A pale version of me reflects in the mirror—large eyes, dark circles underneath, bloodless cheeks. A simple white sheath dress I pulled from a closet—Mom's old dress.

When I was little, I'd look through photos of my parents' wedding. The great Linus Anderson's arranged marriage with Joanna Milton was the social event of the year, splashed across the newspapers and covered by all media outlets.

They weren't in love then. Dad married Mom because our family used to believe in some curse about the wife of the eldest son dying an untimely death should they fall in love. It was ridiculous, but with a string of unfortunate deaths over the years and the superstitious lot of old-money folks, I never questioned it.

Mom died when I was a baby. Dad fell completely apart, or so I was told. They were in love then. It surprised everyone.

But it never surprised me.

I could see it when I looked at their photos. The way Dad smiled at Mom in her stunning wedding dress with the long cathedral train, how she snuck a glance at him when they were cutting their three-tiered cake, a shy smile on her face. Perhaps it wasn't love at that moment, but the signs were there.

It was romantic. It was fated.

Despite the morbid and sad ending, I wanted that for myself. The once in a lifetime love.

But I never thought love wouldn't find me. That instead, I'd take part in an arranged marriage.

Never thought I might have a morbid ending of my very own.

Yet here I am.

"Don't do this, Lana. Please, I beg you." Belle clasps my shoulder and looks at me through the mirror. Tears gather in her eyes.

"I have to." My throat prickles. I look away. "There's no other choice."

And there isn't, and the bastard knows. He listed my choices—going to the cops or fleeing. But he's right. With what I know about The Association and how powerful they are, running might send us straight to our deaths. And with my siblings, my nieces and nephews, can we hide forever?

How can I guarantee their safety?

I'm turning thirty-five in a few months. I can do this for a few months. And the day I turn thirty-five and they get whatever it is they're after, I can put this behind us.

"There is. We'll go into hiding. Change our names," Belle pleads. "Heck, I'll get a bad spray tan, dye my hair blond, and wear gray contacts for the rest of my life. Don't marry the bastard."

An inappropriate snort tumbles out of me.

"You'd look ridiculous, Belle." She's half-Chinese, half-white, and her jet black hair and ivory skin are utterly gorgeous.

"We'll think of something. I'll call the others. All of us together—we'll figure it out."

I pat her hand and give it a squeeze. "Don't. Maxwell and Rex already promised me they wouldn't tell the others, and I need you to do the same."

A crow caws in the distance as I turn and face her. "They can't change anything. Don't make them worry. They're already scared enough with the vault heist and Maxwell getting shot. Let them think it was all a misunderstanding, that criminals broke in and kidnapped me, but Elias came to our rescue. Like he did before. Many times."

I force out my next words. "Tell them we've been...in love this entire time. That this brush with death caused us to elope. That I'm doing something I've never done before. Uproot what's expected of me to live my life. Tell them I'm happy. You saw happy tears in my eyes.

Don't make them worry when they can't do anything about it. Please, Belle. Promise me."

My good friend and sister-in-law wraps me in her arms. "You don't deserve this."

"No one does." I pat her back, hating how my voice wobbles. "But I'll survive. That asshole thinks he's won for now, but I won't go down easily. I'll get out of this. This isn't over."

Far from it. That's the one thought keeping me sane right now.

We'll play pretend. Get married. Leave New York and move into his home in Chicago so he could keep his eyes on me. Stay married until I turn thirty-five and wait for whatever's supposed to happen. In the meantime, I'll dig around, find leverage, evidence, clues. I'll gather the troops, and when the right moment strikes, I'll pull the rug from under the spymaster myself and shoot him in the face.

"Trust me, Belle." Steel infusing my voice, I grab her arms and pull back. "I'll make his life a living hell."

Belle stares at me, the concern in her hazel eyes slowly morphing into strength. She nods.

"Go kick ass. I'm always a call away."

A new resolve straightens my spine. I look out the window, taking in the overcast skies and the garden of bare thorns and twisted branches. The world is damp and gray, befitting a wedding like this.

Nature can mourn my predicament.

I won't.

A pity party won't change anything.

"Zip up my dress, please. Let's get this show on the road."

There'll be a small film crew there. The Berishas want proof we're getting married.

They want a wedding? I'll give them one.

Elias, clad in his usual three-piece glory, is standing at the mouth of the hedge maze, which starts in the heart of the rose garden. In spring, this place will come alive. Multicolored roses will bloom, their heavenly fragrance washing over me whenever I visit. I can hear Levi's giggles as I chase him through the maze, my siblings and friends squabbling behind me, having afternoon tea.

But now, the atmosphere in the rose garden is somber.

Belle speaks to Maxwell softly, my brother looking years older in his wheelchair by the central fountain. Rex paces in front of them, raking his fingers through his hair. A woman with a cello sits in the far corner, her eyes darting from side to side, clearly petrified.

Thank goodness Levi is at a playdate. I can hold myself together, but I'm afraid one look at his innocent eyes and I'll crack.

An imposing man with dark hair and a square jaw, wearing all black with a white clerical collar at his neck, is speaking with Elias.

He must be Elias's priest.

Does he know this is a farce? That I'm being forced to do this?

The priest glances up, his sharp eyes catching mine. A small frown creases his forehead, and he rolls down his shirtsleeves, covering up the swath of ink on both forearms.

Tattoos. This holy man has tattoos.

Elias whips his head in my direction.

His lips stop moving.

For a brief flash, they part. A sharp inhale. Those green eyes flare with heat. His hand flexes at his side.

The priest says something, but the enigmatic monster doesn't appear to hear him.

His attention is one hundred percent solely riveted on me.

A strange swooping sensation appears in my stomach, followed by my quickening pulse.

Nerves. It has to be nerves. After all, arranged marriage or not, I've never been married before.

Someone hands me a bouquet, breaking my eye contact with him. Beautiful blood-red roses. My favorite.

I thank Agnes, who gives me a sad, sympathetic smile.

Maxwell wheels himself over. "One word from you, and I'll shoot the bastard dead. You don't need to do this."

"I have to. It's the right choice."

My brother stares at me, his eyes softening. "We'll get you out."

"I know you will." I smile, my voice thick.

He adjusts his chair, lining it next to me. I look at him in surprise.

"What? Shit show marriage or not, it's not every day my sister gets married. With Dad not here, I'm walking—no—wheeling you down the aisle."

A snort slips out of me, and he chuckles. We begin our trip up the makeshift aisle. It feels like walking up to a guillotine.

It's then I hear it.

The mournful strains of the cello stop me in my tracks.

It's not Pachelbel's "Canon in D" or "Bridal Chorus" by Wagner. It's not Mendelssohn's "Wedding March" or the other usual suspects.

Instead, it's a melody emblazoned inside my heart. Every note I've long memorized. A piece I stopped listening to after a certain boy disappeared from my life when I was fifteen.

Beethoven's "Für Elise."

Unwittingly, I clasp my hand over Kian's emerald pendant. I put it on as a show of defiance, someone else's gift over my heart when I'm marrying another man.

Tears spring into my eyes, the sudden wave of grief coming from nowhere. Back then, I had dreams—love, marriage, growing old and bickering over TV channels.

He stole them from me.

I grit my teeth and glance up, meeting my soon-to-be husband's searing gaze.

I promptly lose my breath.

Elias stares at me—dark, rioting emotions clashing in his eyes. There are pain and grief, anger and frustration. He looks hauntingly alone.

But for a moment, a millisecond, I see a flash of something else.

Unbridled joy.

My heart convulses; the sharp pain has me gripping the pendant tighter. It makes no sense. Must be a trick of the daylight. Or my calamitous emotions impacting my vision.

"Lana?" Maxwell's voice zaps me out of my thoughts.

"Sorry. Let's do this."

With the necklace heavy on my chest, I walk up the aisle to the lonely man standing there.

A pulse drums against his temple, his gaze never leaving mine. His attention is a brand, and I feel its invisible burn on my skin.

With every step closer to this monster, the Shadow King, my body comes alive.

The brush of my tweed dress against my skin morphs into a caress.

The scent of wet grass and rain is a love letter to my nose.

The music...my "Für Elise," becomes a promise whispered into my ear.

He's my enemy. I hate him. But those words don't land.

Instead, sultry heat unfurls from deep within me, spreading to my core, my legs, all the way to my fingertips.

Whatever strangeness is happening, it's clearly impacting Elias as well.

A flush crawls up his neck, those gorgeous eyes becoming impossibly more vibrant and scorching. His fingers curl and unfurl, the power in his tall frame seeming to condense.

Tighter. And tighter.

Like he's a second away from bursting out of his seams.

I close my eyes when I stand next to him, barely noticing Maxwell wheeling himself away.

I hear nothing other than the thundering of my heart.

My palms sweat and my breathing grows shallow.

The priest says words I don't understand. I repeat them. Elias does the same.

"Do you take Lana Elise Farrah Anderson to be your wife? Do you promise to be faithful to her in good times and in bad, in sickness and in health, to love her and to honor her all the days of your life?"

The garden comes back into focus.

Elias stiffens, his throat rippling as he swallows. "I do."

I gasp, my pulse quickening. This is happening.

The priest turns to me. "Do you take Elias Kent to be your husband? Do you promise to be faithful to him in good times and in bad, in sickness and in health, to love him and to honor him all the days of your life?"

My hands tremble as I grip my bouquet. I want to look away from his searing eyes, but they hold me captive.

"I-I do," I whisper.

His lips part, and the tiniest exhale escapes him, like he's been holding his breath.

The priest drones on, more words, more phrases I barely pay attention to. We exchange rings—a simple diamond band for me and a plain silver band for him.

Before I know it, we face each other, the ceremony distilling to this one irrevocable act.

Elias steps up to me, an otherworldly energy rolling off his frame. His menacing scar writhes as he works his jaw. Wordlessly, he takes off his gloves and tosses them to the ground.

His eyes never leaving mine, he slowly lifts his hand.

A hiss escapes his lips when he touches my cheek. Cradles it like a lover would.

I gasp, a thousand sensations coursing through my body, coiling and gathering between my legs.

My breasts feel heavy, my body craving something I've never felt before, a sudden desperation to close the remaining distance between us.

And do what?

I've lost my mind.

Elias's thumb travels to my lips. The softest caress, almost like a kiss, then trails down my neck. For a moment, his touch lingers there. His eyes darken, his finger thumbing my pulse, which is beating a traitorous dance for him. His breath hitches, almost imperceptible, but I feel it scraping my skin.

The small crowd behind us murmurs, but I barely hear them.

Because he's cupping my neck like he's testing its strength, like a panther playing with its food before digging its talons in to sever the major artery.

I don't breathe. I can't breathe. I'm suspended between wanting him to bite down and ruin me or wanting to flee.

But then he shifts, his fingers softening, another lingering downward graze.

Until he reaches my pendant.

Kian's pendant resting over my heart.

I flinch, suddenly realizing how wrong everything is. This wedding. This marriage. This situation we find ourselves in.

I think about the dreams of love I used to have, about the boy with blond hair and a pretty face who carved love notes into tree trunks. The boy who taught me to have patience for puzzles.

Nothing can prepare me for the puzzle of the man before me now.

Frustrated, I grab my pendant, needing it off me. It's wrong to wear the symbol of my innocent first love on a day when love stories die.

"Leave it on."

Elias places his hand on top of mine, clasping the pendant.

"It's beautiful, just like you."

My heart flips, my lips parting in surprise. For a moment, I forget this is a farce. I forget what he did to Maxwell, to me. I forget about the bloodshed.

I'm ensnared by those green eyes, the same shade that reminds me of my first love.

His gaze darkens, and taking advantage of my momentary weakness, he swoops down and captures my lips with his.

The deep, drugging kiss incinerates every atom in my body. Soft lips, the briefest graze of tongue. The sultry spice of his taste—whiskey and something more. An addictive groan rumbles from his chest.

It's over as quickly as it begins.

He sets me back and I'm breathless, my thighs clenching, core aching, the darkest impulse to pull him back to me to continue what we started.

"May I present to you, Mr. and Mrs. Elias Kent," the priest announces.

A camera hovers by my side, knocking me back into reality.

I'm married.

Married to the monster. The Shadow King.

Chapter 15: POSSESSION

ELIAS

I TRACE THE FEMININE swirls on the marriage certificate, my finger trembling. A cold gust scrapes over my skin as I stand alone in the garden after the ceremony.

Lana Elise Farrah Anderson Kent.

Her scent lingers—roses, invisible here but burned into my memory.

Once, I couldn't even read these words. I never imagined they'd be tied to my name.

"Lana Elise," I whisper, grazing the elegant loops of her signature.

She's *mine*.

And God help the world if it tries to take her away from me.

Chapter 16: INTERLUDE—LETTERS ON THE LAKE

KIAN

Past: Chicago, Twenty Years Ago

ONCE UPON A TIME, her name had only existed as letters traced on my palm while our feet dangled in the freezing lake. Little did I know, her name would be permanently embedded in my heart.

"Aren't you worried you'll get in trouble? You ditched your class again," I had asked her, my legs dipping into the icy water of Lake Michigan.

"I told them I was sick and would sleep in. No one questioned it." Elise scrunched her nose. She met me again three days after I was caught shoplifting at the antique store. "It's boring. Museums and stuff. I've seen them all. If they took me to a library, that'd be a different story."

"Books?"

I must've made a face because she laughed. "What, you don't like to read?"

Shame flamed my face. Those damn letters swirled in my vision. "Hate it. I'm dyslexic."

"I'll teach you." She smiled, and I shrugged, not knowing what to say.

"No time. And I wouldn't get it, anyway."

A frown appeared on her lips. She stared at the bruises on my knees and the bandages on my fingertips from the needle pricks at the sweatshop.

Elise's soft fingers grazed the wounds, and I shuddered. A breeze from the lake ruffled my hair.

She traced an *E* on my palm. "Feel it." Then the other letters. *LISE.* "Slow and steady."

"That's cheating," I whispered.

No one had ever touched me like this. Kind. Caring. Like I deserved it.

"I wish they didn't make you kneel for so long."

"It's nothing." I'd been through worse at the sweatshop. Whips to my hands and legs if I was too slow. Every dollar counted at home.

Elise leaned her head against my shoulder and hummed a tune I didn't recognize.

"What's that?"

"Beethoven's 'Für Elise.'" She continued her doodles on my hand.

I stilled, my heart jolting like it wanted to claw out of my chest to reach her.

"You're different from the boys at home. They're spoiled, rich brats. Spending money they didn't earn." She took my hands in hers, rubbing life back into them.

Her eyes widened comically wide.

"What?" I grunted.

"You think the writer of that song, 'The Twelve Days of Christmas,' was a rich, spoiled brat?"

I snorted. "*What?*"

Elise grinned and clutched my hand tightly. "Think about it! The stupid lyrics. A partridge in a pear tree? Lords leaping? Milkmaids? Why would anyone want to give their true love all that crap for Christmas? Or better yet, who'd think that was a good idea? Someone with a lot of money and nothing better to do."

She pursed her lips like she were taking this seriously. "Although I'd give anything to see this live. It must look ridiculous."

Something tingled in my chest. She was so adorable. "So you'd say no to the five golden rings too?"

"Oh, the rings I'll keep," she answered resolutely. I laughed, and she narrowed her eyes. "You're making fun of me!"

Biting my lip, I shook my head, feeling lucky I got to experience the world through her eyes, even if just for a moment.

We smiled at each other, and she linked our fingers together.

"You ever think about what you want to be when you grow up?" she asked.

"Alive." I grimaced because that sounded too sad for my princess's ears. "Fix things. Animals, maybe?"

"You'd be good at that."

My heart fluttered. No one had ever said that to me before.

I hummed and kicked my feet in the water. My palms sweated, but I still lifted my arm to curl around her.

Would she let me?

She giggled when I touched her gently on her shoulder. "The other day, I said you were short for your age. But it's not so bad being shorter. Just the right height for me. Maybe you missed puberty because you were waiting for me."

She then sighed and snuggled closer.

It was then her rosewater scent seared into my memory.

Chapter 17: CITY OF GHOSTS

LANA

Present: Chicago

After the ceremony, Elias called for a car, and it took us straight to the airport, where a private jet was waiting. I asked him why we were moving to Chicago, and he only replied with two clipped sentences.

"Not your concern. Do as you're told."

Anger burned through my veins. But what should I expect from the man who kidnapped me?

The plane ride was thick with silence. I refused to talk to him—my new husband—and he, likewise, didn't engage with me. My heart was heavy, my mind cluttered with fragments of the life I'd just left behind.

I wasn't ready.

Moisture gathered in my eyes as I thought about my family—my brothers, all four of them, even though they drove me crazy with their overbearing ways. Their wives, the best girlfriends I'd ever had. My half sisters. The nieces and nephews I adored and would give up my life for in an instant.

There's grief and heartache when you're forced to say goodbye before you're ready.

But that's life. If I could turn back time, if I knew this was coming, I would still make the same choice.

I would protect my family at all costs.

A town car was waiting when we landed. Men in dark suits, hands hovering near their guns, stood guard next to it. They loaded our luggage into the trunk. I could've sworn I heard an animal mewling.

I must be going out of my mind.

Now, I sit in the back of the dark vehicle beside my silent husband, barely registering their clipped conversations. He's reading a book, his finger tracing the words slowly. If this were a normal occasion with a stranger, I'd ask what he was reading.

But it isn't. He ignores me, and I do the same.

But I feel him. Elias.

I feel his heat, the strength radiating from his body, even though he hasn't said a word to me.

His attention presses against my skin like a physical touch. His gaze bores into the back of my head as I stare out the window. And I smell him too—vetiver and dry smoke, a scent uniquely his. I know how soft his lips can be, how fire burns inside a seemingly cold man.

I wish I could say I hated it—this strange awareness of the man who's my enemy. But in this city, far from home and the people I love, Elias's presence brought me comfort.

It's twisted. Sick. Fucked up. But at least I'm not alone.

The skyscrapers blur past the window. It's been years since I've been to the city.

My hands are clammy. I have a goal in mind, but now that I'm actually here, I don't know how to go about accomplishing it.

One step at a time, Lana.

The car slows. We turn into a neighborhood that has seen better days. Barren trees lined the streets; Gothic facades sagged with age. Storefronts are half-boarded up, dirty puddles pooling on the ground. A heavy fog cloaks the distance. I can barely see five feet out the window.

Saints Hollow.

The neighborhood used to be rich, or so they say. But the Spanish Flu in the early nineteen hundreds took most of its residents. Over the years, new migrants would come, but no one stayed, leaving only a husk of what could've been a beautiful area on the outskirts of the city.

I've been here before, almost twenty years ago. Kian lived here.

The air still smells of rust and rain with a tinge of engine grease, the same scent that clung to his jacket when he first kissed me.

I remember convincing my family to let me do a year of boarding school in Chicago after the spring break when I met him. The school had the best debutante program. Never too early to network, right?

I had spent every free moment with him.

When we walked these streets, Kian would grip my hand, tugging me against him, making sure I was safe. He'd make me walk on the side of the buildings, away from the traffic, because he was thoughtful that way.

He used to tell me, "*This neighborhood isn't for a girl like you. You belong in places like Ashbourne Heights.*" Because I could get the best of the best there—imported cars, houses with butlers, everything gleaming and new.

But I didn't want Ashbourne Heights. I came from a world like that. What I wanted was to be with him.

Green eyes, the color of four-leaf clovers, meet mine.

"Really? And why is that?" He smiles, baring one small dimple.

I nudge him, my cheeks heating. "Who'd take me to play with kittens at the shelter? Or listen to my wild theories about ghosts in our rose garden back home?"

"Kittens, huh? So that's all I'm good for."

"Shut up." I grin. "Someday you'd open a vet office, and I'd play with kittens all day long."

He chuckles, his straw-blond hair falling over his eyes. Tentatively, I brush it back. His dark roots are showing. I wonder how he'd look with his natural color.

"You know, you're quite pretty."

He groans. "That's the last thing a guy wants to hear."

"Pretty boy." I laugh and drag my finger over his smooth skin. How did he escape getting pimples?

My phone buzzes.

Headmistress Larkin

Car service in half an hour. Debutante's ball. Wear the blue.

I grip my phone, stare at the message, then turn it off.

"You need to run." He sounds forlorn.

"Nope. Going to miss it."

His head jerks. "But you'll get into trouble."

"Maybe I want to." I smile at him, ignoring the guilt about flaking on a high-society event. "Maybe I want you to teach me how to sew and show me how to ride on your bike's handlebars."

Kian laughs, glancing at his rusted black bicycle. Then his face turns serious.

"You should go," he murmurs, his eyes sad. "You don't belong here with me. I can't give you anything."

"You've already given me everything." I press my hand over my heart.

His breath hitches, his beautiful eyes flaring with something deep and dark.

Slowly, he brings his hand up and cups my face.

I shiver.

He swallows, clearly mistaking my tremble for me being cold, and shrugs off his jean jacket.

"No—it's freezing, you'll be—"

"Shhh. Let me be good at this too." He slides the jacket over my shoulders and winks.

The past loosens its grip as the car stops. I get out, a gasp lodged in my throat.

A tall, modern building rises in front of me. Three stories of black limestone, thick fog swirling around its exterior, ivy choking the awnings, smothering the many secrets hidden behind its walls. It's nature's poor attempt at shielding this fortress from prying eyes.

"Welcome home," Elias says.

His first words to me since we kissed at the altar.

His gaze is unreadable, jaw tight as the doors open and we step inside.

The house is quiet and gloomy, opulent but sterile. Black marble lines the walls, and there are dark hardwoods and paneling everywhere.

A man materializes to my right—inky black hair, a lock of it grazing a black half-mask covering the bottom half of his face with a cutout for his lips. He's Asian, and with his tall frame and alert gaze, he reminds me of a superhero. Or a villain.

A subtle smile plays on his lips, as if he can read my thoughts. He takes my luggage and makes his way up the stairs.

Elias pauses at the staircase.

"You can go anywhere except the third floor. That's off-limits. Ren," he gestures to the masked man, "will be with you at all times.

He'll give you a new phone with a tracker. Don't even think about ditching it, because I'll know."

Indignation burns inside me. I roll my eyes. "Anything else, O' Shadow King?"

"You can't go out. A stroll in the yard is fine, but that's it."

I gasp. "You can't hold me prisoner in here!" The deal was to marry him and stay in the same house, so this is bullshit.

"Watch me." His face hardens, and he steps toward me. "Don't even think about disobeying. I'm the king of the underworld for a reason. Defy me, and your brothers die."

The air between us vibrates with tension.

I shrink against the banister, wondering how I could've forgotten what the man did. The violence and bloodshed. Killing people without blinking.

He drops his voice into a menacing whisper. "Everything you do, you must clear it with Ren. Security cameras are everywhere." He motions to the black domes affixed to the ceiling. "Don't try anything."

Then he stalks off, his steps echoing against the marble.

My legs tremble, and I plaster myself against the wall, needing support.

God, I hate this infuriating asshole.

This is temporary. Five more months until I'm thirty-five. Five months to figure out what The Association wants with me. What could my mother have written in her letter? I asked my brothers, and they had no clue either.

But I'll find out. Because if there's one thing Lana Anderson isn't, it's someone who wallows and cries.

I draw a deep breath, steel my nerves, and start up the stairs. Ren meets me on the second-floor landing and leads me down an equally sterile hallway to the room on the farthest right.

He hands me a phone. A message blinks back at me.

Ren

This is your suite.

I stare at the words on the screen.

"You don't speak?"

A sharp nod.

"But you can hear."

Another nod.

Ren

I hear just fine.

He swings open the door to my bedroom.

Like everything else in the house, it's modern luxury with neutral wallpaper with gold filigree, chrome furnishings, and a simple crystal chandelier. There's a king-sized bed with a dove-gray leather headboard and one lavender armchair, similar to the one I have at home, by the bay windows. Tucked away in another corner is a desk.

Ren hands me a folder. Inside are drafts of press releases for the Berisha and Sons Company about land purchases, building permits, upcoming mergers, earnings reports, and things of that nature.

I'm familiar with these things from my time at Fleur, which unfortunately I had to resign because of my marriage to Elias. It wouldn't look good to have a C-suite employee married to a known criminal.

Among the issues, it's been hard to let go of that part of my life—having a career. While it didn't fill the emptiness inside me, it was something I took pride in.

Ren types on his phone.

Ren

Elias said, "Make yourself useful." Text me if you have questions. I'm on speed dial two.

The Shadow King has thought of everything, apparently. From the priest, the rings—I stare at the simple diamond wedding band—to now...assignments.

I'd laugh if I weren't so pissed off.

He hands me a laptop and points to the antique desk in the corner—the only piece of furniture that looks out of place in this otherwise modern room. Something about it seems familiar, but I can't place it.

Ren

Elias keeps a small team. Hannah, the cook and housekeeper, will meet you later. Don't try to leave. I don't like chasing people.

His lips twitch.

Ren

I'm much better at shooting them.

He disappears before I can ask him questions. Who is he? Why does he have a mask on? Where's Elias going to sleep?

The last question has my pulse reeling.

He's not expecting a wedding night, is he?

Because if he comes near me, I'll cut his dick off.

Gritting my teeth, I cross the room to the desk and yank open the drawer, grinning when I find a pair of scissors.

This will do.

I slide it into my jacket pocket.

But then, I notice something on the corner of the desk. A small red box topped with a black bow.

My heart flutters because I know that box.

Geraldine's Chocolates.

How does he know?

Seriously, Lana, does it matter how he knows? The man probably keeps food logs of everything we eat, the devil.

My stomach growls. I ate nothing the entire flight, and now my biggest weakness is calling my name.

I peel off the lid, biting down a squeal when I see a dozen of their limited-edition champagne roses confections.

The addictive sweetness hits my taste buds, and my mood immediately improves.

But then, I start hallucinating.

"Meow."

The chocolates are laced. That has to be what's happening.

There's no way the cold mobster has this adorable little creature who just wandered out of my walk-in closet like it was waiting for me.

A beautiful calico cat—brown, orange, and black patches. Soft white fur.

"Meow."

I crouch and offer my hand. It rubs its graceful body against my fingers.

"What are you doing here with the devil?"

Oh! I recall the animal noises I heard in the car. They must be from the cat.

"You know, I saw a cat just like you the other—"

A gasp tumbles out of me. I pick up the feline, looking at her right side, her left, at the very familiar red collar around her neck.

It's the same cat from the café! The place that burned down.

The cat purrs, knocking me out of my thoughts. How does Elias have the cat?

Confusion bubbles in my chest. I snuggle the cat, relishing its warmth.

And slowly, the tightness in my chest eases. Cat, scissors, chocolates. Things are off to a better start than I originally thought.

First, contact my family.

Then I'll figure out a plan—a plan that *definitely* involves the off-limits third floor.

Chapter 18: DETECTIVE WIFE

LANA

THE BASTARD *BARRICADED* THE staircase to the third floor.

"Ugh." I grunt as I try—and fail for the third time this past week since we moved here—to dislodge the wood planks he installed in front of the landing.

There's a temporary door, but it's dead bolted.

I need a Plan B. Maybe I can convince Hannah to help me? I know she won't tell me anything because I've tried prying her for info on the Shadow King. But maybe she can buy me a hacksaw or something.

I growl. *Like that isn't suspicious. At all.*

Someone snorts behind me.

I whirl around, finding Ren leaning against the wall, twirling his cell phone.

He moves silently too, just like a certain someone.

Cece, *my* cat, rubs her lithe body against my jailer like she likes him.

Traitor.

Tail lifted gracefully, Cece prances away, but not before looking at me and giving me an "I'm innocent" meow.

I scowl at the barricade. "Seriously, what's he hiding up there? Dead body? A mentally ill wife who makes creepy sounds at night?"

He arches his brow and types on his phone.

Ren

Spoiler alert. And *Jane Eyre*, really?

My jaw drops.

Ren

When you spend this much time with the man, you read. A lot.

"The dealer of secrets likes books?" My mind flips to him thumbing his novel in the car last week when we first arrived.

I hate the way my heart flutters at the idea—a man reading is the sexiest thing ever. I may be a subscriber to the "Hot Men Reading in Public" thread online.

Ren

You wouldn't be asking if you'd seen the library, which is up there.

He motions to the barricade and rolls his eyes.

Ren

He's doing this to piss you off. I've never seen him so amused.

My eyes narrow, and I glare at the security camera.

It blinks. Once. Twice.

A growl rumbles from my chest. The asshole is watching us.

A snicker draws my gaze back to Ren, who shakes his head, jaw twitching behind his mask. He types on his phone again.

Ren

I'll talk to him. Just…for the love of God, behave. I really don't want to shadow you everywhere.

Brow cocked, he unfurls himself from the wall and saunters down the hallway, but not before I catch him pulling a bottle from his pocket, uncapping it, and tossing something into his mouth.

Pills? Vitamins?

"I'm well-behaved! The best damn prisoner you've ever had!" I holler after him.

Then I slap my forehead.

Being trapped indoors for a week is driving me out of my mind.

Best damn prisoner? Really, Lana?

That's what growing up with four competitive older brothers does to you—makes you want to be the best at everything.

Shaking my head, I prowl down the hall, opening doors, peeking into empty rooms. Between completing the random PR assignments Elias has given me since we arrived, I've spent my hours snooping through every inch of this house that's unlocked and available to me.

So, I already know there's nothing here.

Bedrooms. Lounges. More bedrooms. No half-shredded documents. No sticky notes with imprints of important messages.

No clues. Heck, I have no clue what I hope to find, but I have to trust I'll recognize crucial info when I see it.

My stomach rumbles, and I glance at the modern clock at the end of the wall. Eleven.

Can I sneak a banana from the kitchen without Hannah noticing?

I'll need fortitude for my food strike later, when she inevitably tempts me with some fancy Italian feast.

Okay, maybe I'm not the best prisoner. But not eating is the only way I can think of to rebel against this situation. I have to show my discontent somehow.

Not like the bastard cares.

I traipse down the stairs, past the empty living room toward his office.

On a whim, I press my ear against his door, listening for sounds.

It's quiet.

My pulse rattles as I reach for the doorknob and turn, fully expecting it to be locked—

Click.

It opens.

The light is on in the adjoining bathroom, but the door is wide open and no one's inside.

Swallowing my gasp, I tiptoe inside the masculine space, walls paneled in black wood and leather, illuminated only by the pale daylight peeking through the gaps of the dark curtains. A treadmill rests in the far corner next to a lounge area.

Built-in bookshelves are filled with books—Ren was right, the mobster likes to read—notepads and folders stack neatly on a stately walnut desk. A lone laptop is perched on top, flipped open.

I bite back my squeal of excitement and hurry over, first checking the notepads for pen marks or messages.

Damn it. They're pristine. No clues here.

The folders contain nothing interesting—articles about the stock market and prominent people—probably research he's doing on his next marks.

There's a slip of paper tucked beneath it. A hastily drawn diagram with random words.

The Council, six different last names, one of which is the Berishas, a list of companies, and at the bottom, phrases that put things into perspective.

Russian Bratva, Irish Mob, Chinese Triads, Italian Mafia, Albanian Mob.

This has to be a big-picture diagram of The Association's structure. My pulse quickens as I review it again, trying to make sense of it. I recognize the last names under The Council—some of the wealthiest families in the world who are part of my family's old-money circles. The company names are Fortune 500 conglomerates owned or affiliated with them.

My mouth dries, and I swallow.

That's it.

That's why The Association is so dangerous, why they get away with all these heinous crimes. They control the wealth and de facto governments. And now it looks like they control the gangs too.

Mind reeling, I return the paper to its original spot and continue searching.

Most of the drawers are locked, with the only one unlocked being a perfectly organized, color-coded stationery drawer. Ten black pens. Ten blue pens. Ten red pens. More sticky pads. Small box of paperclips.

The devil is precise.

I check the laptop next, but unfortunately, a facial scan flashes the moment I press a key.

So, that's a no-go.

Wishing I had a voodoo doll with me so I could jab my frustrations into it, I turn to the bookshelves to check out his selections.

Philosophy. Biographies. Sun Tzu's *The Art of War* and Niccolò Machiavelli's *The Prince*.

Figures. The dealer of secrets gets his education from the greatest strategists in history.

I pull out a book I've seen before but haven't read.

Dale Carnegie's *How to Win Friends & Influence People*.

I scoff and mutter, "Like he needs to make friends, the manipulating, emotionless, spineless—"

"Wouldn't finish that sentence if I were you."

I freeze. My breath hitches as the scent of vetiver, smoke, and salt wafts to my nose. Then, a column of heat appears at my back.

My heart twists and jumps like it's competing in the Olympic qualifiers.

Clearing my throat, I stuff the book back on the shelf and turn around.

My voice deserts me.

Elias, *my husband*, is standing fresh from exercising, his half-naked, glistening body inches away from me, a towel curled around his neck.

Fires ignite on my skin, heat suffusing my face.

My feet stumble, my back plastering against the shelves for support.

Muscles. Endless stretches of sinewy muscle.

And ink. Ivy, vines, roses coiling up his arms, swirling over his chest. A lone Chinese character sits above his right pec—old, inked deep. It must be meaningful.

Sweat drips down his body, writhing a sultry path down his broad chest, the grooves of his abs, a trail of dark hair disappearing beneath his low-slung gray sweatpants.

Then there's the heavy bulge appearing to grow by the second.

My lungs try but fail to retain oxygen. My fingers grip the hem of my shirt.

Anything other than pouncing on this virile man in front of me.

"A deviant," he rasps.

"Wh-What?"

I snap my gaze up, meeting his intense eyes—pupils invading the green of his irises. A droplet of sweat drips from his dark hair, trailing down the bridge of his nose to his full lips. His shadow looms over me, trapping me in a purgatory of wicked temptations.

"You want freedom, but you don't follow the rules," he murmurs, his gaze snared on my lips. "Now, how can this partnership work out?"

He dips his tongue out. Like he's hungry. Famished for something.

My core clenches.

Then his words register.

"Partnership!" Fury chases up my spine like a blast of frigid water, cooling whatever lapse of sanity just transpired. "If *this* is your idea of partnership—locking me up inside a spooky mansion like some Victorian heroine—think again."

His eyes flare. He shifts, the scary scar on his cheek twisting under the dim light.

"What we have is not a partnership. It's a kidnapping. And if you think I'm going to sit around and let you bulldoze me, you've got another thing coming."

His lips twitch, like he's struggling not to laugh.

I want to strangle him and kiss him in equal measure.

The thought horrifies me, and I shove past him, needing to escape the chaos inside me.

"Elias Kent, we're just warming up. You're up to something—something important enough for you to risk everything—and I'm going to find out what that is."

Whirling around at the threshold, I glare at him.

But his expression has me scrambling back—a prey who knows she's pushed too far.

His nostrils flare, his lips flattening into a thin line.

A cold current sweeps the room as his body stills—lethal and quiet, the way a lion lies low before it strikes.

Elias rolls his neck, the joints crackling through the air.

"Wouldn't you want to know?" he murmurs, voice gritty. "But you never will. Because you're right. I was mistaken. This—" he jabs his finger on the table, "—will *never* be a partnership."

Elias bares his teeth, a cruel sneer befitting the king of the underworld.

"If you value your life, don't let me catch you in here again."

Chapter 19: THE CATACOMBS' MASK

ELIAS

REN'S WORDS HAMMER THROUGH my mind as I descend the spiral stairs leading into the underground labyrinth beneath Saint Michael the Redeemer three days after I caught the vixen snooping around my office.

Looking too delectable and at home—*my* home—in her oversized T-shirt and leggings.

"She's been asking to go to the Hollow Gardens. Something about a special tree. I told her the place was closed for reno."

Our words were carved into the tree two decades ago. She's thinking about Kian.

Ever since last week when I almost succumbed to my basest impulses to kiss her pouty lips in the office, I've kept myself busy, avoiding Lana as much as I can. I don't entertain the idea of sleeping in the same room as her.

I'm afraid if I touch that lithe body of hers, I won't be able to stop myself.

But I've seen the security footage. My princess is restless.

She continues her amateur detective hour—checking locked doors, drawers, anything forbidden. When I checked my feed this morning, she was digging through the recycling bin in the kitchen. As if I'd ever throw out anything important that way.

That devious streak of hers hasn't dimmed.

I should be pissed that she's actively disobeying me. If she were anyone else, she'd be buried six feet under.

But fury doesn't ignite in my gut.

It's because I expected this from her, of course. That has to be it. Nothing more. I want to see how far she'll take her investigation.

And she's spending a lot of time with the damn cat. The feline follows her everywhere like she's decided she's a dog. Lana saves all her smiles and snuggles for her.

Damn cat. Why did I rescue it again?

You know why, you sick psycho. She liked—

I don't let myself finish the thought.

I only allow myself twenty-eight minutes a day to let my impulses run free. And most of those twenty-eight minutes are spent watching Lana.

At seven on the dot, Hannah drags her to the dining room. One stubborn vixen versus a five-foot tall Italian tornado. Hannah sets out a feast—minestrone soup, grilled chicken pesto, breadsticks, and tiramisu.

But my *zemër* barely eats.

Three bites, maybe four, before she pushes the plates away, a hand on her stomach.

Then she stares at the camera, the arrogant tilt of her chin daring me to find her.

A hunger strike.

I have half a mind to drag her into the kitchen, hold her on my lap and feed her myself. See the pink return to her cheeks. My groin twitches thinking about her curvy ass on my thighs.

Hannah's worried, and I ignore the twist in my gut. While Lana's personality has remained the same, she's getting too frail.

The stubborn woman. Maybe I need to give her some freedom.

I tell myself it's only for appearances. A sickly looking wife won't impress The Association. I didn't marry her so she'd slowly kill herself under my watch.

If I can't control a woman, how will they ever trust me with their kill ledgers?

Obsession is a disease that's easily fed.

But fuck, having her in my home, sleeping three doors away from me, tests limits I didn't know existed.

So, I've buried myself in work.

Meetings. Blackmails. Bartering secrets on behalf of the Berishas.

Folks have come out of the woodwork to congratulate me on my marriage. The Berishas have even sent over a bottle of their best Raki.

The fucking bastards. Like they didn't force me into this move.

And now it's time to meet with the rest of The Antihero Syndicate.

The air grows colder as I pass through the Hall of Saints, the marble statues of the twelve disciples frozen in prayer. The scent of wax and incense follows me as I turn into The Syndicate chamber.

Three men sit around an oval obsidian table inlaid with gold chess pieces.

Aleksei grins beneath his LED mask. "Well, well, well. Our fearless leader has joined us." He yanks the mask off and ruffles his shorn brown hair, his neck tattoos twisting like ghosts.

The masks are necessary—keeping identities secret in public or when we exit our cars to meet here. We can't have The Association knowing we have members of the Bratva, the Irish mob, the Italian Mafia, and the Chinese Triads conspiring against them. After all, these gangs are their foot soldiers. It doesn't hurt that there's a prominent theater group in the building next door, so no one bats an eye at costumes and masks.

"Marriage. How antiquated," Sebastian drawls, immaculate in his navy pinstripe suit, styled dirty-blond hair, silver mask set aside.

"You're supposed to congratulate the man." Aleksei grins. "I'm far from normal, but even I know that. We need to prep you better. Hide your psychopath. Give us a smile. Say, 'Congratulations, I'm so happy for—'"

He chokes. "I can't. Even I can't do this. Elias looks like he'll kill me. We'll prep you better next time, Sebastian."

Sebastian's pen ticks against a stack of papers. The mob lawyer looks wholly uninterested in everything around him.

Ren snorts and twirls his gun, his leather jacket creaking when he props his feet up on the table.

"Off," Sebastian snaps.

Ren sighs. "*You said—*"

He stops signing when Sebastian arches his brow. With a growl, Ren pulls out his cell phone and starts typing.

Ren

It'd be more efficient if you stopped being so stubborn. Everyone here knows sign language. You've had more than a decade to learn.

Sebastian scoffs. "I'm not learning a new language just for you. That's inefficient. And get your damn feet off the table."

The assassin swings his feet off and shakes his head.

Ren

You were working on your obsessions.

"The key word is 'obsessions,' plural. This isn't one. Cleanliness and hygiene are common sense."

A low growl ripples from Ren's throat.

Ren

Mob lawyers. I hate mob lawyers. Twisting words. This is why I don't talk. Bullets are more efficient.

"Gentlemen," I say. I'm one second away from emptying my clip into these idiots. "Shall we begin?"

"Wouldn't miss it for the world," Rafe murmurs, stepping out from a hidden panel, his black clerical shirt and white collar the only things that make sense in this place of holy worship.

The church was built after the Great Chicago Fire of 1871. Tunnels were dug to store valuables and bodies, and later, during Prohibition, bootleggers expanded them for smuggling between major drop points in the city.

It's perfect for us now—a gang of miscreants aside from Father Rafael Mancini, or Rafe as we call him—out of sight of prying eyes, deep underground where surveillance is difficult.

"Come on, let's see that pretty face," Aleksei says gleefully.

He reaches for Ren's mask.

A gun barrel answers him.

"*One more move and I'll drop you,*" Ren signs.

Ren doesn't like to be touched, and he has an unhealthy attachment to his mask.

Aleksei laughs. "Foreplay. Too bad I don't swing that way."

I sigh. In New York, I have the bickering Anderson brothers. In Chicago, I have these lunatics.

Had. I correct myself, a dull ache flaring in my chest. *I've sacrificed my friendship with the Andersons.*

"Pray more. That may calm your bloodlust," Rafe murmurs, his lips twitching. He clearly senses I'm at my wit's end. "May even improve your relationship with your wife."

Despite his marrying us, he disapproves of the forced arrangement.

"Starting without me?" a soft, smoky voice interjects.

Sofia.

She peels off her black domino mask, her black hair falling loose. Her perfume today is incense, which means she's in a foul mood.

"You okay?" I ask.

Sofia's smile doesn't reach her eyes. There's a shadow in them, the same darkness haunting her since our parents' deaths.

Guilt punches my solar plexus.

I was the eldest. I should've protected her and little Beatrice. But I didn't. Instead, I chased a beautiful princess—someone I had no business being with.

"You're thinking too much," Sofia says.

My teeth score my lower lip.

We take our places. Sofia in the corner, where the queen sits; Sebastian, the bishop, next to her; Ren, who faces the door as the knight; Rafe, the silent king to my right; and me, in the center as the rook.

It's all a game of chess.

"For the vow," I say.

They answer in unison, "No mercy. Our ruin for their fall."

All of us have vendettas against The Association.

"What's your next move?" Sebastian says, his stare glacial as usual, but there's a flicker of something resembling concern.

"Grunt work. Trading favors. Port deals. Putting out fires at their clubs."

"They're testing you."

I nod. The Berishas aren't stupid. I've spent years with the Andersons, thwarting The Association's attempts at luring them in. This sudden change of heart? They aren't buying it yet.

"Too slow," Aleksei complains. "Bots would take over the world before you get in."

"And what do you suggest? Go boom?" Ren arches his brow.

"You know it. If it explodes, it's working." Aleksei grins. "I know you love me."

"Why did you rescue him again?" Ren glares at me and winces, rubbing his chest.

The smile slips off Aleksei's lips. A shadow crosses his eyes.

I clench my hands into fists.

Aleksei was an innocent casualty in my quest for revenge. His family aided the Albanians in finding my parents.

I killed them ten years ago without hesitation, but I couldn't bring myself to harm the broody teenager.

"A life for a life," Aleksei answers Ren, his sad eyes aimed at me. "I bet he regrets it now."

"I don't enjoy having the pace of the game controlled by them." Sebastian steers our conversation back to the main topic while fiddling with his silver pen.

It's not really a pen. It's a poisonous knife I gifted him last Christmas. And if I knew he were capable of emotion, I'd say he was eternally grateful.

What I got from him was a receipt. Lana's receipt from her last trip to Paris with her little note: *You have the best smile. Thank you for your wonderful service.* I wanted to strangle him. He grinned, the rare sight completely disturbing.

"They moved up the Benefaction Ball," Sofia cuts in. "September first."

"How do you know?" Aleksei asks, apparently distressed he didn't get the intel first. "It's not in any of their comms."

My sister takes out a deep-red lipstick and starts applying it. "I have my ways. I smile. Burn things. Men are easy to manipulate." She doles out a dark smile.

For a moment, I remember the little girl who'd follow me around in a cramped apartment, asking me to be part of her tea party.

That girl is long gone. I click my lighter, staring at the flame that appears.

Something so small, capable of inflicting such devastating destruction.

The Association will burn in hell for this.

"You two and your cloak and dagger shit," Aleksei grumbles, fishes out his phone, and madly types on it.

Probably engineering some virus for his bosses in the Bratva.

"The Carusos will be there this year," Sofia adds. "They never attend."

Something big is happening. The Carusos, while holding the controlling power of The Six, are famous for hiding in the shadows. If they are making a public appearance, we need to be there. I might find more info about the kill ledger, or anything I can use to root out the killer.

"We need to get you in," Sebastian says, obviously thinking the same thing.

Rafe stares at the crucifix on the wall. "If you make a move now, they'll be suspicious."

"Don't worry," Aleksei chirps. "We aren't suggesting murder...yet."

Rafe pinches his nose and sighs. "I swear—"

"Why are you here, Rafe? A holy man with the most unholy people," Sebastian asks, a sudden interest in his gaze. Nothing like a conundrum to perk the unfeeling bastard up. "There has to be a reason."

"Even the damned need to see the light." Rafe plays with the cross around his neck.

"I think it's too late for us." Ren points to the ceiling. *"We've reserved seats in hell."*

"Finally, common sense," Sebastian comments.

Ren bolts up and arches a brow, a sly smile curving his lips.

The mob lawyer blinks and clears his throat. "Don't get your panties in a twist, Ren. I was making an educated guess, not like I know sign language."

"I never agree with Ren, but I agree with him this time," Aleksei comments, his attention still on his phone. "I reserve one of the first five circles of hell."

"Uniting us sinners already, maybe there is a God," Sofia drawls.

"No one is beyond saving." Rafe smiles sadly.

He means it.

In an ironic twist, it was Rafe who formed The Antihero Syndicate. Not officially, but each of us stumbled into his path for various reasons. He found me delirious with fever after I escaped my family's massacre. I brought Aleksei in years later. He offered Sofia sanctuary at the church after I rescued her from her handler.

He was the first person she'd talked to, even though he refused to tell me what she told him. While he hasn't taken his final vows to become an ordained priest yet—he's technically a transitional deacon—he follows the confessional rules, and in this case, the private "counsel" since he's not allowed to take confessions.

A technicality no one here or in this community cares about. There's a priest shortage in the church, and the parishioners are more than happy to call him Father Rafe.

"Boom!" Aleksei announces, a wild grin on his face. He slams his phone onto the table. "A present to solve your problems."

My phone buzzes.

Edon

Call me. All our shipments got frozen. Unacceptable.

Aleksei plops his feet on the table, earning him a glare from Sebastian. "Genius. I'm a genius. Why doesn't anyone know that?"

"What did you do?" Ren jabs him with the barrel of his gun.

"Might have caused a war between our country and five others in Eastern Europe," Aleksei says. "They really should fortify their firewalls. It wasn't hard feeding them info about imminent assassinations."

Sebastian glances up from his phone and offers a chilling smile. "A day of miracles."

The other phones start pinging as the rest of us stare at our screens.

"But doesn't The Association control these governments?" Rafe asks.

"They do. But the powerful are always paranoid." Sebastian twirls his pen.

"And you get to save the day." Ren shakes his head, an admiring glint in his eyes. He chucks his mask onto the table.

Aleksei mock gasps. "The lethal assassin is gifting me with the honor of his face."

"Fuck you," Ren signs.

I stare at Edon's message and type back.

Elias

I was waiting for your call. I'll take care of it, but on my terms.

Chapter 20: THANKSGIVING

LANA

I'M TRAPPED HERE.

Unable to focus, I set down a book I'd taken from the living room bookshelf.

Radical Acceptance in Dark Times

I wonder if the asshole left that there as a message for me. Radical acceptance, my ass.

It's been two and a half weeks since we moved to Chicago, and aside from avoiding me like I'm contagious with the plague, he only communicates via texts or Ren. My silent bodyguard looks like he wants to put a bullet in his head to end his misery.

I don't blame him.

Something needs to change. I can't spend day after day waiting for PR assignments to pass the time, having no meaningful conversation with anyone.

I miss noise. I miss little Levi's giggles. I miss my brothers' bickering and gossiping with my girlfriends.

Thanksgiving is next week. I've never spent the holiday away from my family, and I miss them so damn much.

I've been accommodating—absolutely the *perfect* prisoner, really. I haven't gone out. I've completed every task he sends my way. And while Elias has finally removed the barricade—suspicious in and of itself, but I've stopped trying to figure out his games—I haven't even tried the third floor yet.

Because I want something from him.

I just want to go home for the holiday. One little trip back home is perfectly reasonable. If he doesn't want this marriage to be a living hell for both of us, he has to compromise.

Balling my hands into fists, I head downstairs. I'm going to find my husband and make my case. Then I'll see my family.

The infuriating man strides out of his office as I reach the hall. He looks too good in a tailored shirt and vest, collar unbuttoned, a hint of skin glinting under the light.

His gaze narrows the second he spots me.

"I have a proposal," I begin.

"No."

I pinch the bridge of my nose, forcing calmness. "You haven't even listened to it."

"I don't need to. The answer is no. Simple. Or are you hard of hearing?"

Air hisses through my teeth. "Is this how it's going to be? I can't go anywhere, do anything? I'm to sit around until the end of February?"

"My spoiled princess getting bored?" He flicks his lighter open.

Click.

"I can't stay locked up like this. I'm going crazy. I want to go home for Thanksgiving."

"No."

"This might be foreign to you, Elias, but I have a family. They love me. I love them. I miss them—"

"Don't you tell me about *family!*"

He slams his fist into the wall, and I jump.

A muscle beats at his temple. His chest heaves as if the air hurts.

For a second, I see pain in his eyes—then it's gone like a ghostly apparition.

"You're not going anywhere." He exhales, his anger vanishing too.

I swallow. "I-I'm trying to be reasonable. Even if I don't go home, we need to work together to get out of this situation."

Click. The damn annoying lighter again.

Fury tightens behind my shoulder blades. "You can't possibly want to be married to me! I was there in the room, Elias. The Berishas forced you into it. I swear, if we just—"

"There is no '*we*,' Lana. Let me make that very clear." His eyes flash, and the hallway shrinks. "You aren't going to mess this up for me."

Mess this up for him?

I clamp my teeth on my cheek, barely registering the sting. Uprooting my entire life is an *inconvenience* for him?

Click.

I snatch the infuriating lighter, ready to hurl it down the hall.

In a blur of motion, Elias grabs my wrist mid-throw.

"Don't. You. Dare."

His voice is pure venom. Wrath and thunder.

"I won't have anyone, including you, jeopardize what I've worked for. And that includes going home and giving your brothers a chance to play hero and fuck things up."

He leans in until barely an inch separates us. He steals the air from my lungs.

"Don't try anything funny. Obey, or your family dies."

Then he stalks off, leaving silence in his wake.

Snow blankets the world outside the window on Thanksgiving, daylight fading fast into winter gloom.

The fireplace roars in my room, but I'm chilled to the bone.

My eyes sting as I look at the care package spread before me.

Geraldine's Chocolates courtesy of Belle; a slice of carrot cake from Estelles, Taylor's favorite; Grace included a photo album of her baby. Olivia sent over aromatherapy lotions with a note saying she and Rex miss me and the lavender is very calming if Elias pisses me off. Alexis bundled up trinkets from her travels.

They think I'm sick with the flu. That's why I couldn't fly home for Thanksgiving.

Ever since my argument with Elias, our relationship—if you can even call it that—has plunged from cold to subarctic.

Cece meows as if to let me know she's here. I scoop her up and hug her to my chest before crossing the room to the windows.

I fiddle with my emerald pendant and listen to the soft purrs of my cat.

Another reason this Thanksgiving feels heavy—it falls on November twenty-fourth this year.

Kian's birthday.

Back home, I'd light a candle on a slice of cake and blow it out.

I hope he's alive and happy, celebrating with his loved ones.

What happened to you, Kian?

That's the thing about loss—it sneaks up on you when you least expect it. And when you have no closure? The ache never ends.

Wind beats against the glass pane, snow swirling in the air. Hollow Gardens is nearby. If only I could go out, I'd light the candle there, by our tree, our carving.

But I can't, because the bastard won't let me leave.

I picture Elias again, the terrifying man I now call my husband. He used to be a puzzle I wanted to solve because I thought there was more than meets the eye.

"Ew, numbers." I peek over Kian's shoulder, watching him scratch his pencil against paper.

It looks like a grid. Tic-tac-toe with numbers?

"Words are hard for me," he says. He wraps his arm around me when I climb onto his lap. "But with numbers, we get along."

"What's this?"

He erases a number and writes another one in its place. "Sudoku. You need to add to nine."

"Sounds boring. I'd rather read."

Kian chuckles and kisses my hair. "Puzzles are like books, I think. There's a mystery to solve. And mysteries are always worth solving."

His words echo in my mind and I shake myself. Elias isn't a puzzle.

He's just mad.

I won't let a madman ruin my day.

Determined, I stomp to my goodies, pick up the carrot cake, and head downstairs for a candle.

Minutes later, I round the corner toward the kitchen.

"Fuck!"

The crash of glass shattering cuts through the quiet.

Then a deep, delirious chuckle. Someone mutters under his breath.

Elias.

Glass clinks. Liquid sloshes.

I square my shoulders and step in, fully intending to ignore the man and grab my supplies.

But the sight stops me cold.

He's slumped over the granite island, his normally tamed hair a disheveled mess, his dress shirt halfway unbuttoned. He looks like he's brawled with a tornado and escaped with his life.

But it's his eyes that stop me. The agony in them. The self-derision.

And a broken whiskey bottle, a victim on the floor.

"Wife," he slurs. "Why are you down here?"

That's when I notice the crimson streaking down his hand.

"You cut yourself!"

I set down the cake and grab the first-aid supplies I discovered last week.

I should ignore him, let the man hurt himself, but against all logic, I can't. Not when he looks so broken.

Elias stills when I pull up a stool next to him. He hisses as I lift his hand and carefully clean the wound with wipes.

"Why are you doing this?" he rasps, his whiskey breath drifting over my skin. Awareness thrums between us like a living being. "If I bleed out, that'd make your life easier, wouldn't it?"

I snort, wrapping the bandages. "You aren't bleeding out from that. If only it were that easy."

"Then why help me?" He chuckles darkly. "You hate me, don't you? Because I hate you."

My lungs tighten, a dull ache flaring. I tell myself his words don't hurt.

But then I look up.

His green eyes, glazed with pain and something else, lock on my parted lips. My mouth dries. Elias dips his head slightly and trails a finger over my cheek.

A gasp escapes me. Liquid warmth pulses through my body in shivering waves.

"I hate you so much, Lana," he repeats.

I flinch, drop his bandages, and step back. "Seriously, why do I even try?"

Shaking my head, I add, "Bandage yourself. Bleed out for all I care."

But before I can take another step, he grips my wrist and yanks me onto his lap.

"What on earth?" I struggle in his hold, but he's too damn strong.

"Stop."

"Stop what?"

"Moving. Leaving. Whatever." Elias presses me against him, his breathing rough. "Don't leave. *Please*."

The anguish in his tone stops me. He tightens his hold as the air between us heats.

"Why? Why do you hate me?" A sharp pinch catches behind my sternum. I glance into his eyes. "What did I ever do to you?"

Elias clenches his jaw while his gaze skates over my face before settling on my lips.

He doesn't answer me.

But he doesn't look at me with hate. He looks at me like I'm precious. Like I'm a dream he can't believe is real.

My heart throbs now, the ache stealing my words. There's confusion too, because I don't understand what my sins are, but I know they're real to him.

This is nuts. I don't care what he thinks of me.

But still, I finish wrapping up his wound.

"All done." I affix the tape and get off his lap.

He doesn't let me.

Instead, he digs his fingers into my waist—almost painful—but then my body comes alive. My skin tightens as I take in his broad chest, the pulse throbbing in his neck, and those emerald-green eyes, wild and untamed.

"Lana," he whispers.

My lips part. His eyes zero in on the motion.

The world swirls as my vision narrows. His face dips closer. My eyes flutter shut when his hot lips brand my neck.

Sparks explode at the point of contact, and I moan. My legs clench to relieve the sudden pulsing in my pussy.

Elias growls and manhandles me until I straddle him.

"What am I going to do with you?" he says, then drags his hand down my back and over my ass. "Fuck me."

My panties dampen. Common sense flees the scene. I can't help but move on his lap.

Once. Twice. Small gyrations that drive him wild.

A warning flickers in my mind. *I'm his prisoner. He's a monster.*

But my body has other ideas. It wants this virile man to touch me, to hold me like he wants to possess me and never let go.

"Elias." I bare my neck to him. "I don't. I need—"

"Yes, princess." He reaches up and palms my tits, playing with my beaded nipples. I whimper. I need more. So much more. "What do you need from the man who hates you?"

His words are a slap across my face, snapping me out of my haze.

I scurry off him, and the cold air crashes between us like a tsunami.

I miss his warmth.

My lips are swollen even though he didn't kiss my mouth, and I refuse to analyze the regret that follows.

What am I doing? He's my enemy. And I'm down here to grab a candle for Kian.

Kian, the sweet boy who would never hold me captive.

Shaking myself, I hurry to the drawer by the dishwasher. I spotted some candles and a lighter there before. I grab them, a fork, and pick up the cake, eager to flee the stifling room.

"I'm sorry."

His words halt my escape, and I swallow my gasp. I've never heard Elias Kent apologize before.

"I'm drunk. Ignore me. Nothing I say means anything right now."

Another beat of silence.

"What's the cake for?" Elias exhales. "Please. Come back."

I stare at the carrot cake, the earlier lust finally fading to the background.

Tears prickle my eyes again because loss once again reminds me of its presence. Faces of people who are not here with me—Mom, Kian, Dad, my siblings—flash behind my eyelids. Maybe it's loneliness, maybe it's Thanksgiving and I'm away from home, but I don't want to be alone.

"I don't know what's going on with you, but I won't take your bullshit." Slowly, I turn back and take a seat across from him. "You're skating on thin ice."

Those beautiful green eyes warm a smidgen, and he nods. A truce.

"The cake is a tradition." Carefully, I remove the plastic lid and stick the candle in the middle. I click on the lighter, but it sputters uselessly.

"Here, let me." He reaches over with his silver lighter and lights the candle.

My heart heavy, I stare at the lonely flame emitting its warm glow. It can't chase away the darkness in this house.

"Today is November twenty-fourth," I murmur, needing to confide in someone. Elias is halfway to drunk, so he probably wouldn't remember it tomorrow, anyway. "It's the birthday of someone important. I light a candle for him every year."

His breath hitches, and I look up, finding his gaze dark and riveted on me.

"Someone important?" His fingers are white-knuckled around his tumbler.

"Yes." Heat creeps up my face at his intensity. I want to look away but can't. In this moment, I'm a willing prisoner. "He's someone I miss a lot. Someone who wasn't family, who loved me for me, not because of my name or my money."

Elias's throat ripples and nostrils flare. The flickering flame casts his face in shadows, but emotions still swirl in his eyes.

I'm hit with an urge to solve him again. The same feeling that something lies beneath the surface. Something worthwhile.

I grip my pendant, and his gaze flicks to it.

"He gave that to you." A statement, not a question.

I nod.

"And you kept it all these years."

"He's not someone you forget," I reply.

The air stills as we stare at each other, both of us snared in its intricate web.

For a heartbeat, the violence, the fake marriage, all fall away. I stop remembering how much I hate the man before me, who's looking at me like he's beholding the cosmos.

The ache eases a smidge in my chest.

I close my eyes, needing to break our connection, and make a wish.

Kian, wherever you are, I hope you're happy. I hope all your dreams came true.

"Happy Thanksgiving, Elias," I whisper.

Then I blow out the candle. The darkness sings, warm for once, before swallowing us whole.

Chapter 21: DANCE WITH PHANTOMS

LANA

THE SHADOW KING IS in a good mood these days. I wonder if Thanksgiving two weeks ago had thawed something between us. But the man has made no mention of it, nor has he tried to touch me ever since.

It's enough to make me question my sanity—if those heated caresses and rough words were figments of my imagination.

But I know they aren't.

I've spent too many sleepless nights tossing and turning in my bed, thinking of how good it felt to be held by him.

How easy it was to burn out of control.

Physical reactions, that's all they are. I have one goal—to get out of this alive. Screw the man.

Now, Elias doesn't even blink when I stroll past him in his office as I head up to the third floor. A devious streak inside me wants to drive him crazy.

I taunt him with a sway of my hips, *"Come catch me,"* or thunder up the stairs in my stilettos just to drive him nuts with the noise, but he ignores me. If it weren't for the twitch of his jaw and the clicking of his lighter, I'd think I wasn't getting to him.

Then there's the silent bodyguard who still follows me everywhere when I'm outside the mansion. But when I'm inside, he gives me privacy. Ren and I have reached an understanding: I won't test him and he'll leave me alone.

Frankly, I'm not dumb. If I run, we're back to square one. Those cold-blooded murderers in The Association will hunt me down or go after my family, which is precisely why I'm in this predicament in the first place.

Frustrated, I climb the stairs again.

The third floor is "forbidden," which only means I now come here daily. So far, Elias's threats don't have bite. If it's truly forbidden, he wouldn't have removed the barricade, right?

The first time I came up here, all six doors were locked. Oddly, five of them are on one side of the hallway. Then, over the next few weeks, suspiciously, five doors would click open, one by one, right as I passed them. I'd look up at the camera in the corner, seeing the red light blink, just as it does now.

He's watching me. I know he is.

I give the camera the middle finger, and it blinks again.

I can almost hear his dark chuckles.

Elias is taunting me back. *I know you're snooping. I control the flow of information, not you.*

Over time, I've explored the open rooms—a small study, three guest bedrooms, and the last one, the room Ren mentioned before, is my favorite place in this cold, dark house.

An enormous library.

It's like the ones in Europe—ornate, gold leaf decorating the ceilings, antique sconces on the walls, filled to the brim with books, completely out of place in this modern home.

The mobster definitely loves reading.

Cece pads at my side, tail brushing my calf. I've asked the devil why he has the cat and if she's from the Albanian café, but no surprise, he doesn't answer my questions. Either way, I'm grateful for her. It's like she understands me; she knows I have nobody here.

I don't contact home other than occasional messages to tell them I'm okay. I cut the brief calls short because I don't want them to worry. If my brothers sense an ounce of sadness or desperation, they'll come get me, safety be damned.

So I tell them Elias and I have a comfortable relationship, that we're roommates who barely see each other. I tell my friends we're in the thick of our honeymoon phase and he's whisking me around the world. And with time zone differences, I can't call often. I send staged photos: stock images of a couple holding hands, chocolates that mysteriously end up in my bedroom every morning, and lots of photos of the calico cat.

It's quiet this morning. Hannah fussed over my breakfast like the mother I'd never had. Moments like these make my heart clench. I wish I remembered my mother. I wish I could taste her food, which Rex always said was delicious.

I'm eating again. Hannah's food is divine, so why keep punishing myself if the Shadow King doesn't care if I starve to death?

A few guards patrol the perimeter and, of course, Ren lurks about, his movements precise and purposeful, which tells me he's just like Elias: lethal, violent, if not more dangerous.

I stop in front of the mysterious locked door on the third floor, the only door on the right side of the hallway.

Two locks. The first looks simple. I kneel and tug a bobby pin from my hair, trying to remember the steps for picking a lock from the videos I've watched.

My answers must be inside, right?

If this works, then I'll work on the keypad, which looks like a cipher. I see faint wear on the number two. My blood thrums at the idea of a puzzle. No new puzzle boxes have shown up from my mysterious admirer. Perhaps they didn't realize I got married and moved away.

I insert my bobby pin into the key slot and press my ear against the wood.

Wiggle it right. Then left. A lift. Another click.

I twist the knob. It doesn't budge.

Releasing a sigh, I try again. Left. Then right. I add a second bobby pin the way I've seen the experts do it.

Still nothing.

Cece meows, clearly annoyed on my behalf.

My phone buzzes.

Shadow King

> If you're done playing spy woman, I have a job for you. Come to the office.

Anger constricts my chest. What the hell is this? He's been sending me more press releases to proofread, market research, and crap for the Berishas I can do in my sleep. I was the Chief of PR at Fleur, and he's making me do grunt work I typically assign to interns. I alternate between being insulted and being bored out of my mind.

The damn bastard. I agreed to marry him to protect my family, not to work for him. Especially if he won't even let me leave the house.

Gritting my teeth, I stand and kick the door for good measure.

"Ow!" *Genius move, Lana*. I grab my foot and hobble down the stairs.

Elias arches a brow when he sees me limping into his office. "What did you do? Try to kick in the door?"

His lip twitches. The bastard is trying not to laugh.

I stomp forward, biting back a wince with each step. He leans back in his chair and swivels toward me, an air of nonchalance in his frame. He looks too damn good in his crisp white shirt, unbuttoned to the chest, revealing his deliciously cut muscles. Then he taps his lighter against the armrest.

Tap. Tap. Tap.

The movements quicken the closer I get, drawing my attention to his corded forearms, the perfect veins and tatted vines running up his skin like a map I want to memorize.

Suddenly, I forget why I'm here. My fingers itch to turn his arm over, to examine his tattoos up close. A perverse need surges through me—to lick the vines, to taste his skin.

A dark chuckle. Then body heat and vetiver as he hauls me onto his lap, and dangles his arm in front of me like a treat.

"Bite it."

My gaze snaps up, finding his eyes—the greens darkening like a forest at night—snared on mine.

"You're ridiculous," I say.

"And yet, you're considering it."

I swallow.

"Go on, princess. Take a bite," he rasps. His eyes dip to my parted lips. "Don't be a pussy like last time."

The bastard is referring to our moment in the foyer when I wanted to slice his throat.

My core clenches. I try to remind myself why I hate him.

He's overbearing and a criminal. He shot my brother and chained me in marriage.

I repeat the thoughts. *Yes, that's it.* Sparks shoot up my spine.

I shove him away.

He doesn't let go.

"What on earth is wrong with you? Can't get women so you have to manhandle one?"

"That mouth of yours. I should punish you."

He spans his large hands around my waist and grips it tighter, pinning me down on his lap.

Right on top of something hard, thick, and undeniable.

He's turned on.

A startled sound slips out of me—half whimper, half moan.

"You sadistic piece of shit," I rasp as I wiggle on his lap.

"You're welcome." He pins my hands behind me. "Stop fighting me."

"Make me, Elias. I fucking dare you."

"You like it though. I can see it." Elias dips his lips to my ear. "You're turned on. Just like Thanksgiving."

I shiver. "You're delusional."

"Am I? Or are you lying to yourself?"

He kneads my waist, his fingers dipping under my oversized sweater, grazing my skin.

Tiny flames lick outward. My breathing stutters.

"You hate me. I loathe you," he says, his voice rough. "I stole you from your family, took away your freedom. I shot Maxwell. Take your revenge. Be *vicious*."

Is this how Persephone felt when Hades pulled her into the depths of hell?

My eyes flicker up to his again, seeing the taunt and challenge in them.

He thinks I won't hurt him? He wants viciousness?

My jaw tightens. I sock him across the face like my self-defense instructor taught me.

Elias wipes his mouth, his hand coming away with blood.

"Again," he growls.

"You want me to hurt you?" I gape and climb off him.

"I want you to mean it. You can do better, Lana."

This time, he doesn't make it easy. He pounces on me and locks my hands behind my back. His eyes darken with unholy fire.

I yell and knee him where it hurts.

"Fuck!" He drops me, staggers back, and groans from obvious pain.

"Good. Stay down."

A high like no other burns through my veins.

"Is this vicious enough for you?" I ready myself to deliver another right hook across the bastard's face.

He blocks me with his arm. A deranged smile splits his lips.

"Not even close, princess."

Fury surges up my spine, and I jam my elbow into his chest.

"Harder." He blocks my next kicks and hits.

"You're nuts."

"And you're beautiful when you're angry."

I throw out a left hook. It lands on his cheek with a satisfying smack.

Admiration reflects in those green eyes, and I ignore the excited flutters in my stomach.

"Tell me to stop," I grit out.

"No."

Spinning around, I follow with a right jab. But this time, he catches it, uses my wrist as leverage, and turns me so my back plasters against his front.

A scream rips out from my throat as I jab my heel into his foot. His grip loosens, and as he reaches for me, I headbutt him, hitting him square in the nose.

A pained hiss escapes his lips as he stares at the blood dripping onto the floor.

Adrenaline pulses through me, my senses heightened.

I settle into a defensive stance. "Want more, bastard?"

Elias's shoulders shake. Then a low chuckle rumbles through the room. Unwittingly, I take a step back, knowing I've unleashed something.

"You have no idea," he murmurs.

Slowly, he lifts his head. His eyes take on a maniacal glint as his lips curve into a twisted smile. He wipes the blood from his nose.

"You're turning me on, princess." He prowls toward me, his hoarse voice sending ripples down my body.

My nipples peak and my body heats.

"Monster." I back up until I hit his chair.

"Say it again," he says softly. "Tell me you want to kill me."

Another dark chuckle.

Then a flash of black and green—too quickly for me to react—he twists me around until I'm sitting on top of his lap on the chair again.

"Not vicious enough," he says, pinning me in place with one arm while taunting me with the other like a dare.

He thinks I won't do it?

I snatch his arm and bite down.

Hard.

He hisses, his nostrils flaring, but he doesn't move. He doesn't yell or push me off.

Instead, his lips curl and eyes flash. Then an arrogant smirk. *That's all you got?*

The shaft between his legs grows harder.

I bite until copper floods my tongue. Warm, wet liquid slides over my lips, down my chin, my neck.

He grunts, his fingers digging into my waist, a sharp pain mixing with the heady warmth swirling in my veins.

I don't know what comes over me. A lapse of sanity. The Shadow King infecting my mind with whatever sickness he has.

I grind myself against him, savoring his hard muscles clenching underneath me. Roll my hips once. Twice. Slow figure eights over his length.

I want to unravel him and obliterate the detached control he wears like a second skin.

Heat curls in my core, gathering at my clit. My lips part, and I moan.

"Fuck," he rasps. "Look at me."

"Make. Me." My response is breathy.

"Gladly." He drags me closer and buries his face at the base of my throat. His nose grazes the tender flesh where my pulse throbs a rickety rhythm. I hear his desperate breaths, like he's famished for my scent. Like I'm his salvation.

A tortured groan wrenches from him—desperate and aching. He bands his arms around me and moves me up and down, up and down, a sinewy rhythm over the thick cock in his pants.

Logic burns away, my body incinerated by madness. With his blood on my tongue, his cologne in my nostrils, I'm overwhelmed with everything that's Elias Kent.

Flames singe between my legs and burgeon into an inferno as he grows harder against me, his warm tip dampening, digging into my core, seeking entrance. My mind spins and muscles tighten, a guitar string wound over and over again until it's taut to the point of breaking.

I writhe over him, our movements natural, like we were made to do this.

Made to drive each other mad.

"My *zemër*," he grunts into my neck, his hand traveling down to my ass before he cups it and squeezes.

Zemër? What's that? The thought vanishes like smoke on a rainy day when he presses his lips to the hollow of my throat. I whimper.

"I *hate* you," he says. Another loud, masculine groan of approval. "You drive me insane. And I've fucked my hand raw to the thought of you on my lap."

"Elias," I moan and chase the sensations—the climbing sparks around my clit.

"Let go, Lana. Feel what I do to you."

My back arches, my pussy wet, accepting his hard thrusts like it's my only purpose—

This elusive pinnacle, this explosion, I can see it, feel it—

He wrenches me off his lap.

What? Why did he stop?

Cold air knives down my spine. My legs tremble, and feet find purchase. I want to claw him back to me and feel his body against mine. I want to kiss him and punch him and finish what we started.

The room swirls as I heave out heavy breaths. Elias glares at me, his feral dark eyes burning like hot coals.

Then there's the blood.

The crimson liquid drips out of my bite mark and streaks over his white dress shirt in crescents.

Who am I?

"Get out," he growls and hurls a folder at me I barely catch in time. "Press releases. A magazine interview. A deal between your family and the Berishas. Due tomorrow."

I wipe my mouth with the back of my hand. My taste buds are singing, nerves ringing. Temporarily losing my voice, I glance away, my gaze catching on a document on his desk.

Saints Hollow Conservancy—Hollow Gardens Acquisition Permit.

Dates circled in red. Photos of the park tucked above.

My heart twists and spasms. Hollow Gardens. The tree. Kian.

What was I thinking? Have I lost my mind?

"I-I want to leave the house. I'll take Ren. Please. I can't stand being trapped here anymore."

The second after is heavy with tension.

"Fine. Now, get out!"

I turn around and flee.

Chapter 22: HOLLOW IN MY HEART

LANA

"I KNOW YOU SAID it's closed, but I still want to go," I murmur from the backseat.

Ren's eyes meet mine in the rearview mirror, and he sighs.

After the *incident* in his office—temporary insanity or Stockholm Syndrome, take your pick—Elias is dodging me again.

But at least I can leave the house now.

The realization sits wrong. Did I buy my freedom by grinding against my jailer? And what does it say about me if I want to do it again?

Because the sounds of his strangled breaths and the burn of his hands on my body, like getting me off was his sole purpose? They're carved into my mind, and creep in when the house is quiet. And I refuse to untangle my complicated knot of emotions.

To distract myself from these unhelpful thoughts and to do something I've always wanted to do but couldn't while I was imprisoned, I asked Ren to take me to Hollow Gardens for my first outing.

Ren grunts his disapproval again, pointing at the darkening skies.

It looks like it might snow—the weather in Chicago is as volatile as the man I married.

"I'll make it quick. I just need to do something," I reassure him, clutching the small box in my hand.

A slice of Hannah's tiramisu.

It's been my biggest regret since moving to Chicago—not lighting a candle for Kian by our elm tree at Hollow Gardens for his birthday.

Wrought-iron gates, tipped with the gray sludge of dirty snow, loom before us. My heart clenches, ghosts of the past twirling behind my eyelids.

Before the car comes to a stop, I wrench open the door and hop out.

My boots clomp on the snow piled on the curb, and my lungs heave in icy needles of winter air. A sudden gust almost knocks me off my feet as snow drifts from the sky. I wrap my jacket tighter around my body as I follow the fence to the towering metal sign with the gothic lettering.

Hollow Gardens.

The letters are rusted with age.

I shake the gates.

But as Ren said, it's locked.

A yellow sign hangs to the side—under renovation.

My mind shifts to the permit I saw on Elias's desk. Why would he have it? What does he want with the park?

My breath comes out in a cloud of white. I spot our elm tree in the distance, its barren branches straining toward the sky.

Memories flicker through my mind.

Kian's bleached blond hair covering his brilliant green eyes. How he'd cup my icy hands in his, blowing warmth into them. The gentle smile curving his lips when he'd give me pricey chocolates out of his budget—Geraldine's—every time we'd meet here.

But he'd always say, "Anything for your smile."

There were no five-course meals, no fancy cars. But there was one thing he gave me that no man unrelated to me ever did before or after him.

Genuine love. One stripped of my last name or bank account.

When I first met him, I went by my middle name because I didn't want to be *the* Lana Anderson, the precious Anderson princess. I wanted to be me—just me.

And Kian? He made me feel his Elise was enough.

And in those stolen moments—strolls in the park, dreams of the future—his presence and love were priceless.

Kian would look at me the way Dad stared at Mom in our photo albums.

And then he disappeared. I had no closure. My heart never moved on.

The wind lets out a mournful wail. My mitten-clad hands shake as I pull them off, fingers stiff.

Quickly, I open the box, push in a candle, and reach for the lighter in my pocket.

It sputters on, but a gust steals the flame away.

"Come on," I mutter, sparking it again.

But nature doesn't cooperate. Instead, frigid wind and thickening snow stab my face like glass shards.

Then, the snow stops.

Vetiver and smoke drift to my nose. My skin hums with awareness.

A spot of red—his umbrella—shields me from the elements, like some echo of a memory I can't catch.

Elias stands next to me, silent in his gentleman gangster attire, all harsh lines and strong angles, complete with leather gloves.

He pulls his lighter out of his pocket, flips it open, and lights the candle for me.

My heart hammers against my rib cage.

Suddenly, I'm lightheaded.

"Why are you here?" I whisper. "And why do you have the acquisition permit for the gardens?"

He doesn't answer either question. Gaze inscrutable, he faces me instead, his body blocking the howling wind, his umbrella protecting me from the harsh elements.

His smoldering eyes drift to the emerald pendant around my neck.

Slowly, he scrapes one finger down my cheek, lighting tiny fires on my skin.

I shiver.

"I protect what's mine," he murmurs, unbuttoning his coat.

Gently, he places it over my shoulders, wrapping me in its warmth.

A sense of déjà vu falls over me, but I can't place it.

He holds my gaze for a few heavy beats, his throat rippling, like he wants to tell me something, to bare his soul and reveal his secrets.

But a rough exhale escapes his lips instead.

Wordlessly, Elias lifts the dessert and blows out the candle.

My breath hitches. Something sharp and guilty twists in my chest.

This was supposed to be Kian's flame, not his.

But then, it also feels...right.

He curls my hand around the umbrella handle.

"A blizzard is heading our way," he rasps. "Don't stay out too long. You'll get sick."

Before I can answer, the Shadow King ducks out from under the umbrella into the wind-whipped snow, letting it coat his hair and clothes while I stand there dry and wrapped in his coat.

A hollow ache flares behind my sternum as I watch his lonely silhouette disappear into the mist.

Chapter 23: INTERLUDE—HOLLOW GARDENS

KIAN

Past: Chicago, Twenty Years Ago

I SHOULD'VE KNOWN DANGER was near.

There were warning signs. But I didn't recognize them back then.

My happiness had deflated the moment I saw the black luggage stacked like little coffins by the front door. I lifted one. *Empty.* Relief crashed through me.

"Make sure to pick up the flowers for Mom, son," Dad muttered as he grabbed his silver lighter and brushed past me to put on his shoes. He'd signed up for an extra shift at the shop so he could make Mom's birthday tonight special.

"Sure. Will do it on my way back." I still couldn't look away from the suitcases.

"Better to be safe than sorry." Dad eyed the luggage.

"But why? It's not like we're important or have money. We don't need to be so paranoid."

Dad grunted but didn't say more.

He never did.

I used to roll with it—new apartments, new schools, new streets.

But now I had someone—someone who made me dream about things besides money for our next meal.

And I didn't want to leave the city that gave me my Elise.

We stepped out of the building into the biting cold.

I went right to grab my bike. Dad went left.

"The flowers, son. Florist closes at four today," Dad hollered.

"Got it!" I turned around and gave him a mock salute.

Dad chuckled, his eyes scanning my face. "That special girl of yours..."

I stopped, dread coiling in my gut. Mom disapproved of Elise, saying we were worlds apart and I'd end up heartbroken.

"A man's greatest accomplishment is finding a good woman." His eyes softened the way they do when he thought of Mom. "Your Elise...if she's your special someone, do what you can to keep her by your side. Good women don't come along often."

Her sweet smile flashed across my mind. My chest warmed.

"Got it, Dad."

He grunted and turned away, whistling as he walked toward the bus station. A flash of silver arched through the air. Dad chuckled, catching the lighter he had tossed up moments ago.

Elise stood at the gate, bundled up in a thick wool dress and snow boots, a fuzzy scarf around her neck. Her red umbrella was tucked under her arm. Her cheeks pinkened, a smile splitting her lips when she saw me.

"Kian!"

My heart fluttered as I parked my bike and rushed toward her.

Slightly out of breath, I took her hands in mine.

They were cold—too cold. I swiftly rubbed her fingers, then brought them up to my lips to heat them with my breath.

She hummed her favorite melody—Beethoven's song—as we strode into the gardens. The trees were barren, the weathered benches thick with snow, but there were still people loitering about.

After all, it was one of the few places kids could run and scream without getting side-eyed by the Albanian mob. The park was off-limits.

"Sorry we couldn't go anywhere nice." Shame thickened my voice.

"This is perfect." She shuffled closer to me and let out a happy sigh. "Absolutely perfect."

We strolled on the outer loop, past the marble angels with wings unfurled, and thorny bushes that would bloom her favorite flowers—roses—in spring.

She fished out a book and started reading.

"And when he opened his eyes, he realized his dark world had light. That, for once, his thirst wasn't for death but for a woman bright with life. That he'd—"

I chuckled.

"What?" She elbowed me.

"That book again. It's so dramatic."

Elise gasped. "Hades and Persephone's story isn't dramatic! It's a classic. It survived thousands of years, Kian Leste. It's one of the most famous Greek myths—"

"Fine. Fine. I'm sorry, my goddess." I exaggerated a bow. "How will I ever redeem myself in your eyes?"

I tucked a chocolate into her palm. Her eyes brightened. Caramel flavored today.

"Someone's been paying attention to my stories." She stuffed the chocolate into her mouth. "This is *sooo* good."

"I pay attention to everything you say." Heat crawled up my face, but it was true. "Someday, I'll read to you instead of the other way around. I've been practicing."

Shame settled deeper inside me, but I forced out a smile. Elise never cared that I couldn't read well.

Only I did.

But someday that'd change.

"You have?" She jumped and closed her book. "Yay. Maybe you'll find a favorite book or two. It really is the best thing ever."

Elise beamed and laced her fingers with mine once more.

We strolled off the beaten path.

"Your family's Albanian, but Leste isn't Albanian," she commented.

"That's random."

"I'm curious!" She scrunched her nose adoringly. "My family's from the UK. But that's obvious...Anderson, right?"

"Hm. Technically, we are the Lleshis. But Dad said immigration got it wrong when Grandpa moved over. Somehow became the Lestes. Not that I could confirm this. Never met Grandpa. Although Dad said Grandpa was wealthy and powerful." I shook my head. "Urban legend, really."

"Maybe someday you could find out your family's history."

I hummed noncommittally. I was more interested in creating my own history with her.

"Maybe someday I could become a powerful, rich man," I joked.

"A good man. That's more important."

My lips hitched as I tugged her to a stop. "But how would I make your dreams come true without money?"

She grinned. "I could make my own dreams come true. You just come along for the ride. Although..." A frown marred her forehead. "I don't know what my dreams are. It's probably good to have one. A goal."

My dream is you.

The thought barreled in from nowhere, sending my heart into a tailspin.

I swallowed, my fingers twitching, my chest suddenly swelling with feelings that had been building since almost a year ago when I met her.

Dad's words echoed in my mind. *Do what you can to keep her by your side.*

An impulse surged through my veins, and I looked around, my eyes widening when an idea took root.

"Come."

I grabbed her hand and tugged her toward the far end of the park, to the biggest elm tree that had been there forever.

Sturdy. Unwavering.

I fished out my pocketknife and carved a heart and my words onto the tree.

Elise gasped, her roses scenting the air.

"Too much too soon?" I asked, my pulse thundering.

She grabbed the knife from me and added her own word underneath mine.

"There. Etched forever."

My gaze snapped to hers, heat barreling through my chest.

"Really?" I rasped.

She nodded, a blush blooming on her cheeks.

I traced our carvings, my mind flashing to the suitcases by our front door.

"Elise," I had whispered, my hand cupping her face. "If anything ever happens, I'll find my way back to you."

"Nothing will ever happen," she whispered, her eyes steadfast.

"I..." My lungs strained in an inhale. "I love you, Elise."

Her beautiful gray eyes glistened, a sweet smile curving her lips. She rose on her tiptoes and pressed a soft kiss on my cheek.

"I love you too."

I kept my promise from that day. I just didn't know how much it would cost me.

Chapter 24: THE LIBRARY

ELIAS

Present: Chicago

THE FAMILIAR MELODY STOPS me in my tracks as I walk past the partially opened door to the library.

Beethoven's "Für Elise."

Lana sits in her usual spot on the chaise lounge, cozy in a warm, fuzzy sweater dress that shows off her long legs. A bottle of wine and a glass sit on the side table.

She's humming under her breath as her fingers flip through the pages of a familiar book.

Then she empties her glass and lets out a very unladylike burp before reaching for the bottle to pour more.

Only to find it empty.

She growls like a puppy being denied her favorite toy. Lips pursed, she gets up, but sways and quickly sits back down.

"Oops." Lana hiccups, then mutters, "I'm so buzzed. Shouldn't drink that much. But it's boring here. *Boring*."

Something warm gathers behind my rib cage.

My chest tightens. I slide my hand into my pocket and grip my lighter.

I should walk away. I should think about her role in my family's deaths and why I married her. She's leverage. A means to an end.

But I haven't had my twenty-eight minutes today yet. So I pull out my phone, set a timer, and watch her again.

Clearly tired, she yawns and stretches on the chaise, her book falling to the floor. Her dress rides up on her thighs and stretches over her luscious curves.

Blood surges to my cock and I relive the way she feels in my arms, her needy sounds when she's turned on, the fire in her eyes when she fights me with everything she has. Gripping the doorway for support, I memorize every delectable inch of her, looking so gorgeous and safe in *my* home.

For a moment, I'm transported to the past. This was Kian's dream, having Elise safe in his home, creating a life together.

It will never happen.

And when she turns thirty-five and I get my hands on the package, we'll part ways. She'll go on and find a nice man with good connections, have the babies I know she loves, judging from the way she is with her nieces and nephews.

I will never see her again.

The tightening sensation worsens. I loosen my tie, needing oxygen to release me from this pain.

She turns a page—then stillness. Lana's gaze drifts to me.

"All that ogling, and I might think you're in love with me," she mutters and reaches for her book on the floor, only to miss it.

"You're drunk." I arch my brow. "And I wasn't staring."

A teasing smile curves her lips and the sight of it—no animosity or hatred, like she's forgotten what I did to her—temporarily robs me of speech.

"And I-I'm," another hiccup, "currently not being held prisoner against my will."

"You signed up for this."

"You forced me into it."

My lips twitch in amusement. "It's for the greater good."

"Is it now?" She narrows her eyes. "I have a feeling it serves your agenda more than it protects me."

Clearly annoyed, she reaches toward her book again, but her body loses its momentum and pitches forward.

In a few strides, I reach her before she face-plants onto the ground and gently ease her back onto the chaise.

"Ugh. It's embarrassing letting you see me like this," she groans and closes her eyes.

Chuckling, I pick up her book and set it on her lap.

Hades and Persephone again. Some things never change.

"It's not the first time you've been an embarrassment in front of me. I've seen you drunk before. Very unladylike."

Her eyes snap open. "Asshole. And when?"

I sit down on the floor, my fingers twiddling with my lighter. "You don't remember?"

When she doesn't answer me, I glance back, finding an adorable frown on her face as she racks her memory.

Then she sits up and slaps her forehead. "When you started helping at The Orchid ten years ago! That was you, huh? I always thought I heard someone talking to me that night, but I don't remember."

"Because you were drunk. You should be more careful of your surroundings. There are monsters everywhere who'd take advantage."

She snorts. "Look where that's got me. Here. With you. The monster of all monsters."

I stand before I realize what I'm doing, and a second later, I'm hovering over her.

Her eyes go wide as she stares at me.

"I *never* take advantage of women," I rasp.

Her lips part, her wine-scented breath grazes my face. I watch in fascination as a pink flush creeps up her neck to her face, and those startling gray eyes darken as the seconds stretch by.

"When I touch a woman, it's because she wants it."

"B-But in the office, and on Th-Thanksgiving..."

"You didn't walk away." I lean down until barely an inch separates us. "And you *wanted* it, Lana. You wanted every single second of it. I could smell your arousal."

A soft whimper escapes her, and my cock hardens to full mast.

I swallow a groan, my hands clenching the chaise lounge for dear life because if I touch her, I'm done.

She's drunk. She's a means to an end. This is not *part of your twenty-eight minutes.*

But then *she* touches me. Drags a gentle finger over my scar, down my neck, setting me on fire.

Two slender hands mold over my shoulders then slide to my front, where my dress shirt is unbuttoned.

She slips her hands inside my shirt and caresses my pecs.

Skin touching skin.

"So hard. Muscular." Lana continues her tentative exploration. "Your tattoos are so beautiful."

Visions of me pinning her down, ripping her dress, suckling on her damn pointy nipples, and feasting on her wet pussy fill my mind. I want to taste her honey at the source. I want to know what she sounds like when she comes apart with me buried deep inside her.

"Fuck. Stop, Lana. Stop. You're drunk." Sweat beads on my upper lip, but I can't step away.

She hums again. Beethoven's melody. *Our* melody. Her fingers reach for my buttons.

"I said *stop*!" I wrench away with my last remaining willpower. "Are you that desperate for a man, you'd go for someone who treats you like shit?"

Lana flinches, her eyes widening with shock, then hurt. The intoxicated haze clears.

I want to take back the words, but they're necessary. There can't be any feelings between us. Unless it's animosity.

"I *hate* you, Elias Kent. That," she motions to the air between us, "was a drunken mistake. I don't know what I was thinking."

"Make sure it doesn't happen again."

With my thoughts spinning, my inhibitions at a breaking point, I pivot, walk out of the room, and slam the door behind me.

It can never happen again.

Chapter 25: THE APOTHECARY'S BLOOM

LANA

"CAN YOU NOT TALK, or is this a choice?"

Ren shuts the car door behind me without answering. He's in his usual super spy, deadly assassin getup: black leather jacket, black jeans, black boots—everything black. Aside from his wool gloves, the man seems impervious to the winter elements.

Tattoos snake up his throat, thorned vines I spotted on Elias's arms. His mask hides half of his face, but those brown eyes are sharp enough to cut glass.

"Do you have a last name? Why don't you take off your mask?"

He presses a hand to my back, urging me along. An icy December gust flutters my thick wool skirt. The sun peeks from behind the clouds, scattering shards of cool light across the snow-covered cobblestones of Waverly Street, barely ten minutes uphill from Elias's house.

Or, I guess, my gilded cage now.

To the east, Ashbourne Heights gleams with old-money mansions with front-row views of Lake Michigan. To the west, darkness fades into Saints Hollow and its cracked bricks, flickering streetlights, and lingering ghosts.

The mysterious room on the third floor remains locked. I've stopped trying for now. I should just buy a hacksaw, but I'm sure the Shadow King won't let me.

Elias Kent is a conundrum I can't solve. He's violent, a cold-blooded murderer who seems to have some sort of moral code. He's cold one minute and hot the next.

He's someone who'd say, "I hate you," but would give me his coat and umbrella amid strong winds and heavy snow.

And that drunken incident in the library? My skin heats at the spotty memories. I can't believe I came onto him. It was definitely the alcohol and not me.

Absolutely not me, the rational me, that is.

Elias has made himself scarce these days.

Aside from the crude diagram of The Association's org structure, I have found no more dirt on him or the Berishas. No mysterious phone calls or shadowy visitors.

His office? Always locked.

I want to scream at the top of my lungs. Not that anyone would care.

But at least my family is doing well at home. Maxwell has fully recovered, and he and Rex check in on me weekly. They promise me they're looking into the Berishas and The Association. The girls still think I'm jetting across the world.

I want more than anything to go back. Away from this lonely house and its shadowy owner, away from the threat of violence and the uncertainty of my future.

So, to keep myself from going mad, I've started exploring the border of Saints Hollow and Ashbourne Heights.

"My tough, silent bodyguard," I needle Ren. "Do you like chocolate? What's your favorite food? Color? If we're spending so much time together, we should get to know each other, don't you think?"

He snorts and shakes his head, his lips moving silently.

"What are you mouthing? I can't read lips. Are you saying I'm your ray of sunshine? That you're overcome with a need to tell me everything so I can get out of your hair?"

A smile tugs at my lips as I watch him heave an exasperated sigh, his pace quickening as we weave through the crowds toward our destination.

I take in the quaint storefronts, their awnings thick with snow. Construction noise from the next block over interrupts the quiet.

It's bittersweet, being back here so many years later after Kian disappeared.

Some things have changed—the new shops, the hip condos popping up—but a lot has stayed the same. There's still an air of melancholy, a vibe of historic decay in the neighborhood, like it has seen too many losses.

Twenty years ago, a devastating fire burned down half of Saints Hollow.

It was also when my relationship with Kian abruptly ended.

I had returned to New York because Dad had come down with pneumonia. Kian and I were long distance, but I planned to go to college in Chicago to be near him.

Panic seized my chest when I saw the news about the fire. I emailed Kian because he didn't have a cell phone. He never replied. I scoured newspapers online for weeks afterward, pored over obituaries, called hospitals after cheer practice, desperate for news of him and his family.

Then I finally saw, among the list of casualties, his parents' and baby sister's names.

My heart shattered. I was inconsolable. Dad and my brothers even asked their contacts in the city to locate Kian or Sofia.

Nothing.

Those were dark times—tears were my constant companion at night after I played the role of a dutiful daughter during the day.

I missed the boy with a beautiful face, bleached blond hair, and warm green eyes.

Until one day, I got an emerald pendant in the mail.

The emerald pendant.

He was alive.

But there was no note, no explanation. It was a farewell.

Over the years, the same questions haunted me.

What happened to him? Why did he disappear without a trace?

I thought he loved me.

Eventually, I tried to move on. I dated guys here and there, but those relationships never lasted more than a few months. Tanner, the guy I was with the longest—four whopping long months—ghosted me the summer of my junior year in college. Everyone else was more or less the same. Excuses about being too busy. About being intimidated by my brothers.

No one would stay. They'd all vanish. Sometimes, late at night, when the city sounds quieted and my apartment felt all too lonely, I'd wonder.

Is it me? Am I not good enough to make them stay?

A car swerves in my direction, shocking me out of my thoughts.

Tires screech and burning rubber permeates the air. A scream shoots up my throat.

Ren curses. He grabs my waist and shoves me against the brick wall. The impact jolts the air out of my lungs. Pain explodes across my back. Daylight swirls in my vision.

A black car speeds away, gawking onlookers pointing at it.

"You okay?" Ren rasps, his dark brows furrowed.

My pulse bellows in my ears as I strain a breath, disoriented.

A pistol glints in his hand, hidden under his jacket. I didn't even see him pull it.

"Some people can't drive, huh?" I quip.

He narrows his eyes at the street, a muscle ticcing in his jaw.

Something in his expression gets my hackles up, and ice slithers over my skin.

It's an accident, right? I'm from New York. Things like this happen all the time.

"Hey! You can talk!" I nudge him and waggle my eyebrows. "Does this mean you're warming up to me? Yeah? You like me, don't you?"

Ren lets out an exasperated sigh and stays silent, ignoring the quizzical stares from onlookers.

He walks toward the café I passed by a few times last week.

The storefront of Arcana & Bloom beckons me like a box of gourmet truffles. I can never resist good chocolate, after all.

Pastel green double doors are adorned with brass handles. Faux white roses, hydrangeas, and wisteria frame its windows and archways. Little bistro tables sit on the curb, enclosed in clear, heated tents, reminding me of people-watching in Paris as I sip my lattes.

Ren holds the door open with one hand, his phone in the other.

Ren

Well? You going in?

I ignore his question. "So, now that you've talked in my presence and saved my life, how about those questions? How old are you? Do you work for Elias or with him? Are you a dealer of secrets too?"

The infuriating man remains silent. He twitches his nose and leans against the brick wall, trying to disappear into it, but that's impossible. He radiates danger, standing out like a shark in a school of clownfish.

I tap my foot.

Ren

Not going in?

He rolls his eyes.

I mirror his pose and blink at him. Too bad for him, I have all the time in the world.

He sighs, fingers flying over his phone screen.

Ren

I don't like to talk. People talk too much. Silence tells you more.

Seeing I haven't moved, he sends another text.

Ren

I have a last name, but that's none of your business. The mask protects us both. And I work with Elias, not for him. Understood, Your Majesty?

I snort. "Your Majesty should be reserved for the Shadow King himself. I'm just his lowly prisoner."

Before he responds, I rise on my tiptoes and brush a quick kiss on his cheek. "Thank you, Ren."

The grumpy man freezes, his eyes widening as I sweep past him and enter the café.

Immediately, I feel at home.

Warmth and spice welcome me like a hug.

Sage-green walls adorned with twinkling Christmas lights and worn wooden counters make this place seem like a cozy countryside escape.

But then, I see its quirks—brass jars lining multiple shelves, vintage teacups and pots, sunken seating areas with mismatched furniture, multi-color cushions that look like a unicorn crossed with a seventies hippie threw up and this decor is the result. Bookshelves stretch floor to ceiling, filled with novels and knickknacks.

Then there are the flowers, the glorious flowers. Lush purple wisteria drips from the ceiling, orange roses climb lattices, and ivy curls along the walls. I don't even know how they keep them alive in the middle of winter.

I breathe in the nutty scent of coffee and spice mixing with the sweetness of the bouquets.

A memory stirs.

"So you're an Anderson—you can have anything. What do you want that you don't already have? Have you decided on a dream?" Kian asks.

We're in his backyard, my feet resting against the beat-up tire we used as a chair. Sofia chats with a friend, laughing in the background. His mom, a petite woman, watches me with narrowed eyes and a tight smile.

"Well," I say, "I don't really care about the money. I guess I want what my parents had. Love. People say it killed her, but from her journal entries, she was happy. I'd risk it all for a love like that too."

He's contemplative. "What about something tangible?"

Inhaling the sweet air, I climb onto a makeshift swing, kick out my legs, and feel the breeze flutter my hair.

"Other than that music box, which I'm not getting until my birthday because I want the anticipation...I suppose I want a place of my own. Something I can decorate."

His heat brushes against my back as he pushes me. Higher and higher. I soar through the air like the ravens flying overhead.

"I want a gorgeous library with walls of books. One of those beautiful antique desks with cherubs on the legs. A music room. And..." I stop, excitement bubbling, and leap off the swing.

Kian's already there, like he's predicted my next move.

He catches me easily.

"What?" He grazes my cheek with his finger. I shiver.

"An indoor garden," I say. "Like a greenhouse filled with roses, more books, a comfortable chair, the best hot chocolate, and big windows I can watch the stars from."

"That's...very specific." A smirk tugs at his lips.

"What can I say? I have standards."

"And yet you chose me."

"And yet I chose you," I whisper.

The hiss of the espresso machine drags me back to the present.

A redhead reminding me of a certain fairytale mermaid frowns behind the counter.

She mutters something to the machine. Then she scowls.

"Just whack it," I call out, grinning. "Hit it like you hate it."

Amusement glints in her green eyes. "You break it, you buy it."

"But you're the one hitting it."

I sit at the counter and glance at the chalkboard behind her—the drink offerings.

The Velvet Hex. The Obsidian Heart. The Alchemist Kiss. Moonpetal Elixir.

What the heck?

Whack.

The coffee machine splutters and purrs, and soon the scent of freshly ground espresso fills the air.

"Damn. It works."

"Told you. Works with everything." I may have whacked one of Maxwell's race cars a few years ago when it wouldn't unlock. I could've sworn I was a dead woman.

But then it worked. Ha!

"So, what can I get you? First time here?" The redhead grins as she ties on a green apron.

"Just moved here, actually." I look around, taking in the people quietly chatting, a brunette with ivory skin in a turtleneck stocking books on shelves, and the rows of spice jars—willow bark, lemon balm, calendula, echinacea, among other things. "What is this place? Bookstore and coffee shop mixed with *Practical Magic?*"

She grins. "Exactly. It's one of a kind. Aria," she points to the brunette, "and I came up with it. We wanted our favorite things in one place. I'm Scarlett." She sticks out her hand.

I shake it and smile. It feels good—chatting with regular people, getting a drink at a new café. Normal life things.

Brow arched, I motion to her hair. "Scarlett...with red hair."

She mock groans and sighs. "I was named after Scarlett O'Hara from *Gone with the Wind.* My parents didn't think things through."

Scarlett tells me she and Aria met in the University of Chicago's nursing program. Aria graduated and is now a nurse at Chicago Memorial. Scarlett took her family's investment and opened this shop instead. She wanted to use her herbology obsession to make weirdly perfect drinks and build a place where people want to linger and read. Aria hangs out here on her days off.

"Special perennial plants. Experimental strains." She motions to the flowers.

"And trust me, my drinks are magic. Head cold? Bad luck in the love department?" She leans in and points to the jars behind her. "I've got you covered."

"And some awesome books to read while you're at it." Aria drifts over and sits next to me.

She gives me an impish smile. "I saw you before with that scary dude outside. What are you? Part of the mafia? They are around here, you know."

I swallow, my mind flashing to The Association, and that pause has her eyes widening.

"No way! Not judging though."

"All are welcome here," Scarlett comments. "We have a mix of folks from different 'backgrounds' in Saints Hollow. This is a safe haven."

"It's not really like that." Heat crawls up my neck. There go my plans of making new friends. "Ren looks scary, but—"

"Hot. Killer vibes. Model body, though. Dude, see those shoulders. And that mask. I'm a sucker for men in masks." Aria grins.

"Don't let Blake hear that. You're engaged, missy," Scarlett teases.

Aria flushes and explains, "Blake's a surgeon at the hospital, and he—"

"Is not a killer but does wear a mask." Scarlett snickers. "A surgical mask, so it's different."

"Heeey. Surgical masks are...hot."

"If you say so."

Aria eyes Ren again. "Why doesn't he come in? It's freezing outside."

"Genetically modified, maybe. A super soldier. He looks tense. I think he needs chamomile and ashwagandha in his coffee," Scarlett muses.

The girls banter, and I blink.

Aria leans in and whispers, "Every book has a good story. Even the scary ones. I *love* the scary ones."

"But she picked a golden retriever, make that make sense," Scarlett stage whispers. "Honestly, I think she's seen too much shit at the ER and it's messed with her common sense."

Something inside me loosens—an ache that's taken residence under my ribs since the wedding. For a moment, I feel like my old self again.

The two girls chat about hospital gossip. Aria talks about the new research wing under construction. I bite back a smile, not mentioning my family's donation is paying for it. Instead, I make a mental note to email Chicago Memorial's PR department and connect them with my replacement at Fleur for their joint media tour.

"I'm homesick," I begin, and they swivel their heads toward me. "Any cures?"

Scarlett winks, her bangles jangling on her wrist. "I've got just the drink for you."

"Welcome to your home away from home." Aria runs to the shelves and returns with a book.

Wuthering Heights by Emily Brontë.

"Matching me with heartbreak?" I say wryly. My mind flashes to a man with dark hair and a dangerous scar, who clutches me against him like he never wants to let go.

Aria smiles. "No. More like obsession and eternal love. And gothic, spooky atmospheres. Something you can sink your teeth into."

An old ache flares. The images merge inside my mind—warm green eyes morphing into cutting emeralds, lost promises and words carved on a tree.

"Hey! We're going to a new club in two weeks. It's so hard to get in. You should come with. You can meet Blake!" Aria exclaims.

I stare at the friendly faces and shove my melancholy away.

New friends in a new place. Action, not reaction.

"Sure." I grin. Maybe a night out will turn things around. And if my overbearing husband has an issue with it, that's his problem, not mine.

The girls squeal, and I glance outside.

A dark sedan with tinted windows idles at the curb across the street, exhaust puffing out in dark plumes. Hair rises on my forearms. Ren stands sentry, his hand clutching his phone, his jaw clenched, brows pinched.

Like he's worried.

Chapter 26: PRISON BREAK

LANA

MY HAPPINESS DIMS THE moment I return to the house.

Elias leans against the foyer wall, which is strange to begin with. The man usually barricades himself inside his office.

Is he waiting for me?

My heart trembles like it's excited.

You're nuts, Lana. Nothing good can come from the Shadow King waiting for you. We are not *excited about him. At all.*

He hums under his breath, one hand holding a crimson book, the other playing with his damn lighter again. He stills, appearing to be completely engrossed in his reading.

The man isn't a fast reader, judging by how quickly he turns the pages. His finger trails over the paper. He studies the text like he's trying to memorize it. Or peel apart the words and find the hidden meaning underneath.

Who knows? I wouldn't put it past him. He's probably memorizing for fun, the unhinged monster.

Click. Click. Click.

A muscle twitches in his cheek—a ghost of a smile. What *is* he reading?

I hate how the afternoon light drapes over his towering frame, how put together he is in his crisp white shirt, perfectly fitted double-breasted vest—a stunning forest green color this time—and gray dress pants.

"Careful there. All that ogling and I might think you're in love with me," he says, his obsidian hair glinting under the pendant light. He snaps his book shut.

"Stop copying me."

"I didn't do anything." He smirks.

"I said that in the library...and yes, I still remember my temporary lapse of judgment." My face warms. "You don't have to worry. You're the last person I'll ever fall in love with."

He stares at his lighter for a beat, slowly sliding it into his pocket.

When he looks up, those green eyes are cold as ice.

"Had a fun outing?" he asks.

"Why does it matter to you? You're my husband in name only."

His voice drops. "Do you want it *not* to be in name only?"

He steps closer, each step shrinking the room. A current runs through my body.

Fight or flight.

"Is that what you want, Lana?"

He closes the distance. Space ceases to exist.

"N-No." I back up until I hit the door. "You're ridiculous."

Slowly, Elias brings his hands up, caging me in. My breath stutters as I look up at him.

"I seem to recall someone being enthusiastic that night in the library. Or in the kitchen. Or in my office. Moving on my cock like you were desperate." Body slowly pressing against mine, just a graze, a taunt, he murmurs, "Three times, Lana. Is that it? Is my wife lonely and horny? Am I not doing my husbandly duties?"

Heat flares through me at his words and the dark promise in his eyes.

My mouth dries. I wet my lips, and his gaze drops to the movement. A rough sound rumbles in his throat.

An ache flares between my legs.

What's wrong with me? He's the enemy.

A shadow encroaches on his irises like mist rolling in on a winter night.

Every part of him stills.

A predator lying in wait.

My hands move before my mind registers. I touch him—graze the silk emerald tie under his vest, feeling the sturdy muscles rippling underneath his shirt.

"That's it, *wife*," he rasps, leaning down, his lips hovering an inch from mine. "Pupils dilated. Pulse beating madly in your throat. The flush...beautiful pink flush. You want me, the man you hate, don't you?

Is this what you dream about late at night, your body hot, aching, your soft skin rubbing against the sheets?"

A moan perches on the tip of my tongue. I'm hot. Burning.

I dig my body into the wall, fighting my basest impulse to arch up, to sample those perfectly curved lips.

To bury myself in his darkness.

The thought snaps me, just barely, out of his spell.

"You wish, asshole! You have no place in my dreams."

He releases me with a low chuckle. "Dreams. Nightmares are probably more apt."

His eyes dim—sadness, but that can't be right. He strides toward his office. I follow, my control clearly nonexistent.

"Why are you talking to me suddenly? Were you waiting for me?"

He looks over his shoulder. "I'm leaving next week. Ren also has things to take care of. You are *not* to leave this house in my absence."

"No way. I'm not doing this again. It's bad enough I'm married to you. I won't be chained here like I'm in jail."

"You'll do as I say. For your own good." He stalks off.

My jaw drops. *Oh no, you don't.* I chase after him, but his strides are too quick. He slams the office door in my face.

I bang on it with my fist.

"Elias Kent, you open the door this instant! You need to get something straight. We're in this arrangement because you and your cronies need something from me. I'm doing you all a favor. Not the other way around."

He doesn't answer. I only hear that aggravating lighter. *Click, click, click.*

It's been six days since he disappeared to God-knows-where.

Six days of pacing this mausoleum of a mansion, going through each unlocked room like a bored ghost. Six days of trying new lock-breaking exercises to break into the impenetrable room on the third floor. Six days of Hannah trying to convince me Elias is a good man because he took her in ten years ago as she was about to be evicted from her apartment with two young grandkids to feed. Her daughter died in a car accident, and the deadbeat father was nowhere to be seen.

I have to admit, the thought of Elias helping sweet Hannah out brings a smile to my face.

But then I remember he's Elias Kent.

I wouldn't be surprised if he singled her out because of her superior cooking skills.

Scrunching my nose, I peek through the curtains of my bedroom and spot the black sedan in its usual spot across the street. Snowflakes fall from the sky.

The government car.

For the past six days, that sedan has been parked out there every single day. Exhaust puffs into the air. A shadow of someone sits inside.

It's strange.

This morning I texted Emerson a photo of the car and its plate.

He replied, *These are government plates. Different from the car that followed you in New York City. Do you need me to look further?*

I told him no. But the message lingers.

Are they tailing me, or following Ren? Why would the government follow me? Who was following me in New York?

I think back to my brush with death outside the café. Ren's worried face when he spotted the car.

Chewing my lip, I eye the stack of romances on my nightstand. I can spend my time with hot dudes with chiseled chests who can growl like nobody's business, or I can act on the madcap idea I came up with two days ago when I saw the mysterious car yet again.

The house is quiet. Really quiet. Not the watchful silence of my imprisonment, with the prickly sensation of someone—the cameras or Hannah—watching my every move.

Elias is coming back tomorrow. Ren has disappeared, and Hannah, last I checked, has Sinatra crooning from her phone while she prepares a feast for tonight.

This is my chance to get answers.

It's a huge risk to do what I'm about to do. If The Association finds out, they'll kill me or my family.

But I've never been the passive type. I can't wait for someone to rescue me.

And with the opportunity in my face, I have to trust my gut.

My gaze darts to the camera closest to me. No blinking red light.

My asshole husband probably thinks I've given up searching for answers. Maybe he thinks I'm too chicken to do more.

A slow smile tugs at my lips.

Oops, Shadow King.

Seems you've underestimated your good little wife.

I glance at the clock, its second hand ticking, reminding me I'm running out of time before my jailer returns.

Time to take a risk.

"Meow," Cece voices her concern.

"I'll be fine. Be good. I'll be back soon." I set her on the windowsill, her favorite spot.

Carefully, I pull on my down jacket and traipse down the stairs.

I unlock the front door. The click is soft, but it echoes in the marble foyer. I hold my breath, gaze snapping around. No one comes, and I slip out.

The sky is overcast, a light mist shrouding the air. The weather may be freezing, but it's on my side.

One good thing about being trapped indoors and being bored out of my mind is I've observed the guards and their routines, written down their schedules.

Yesterday, I spent the whole day haunting the window, noting every lap, tracking cigarette and cell phone breaks.

There's a small window now—one precise minute—where one guard walks toward the backyard pool, the other circling the perimeter. Their patrols run the same way throughout the day. I timed it. A precise pattern. If I don't go now, I won't go at all.

I dart along the fence, boots clomping on thick snow. The tall evergreen trees screen me from the main lawn. Branches scratch my calves, and I hiss in pain. Quickly, I make it to the front, but I don't take the main gate where the guard tower is. Instead, I slip toward the smaller door the gardeners use.

Voices travel to my ears. I duck behind a hedge, heart beating out of my chest.

Shit. I glance through the small gap between the leaves and the pockets of snow. They finished their patrol sooner.

Or I was too slow.

The man speaks into his walkie-talkie, his gaze sharp. He turns his head in my direction.

I curl into a ball and hold myself still. The sharp twigs dig deep into my flesh.

Please don't see me.

A few seconds pass, then I hear his footsteps as he walks out of view.

Blowing out a breath, I tiptoe to the small door, fish out a hairpin, and fiddle with the lock.

Click. It opens.

I slip onto the quiet street, scan left and right. No neighbors. No guards.

I dash toward the sedan.

Then the door opens before I reach it.

A striking man steps out. Gray wool coat. Black tie. Sleek gray suit. Espresso-brown hair, short on the sides, longer on top, perfectly tamed. Intelligent brown eyes behind black-framed glasses.

"Ms. Anderson," he says. "Finally, we meet."

"Who are you, and why have you been following me?" Adrenaline spikes and my pulse riots.

He smiles, draws a black wallet from inside his jacket, and flips it open. "Special Agent Tristan Clarke, FBI, Criminal Investigative Division, at your service. We need to talk. Time is of the essence, and your life is in danger. Will you come with me?"

Indecision wobbles inside me. Something pinches my gut. I glance back at the looming mansion—my prison—and think about the enigmatic man who is my husband in name.

Why am I waffling? Why do I feel *loyal* to Elias? He's a criminal.

Remember the vault. The people he killed. The gun he pressed against your head.

I'm losing my mind.

Drawing a quick breath, I slide into the backseat. "Don't make me regret this, Special Agent."

Chapter 27: A GAME OF CHESS

ELIAS

THE CRACK OF HIS jawbone shattering vibrates inside the small cell of a nondescript warehouse at the edge of Saints Hollow. I sit in a dark corner, ankle to my knee, watching Niko deliver another sharp right hook to the handler's face.

I tsk. That one was weak. Bad angle. I could've done better.

"I swear I know nothing!" the man sputters, sweat dripping down his forehead.

Niko—the number two enforcer under the deranged Bakim of the Albanian mob—arches a dark brow at me.

I press my lips together. "I don't buy it. Do you?"

Niko cracks a small smile and drags the man up by his collar. "Tell us who gave you the USB."

The Berishas think the encrypted messages, which stopped their "shipments," came from a USB drive.

A drive I planted, courtesy of Aleksei.

"An inside job." He grins. "Nothing freaks these people out more than a mole."

"I swear it's not me. You've got the wrong guy!"

"Only you knew about the shipments from Estonia and Croatia. It's strange, isn't it? The moment you disappeared was when all the shit went down?"

He lands another hard punch into the man's stomach.

A wet plop. A rancid smell.

Shit, the bastard vomited.

I twirl my gloved finger in the air and tell Niko, "I don't know about you, but this is going nowhere, and I have an appointment to get to. Speed it up."

Niko grunts and excuses himself to go outside, no doubt to bring in some power tools.

As the door slams shut, the man—Akim, I think; these assholes are all the same—stares at me, blood pooling at the corner of his lips.

"M-Mr. Kent, believe me! I didn't send the virus. I had an emergency at home. When I came back, they told me the servers were hacked. Please! Tell them it wasn't me."

I sigh. I almost feel sorry for the bastard since he's our fall guy.

If I had a conscience, that is.

But since I don't, I get up from my chair and amble toward him. Something must've given me away because the man shrinks.

"Mr. Kent..." His voice cracks.

I catch his chin, tilt his face up, and pat his cheek. "Do you know what I hate more than anything?"

My words are a quiet whisper. The man stills, his sour breath puffing against my face.

I lean closer. "I hate crimes against women. People like you *disgust* me to the core. If I had my way, I'd peel every inch of skin from your body just so I could hear you scream. And that'd only be an ounce of the torture you put those women through."

Akim's breath quickens. "But you work for the Berishas! You're part of The Association!"

I smile and step back, wiping my gloves with a napkin.

The door opens, and Niko walks back into the room, holding a toolbox.

"I got it from here," I tell him.

He hesitates. "You sure?"

Oh yes, I'm fucking sure.

Niko's eyes narrow with something like understanding. He hands me the toolbox and leaves.

"So many choices," I tsk under my breath as I flip through the tools, "what shall I use?"

Akim whimpers, pleas blubbering from his mouth.

Useless, spineless idiot.

I hold up a sharp tactical knife and walk back to him. It gleams under the fluorescent light.

I check my watch. "Too bad. I don't have time to play with you today."

"No please! Talk to Dalmat Hoxha. He'd know more. I swear it wasn't—"

Hoxha. The Albanian mob secretary. Of course. Sick satisfaction warms my chest as I find my next target.

"You." I press my boot on his chest and bear down, watching with satisfaction as he gasps for breath, his face turning red. "I know it wasn't you."

Rule one: look them in the eye.

I stare straight at him. The rage I've tethered away comes roaring back to the surface.

Rules two and three: Tell them their sins and no innocents.

I lower my voice, a raw whisper. "It might not have been you, but your sins are just the same. Those women you hurt? Now, who will avenge them?"

My fingers curl around his neck, feeling the tendons yield beneath my grip. The bones crack and give. He struggles against his binds, eyes widening, bloodshot and wild.

"S-Stop...h-help—"

I lean in. "I sent the virus."

His eyes widen and I plunge the knife, the hilt slamming into his chest. Wet gurgles reach my ears. Then fruitless struggles.

When he stops moving, the room stills, thick and silent. I step back and slowly peel off my gloves—another pair ruined—and toss them into the metal bin.

Flicking open my lighter, I hold it to my handkerchief. Flames catch. I drop it into the bin, watching the fire devour the evidence.

A hollow satisfaction fills my gut as I step outside. Niko watches me from the hallway.

"Well," I say, "tell the Berishas it's done. He wanted to get a cut of the shipment for himself. Go check his bank account."

They'll see the three extra zeros I transferred over. Untraceable, of course.

Niko's assessing gaze pauses on my face.

"Questions?" I ask.

He shakes his head, eyes narrowed in anger.

"Teenagers," he mutters. "Thirteen-year-olds. That was the last batch. The bastard got what's coming."

Anger climbs inside me. I think of Sofia—eyes haunted and lifeless, frame frail when I found her all those years ago. How close I was to losing her.

Niko grunts his approval and stalks off.

I can't help but wonder why someone who clearly hates this life would stay with the Albanian mob.

Just as I slide into the backseat of my car, my phone pings.

Knight Ren

It worked. She's on the run. Want me to go after her?

Ren attached a few photos—Lana getting into a black car.

A flare rises behind my ribs when I take in her face—the desperation, the fear when she glanced back at the house, like she thought we were going to hurt her. Like she truly believed she was running for her life.

I push down the emotions rising inside me. I won't analyze why it hurts to breathe.

You hate her, Elias. Remember what she did. Remember why Kian ceased to exist.

But she never forgot me. I may have been drunk on my birthday, but I remember every second. There was sorrow in her eyes when she lit the candle.

Then another image flashes behind my eyelids—the heartache on her face days later in front of Hollow Gardens.

For me.

My conscience, something I thought was long dead, flickers to life. Conscience kills in my reality.

I harden myself and type a response.

Rook Elias

No, let her go. This way, we'll see how much the feds have on us.

Knight Ren

Noted. Did I mention you're a scary asshole?

I chuckle, motioning for John to drive.

Rook Elias

Chess is only scary if you're the piece being sacrificed.

Chapter 28: A NEW PLAYER

LANA

THE FED TAKES ME to a small café overlooking Lake Michigan on the north side, far enough from Ashbourne Heights and Saints Hollow where no one we know will "happen" to drop by. The place is empty, but the heater is thankfully on. With its dated furnishings—peeling floral wallpaper, faded leather seats—it feels like a ghost town.

"Well, I didn't expect this, Special Agent Clarke. This is unusual," I comment as he hands me a cup of tea. "Do you treat all your interviewees this way? Take them out for tea in the middle of nowhere? I was expecting four white walls, fluorescent lights, and really bad coffee."

He laughs, removes his gloves, and settles into the seat in front of me. "Tristan. Call me Tristan."

His lips curve into a small smile, which normally should make me feel better, but there's a hardness in him that gets my hackles up.

"I figured you're used to more refined tastes, being an Anderson and all." He stirs his drink but doesn't take a sip.

"So was it you following me in New York City?"

"No. But you know my younger brother." He stops stirring.

My mind whirs, going through my directory of names, when shock registers. The last name *Clarke*. "Emerson? My PI is your brother?"

"Small world. Almost meant to be, don't you think?" Another smirk. This is someone who rations his emotions. *Much like another man you know.* I push the thought away. "And I had colleagues keep tabs on your family. The Bureau does that for high-profile people who have frequent brushes with the law."

"That's not fair! We were victims. It was—" I stop myself, not knowing how much I should share about The Association.

He stills, his brown eyes steady on mine. "Go on. You want to say it. The Association, right?"

"If you already have all the answers, then why am I here?"

"Well, to be frank with you, Miss Anderson—" He pauses, then cocks his brow. "Or should I call you *Mrs.* Kent?"

"Lana will be fine."

"Lana, then." He leans back. "You're an intelligent woman, so I won't beat around the bush. I've had my eye on The Association's activities for a while, but things are delicate given their connections. Unless we have definitive proof, my hands are tied."

His jaw tics. Then, he flashes an icy smile again. *Fake.* I do it when I face the press.

"You aren't telling me everything." I lean forward, hands clasped on the table. "You see, Tristan. I spent years in PR, hearing bullshit and spinning bullshit. You're hiding something. And this? As much as I like to think I get special treatment, I don't think that's it. This is all off the books, isn't it?"

Silence falls as Tristan holds my gaze, the earlier softness vanishing into the ether.

Yes. This is personal. A vendetta.

"Smart woman. Why *would* you marry Elias Kent?" he muses.

Heat creeps up my neck. I hate how my emotions are haywire when it comes to my husband.

"I don't know what to tell you," I admit. "I don't know anything about The Association. I was hoping you'd tell me something I could use."

"To do what? You're married to the dealer of secrets himself. The man's as slippery as a snake, and we haven't been able to find anything on him. All we know is whenever he's involved, things get questionable and evidence disappears. What were you going to do with this," he air quotes with his fingers, "'information' you think I'll provide you?"

Blackmail the bastard back. Figure out what The Association wants with me when I turn thirty-five and escape.

Alive.

Tristan's eyes sharpen at what he sees on my face. "You know something, Lana. Tell me. I can get you out of this."

I bite my cheek, thinking about the man who threatened to blow my brains out at the vault, who comforted me amid the bloodshed, like he knew I was terrified.

Even to this day, I can't reconcile that cold-blooded man with the arrogant mobster who helped my siblings repeatedly and showed up with Christmas gifts for the little ones.

The bastard even got Levi a toy train with real steam coming out. The little guy looked at him like he were a hero. And I hate to admit—Elias is a pro with guns. How could he miss *all* of Maxwell's vital organs with both shots?

"You're going to help me alone? Or do you mean the Feds?" *What can one man do that my brothers can't?*

Tristan doesn't answer me, his expression shuttering again.

"I promise you, you're safe with me. Let me help you."

Indecision wavers inside me, and snapshots of the last few months play in my mind. How Elias held me on his lap in the office and inhaled my scent like it was something he'd been chasing all his life. Then there's the gentleness in his voice and eyes that whispered secrets on Thanksgiving and in front of Hollow Gardens. Like he too was carrying invisible pain, and he wanted to show me his scars but couldn't.

He had never hurt me, had he?

Good God, Lana. This has to be Stockholm Syndrome. There's no way I'm feeling any compassion for that man.

But when I open my mouth, nothing comes out. Tristan's watching me too closely, and instead of pushing, he takes out his phone and swipes to a video.

"Let me show you something. This might change your mind."

A feed with a time stamp from three days ago shows up. Elias was on his "trip." Decked out in another three-piece suit, he stands tall in the middle of a fancy room, a lone spotlight shining on him. Men sit in the corners, but I can't see their faces.

"Do you swear to uphold your oath and loyalty to The Association?" someone murmurs from off-camera, the voice muffled.

"I do," he replies.

"Do you swear that The Association will come above all other priorities?"

"I do."

"Do you know the repercussions if you betray The Association?"

Silence. A faint clicking. The glint of silver in his clenched hand—his lighter.

Elias clears his throat. "Extirpation. If I betray The Association, my bloodline will be exterminated. All relatives, blood or not. The entire family line."

My veins turn to ice. The words echo in my mind: *Extirpated. All relatives, blood or not. Entire family line.*

I'm married to him. I'm his family now. My siblings, nieces, and nephews are all related to him by marriage.

If Elias betrays The Association, they all die.

No. I collapse back into my chair. My stomach heaves. I grip the edge of the table for support.

"Good. Now kneel for your final oath," the man says.

Elias freezes, just slightly. If he hadn't been around my family for the past decade, I wouldn't have noticed it.

"No." He straightens. His fingers tighten around the lighter. "I never kneel for anything or anyone."

My pulse shoots up. I can't see much in the frame, but I feel the hostility in the air like I were physically there.

"What do you mean, no?"

"No, is no. Take it or leave it."

Another beat of silence. Muffled voices murmur offscreen. A low argument. Cold dread gathers in my chest, and I clutch the tablecloth in front of me. I tell myself it's because I'm terrified of The Association and not because I'm scared about what they'll do to him.

"This can be classified as a betrayal of The Association," the man muses, voice sinister. "Of which you just told us the consequences."

Elias stills, so much I don't even see his chest move. Then, a low, rough chuckle raises the hairs on my forearms. "You're smarter than that. You need me."

"You're calm about this," the same voice murmurs. "A sick motherfucker. You're lucky we want you on our side."

Elias curves his lips, the smile terrifying.

"Your Rite is complete, Mr. Kent. Welcome to The Association, where all the power you can imagine will be yours."

I don't see his response because Tristan clicks the phone shut. Air rushes out of me, and I force myself to let go of the tablecloth.

"A camera in a floral arrangement. A rare oversight for them." Tristan looks at me, clearly sympathetic. "Do you understand what you're up against, Miss Anderson?"

He's using my maiden name again.

"You can't do this alone," he continues. "Your life is at stake. Your family's lives are at stake. You're married to the enemy—a very dangerous man who would risk everything, even the lives of everyone he cares about, for power. Don't you find that terrifying?"

A breath rattles out of me. I grip my cup and bring it to my lips, needing to do something with my hands. The liquid is cold. Bitter. The china clatters when I set it down.

"Wh-What do you want me to do?" I whisper.

"Spy for me. Take pictures. Notes. I'll walk you through it."

My mind is a mess. If I help Tristan, I'm betraying Elias, and the king of the underworld shows no mercy. But if I don't, I'm leaving my family at the mercy of The Association. Either way, we might all die.

I'm in way over my head.

"Lana," he rasps.

The concerned tone in Tristan's voice snags my attention.

A muscle tics in his jaw, and for a moment, the emotion swimming in his eyes is clear.

It's pain.

"I know it's overwhelming," he says. "I know you don't trust me. But I really don't want to see you hurt. Think about your family, the people who care about and love you. If anything happens to you, how will they go on?"

A lump thickens in my throat. Images of my family flash in my mind and my heart constricts.

"Let me help you." Tristan slips me a card with his contact information. "That's my private line. Encrypted. Call me anytime."

Before I can respond, he stiffens. Slowly he rises, his hand reaching for his holster as he looks at something behind me.

I smell it before I turn—the familiar scent of vetiver and smoke. My skin prickles. My spine locks.

Elias.

"Well, well, well. Tristan Clarke." His tone is calm but dangerous. "It's rude of you to invite my wife out for tea without letting me know. And a gun," Elias tsks, "really?"

"It's Special Agent Clarke to you. Your wife has a mind of her own. She can make her own decisions."

The two men stare each other down.

My mind riots, excuses tangling on my tongue.

Elias steps to my right, the sound of his shoes hitting the floor—*thump, thump, thump*—matching the rhythm of my heartbeat. He looks down at me, his gaze suddenly soft as he lifts a gloved finger and traces my cheek, sending a shiver down my spine.

"My princess," he murmurs. "Did you miss me?"

"Elias—"

"It's okay. I don't blame you." His voice is smooth, almost gentle. He sounds like he's soothing a spooked animal instead of catching his wife with the FBI.

Elias murmurs, "You're just looking out for me, Lana. I'm not mad. What does the fed want with our newlywed bliss?"

"I didn't tell him anything, Elias. I—"

"I know you didn't, princess."

He leans down and presses a soft kiss on the tender spot where my ear meets my neck. It's like a reward for passing a test I wasn't aware I was taking.

Heat blooms low and dangerous, warming me from within. I tremble.

"It's time for us to go," he says, his voice steady. "Leave *Special Agent* Clarke to enjoy his wild goose chase by himself."

He laces his fingers through mine, firm—an unspoken command.

I get up quickly, heart pounding, and glance back at the federal agent. His eyes narrow at the sight of our joined hands.

"Think about what I said, Mrs. Kent," Tristan says, his tone tight. His card weighs heavily in my pocket.

Then, with a thin smile, he addresses Elias, "Always a pleasure, Mr. Kent. May our paths cross again soon."

Elias smirks, his eyes remaining dark. "Count on it. Unless I find you first."

Chapter 29: SAINTS DON'T DANCE

LANA

A SHIVER MOVES THROUGH me as I step out of the car into a cutting night breeze. Multicolor lights blink in the distance. Christmas songs blast from the radio.

I think about home. My family is preparing for the annual Christmas Ball at The Orchid. Levi has probably made a list of toys he wants from Santa. I breathe through the ache behind my sternum. My family will be there once all of this is over.

When I'm free.

The Nocturne Rose, a refurbished meatpacking warehouse turned nightclub in the Fulton Market District, looms ahead. John, my bodyguard for the night, since Ren is still away, shadows me.

I guess I should be thankful Elias still lets me out of the house after my outing with the fed.

If anything, the asshole seems amused and nonchalant about it all, like he's gotten some answers he's been seeking.

"I'm not worried at all," Elias says in the car after my meeting with Agent Clarke. "Both you and the feds have nothing on me."

"You're too sure of yourself."

He leans down and trails a glove-clad finger across my cheek. I curse myself for the goosebumps erupting over my arms.

Elias's eyes darken. His gaze drops to my parted lips.

"You won't betray me. You don't have it in you."

He probably thinks I'll be a useless spy, the damn bastard.

Aria and Scarlett from the café are already inside. Sickly sweet perfume chokes me the moment I step through the doors. Sultry hip-hop beats vibrate the walls, and soon, I find my mood lifting as I search for the girls.

The club has two floors, all dark concrete and unfinished metal. It's expensive but unrefined, unlike the clubs my family owns.

But the people packed like sardines on the ground floor obviously don't care. Open balconies and cage-like alcoves on the second floor wrap around the dance floor for the elite to watch the crowd.

"Lana!"

Aria squeals and wraps me in a hug. A tall blond man with kind eyes hovers behind her. That must be Blake, the surgeon fiancé.

Her eyes, rimmed with gold glitter, widen. "Dude, you look amazing! I could never pull off that dress."

"You're a petite dynamite." I laugh.

"But lacking in the chest department." She eyes my cleavage revealed by the deep V-neckline of my black mini dress.

Whack!

"Ow!" Aria sticks her tongue out and bats Scarlett's hand away from where she playfully smacked her arm.

"You're right. This works for everything." Scarlett grins at me, then turns to her friend. "Quit ogling other people's tits."

My lips quirk, and I throw my arms around them. "You'll be thankful in twenty years when mine sag and yours are still cute and perky."

Blake laughs and extends his hand. "Blake Amscot, cardiologist slash chaos victim."

"Hey!" Aria grumbles. "I'm excitement. Not chaos."

He kisses her forehead, affection warming his eyes. His phone rings, and a frown crosses his face. "It's the hospital. Emergency surgery. Sorry, have to run, honey."

Aria sighs and stares after her man. "The life of a medical professional."

"So honorable though," I say.

Glass shatters in the background, and people holler. I flinch, but the girls drag me to the bar before I can look.

Two shot glasses slide in front of me.

"Here's to new friendships and kick-ass lives," Aria says, cheeks flushed under the neon lights.

She frowns, then pouts in my direction. "Ugh. And parents who don't think you're trash."

I blink. "Shit. That bad?"

Scarlett leans over and whispers, "Blake's parents are snobs. They want him to marry a doctor."

I shudder. I know that type.

Aria groans. "And I'm stuck dealing with them for the rest of my life." Aria bangs her head against the bar top.

The sound jolts through my chest, then morphs into something else entirely.

The walls rattle as the front door slams shut.

"You can't be with her, Kian. She's an Anderson."

"Mom, stop it. She's here. She can hear you." Kian's voice spikes with agitation.

I curl into a ball, not understanding why Mrs. Leste hates me. Am I not good enough for him?

The question still echoes, but I won't ever know the answer.

"How many did you have? You're bright red." Scarlett pokes Aria. "You're getting a detox tea tomorrow."

"Screw tomorrow! I'm forgetting my troubles tonight. Cheers, girls!" Aria sits back up, nodding to the music.

I raise my glass and down the shot of vodka, pretending the burn isn't from a memory I should've long forgotten.

Then we down one more shot. My body is pleasantly warm, my mind feathering at the edges. I reach for another drink.

"Easy there. I got you something else." Scarlett slides over a shot glass with amber liquid.

I sip it. Sweet, refreshing. Non-alcoholic. A calming warmth floats through my veins. "You're a magician."

She winks. "Herbalist."

"So, Lana. Why do you always have someone shadowing you?" Scarlett asks, eyeing John, who's nursing a water at the far side of the bar. "Are you a celebrity or something?"

Some lady holds up her phone, and I cringe. I've been made. It's a miracle the girls haven't figured out I'm from *the* Anderson family yet.

Aria tosses a napkin onto her camera. "Dude. Privacy, please." She squeezes between us and blocks her view.

"It's complicated," I reply, finishing the rest of my drink. "I'm from a big family. Bodyguards come standard."

Scarlett squints. "Hold on. Your last name's Anderson. Body-guards. Big family. Shit." She elbows Aria, who's bopping to the beat of the music. "Lana's the Anderson princess!"

"Huh?" Aria stops. Her mouth drops open. "That's why you look familiar! Oh my God, didn't you marry some mobster?"

I sigh. But friendships should be based on honesty.

"*Complicated*," I grumble.

"I'll say," Aria hooks her arm through mine. Scarlett takes the other. "Doesn't matter, you're still awesome. Let's dance our troubles away!"

She drags us toward the dance floor. Scarlett tugs my arm, slowing my steps.

"Hey," she whispers, her eyes kind, "we're here for you. What-ever's going on. No judgment. And if your 'complicated situation' needs to be uncomplicated...I might have some deadly belladon-na."

I snort and squeeze her hand.

Five songs later, my feet ache and my voice is hoarse from laugh-ing. I've learned that Aria can't handle her alcohol, which she blames on the Asian glow, as she's a quarter Korean. She also has a penchant for bad boys, but Blake is her exception. Scarlett has a big family like me. She may be whimsical, but her mind is sharp.

I've found my gang.

We invent a ritual. A good book, a perfect drink, and a dare whenever we feel down.

The bass drops, and the crowd surges. For the first time since the wedding, I feel light as a bird.

Until pressure builds in my bladder.

"Going to the restroom. Be right back!" I holler at the girls.

"Want company?" Scarlett asks.

"No, I'm fine. Stay here; have fun."

John moves to follow, but I shake my head and point to the restroom, which is well within his sightlines.

He nods and goes back to drinking his water.

I make my way to the back, passing by a spiral staircase cordoned off by a velvet rope. Two towering men with hard eyes and dark suits stand in front of it, their hands resting near their holsters.

Something's happening on the second floor.

I duck into the restroom and complete my business in the stall when voices drift in.

"They won't let us go up there." Two girls walk in.

"VIPs?"

"I think so. The two single Berisha brothers are with their crowd."

"Ooh! Ilir and Dritan? Billionaires. Worth the risk."

"Tell me about it." The faucet turns on. "The guards said no. A private meeting, apparently."

The Berishas.

The haze in my mind vanishes. My pulse spikes.

More noises reach my ears—the towel dispenser, heels clacking on the concrete floor. Then the door swings open, and silence returns.

I step out and wash my hands, catching my reflection—flushed cheeks and wild hair.

From the crude diagram of The Association in Elias's office, the Berishas are up there in the org chart.

And they need something from me, which means, in a twisted way, I'm *safe* right now.

Tristan's words at the café hammer into my mind. I can't get out of this alone. My brothers, as rich and powerful as they are, can only do so much.

John is out front, the girls still partying it up.

I can go back and play it safe.

Or I can take a risk and find out what the Berishas are meeting about.

I scan the bathroom, noticing a small service door, the same design our family clubs use for staff exits.

Decision made, I slip out the small exit, then loop around to the dance floor.

The girls spot me, and I pull them aside.

"Need your help. And no questions. You in?"

Aria blinks. Scarlett nods. "I meant what I said. We're here for you, Lana."

"Let's uncomplicate my complicated situation."

Heat flares in my chest. I gather them closer and tell them my plan.

Minutes later, the three of us walk toward the guarded staircase.

Aria giggles, her flushed face and glazed eyes totally selling her drunk act as she sways into Scarlett, who looks like she's having a hard time managing the five-foot tall bombshell.

The guards frown, their gazes fixed on the duo. I slip to the perimeter, keeping to the shadows.

"Handsome, you look like you're very good with a gun," Aria purrs, walking her fingers up the first guard's chest. "I love men with *big* guns. Do you have a big gun?"

I bite my lip to keep from snorting.

She sways, and a dramatic drop follows.

Scarlett, equally bad—or good—at acting, gasps. "Oh, shit."

Her drink tumbles out of her grip and splashes over the second guard's suit.

Curses fly. The men step back and pull the girls aside.

There's my window.

I dart to the staircase, catching Aria's wink as I dash upstairs, my heart pounding.

Holy shit. It worked.

It's quieter up here, the music and crowds a faded backdrop.

Deep voices and glasses clinking reach my ears as I slow my climb. My smile disappears, fear tightening my lungs.

"You can't trust him. Something's off."

"He's the dealer of secrets. Of course you can't trust him."

My mouth dries. They're talking about Elias. Quickly, I take out my phone and start a recording.

"Ilir, you're quiet. What do you think?" the first voice asks.

A click, followed by the smoky scent of a cigar. I press myself against the wall as I reach the landing. They're just around the corner in one of those alcoves I spotted earlier.

"He has my father convinced. They're inviting him to the Benefaction." A low drawl—cultured, but with an accent. "But I don't think the rest of The Six trust him yet."

The Six. I saw that on the diagram.

I frown and press closer.

"Shit. We can't let him win over the Carusos. They'll be there this year."

The Carusos. Elusive financiers. Their name was on the diagram too.

"Rumor has it Gabriel Caruso is making a play to take over The Association," Ilir says. "We can't let him align with Kent. What if he turns on us?"

"Gabriel? Daddy's yes-man? Like The Scheduler would let that happen."

"You think there'll be a coup?" another unfamiliar voice asks.

"Definitely. If not now, then later. The Carusos are weakening ever since you know...what happened with their heir," Ilir responds.

Heir? Gabriel? The Scheduler? This all sounds Greek to me.

My pulse quickens, and I tiptoe closer.

The stench hits first—cloying mint layered over expensive cologne and cigarettes.

The hairs on the back of my neck stand.

A large hand clamps around my waist. A wet exhale brushes my ear. I jerk, a strangled sound catching in my throat.

"Looks like you're lost, darling."

Chapter 30: THE FINE LINE

LANA

I FREEZE, TREPIDATION BURYING me like an avalanche.

But poise and calm—all ingredients of an excellent head of PR—are second nature to me. And so I curve my lips into a generous smile and turn.

A heavyset man with dark eyes and a buzz cut leers, his gaze roving lazily down my body.

Lingering at my breasts.

Repulsed, I fight the urge to cover myself. "I'm sorry. I definitely lost my way."

I bat my eyelashes for good measure.

His attention snaps back to my face. The man frowns, and I inwardly groan.

"Well, what's this? The infamous Lana Anderson?" He drags his chubby finger up my arm. "Beautiful. I can see why the devil himself married you."

"I-I don't think I've had the pleasure." Acid rushes up my esophagus.

"Shkelzen Berisha." His grin turns obscene. "You've met my cousin, Agron. He said you looked fetching wearing only a man's dress shirt."

The bastard shackles my wrist in his grip.

Fury sparks at the base of my spine, licking up. Memories flash—being dragged by the hair into a room and finding out I'm to be married.

"Let go of me." My voice is steel now.

No more nice princess.

"Or what?" he mocks, thumb circling my pulse. "You'll scream? Run to Daddy?"

Shkelzen steps up, his whiskey breath assaulting my senses. I grit my teeth.

"Oh right," he murmurs. "You can't. You want to protect them."

I grab his meaty wrist with my free hand and dig in my nails.

He winces, his face mottling.

"You need me as much as I need you." I twist his wrist sharply toward the thumb joint. "Let go of me. Or you'll regret it."

"You bitch!" He raises his hand and—

Click.

"Drop her hand, or you won't have one."

A lethal whisper. Vetiver. Smoke. The lighter.

Elias.

Relief crashes through me. I snap my gaze to the man ascending the staircase, stepping into view.

Elias is a vision of wrath and power—dark hair, all-black suit aside from a flash of green—his handkerchief. His eyes glitter with unholy intentions and his jaw is tight.

He flicks open his lighter. A flame appears. The flash of light clashes against the severe scar carving up his face.

"*Now*," he commands.

He snaps the lighter shut.

Shkelzen drops me and staggers back. Sweat beads on his forehead.

"The frigid bitch, you can have—"

Elias arches his brow, unhurried. In a split second, he unholsters his gun and points it at the man's face.

"You sure you want to finish that sentence?" he rasps. He cocks his weapon.

There's a lethal calmness to him, the violence promised in his words sparking a fire between my legs, licking, swirling up my body.

Madness. This is madness.

Blood drains from Shkelzen's face. His eyes dart to me. What a coward.

I think about the men nearby, what I overheard. If Elias killed him, everything would go to hell.

"Last words?" Elias murmurs.

I grab his arm. "Don't. He's not worth it."

He ignores me, his deadly gaze still leveled at the man.

"Not worth it," I repeat, softer. "Assholes are a dime a dozen. I'm fine. *Please*, Elias."

After a long beat, Elias slowly lowers his weapon. He still doesn't address me but steps up to the slimeball.

A hiss cuts through the air.

He grips Shkelzen's hand—the one he used to touch me—and burns it with his lighter. The asshole emits a strangled howl.

A charred smell reaches my nostrils. My stomach roils.

"No second chances." He tosses the man back, who's clutching his injured hand as if he were permanently maimed. "Tell your cousins if they've got a problem with me, they can find me themselves. Don't gossip like high school girls."

Without another word, he grabs my hand and drags me down the stairs.

"Slow down." I stagger down the steps. "Elias, seriously. I was fine. I could've handled him. You think he was the first asshole to touch me that way?"

He stops dead in his tracks and spins around. I slam into him.

"Names," he seethes, his eyes murderous, "give me their names."

"What?"

"Who touched you that way? They won't live to see another day."

I gasp, a deep pulse throbbing in my core. My senses finally register the six-plus-feet of powerful, muscular male in front of me, anger rolling off him—a thunderstorm threatening to wreck anything in its path.

"Why do you care?" I whisper. "You loathe me. That's what you said. You shot my brother. Pointed a gun at me. I'm a means to an end."

My ribs tighten, fury singeing my insides. I jab his chest, angry at the situation just now, the marriage I'm in, the dreams lost. "Why do you care, Elias?"

His eyes flash and nostrils twitch. Without answering, he hauls me down the rest of the stairs at breakneck speed, yanks open the first door he finds, pushes me inside, and closes it behind us.

Our breaths tangle in the dark room, an office of some sort. Only a sliver of light seeps under the door.

But I feel him—all of him—crowding me in.

He shackles my wrist above my head against the door.

Unlike the revulsion I felt earlier when the asshole assaulted me, Elias's touch only sparks heat.

"I *don't* care," he seethes, venom dripping from his words. "Remember, I *hate* you."

His poisonous words sound like love sonnets to my twisted heart.

Elias tightens his hold and presses his body against me, letting me feel all of him.

Rock-hard muscles, barely tethered control, fire and brimstone.

I should shove him away. I hate his guts.

But instead, I moan. My body sings, my mind going dark. "Yes."

Elias's breath hitches. He buries his nose in my neck, just like he did in the office.

Another guttural groan. A desperate inhale.

"Roses," he mutters, "sweet motherfucking roses."

He lets out a masculine growl of satisfaction. My thighs clench, my pussy aching. I want to wrap my legs around him and dig my heels into his back.

Wetness slicks from my core and I arch my back, needing friction and his touch, needing more angry words and frenzied grunts.

I moan again.

"Fuck!" He smashes his fist against the door. It rattles. I flinch.

Elias's face is inches away from mine. I drag my gaze down the dim silhouette of his strong nose, over his raised scar, resting on his full lips.

Everything aches.

Another needy whimper slips out of me.

"Lana," he growls, and bears down, finally giving me all his delicious weight and heat, letting me feel his coiled muscles and the weapon between his legs.

"I thought you hated me," I whisper.

I need more. Pressure builds inside my core, frustration climbing inside my chest.

I lose my battle and rub my tits against him, my eyelashes fluttering from the sharp pleasure zinging my nipples. *Yes.* My body begins a soft rhythm, a feminine twist, chasing the sparks to an inevitable ending.

Too many clothes.

My nipples are so hard, they hurt. I want to claw off my top and bare them to him so I can rub my naked body over this virile, dangerous man.

Slowly, I drag one heel up his leg.

He freezes and does the thing where he remains still as a statue, not even breathing.

Emboldened, I drag my heel up, up, up, until I curl it around his buttocks.

Then I cinch it tight against him, pressing my pussy against his cock.

His thick, throbbing cock.

"It doesn't seem like you hate me that much." My words come out slurred, the pressure sharpening in my core. I'm drunk on everything that's Elias Kent.

With a growl, he hefts me up with one hand, drags up my skirt, and clamps his fingers hard into my ass.

He sinks his teeth into my throat, and I scream, the sting morphing into sharp pleasure.

"My wife is a slut, isn't she? You want pain? Pleasure?" He laps at his bite mark, his hips grinding a tortuous rhythm against me. "Want to come all over my cock like a good fucking girl?"

White light sears behind my eyelids. I twitch and tremble, my body entirely held up by his firm grip on my wrists and his weight pinning me against the door.

He moves harder, digging his pants-covered cock into my soaked thong, letting the rigid outline saw through my pussy before pressing against my clit.

My heart thunders, an electrical storm building between my legs. Lightning prickles my nipples as he grinds and grinds.

"Elias." I don't recognize my lust-filled, throaty voice.

The turbulent storm grows, lashing my core that suddenly feels too empty, pulsing, needing him inside me, filling me up, ripping me apart.

A whine tears out of my throat as we move faster and harder against each other, our bodies simulating the most erotic sex I've ever had. The pressure condenses into a tight, tight point.

"Yes, yes, yes," I moan.

Let me fall over the cliff, fall into the flames of hell with him.

"My *zemër*," he grits out, his tall frame trembling, his lips still sucking my tender neck. "Let me hear those sounds. Let me hear you coming for a man you hate."

He bites me again.

I explode, my cry echoing in the dark room. A gush of wetness streams out of me as ecstasy I've never felt before blinds my senses until all I can see, smell, and hear are him.

Elias Kent, the Shadow King, my unwanted husband.

He drags one hard grind of his cock between my legs.

Then he drops me.

I slide to the ground, boneless.

"No one disrespects me or anything I own." Fabric rustles and shoes squeak against the floor.

He opens the door, the club music bellowing in my ears.

Holding my gaze, he slowly cups his groin, gripping his hard-on through the confines of his pants. *He hasn't come.*

He tugs it, and I whimper, remembering how good it felt against me.

"And you're *mine*, wife. Whether I like you or not."

He shrugs off his jacket and tosses it to me. "Cover yourself up and tell your friends goodbye. We're going home."

He stalks off.

My heart pounds as I sit on the ground, my body deliciously thrumming yet unsated, wondering what the heck just happened.

It's twisted. So damn wrong.

And yet, why does it feel so right?

Chapter 31: WORDS BETWEEN SHELVES

ELIAS

THE TIMER TICKS DOWN. Twenty-eight minutes start now.

I rake in a deep breath, the air thick with roses that'll forever remind me of her, and stare at the monitors in front of me.

Fifteen screens—one for each room in the house. But currently, my focus fixes on the top right feed.

The library.

She just tried to break the unbreakable lock on the third floor. Then she cursed, lifted her leg to kick at the door, only to stop herself.

Then she stomps across the hallway to her favorite room here—the one filled with books, of course.

When will she learn she'll only win this game if I let her?

A wry smile tugs at my lips.

Lana frowns and stuffs a bobby pin back into her luscious hair, one wavy strand curling at the base of her throat.

The exact spot I kissed her that night at the club a week ago.

My fingers twitch as I relive the memories. The needy sounds she made. Her pussy grinding against me. How I bet if I slid my fingers underneath that tiny scrap of underwear, she would be soaked.

I could barely stop myself from coming in my pants like a reckless boy.

Like Kian.

Lana mutters something, moves to the shelf on the right, and pulls down the dark-red volume I knew she'd choose.

Greek myths. *Hades and Persephone*. I have to admire the irony that her favorite story mirrors her real life.

Married to the man she hates, someone with a soul darker than the king of the underworld.

Sometimes I tell myself I'm protecting her. The truth is, I just can't stop watching.

I used to tell myself I hated her, that I kept her at arm's length because of the role she played in my family's deaths.

The reason tastes bitter and shallow.

Now...I just keep her.

My chest pinches and I sit up, waiting for her to find the surprise tucked within those pages. It's a risk. One that might give me away. But I want to know. After all, Christmas is in a week and a half.

It's her favorite holiday.

Did Kian leave a permanent imprint on her mind the way Elise did on mine?

Will she finally solve the puzzles I've left for her over the years?

Her lips tip into a smile as she thumbs the leather volume. I've memorized every line.

When the Dark Learned Her Name.

My mind slips into another fragment of the past.

Thump. Thump. Thump.

Dad's hammering in the hallway again, the sounds giving me a migraine, but Elise doesn't seem to care.

Ding dong.

Dad freezes at the doorbell. He and Mom exchange worried glances.

"Everything okay?" Elise asks. "Are you guys expecting someone?"

I scoff. "We never get visitors. In fact, my parents forbid it...except you."

"Really?"

"Yeah. I mean, I told them you were my tutor. They figured out I was lying, but it was worth it." Grinning, I cup her cheek.

"Is that why they have those rules?" Her brows furrow, obviously as confused as I was. I've stopped trying to figure out my parents.

"Yep. 'Don't bring strangers to our door. Don't open the door for strangers. Be careful because there are bad people in the world.'" An exasperated sigh heaves out of me. "They're paranoid. Who knows, maybe we owe money to loan sharks or something. But yeah, better safe than sorry."

The hammering resumes.

Dad just tore the number plate off our front door. He's muttering something about a reno we have no budget for.

I don't buy it; it's sketchy, but I couldn't care less with Elise here.

She stretches happily on my twin-sized bed and points to the words she wants me to read.

"How do you focus with that racket?" I grumble, staring at the letters swimming in front of me. I've practiced so much, but I'm still far behind.

The damn glare on the page. Why is reading so hard?

"I'm tired." Closing my eyes, shame curls inside me and heats my face.

Why would a girl like her waste her time on someone like me? Penniless, with no future.

Soft lips brush my cheek, and my groin flares to life. My eyes snap open, finding her dove-gray gaze, framed by long lashes, dipping to my lips then back.

My chest burns.

"How about this?" she whispers, the scent of her roses filling my lungs. I can survive on her scent alone. "We try one more thing, and if you do it right, I'll let you kiss me."

My heart stutters.

"Yeah?" My voice is hoarse.

I've been dying to kiss her ever since I told her I loved her a few weeks ago.

She nods.

She points to the page again, and this time, she slides a transparent pale-blue plastic sheet over it. "Try again."

The glare softens. The words still.

"Better? I've read that could help."

I swallow, a glimmer of something gathering in my gut, then rushing up my chest. Pride.

"They've stopped swimming, the letters." I place my finger on the page.

"When the Dark Learned Her Name: A Tale of Hades and Persephone," *I slowly read. It's working. The words are staying. "Your favorite story."*

"You did it!" She grins, sets down my book, and climbs onto my lap.

My heart batters against my rib cage. My lungs forget how to breathe.

Slowly, Elise trails her fingers along my jaw, my face. Her thick brown hair falls like a curtain, hiding a shy smile. She leans in and hovers before me.

I close the last inch between us.

My fingers tangle in her hair, the lush strands wrapping around my heart, my mind, her scent of roses forever ingrained into my soul.

Maybe this is when my soul became hers.

I taste her. Her sweetness. Her beauty.

I vow never to kiss anyone else for as long as I live.

My lips tingle as the present rushes back.

Her happy sigh draws my attention back to the screen. She plops onto the navy blue chaise lounge in the corner by the main arched window. It's her favorite spot. Time and time again, I find her asleep there, waking in shock because someone covered her with a blanket. She cracks open the spine of *When the Dark Learned Her Name*. It's a first edition, hand-signed by the author.

A sad smile tilts her lips as she begins reading.

The clock ticks, grains of time sliding through the hourglass.

Lately, it's getting harder and harder to keep to twenty-eight minutes.

Outside these walls, the Berishas are stirring, the cousins still fuming over our meeting at the club. The Benefaction looms. I should be preparing.

Instead, I sit in the dark watching her, the voracious hunger clawing deeper.

The monster wants more.

LANA

My phone buzzes.

Geraldine's Chocolates

Good intel on the audio, but we need more. Keep me posted.

I bite my lip as I stare at Special Agent Tristan Clarke's text message. After the incident at the club, I sent him my recording.

A pinch of guilt niggles behind my rib cage.

This is the right thing to do. Partner with the Feds. But why does it feel so...wrong? I can't possibly be having feelings for the devil. No way.

I set down my phone and eye the black dome in the corner of the ceiling.

The red light blinks at me.

Damn bastard. Voyeur.

This is how he gets his secrets, by spying on everyone.

But anger doesn't burn hot at the thought. Instead, a perverse pleasure sifts through me—the idea that the Shadow King finds me interesting.

How he almost lost his precious control at the club.

Heat unfurls in my lower belly, curling down low. Since he made me come, I want it again. But I can't seem to get there myself.

Late at night, when the house stills and my thoughts go dark, images of him barrel into my mind—his ragged breathing, the power in his body, his hard cock grazing against me just the right way.

I'd squirm, my hand snaking under the covers to play with my slickness, swirling it around my clit. The pressure would build, but ecstasy was always out of reach.

It's like I'm addicted to him.

"Ugh," I grumble, my face hot and mouth parched.

I snap the book shut and sit up.

A postcard slips out.

I frown at the deep-red rose design and flip it over. Strong letters, a masculine scrawl:

To my devious wife,

```
Instead of picking locks, why don't you do
something worthwhile with your time?

Fifth bookshelf down. Row three. You'll
know it when you see it. An early Christmas
present.

E.
```

My eyes snap to the camera again. It blinks once—like a smile—then stills.

"What does the Shadow King want with me?" I mutter under my breath. "Why can't he ever be straightforward?"

Despite my grumbling, excitement gathers in my chest. I tell myself it's because it's Christmas-related, but I know it isn't true.

The thrill of a new riddle lights me up, and I scramble off the chaise.

I head to the back alcove, brushing my hands over the sturdy shelves, the carved rose molding tipped in gold.

"Okay, what am I looking for?" I murmur, standing in front of the shelf in question.

My gaze trails over the books. Culinary arts. Rex would love these. My chest tightens at the thought of my brother. He sent me a photo this morning, his smile strained. Olivia leans against him with the twins in her arms. He's worried about me. But I tell him I'm fine, that Elias and I are getting along.

Apparently, living with the dealer of secrets has turned me into a convincing liar.

Asian cuisine. Mediterranean. Italian pasta. My fingers skim the weathered spines. Didn't know the devil liked cooking too.

Then—a pink volume.

The History of Chocolate.

My mind snaps to the small boxes appearing on my desk each morning. All Geraldine's. All limited-edition flavors.

I slide the volume free, finding a small paper box tucked behind it.

My senses prickle. Foreboding. Excitement. I'm standing on the precipice of something, and my life will never be the same.

Blowing out an exhale, I pick up the box and open the lid.

Tears sting my eyes. My fingers tremble as I lift what's inside.

Something I never thought I'd see again.

A mahogany music box, with a rose inlaid on top, the wood polished and pristine. My heart squeezes painfully as I flip the lid, afraid to hope, afraid to look.

A sparkling red rose of rubies and diamonds meets my gaze.

It's the music box from all those years ago. The one I never got. It disappeared from the shop along with Kian.

"Twelve petals," I whisper, my mind transported far away. "One for each month. Everlasting love."

My vision blurs. I twist the dial on the side.

The beautiful, melancholic notes of "Für Elise" float to my ears.

Our song. Kian and Elise.

How does *he* know?

Sobs rack me. I slide to the floor, thinking about the boy from long ago, the only man I've ever loved.

How does Elias know? How does the bloodthirsty Shadow King know about the boy with a kind heart who wanted to become a vet?

I gasp and set the music box on the floor. Does Elias know where he is? My Kian? Does he know what happened to him?

I shoot up, the song still playing, soft and cruel, as I run for the door.

My feet fly down the two flights of stairs; my heart lodged in my throat.

Where is he? Where's the maddening man when I need him?

I throw open the office door, finding the room dark, the devil nowhere to be seen.

"What's going on, dear?" Hannah calls from the doorway.

"Where is he? Elias?" I grab her shoulders. She blinks, startled. "He's here, right?"

I could've sworn he was here, the blinking red light and all.

"Mr. Kent? He went to the basement after a call. Seemed agitated."

The basement?

I rarely venture down there. I'm not a big fan of dark spaces. I thank Hannah and bolt past her, past the utility hall and the guard station. The nondescript black door next to the laundry gives as I shove it open.

My feet pound the stone steps, past the wine cellar, to the small office in the back.

No one's here.

I clutch my hair, my gaze pinballing around the space. Bookshelf. Desk. Wet bar. This makes no sense. He couldn't have just vanished.

Then I feel it.

A thread of air grazes my ankle.

My breath grows thready as I force myself to quiet, to listen.

Thump. Thump. Thump.

It's faint, but there. Then there's the chilly breeze.

There has to be a hidden passageway. It's Saints Hollow—of course there are tunnels underground.

Determination rushes through me. I tear through the room, tossing books from shelves, looking under the desk, the chair, feeling for any hidden latches or buttons.

Just when despair seizes me, I freeze, my fingers catching on a recess behind the one book I didn't think he'd have.

The Bible.

The bookshelf swings open, revealing a stone tunnel dimly lit by caged bulbs.

My palms sweat, the hairs rising on my forearms. I feel it—the answer to a puzzle I've been trying to solve. Something I was not aware I was even searching for before.

I hasten my steps, my footfalls light as I make my way down the stairs. The air thins and grows frigid. The sounds are louder.

Groans and grunts. Someone yelling. A crash.

I shouldn't be here, my mind warns me, every instinct telling me to turn around and flee.

But I press forward, beckoned by a past I can't let go of.

The boy with soft green eyes and a beautiful smile who complained about his height.

I bet he'd be tall now.

With memories of Kian making me brave, I follow the curve of the tunnel, finally to a room with a door cracked open, light blazing from the gap. Voices sharpen.

"Please! Mr. Kent—"

"The kill ledgers. Who has access?" Elias bellows.

I flinch at the hatred in his voice.

"Th-The Berishas. They move them. The Six all have copies."

What is Elias looking for? What's his endgame?

I press my body against the wall, inching toward the room.

A loud smack. Choking sounds. Metal scraping stone.

"You won't make it out alive. Make your death useful. Where are the ledgers?"

Another blow. I flinch, nausea flooding me.

"Tell me," Elias rasps, "and I'll spare your wife and kids."

I recoil in horror, my fingers digging into the crude stones that have seen too much over the years.

Run, Lana. Run.

My feet root to the ground.

Instead, I'm driven by a need to see the truth of my husband, the Shadow King I made the mistake of thinking could have a soft side.

I push the door a fraction wider.

My heart stops at the visual before me.

Elias is stripped of his jacket and tie, his white dress shirt drenched in sweat and blood. His eyes feral, teeth baring as he hoists a man up by his throat.

The man grunts as Elias drives a knife up beneath his ribs.

Crimson sprays the devil's shirt.

"Time is ticking. Answers now. If you die before you tell me, your family perishes."

"The B-Benefaction!" the man gurgles, eyes swollen, face barely recognizable. "They'll have a copy there. Th-That's all I know. Please—"

A sick, twisted smile curves Elias's lips, his scar marred by blood spatter.

My hand slips on the doorknob. I stumble inside.

Elias's cold, flat eyes snag mine, then flare with shock.

"H-Help me!" the man screams.

"Out!" Elias roars, grabbing the gun off the table.

Horrified, I spin around just as a shot explodes through the air. The man collapses, the thud echoing in my mind.

I burst through the door, fleeing the way I came.

Strains of “Für Elise” warp with sounds of murder as tears fall down my cheeks.

I not only married a monster.

I married a hellish nightmare, and I don’t know how I’m supposed to survive this.

Chapter 32: RUIN ME

ELIAS

PANIC SEIZES MY CHEST as I drop Dalmat Hoxha. A single shot between the eyes ends his miserable existence.

My immediate impulse is to bolt after her.

Lana. She saw everything. Now she knows what kind of sick, twisted monster she married.

But I stop myself. My fingers grip the cold metal chair, knuckles white. Rage and bloodlust pulse through me like poison. Her terrified screams blow out my eardrums, detonating inside my skull.

Good. That's what should happen. Because nothing good can come out of this "relationship." That's what I want to happen. Because she should hate me like I'm supposed to hate her.

Hate. Who am I deluding? That ship sailed long ago.

My shoulders lock, muscles trembling as I force out slow, even breaths. The scent of blood and rot clings to me, the weight of the gun still heavy in my hand.

I was already in a pissed-off mood when Ren hauled the elusive recordkeeper into St. Michael's catacombs through the Lake Michigan tunnel. The motherfucker was on the run. According to Aleksei, he stole two million from the Berishas and had a ten million bounty on his head.

But what truly signed his death warrant was interrupting my twenty-eight minutes with Lana.

When she eyed me through the camera in defiance, like she knew I was watching, every cell in my body stood at attention.

Thoughts of the Berishas, The Association, revenge? Nowhere to be seen.

Then she dragged her teeth across her bottom lip, slow and deliberate, her large, doe-like eyes smoldering with heat, her skin flushed as she trailed a finger over her creamy cleavage.

My cock roared to full mast. I had half a mind to stalk out of the room and go to her.

To claim my wife in every way I've denied myself.

Then the damn bastard had to come and ruin it all.

But this is good. This is fine. Pain is focus. Pain is drive.

Desire? Only for the weak.

The words don't stick.

"Ren!" I snarl, tossing the gun on the desk. The metal clangs loudly against steel.

The assassin materializes in the doorway instantly, his black mask revealing only his eyes.

"You couldn't have stopped her?"

He twirls his gun in his hand and shrugs. *"You said, 'Don't disturb me for anything.' I can follow instructions."*

I reach him in a few strides and shove him against the wall. "You never follow instructions."

"You're mistaking me for Aleksei." Ren doles out a lazy grin, but anger sharpens his eyes.

His leg snaps out, a center blow to my chest.

Air knocks out of my lungs.

Nostrils flaring, he pushes forward. He sounds out of breath. Too out of breath. *"She deserves to know. You shouldn't keep her in the dark."*

"Why the conscience?" I hiss, pulling him off me, and stalk away. "Remember the vow?"

"For the vow. No mercy. Our ruin for their fall," he seethes, his voice rough and unused. Almost inhuman.

It's the first time I've heard him speak in three years. Shock cuts through my fury.

My eyes flare as he bares his teeth and pulls off his mask. Brown eyes pin mine. The same madness that floods my veins burns in his eyes. Pockmarks disguised by tattoos go up to his right jaw and temple.

We're the same. Both ruined, both damned. That's why I'm closest to him.

"She never took the vow. She deserves more." Ren jams the butt of his gun into my chest. I want to tell him to pull the trigger. Because I'm a sadist and a masochist all rolled into one.

I'm not even human anymore.

"The cat-and-mouse game you're playing? You're toying with her heart," Ren spits. "Remember rule number three? No innocents. But I hate to break it to you. Lana? She's *innocent!*"

I recoil, his words landing like bullets.

"So yeah," Ren switches back to signing, grabs his mask from the floor and jams it back on, *"I let her come in and see you in your full fucking glory. Who the Shadow King really is. You clean up your shit this time."*

With his face leached of color, he storms out, his boots echoing in the tunnel.

Silence falls. I sink into the chair, staring at the corpse sprawled across the floor, lying in a pool of his own blood.

I'm Elias Kent. Ruthless. Cold-blooded murderer.

I'm Elias fucking Kent, and I only exist for revenge and retribution.

My lighter slides out of my pocket. I click it open. The sound does nothing to soothe the pain carving up my chest, stabbing at the organ trying to resuscitate after twenty long years.

I don't feel. I don't love. I need to hate her.

I'm Elias—

Then I still.

My heart, that useless, traitorous beast, jolts to life.

My lungs seize. I pull in a breath.

Because I smell it.

Sweet roses that have no place in the stench of death and decay.

Soft footsteps. Careful. Graceful like fairies. Butterflies.

The air in the room shifts and vibrates into something wild. Something uncontainable.

"Elias," she whispers.

My head lifts. She stands at the doorway, eyes bloodshot, thick brown hair tumbling over her shoulders, her sweater speckled with blood and tears.

She trembles like a flower, fragile but defiant against a hurricane.

She came back.

LANA

I've completely lost my mind.

That's the only explanation for why I'm standing in front of a murderer, my husband, after bolting back to the library upstairs to claim my music box.

I meant to take the first flight back to New York; The Association be damned.

But when I picked up the wooden box and felt its weight in my hand, I couldn't leave.

Not without answers about Kian.

And as proof of my descent into lunacy, I couldn't leave *him* either.

I tell myself the man Elias killed was a bad guy. Part of The Association. But the brutal way Elias did it? The sadistic glint in his eyes when I caught him?

It terrified me.

A sane person would've run and kept running. So why am I still here?

Because underneath the savagery I just witnessed, past the blood and the violence, I saw something else.

Grief. Heartbreak. A man who lost too much and couldn't find his way back.

So, against all common sense, with my pulse rioting, I descended the stairs again, music box clutched to my chest.

And when I saw him, broken and ravaged, my heart stopped trying to flee.

He was slumped in the chair, blood soaking his shirt, sweat slicking his hair.

Completely devastated.

"Elias." My voice is barely a whisper, but his head snaps up.

He hitches a breath. Sharp, as if it hurts.

I move toward him, my steps careful. My body thrums with static, the zinging energy in the air moments before a tornado hits.

And yet, none of it is fear.

I should be terrified. He's a monster. He's dangerous and vicious.

But I'm not.

Slowly, Elias rises, uncoiling his powerful frame until he towers over me. He fills the room with his presence.

My skin prickles, my vision narrows as I arch my head back to look at him.

My husband.

"Why did you come back?" he rasps, hands fisted at his sides.

Anguish. I hear it in his voice, loud and clear. My heart shreds into pieces.

I slowly lift my hand and wipe the blood from his face. A tortured hiss escapes his lips. "What are you hiding, Elias? What are you planning?"

There has to be a reason for this bloodshed. Deep down, perhaps I've never really believed the man who's been loyal to my family for the past decade could be that unhinged and brutal for no reason.

Maybe this entire time, I still hope for one impossible thing.

That somewhere inside the Shadow King has a soul worth saving.

"Tell me, Elias." My gaze sweeps over the hard planes of his face, fingers trailing the raised scar that still looks painful.

The sight of the corpse's legs behind the table makes me gasp.

He immediately moves closer, blocking my view.

"It's none of your business, *zemër*." His fingers tremble as he covers my hand with his blood-smeared one, pinning it to his cheek. "Don't pretend you care."

"Maybe you need someone to care about you," I whisper, my heart resuming its chaotic rhythm.

Time splinters into fragments. Elias freezes, and I hold my breath.

I hear a faucet leak from somewhere in the distance. *Drip. Drip. Drip.*

His lashes lift, revealing deep emerald irises rimmed with molten gold flecks, sunlight trapped in an evergreen forest.

Eyes I've only seen long ago in another life.

A lever slides into position—the final click unlocking the invisible puzzle buried for all these years in the deepest recesses of my heart.

I lift the music box between us, my hand trembling. Elias's eyes widen, his grip on my fingers tightening.

"How did you get this, Elias?" I whisper. "How did you know? Where's Kian?"

Agony flashes in his eyes, and his throat ripples.

He doesn't answer me.

"How, Elias? How?" My hand slides from his face to his shoulder. I shake him, desperation stabbing wounds into my chest. "Tell me."

Another dead silence, thick and unrelenting.

A deep, tortured sound rumbles from his chest. A dark chuckle. A flash of teeth. His entire body shakes as if I'm the punchline to a joke I'm not privy to.

Then he stops. His nostrils flare.

He dips down, his lips inches from my ear.

"I think you know the answer, my *zemër*." His breath brushes my face, and I shiver. "I guess puberty did find me after all...*Elise*."

I flinch. Electrocuted. Death by surprise or terror.

Staggering back, I shake my head. Elias straightens slowly, his face lifting to the light, illuminating the strong, masculine jaw, the five o'clock shadow, and the rigid scar bisecting his cheek.

His eyes.

Those breathtaking green eyes. The ones that always seem like they can see through me.

No. It can't be. How have I not noticed them until now?

Images of a beautiful boy flash behind my eyelids—his soft skin, even softer eyes, his dazzling smile, his gentle touch.

They morph into the man before me—all hard angles, tethered power, leashed control. He looks completely different, and yet, the echo's there.

How could I've missed it? How did I not know the boy I never forgot was beside me all along?

"K-Kian?" I stumble toward him, driven by pure instinct. Moisture mists my eyes. "Kian? Wh-What happened to you? What's going on?"

Click.

Gaze pinned on me, he flicks his lighter. But his usual grace isn't there. His cheek twitches, chest rising and falling in a chaotic rhythm. The lighter clicks quicken.

Then he hurls it to the ground. The loud clang jolts me in place.

"Surprise," he rasps. "Scared yet, Elise?"

Chapter 33: THE LINE BETWEEN LOVE AND HATE

LANA

MY HEAD SPINS. I lose my voice.

I can't reconcile the sweet Kian with the brutal Elias. What happened to him? How did the boy who wanted to save lives become the man who takes them?

A mocking smile curves his lips as he advances toward me.

Unwittingly, I back up, my breaths thready. Every sense sharpens, zeroed in on the predator showing me his true colors.

This can't be.

We stand under the elm tree in Hollow Gardens, looking at our carving.

"I don't want you to leave," Kian murmurs, linking his fingers with mine.

My insides twist, and I fight the urge to cry.

"I don't want to go either." My lips tremble and I face him. "But don't worry. I'll come back for college. You can be a vet, and I'll be happy as long as we're together."

His eyes glitter, green eyes rimmed with gold. I brush his hair over his ear. It's so long now, the brown roots creep into the blond, telling us our time is up.

"You promise?" he rasps, voice thick. "What if I can't save up the money—"

I press my finger to his lips. "We'll find a way. But for now," we face the tree again, and I trace the etched words, "we still have my birthday next week. One last celebration."

His heat presses upon me, jolting me back to the present. The eyes. The divot on his chin. The similarities, while not plentiful, are there. It is the same person, but my mind refuses to accept it.

A dark laugh slips from Elias's lips, cruel and cold. "Kian's *dead.* He died with them."

His words spear into my chest, the pain robbing me of my breath.

He leans down until we're a hairbreadth apart. His cologne of vetiver and smoke, now polluted with the metallic sting of blood, fills my nose.

"I don't believe you." Not looking at him, I shake my head.

Denial is the only course of hope.

Elias shakes my shoulders. "He's *dead.* You killed him! He died the day Saints Hollow burned down. Elise and Kian? Fairytales for kids who didn't know better. This?" He gestures at the corpse on the floor. "This is real life."

His words are nonsensical. Mad ravings from a lunatic.

"Don't you dare pin this on me!" I slam my fists against his chest, fury finally surging up my spine like a tidal wave. "I didn't *leave* you. I left, but didn't—"

But then I make the mistake of looking up.

Pain floods those emerald eyes. Hands caging me in, arms shaking from restraint, he stares at me as if I stole his world from him.

He stares at me as if he were on the brink of death and I was his last breath of oxygen.

My tragic heart, lovesick and broken, makes the mistake of latching onto the one man who was once my everything, who, even now, under a different identity, makes me feel too much.

My body awakens. "Für Elise" hums in my mind.

Some songs you only need to hear once to remember for the rest of your life.

My hands move on their own. I fist his shirt and pull him flush against me.

"I will *never* give up on you, Kian," I whisper.

A sharp exhale. A beat suspended in midair.

He crashes down, one hand cupping my face, the other fisting my hair, and claims my lips in a savage, desperate kiss.

Heat floods my body, my nerves singeing with light. Our mouths tangle, teeth biting, hands clawing at each other, the madness invading every cell, obliterating every morsel of logic. He grunts as I dig my nails into his back, unable to find purchase.

Clearly frustrated, he rips open his shirt, sending buttons pinging onto the ground.

A whimper escapes me as I finally touch his heated flesh. I climb onto him, wrapping my legs tight around his waist. His tongue dominates my mouth, tasting, dueling, savoring every sound I make.

"What's my name?" he rasps as we break apart for air.

Mind drunk with lust, I pull his hair, needing his kiss again.

"My name," he bellows, his hands gripping the front of my sweater.

My vision blurs as I stare at him, nails raking over his scalp. "Kian. Kian Leste."

A growl tears out of him. "Wrong answer."

He consumes my lips once more, biting down hard until pain sears through me.

"E-Elias!" I cry, and he rewards me with a swipe of tongue, the ache bleeding into pleasure.

"Tell me you want this." The fabric gives. A small tear at my neckline.

I claw at him, any part I can reach, desperation teeming in my blood.

"Say it!" Another rip.

"Please..." I clutch his nape, needing his kiss more than I need air. "Yes...yes..."

"Who?" He nips my ear, and wetness seeps out of my thong. "Who's going to fuck you? Who are you asking to invade your pussy with his throbbing cock?"

Another gasp. A pressure begins deep in my belly. I grind myself against his torso, rubbing my core up and down his muscles.

It's not enough. I need more.

"Elias. Please shut up and fuck me."

A roar of satisfaction grinds out of his throat. He rips my sweater in half. Cold air pebbles my nipples followed by hot, wet suction.

I cry, clutching his dark locks as he latches onto my breast like he needs it to survive.

He pinches my other nipple, flicks it lightly, then roughly. Another pinch. I soak through my thong.

My wetness runs down my thighs. If I were sane, I'd be embarrassed.

But it doesn't matter, because the man feasts on me like he's famished.

He curls his fingers around the strings of my underwear and leggings, then with a rough yank, tears them off me.

My skin burns from the friction. My legs tremble around his back. One shoe falls on the floor, the other follows.

Elias drags his lips up my chest, licking the divot of my collarbone, before raking his teeth over the slender column of my neck. He lifts me from the wall completely effortlessly.

The cold steel of the table meets my back. With a rough yank, he pulls me to the edge and spreads my legs wide.

"Look at this beautiful pussy. It's pulsing, needy, weeping for me."

He drags a finger from my clit to the rosebud of my ass. My eyes fly open.

A depraved glint fills his eyes, his pupils nearly swallowing his irises. With his once-slicked hair now in disarray, his dress shirt half open, revealing a sheen of sweat on his writhing pecs, he looks like the actual king of the underworld.

And he's claiming me as his queen.

My core pulses. I squeeze my legs, needing the pressure. Needing something to finish me off.

Smack!

"Elias!" I gasp, sparks appearing in my eyes.

"You don't get to come until I say you do." He rubs the sting away from my pussy lips. "And you definitely don't get to come until I have a taste."

He buries his face between my legs before I can say another word.

A scream tears out of me as pleasure explodes from my core, shattering every cell of my body. Wetness slicks out, my eyes rolling backward, and I thrash on the table.

My mind faintly registers I'm fully naked while he's still clothed, but the depravity only fans the madness.

"My sweet Lana. You taste as sweet as you smell." He groans into my pussy, his tongue lapping at my wetness, each lick sparking aftershocks as I quake before him.

Before I can fully take a breath, the sound of a zipper tears through the air.

Then he's on top of me, arms braced at my sides, head hovering just above me. His cock, hard and thick, wet at the tip, perches at my entrance.

But he holds himself still.

His breaths throttle out of him, his gaze darting over my face, my neck, my body, and back up, like he can't possibly look his fill.

My tongue dips out, mouth watering.

"I need you." I curl my legs around his ass and squeeze. "All of you."

A twitch of his jaw. He still doesn't move. "You protected?"

I forgot about protection.

"Please. Yes. Birth control. You clear?" My nails dig into his back.

A curt nod. His eyes flare, darkening impossibly more. "What's my name?"

An ache pulses in my heart. I know what he wants to hear from me.

What he *needs* to hear from me.

"Elias," I whisper. My heart breaks, knowing he refuses to be Kian.

He hisses then bears down, thrusting into me in one rough stroke.

I scream, pain carving through me as everything catches fire.

He jolts, then freezes. His gaze snaps to mine again.

"How?"

Eyes tearing up, lips trembling, I cradle his cheek. "I just couldn't...never found the right person..."

Yes, I pretend I'm experienced. I've made out with guys, used toys and dildos, but have never gone all the way.

I used to think I was defective. In my thirties and still a virgin. I couldn't bring myself to have sex with anyone. Then I thought to myself, why force the issue? Why didn't I just wait until it felt right?

But now, I think...perhaps I've just been waiting for him.

Clearly overwrought with emotion, he cradles my face like I'm the light he never expected to see. He kisses me tenderly, sweetly, giving me his all.

Hope tremors inside me.

My Kian...he's still in there.

Groaning, he thrusts back in, his motions gentle. "Fuck. You're so tight." A masculine grunt of satisfaction ripples from him. "I-I've imagined—"

He stops and presses another kiss on my lips.

"I should've been more careful," he says softly, reminding me of the boy he said was long gone.

A gentleness so heart-wrenching guides his motions. In this fragment of time, I don't remember why I shouldn't be with him. He slides his hand between us, down my body, and starts a rhythm on my swollen clit.

Firm circles, light flicks, all in tune with his body moving over mine.

Frissons of pleasure begin anew. My muscles tense as I clutch his back, helpless to the climbing sparks.

"E-Elias," I whimper, my hips moving, chasing his thrusts, giving as good as I get.

"Fuck yes," he grunts, his cock hardening, swelling, filling me up. "You're going to come again, princess. I'm going to christen this room with your cum."

My core flutters at his dirty words.

Eyes flashing, he peels his upper body from me, his fingers still working hard at my clit. He snakes his free hand up my body, kneads my breast before sliding back down and resting his palm below my belly.

Then he presses down, letting me feel him. Every single hard and thick inch.

I moan.

His dick powers into me, each piston shredding my nerves, sending me into the stratosphere.

My vision whitens. His fingers quicken around my clit. My legs shake, muscles coil, back arching.

More moans and whimpers fill the air.

"Who am I?" Hips snapping hard against me, his rhythm spins out of control. He curves his body over mine once more.

"Elias." My eyes roll back and teeth chatter.

I'm so close. Oh my fucking God, I'm so close.

The table rattles, its legs squeaking against the floor, adding to the erotic soundtrack of our movements.

"I'm your *husband*."

His cock lengthens. His hand presses deeper into my stomach.

"Feel. Every. Fucking. Inch."

The table groans, and a whine slithers out of my throat.

"Remember," he rasps, face flushed, eyes intense, "I own you."

White static rings in my ears, the submissive streak inside me roaring to life.

"And..."

Thrust.

"You're..."

Thrust.

"My wife!"

He punches his cock extra deep.

A scream perches at the back of my throat. I claw his hand, and he hisses, punishing me only by hammering into me relentlessly, stealing my breath, my soul, my everything.

Thud.

The table hits something.

My eyes snap open, the room coming back into focus. Elias stares at me, sweat dripping down his forehead.

He doesn't pause. He doesn't yield. He doesn't care that the table is banging against a dead body.

Oh my God. I'm naked, having sex with my deranged husband with a corpse next to me. Instead of horror, arousal shoots through my veins like a drug.

My nipples tighten, more wetness slicking out of me, the sounds of skin slapping skin echoing against the walls. I shake, unable to stop the tremors, the ecstasy so close, almost at my fingertips.

"Come, Lana," he growls into my ear. "Come around my cock like a good wife."

I scream and break into a million pieces—a cataclysmic event—my mind suspended somewhere between heaven and hell.

Exhilaration floods my veins as I quake and quake and quake.

He crushes his lips to mine, his hand shackling my wrists above my head.

"I hate you," he growls under his breath. "Fuuuck."

"Liar," I whisper. "You don't fuck someone you hate like this."

But my heart spasms, the pain from his words quickly fading as he presses his full body weight on top of me, like he needs all parts of me touching all parts of him.

His cock twitches and hot cum floods my womb. I clutch him tightly.

I can't let him go. I will never let him go.

As we come down from our high, his semi-hard cock still lodged firmly inside me, common sense finally comes back in fragile wisps.

Kian. Elias. The murders. The violence.

"Tell me you hate me," he presses the words onto my neck with his lips. Gentle and reverent.

A heartbeat. Then two.

"I hate you," I whisper.

I'm the liar.

And I know I'm in too deep.

Chapter 34: ASHES BETWEEN US

LANA

HEAT WRAPS AROUND ME in the sweetest embrace. A delicious ache pulses between my legs. I stretch, the sheets sliding over my bare skin, and open my eyes to daylight spilling through half-drawn curtains.

Black walls. Midnight bedspread. This is Elias's room.

Memories of last night rush back—limbs intertwined, mouths searching, pleasure blurring with pain. His dark voice was a prayer at my throat. The soreness between my thighs sharpens, proof it wasn't a dream. I had sex with Elias Kent, my husband.

More than once.

After the carnage in the dungeon, he wrapped me in his bloody shirt, tucked me against his chest, and carried me upstairs to his bathroom. He gently washed my body, his eyes remorseful when he saw the scratches, the bite marks, the bruises forming from our rough lovemaking.

I couldn't reconcile this man—this brutal killer—with the boy I never forgot.

But when the mist cloaked us from the world, I saw it.

The truth.

Elias might be taller, his jaw sharper, his voice deeper—but those eyes never changed. My sweet, beautiful Kian was there all along.

"How did I not recognize you?" I ask.

He rinses the shampoo out of my hair. "Surgery and puberty. I grew half a foot; my voice dropped. I had my jaw shaved, nose altered—just slightly—because I didn't want to be recognized."

He pauses, his thumb grazing my lips. "And I stayed away from you."

Elias refuses to answer any more questions—about what he said in the dungeon, or the accusation that I killed Kian. He only kisses me, clutching me like he can't believe I exist.

Then he worships me again.

He shuts off the water, wraps me in a towel, and carries me back to his bed. He then spreads my legs and stares at me in that intense way of his.

"Look at you," he rasps. "These tits, your sweet pussy. I've imagined and..."

His words trail off as his hands slide up my body, every graze sending liquid heat through me in shivering waves. He kisses my lips, my jaw, that tender spot at my throat where my pulse beats madly for him.

My mind blanks, soon forgetting the questions, the worries, the puzzle I thought I'd solved just a decoy, the actual bomb still hidden underneath.

Whereas our fucking was raw and brutal in the dungeon, this is gentle and quiet. He kisses every inch of my body, his fingers teasing my slit, then rubbing my swollen nub.

"Shhh," he hushes, reminding me of the insane moment at the vault when he had a gun pointed at my head.

It's bizarre, and now, it feels...right.

Slowly, he inserts his finger inside me. I hiss, tender from before, and he softens his ministrations until my body accepts the intrusion. He then curls his finger just right until sharp light bursts behind my eyelids.

"Elias—" I cry, legs trembling.

He groans his approval. When my eyes flicker open, he has his cock tightly fisted, the tip dark red and leaking as he pumps it in a savage motion. A loud growl tears from his throat, and cum shoots out of his tip.

"Fuck me. Shit." He grunts, his eyes feral. He tugs and tugs, releasing ropes of white on my tits, my stomach, marking me between my legs.

"Mine," he rasps, and my core pulses, needing him again.

It's depraved. It's possession and obsession.

After cleaning me up, he crawls into bed beside me and wraps me in his arms.

"Sleep, Lana," he commands, his voice rough.

The old me would've fought him and told him to mind his tone—the new me?

I melt.

And now, as I look around the empty, unfamiliar room, I shiver.

I'm alone again.

I pat the spot next to me—it's cold. Elias must've left during the night. Slowly, I get out of bed and slip on one of his shirts, relishing his scent, which gives me butterflies.

My God, what's wrong with me?

This changes nothing. He still killed all those people. He nearly killed Maxwell. Am I supposed to be okay with this just because I got a few orgasms?

I should be repulsed and terrified. Elias's world is nothing like the one I was raised in.

But strangely, or perhaps righteously, I'm not afraid of him. It's a gut feeling. Or my heart. Because deep down, I know my Kian would never hurt me.

Someone knocks and opens the door.

"Lana, dear, ready for your lunch?" Hannah pops her head in.

"Lunch? What time is it?"

"It's eleven-thirty."

"Holy crap. I've never slept that long."

I blush when I remember my state of undress. "Where is he?"

"Mr. Kent left last night. Had to go on a trip."

"For how long?" I tug at the hem of his shirt.

"Did he have a message for me?" I hate the wobble in my voice.

"He didn't say," she says softly, her sympathy crawling up my spine like ice.

So this is it? Use me and dump me? Does he really think he owns me like a piece of meat?

I don't think so.

"Thank you, Hannah. I'll be right down." I strain a smile.

That's when I see it—a small box sitting on the dresser.

I read the note taped on top.

`To my devious wife,`

```
Next week, you will attend the Benefaction
with me. Sofia will brief you. Don't forget
why you and your family are still alive.

Don't disappoint me.

E.

P.S. John's been reprimanded for your little
adventure. Don't try it again. Or his death
will be on your hands.
```

Asshole. Grinding my teeth, I pick up the box. It's heavy, slightly bigger than the size of my palm.

The polished wood exterior is inlaid with intricate geometric *yosegi* patterns.

It's a Japanese *Hitmitsu-Bako*—a Japanese secret box!

It's something my secret admirer would—

A gasp sticks in my esophagus.

Of course. The puzzle box.

It was always him. He'd been taunting me with his presence the entire time we were in New York.

He must've thought I was stupid for not figuring out his identity sooner.

But what he told me in the shower...the way he kissed me.

No, Lana. You don't treat someone you care about like this—slipping out of the house like a thief in the night.

Fury mixes with heartbreak until I can't separate the two. Things were simpler when he was only the villain. But now I'm addicted...infected with whatever this ailment is.

I deserve more.

Upset with myself, I hurl the box, the thud echoing my scream.

I stalk toward the door, needing to clear my head before meeting the girls at the café.

But before I cross the threshold, I hesitate and turn back.

I retrieve the box and clutch it to my chest.

Despite everything, my fingers still itch to solve it.

Half an hour later, I'm sitting in Arcana & Bloom, stirring my tea and staring morosely into the cup.

"Something's off with her," Aria whispers. "Ginseng. Give her some. Grandma says it heals everything."

"I'll slip some in next time," Scarlett replies. "Ugh. Look at that hair. Total chaos. And that mismatched sweater..."

"Oh geez," I mutter, looking up.

Two guilty smiles.

"Men problems?" Scarlett teases.

"No, no—*man* problems," Aria corrects, eyes gleaming. "Hot, literal serial-killer man problems. I mean, I haven't seen your husband, but I bet that's what he is."

I snort despite myself. "You're both nuts."

A heavy exhale slips out of me. I need to confide in someone or I'll go mad.

"What would you do if you found out your husband wasn't who you thought he was?"

"Depends on what the secret is," Arias muses. "Is it bad news? Other than, you know, killing people and stuff. As a medical professional, I don't condone that stuff. And don't tell me. I have a bad poker face, and the cops will see through it."

"Aria," Scarlett warns. "Stop being so nosy."

"Not nosy—just living vicariously. I like the scary books!"

My lips twitch.

"He was," I sigh, "somebody I thought was long gone."

"Someone you loved?" Scarlett asks.

"I did." A lump forms in my throat. "And I think part of me still does."

The girls gasp. Aria has stars in her eyes, hugging a book to her chest like she's listening to a fairy tale.

Scarlett squeezes my arm. "And that's a problem because?"

I don't answer them.

How do I explain the side of me that's getting used to the violence and unhingeness, or how my heart still skips a beat whenever he walks into a room? Or how I had mind-blowing sex with him while his hands were stained with someone else's blood?

Instead, I sip my tea. Warmth spreads down my throat, loosening my chest.

"This stuff works," I mumble. "No ginseng needed."

"What did I tell you?" Scarlett winks.

I smile weakly. "Yes, yes. You're an herbalist magician. A sorceress."

The door opens; the bell rings. Heels click slowly across the floor. A floral, exotic perfume suffuses the air.

I glance up and freeze.

Sofia Kent.

She slides off her sunglasses. Red nails gleam under the light. Green eyes, lined in black and framed with thick lashes, snare mine. She's almost unrecognizable in a red sweater dress and thigh-high boots.

God, I'm so stupid. Sofia didn't even change her first name. And puberty and surgery can only transform appearances so much.

"You can close your mouth now, Lana," she says.

The girls shuffle aside, and I introduce them.

Sofia turns to me, her gaze cool. "You look like shit. Do you have a few?"

Scarlett and Aria take the hint and leave.

"Hot damn, what happened to the graceful Sofia from The Orchid?"

"She never existed. It's been a drag pretending otherwise."

Aria sets a cup in front of Sofia.

Sofia pulls a flask from her purse and adds a splash to her tea. I can't help staring. Our paths don't cross often, but she's helped Elias oversee some clubs at The Orchid before. But the Sofia I remember was quiet and sophisticated—someone who blended in. And then there was Kian's younger sister who used to follow me around?

Definitely not this femme fatale in front of me.

"You have questions."

"That's an understatement," I say.

"Well, too bad—we don't have time. You need to prepare for the Benefaction. How much do you know?"

"Not much. Only it's a big event, and the Carusos will be there. Something about The Six, which I presume is important to The Association."

"That's right." She leans in. "The Association is like the Freemasons and Illuminati combined. They have their hands in government, politics, corporations, finance. Their dirty work is done by organized crime, the Bratva, mob—"

"They control everything, I get it."

She arches her brow. "I underestimated you, Lana. Honestly, I never thought you'd survive this long."

"Gee, thanks."

She laughs softly, her eyes warming a smidge. "The Six make up The Council—they oversee the empire. Once a year, they have a ball."

"The Benefaction."

"Exactly. It's when information changes hands and deals are made. Legend says The Association was founded by five families. The sixth was added later for reasons no one knows. This year's ball is special—the Carusos never attend, but they're making an exception. That means something big is coming."

She folds her hands on the table. "Elias is trying to understand how the network works. Your job as his wife is to make sure he looks good in front of The Six."

"And if I don't?" I think about his overbearing note from this morning.

"Word of advice." Sofia leans in, voice turning to steel. "Don't test his patience. Elias has given you more grace than I've ever seen him give anyone, but he has limits. Then things would get ugly."

I breathe out slowly, images of his blood-soaked face slip into my mind.

She sets down an envelope. "Read it. It has background info. Photos of key players. Play the role. Survive. After all, that's why you married my brother, right?"

Her words hit like ice water dumped on my head.

Yes. This whole marriage is a transaction. Sex and orgasms don't factor into it.

I steel my heart and stare at the packet, dread threading a web up around my lungs.

This is just a transaction.

Don't lose track of the terms.

Chapter 35: SHARKS AT THE BALL

ELIAS

I PACE THE FOYER, the lighter in my hand. I stop, click it on, watching the flame appear. The routine should calm me.

It doesn't.

I straighten my tux, fix my bow tie, and pace again.

In less than an hour, I'll meet The Six. My hands ball into fists. Fury, my old friend, thrums under my skin. I imagine putting a bullet in each of them, watching with satisfaction as they drown in their own blood. Then I'll destroy everything they own—tear their houses down, brick by brick, reducing their empire to a pile of ashes.

And that's still not enough.

I blow out a breath. I'm getting ahead of myself. Focus.

Tonight, I have one goal: to find the kill ledger. Dalmat said a copy will be present. From what Aleksei found, this is an insurance policy. By exchanging copies of the ledgers, everyone has dirt on each other.

My phone buzzes. The Syndicate gives me an update for tonight.

Knight Ren

On standby with an AR-15. Winds are calm. Signal if things go south.

Bishop Seb

Sources said it's small, palm-sized.

Pawn Alek

No shit, Sherlock. You think the kill ledger is in a cute notebook?

Bishop Seb

Shut up before I add you to mine.

Knight Ren

"Sources," Sebastian? You mean your family.

Bishop Seb

Sources. Mere DNA doesn't make a family.

Bishop Seb

Cleaners are clearing the floors. Will rendezvous with Rook there.

Pawn Alek

Cleaners you got in because of me. ID swaps and all. Go big or go boom.

King Rafe

I'll pray for you.

Queen Sofi

He doesn't need prayers. He's got me.

My lips twitch. I picture Rafe in his chamber, rosary in hand, praying for our clearly unredeemable souls.

This is the closest I've gotten to finding the name of the person who ordered my family to be slaughtered. Vasil Çela from the Albanian café was a lackey. His partner was the same.

Decades gone. Life wasted. I've given up my soul for revenge, and now I can almost taste it.

Will silence ever replace the screaming?

My knees ache, an old reminder of survival.

The air changes before my thoughts settle. It thrums with sudden awareness.

I stop pacing.

Roses wrap around my senses, dragging me back from the brink.

"I'm ready, Elias."

Her voice is seduction and salvation, innocence laced with steel.

Air rushes out of me as I grit my teeth and turn around.

Lana is a vision in crimson. She can move mountains, drain oceans. She could ask me to jump off a cliff, and I'd do it without hesitation.

And you still want to say you hate her? Please.

The fact that I'm thinking this way is precisely why I made myself scarce after last week.

I exceeded my twenty-eight minutes that day.

I told myself that was for every minute I'd saved up over the years. It was lust, not anything else. After all, lines blur too easily.

Her hips sway, each step revealing her long legs through a thigh-high slit.

Legs, I remember, wrapped around me like a vice, never releasing as I pounded into her.

Heat surges in my groin. Images flashing before me: her sounds, her hot, wet pussy clamping my cock like nirvana. She took me so beautifully amid chaos and blood, a fairy tale turned wicked.

"What did I tell you before?" I ask.

Lana stops inches before me.

"I repeat. What did I tell you before?"

Her brows knit, clearly not understanding. I collar her throat, enjoying her pulse jumping against my palm.

She whimpers, her body compliant. Submissive.

"Remember the club," I rasp into her ear, and crush her frame to mine.

I groan and trail my finger down her neck—down, down, down—until I reach the swell of her cleavage. Then, I cup her breast, find her nipple, and twist.

She cries out, "Elias—"

My dick throbs in my pants, angling toward my stomach.

Yes, Elias is right.

Kian—the boy who dreamed of saving cats and dogs—would never treat a woman this way. He'd never experience the sadistic pleasure of seeing Lana's eyes glazing over, her red lips parted, her hips automatically canting forward like she was seeking my cock.

"You feel this?" I ask, still kneading her breast. "This is what every man will think about when he sees you in that dress. It'll tempt him to do very bad things."

"And if they do...what are you going to do about it?" she whispers.

I want to hoist her over my shoulders, toss her onto the nearest surface, and have my way with her.

Screw the Benefaction, The Six, The Association.

But my thirst for revenge won't quit.

I release her, backing away, every muscle protesting.

Before I turn toward the door, I pause long enough to answer.

"If anyone touches you, he won't live to see another dawn."

LANA

It reminds me of home.

And that horrifies me.

The ballroom of the Berisha's estate is a study in luxury. Black-and-white checkered floors, marble imported from Italy like the ones in the Anderson Estate. Soaring ceilings, gold leaf frescoes of angels dueling with demons. Sparkling ornaments adorn the massive Christmas tree. Lake Michigan acts as a backdrop outside the windows, its calm waters deceptive.

Crowds are dressed in their finest.

This could easily be a function at The Orchid.

These people—I swallow my dismay as I recognize familiar faces and longtime Anderson clients—are *our* people.

And they're monsters.

Soft laughter fills the air. An orchestra plays in the corner.

But I feel their gazes on me.

The dark elite have clear cliques—small groups gathered in corners, talking in hushed tones. I spot the Berishas. Shkelzen raises a glass in my direction, like he didn't assault me at the club.

Sweat beads on my palms. I paste on my PR smile. Years of etiquette classes and putting out fires have taught me at least this.

Never show weakness, especially if you're a woman.

The world would eat you alive otherwise.

"The lovely Lana Anderson. A pity we haven't met before now," a deep voice murmurs to my right.

I turn to the imposing man who has crept up next to me. Tall and broad-shouldered, thick brown hair, his muscular frame poured into an expertly fitted tux. A signet ring with the letter C rests on his finger.

Startling light blue eyes, the color of an iceberg, meet mine.

He'd be handsome except for the hardness in his gaze.

And the fact his last name is Caruso.

"Gabriel Caruso," I extend my hand, smile intact, "I've heard about you. And it's Lana Kent now."

My heart skips a beat. It's the first time I've used Elias's last name.

The enemy of my enemy is my friend. And Sofia is right. Like it or not, Elias is my only ally here.

Gabriel's lips curve, just barely. He grabs a flute of champagne from a passing waiter and hands it to me. "Where's husband dearest?"

"Mingling. Doing manly things." Frustration coils inside me, but I keep my tone light. The damn bastard deposited me in the corner the moment we arrived, only to tell me to stay put until dinner.

"How chivalrous. If I had a wife as beautiful as you, I'd never leave her alone in a den of wolves."

"Don't worry. I know how to kill a man in ten seconds."

That might be a stretch, but it feels good to say.

"The queen of the underworld, how savage," he muses, eyes glinting. "Fitting."

Leaning in, he draws a stiff inhale. Goosebumps ripple down my arms. "You smell good."

I shift to the side. "Apparently, money doesn't buy you manners."

"Or maybe, it makes me more discerning...good at spotting cracks in the foundation." Gabriel presses his body to my side. "Do me a favor. Don't try so hard to stand out. It only makes us want a piece of you."

Unease twists my gut, and he chuckles. "Tread carefully. These waters are rough. Who you align yourself with can have...consequences." Gabriel points his finger at a group of Asians. "Over there...the Kongs. Brutal bastards. If you think the Berishas are cruel, you haven't met them yet."

A rowdy cheer erupts in the room, followed by the clinking of glasses. "The Ivanovs. Control Eastern Europe. Your Berishas hate them. The Russians are buddies with the O'Callaghans. I think it's the alcohol."

"They're not *my* Berishas."

"They aren't? Interesting. Probably a good thing. The Berishas aren't doing well, and they know it." He hums under his breath. "Finally, on your far right are the Alvarezes. Don't be charmed by their good looks. You'll lose a limb before you notice." He raises his glass toward a group of stunning brown-haired men and women.

"And let me guess," I point to the group of dark-haired men and women, who have hair so blond it's almost white, "the Carusos. Your family. The pure angels?"

He clasps his chest, looking wounded. "Why, of course. I'm here welcoming you, aren't I?"

I roll my eyes. "Why are you telling me all this?"

"I have a vested interest in your husband. I'd like him to stay alive...*longer*."

A wiry man walks to the center of the room and checks his watch. He looks familiar. "It's six-thirty. Dinner begins in half an hour."

Gabriel snorts. "The Scheduler. He's a stickler for dates and times, in case you can't tell."

The name tugs the memory from my mind. He was the man at the vault, and during the other night at the club, the Berishas mentioned him being against Gabriel. Something about an impending coup.

"Does he have a name?"

"He does." His lips flatten. "But it's not important. Some people are destined to be inconsequential and to do menial tasks. My family doesn't like the spotlight."

A pillar of heat materializes to my right.

"Caruso," Elias's voice cuts in, tight and deadly, "what are you doing with my wife?"

The wiseass shrugs and steps back. "Keeping her company. A doe like her will be devoured in minutes. A gentleman wouldn't leave the vulnerable unattended."

His smile ices over when he looks at me. "If you ever need an ally, I'm one call away."

He stuffs a card into my hand and walks away.

I gape, flabbergasted.

"What is it with you attracting motherfuckers who give you their numbers?" Elias snaps.

Indignation straightens my spine. "Maybe everyone senses this whole thing is a farce and they want to rescue me, *husband*," I seethe.

I down my drink in one gulp and set it on the table. "I'm going to the restroom. Excuse me."

I feel his gaze burning into my back as I walk away.

Den of wolves, my ass.

It's a sea of sharks—each one smelling blood.

Chapter 36: THE HUNT

ELIAS

"THAT WASN'T VERY SMART." Sebastian sidles up to me at the refreshments table, where I'm currently drowning my anger in whiskey.

Gabriel, the Caruso heir, converses with his siblings, a bunch of good-looking motherfuckers. He arches a brow at me, flashing a taunting smile. I want to kill the bastard for flirting with my wife.

"You standing next to me isn't very smart." I scan the room. "Shouldn't we pretend not to know each other?"

"That's illogical. Everyone knows Elias Kent. It'll be a red flag to pretend otherwise." He chuckles under his breath. "And I'm anything but—"

"Illogical. Yes, I get it."

"I told them I was scoping you out. Networking. They want a piece of you." He clinks his glass against mine and lets out a fake laugh. "Those dirty secrets you hold make you the biggest target in the room."

I glance at him. His slicked-back hair gleams under the candlelight. The fucking smile actually reaches his eyes, the damn psycho.

"Oh, the Berishas look uncomfortable. Edon might pop his artery. Then we'll finally get some entertainment in this godforsaken place," Sebastian quips before he belts out a louder laugh. "Or we can always talk about Sri Lanka. That'll work."

The psycho doesn't need an audience. He's a one-man comedy act, laugh track included.

I smirk. "You're a manipulative bastard."

"Human emotions are boring. Predictable. Now, lean in, whisper something in my ear."

I restrain myself from rolling my eyes, but I don't move. I have standards. I'm not whispering shit in anyone's ear.

Sebastian sighs and twirls his penknife. His voice drops as he leans down and whispers, "Basement and first floor are cleared. Third floor's under reno. That leaves the second floor. Two guards, no visible weapons. Aleksei's looping the cameras at your signal. You have ten minutes."

He downs his drink in one gulp. Someone from the O'Callaghan clan beckons him. "I'm being summoned. Give me a secret. A good one. I need a reaction."

Sebastian specifically instructed me not to tell him secrets beforehand. Because his family knows about his condition, his usual masking doesn't work on them. They watch him for cracks, for tells. He needs shock to sell the illusion of genuine emotions.

I flick my lighter and nod at him to lean in. He does.

"Dimitri Ivanov bartered a deal with your Ronan O'Callaghan. Twenty percent of your next month's weapons imports for him to look the other way. Because Ronan is fucking Yuri Ivanov's daughter. Opportunistic bastard." I click my tongue. "All of you led by your dicks."

Sebastian lets out a slow whistle. "Good one," he murmurs. I can hear the sadistic glee in his voice. "Didn't have to fake that reaction. Uncle Ronan, sixty and bedding a co-ed. Who knew?"

He mock-salutes me with his empty glass before facing the crowd.

But before he slips away, he lowers his voice. "The comment about dicks. Watch where yours lead."

The jab lands, and I don't respond. Instead, I keep my eyes trained on my wife, who's chatting up one of the wives or girlfriends of some nobody. She hurls a seething glare my way.

And God help me, because my cock twitches.

"You motherfucker!" Yuri yells.

Chaos breaks out. Fists fly. Glass shatters. Women scream.

The O'Callaghans and Ivanovs brawl. Boris Ivanov, the Russian patriarch, turns crimson trying to pull his sons from the Irish. The princess in question buries her face in her mom's shoulder.

Sebastian winks. I smile. Here's my window.

Rook Elias

Go boom.

I slip out of the ballroom and head up the stairs, knowing Aleksei has the cameras looped.

The two guards are nowhere to be seen.

"You go right, I go left," a soft voice says at the landing.

Sofia, dressed in a dark green gown, points down the hallway.

"Where did you put them?"

She grins. "A sudden onset of bad diarrhea. Courtesy of a small little prick." She flashes two tiny pins laced with meds, no doubt. "We have five minutes max before they call for replacements."

I nod. "Be careful."

We split. I check room after room—a library, a gallery, both ornate but abandoned.

Fucking show-offs.

Lana would love these rooms.

I shove the stray thought aside and head down the hall. Two bedrooms. The air is musty, so I doubt anyone's been in here for ages.

Before I leave the room, I hear a door creaking. Not Sofia, judging by the heavy footsteps.

I plaster myself against the wall, gun raised, breath held.

A man moves past me, his strides quick.

I peek through the gap. Black tuxedo, tall frame, black mask.

Not one of us. Who's joining the party?

The mystery man moves like a phantom, hand tucked inside his jacket. Holding a weapon, most likely.

He opens the last door and slips in, quietly closing it behind him.

My pulse ricochets. I curse myself for being too slow.

Is this the ledger exchange? Or something else?

Minutes crawl. The man isn't coming out.

My phone buzzes.

Queen Sofi

No ledger. Only bedrooms. You?

Fuck.

I glance at the time. It's been ten minutes. Whatever he's doing, he should be done by now. I can't wait anymore.

Quickly, I walk out of the room, shoulders back. Guilt is easy to spot. Confidence makes people second guess.

I head to the last room, curl my hand around the doorknob, and twist.

It's unlocked.

Gun ready, I walk into the darkness. My eyes readjust. I make out bookshelves, a large desk, and a settee. This is a study. A pristine one at that.

But no one is here. Where did the phantom go?

Sweat drips down my neck. I sweep the room, checking the usual suspects—empty vases, hollow books, anywhere anyone can hide a small USB drive.

It's like trying to find a needle in a haystack.

Then I see it.

A notebook lies open on the coffee table in the far corner. Smoke curls from a blown-out candle.

I cross the room.

My breath freezes when I read the writing.

Better luck next time, Elias.

Or should I say, Kian Leste.

A for effort though.

Here's a consolation prize.

Beneath it, a photograph taken at a deli near my childhood home. An image of a tall man wearing all black.

Time-stamped February twenty-eighth, twenty years ago.

My vision narrows, anger so intense I can taste it. The photo crinkles under my death grip.

I know that face. The eyes. That sickening smile.

Çela's partner, the other killer that day.

Someone's onto me, but I can't bring myself to care.

All I can think of is—kill.

Chapter 37: SHARP EDGES AND SOFT CARESSES

LANA

SILVERWARE CLATTERS ON PLATES. Chairs squeak on parquet floors. A string quartet's version of "Joy to the World" plays in the background. The dinner portion of this ball is in full swing.

The aroma of butter-poached lobster and applewood-smoked quail, or the sweetness of the dark chocolate spiced curry scallops should entice me.

But my stomach twists instead.

I'm all too aware of the empty seat beside me, where my husband should be. As much as I don't want to, a thread of worry tugs at my chest.

Where is Elias? He was supposed to be back before dinner began.

Why are you worried about him? He's a butcher; he can damn well take care of himself.

I poke at the garden salad with my fork.

"Lana dear," a familiar silken voice purrs.

I stiffen and look up. Shkelzen stares at me, the same slimy smile on his face.

"Your husband left you. Probably too tired of your ice-queen act."

"At least he has a queen." I spear some lettuce and stuff it into my mouth.

It was that or stab him in the eye.

He chuckles, nudging Agron. "The Anderson airs. They always thought they were too good for us."

"And yet, here we are." Agron smirks. "Her brothers are doing our bidding now. All to protect their precious younger sister."

He swivels his tumbler, arrogance dripping off his frame. "What was it, cousin? Ten million? Or thirty? The amount of money we laundered through their hotels last month?"

"Fifty. All tied to their name." Shkelzen chuckles, eyes full of victory. "Prime crop, our recent shipment from Lithuania. The girls aren't even eighteen, but have the best tits and ass I've seen in a while."

My knuckles tighten around my fork, face heating from rage.

We Andersons pride ourselves on our good name. We give back to the community. Open shelters. Donate to charities. It's our philosophy.

And now, we're tied to human trafficking.

Because of me.

My shoulders quake, tears burning behind my eyes.

Because of something I'm supposed to get at thirty-five. And I still have zero clue what it is.

We're sitting ducks.

"And now, poor Lana has been dumped by her husband. Frigid bitch. Probably because she can't fuck."

The men laugh. My veins turn to ice.

"At least I'm not fucking you!" I snap, unable to help myself.

Shit. Shit. Shit.

Shkelzen's face darkens. He grabs my wrist and yanks me up.

Glasses knock onto the floor. Shocked gasps erupt in the room.

He twists my arm, and pain steals my breath. Fabric rips—the bastard tore off the strap of my dress. I gasp, clutching the tattered silk with my free hand.

"You fucking *whore*, how dare—"

Bang!

I flinch. Wetness splatters my face. The shot rings in my skull.

Everything freezes for a heartbeat. I look down.

Shkelzen's hand has a gaping hole in it.

Screams of terror erupt. Chaos descends. Chairs knocked on the ground. Guns drawn, the security rushes in.

Movement comes from my right. A flash of black and green—Elias. He slams Shkelzen's face on the table and grabs a steak knife.

Then a gurgled scream and blood.

Lots of blood.

Elias tosses something red onto the floor.

"A tongue!" Someone gasps.

My stomach lurches, but I can't look away.

"What did I tell you last time?" Elias rasps into the bleeding man's ear. "Touch my wife and lose a hand."

Shkelzen howls in agony. He swats at Elias, but it's useless.

"Because you didn't listen, I threw in a tongue removal." Elias yanks Shkelzen up and drags him to my feet.

"Didn't your mom tell you, if you have nothing nice to say, don't say anything at all?" Elias looks up, pinning me with his blazing green eyes. "Apologize to my wife. Wipe the blood from her shoes."

I shake my head, but my husband's glare roots me.

I'm to stay put. This is a matter of respect.

Shkelzen crawls, his bloody hand grazing my shoe. He smudges the blood away with a napkin.

"I-It's fine," I whisper.

When I look up, five guns are pointed at Elias. Edon's face flushes, eyes murderous.

"How dare you?" he rasps.

Agron snarls, his aim unwavering. "I've been waiting a long time to do this."

Elias wipes his hands with a napkin. He stares at his dirty tux in clear dismay.

"Fuck." He tsks under his breath. "Such perfect craftsmanship. Ruined."

Agron jams the muzzle harder into his temple.

A sick smile curves Elias's lips. "I wouldn't do that if I were you."

He nods at the O'Callaghans and Ivanovs, who have paused their earlier brawl. "That was appetizer. Dead man's switch, gentlemen. I have more where that came from. Much more."

Then he faces Edon. "What type of man would I be if I let someone disrespect my wife? And remember what happened in Sri Lanka."

Someone coughs. One of the O'Callaghans shakes with laughter.

Edon's face ashens. He sits down.

"Sit! Continue!" he commands. "Get Shkelzen to a hospital."

People scurry at his command.

Elias dusts off his tux and offers his arm. "Wife. Shall we?"

Wordlessly, I nod, still clutching my ruined dress. I take his arm as he leads me away.

Whispers buzz, silverware clinks. "We Wish You a Merry Christmas" plays now. Normalcy resumes, and someone laughs.

These monsters.

My legs quake as we enter the main hall. But Elias is sturdy. He holds me up.

"Shhh," he hushes me again, the back of his hand grazing my skin.

Like he doesn't want to dirty me with his bloodstained fingers.

"A sewing kit," he barks at an attendant.

He steers me into a dark room and turns on the light. It's a sitting room.

The attendant returns and hands him the kit.

The room tilts when I sit down. My heart won't stop racing. I clutch at my ruined dress like a lifeline.

"Deep breaths," he murmurs, "it'll be okay."

Okay? Nothing about this is okay.

He frowns as he fiddles with the torn fabric. His touch is gentle and reverent.

"I hate that they touched you, my *zemër*," he says softly.

His fingers trail down my arm. Flutters awake in my lower belly.

"What does that mean? *Zemër*?" He's called me that a few times before.

A small smile curves his lips, but he doesn't answer. Instead, a seductive warmth fills his gaze.

My heart races for a different reason. Slowly, he lifts my throbbing wrist and presses a gentle kiss on the red marks left by the asshole. The violence dissolves into tenderness. Desire curls between my legs.

What does this make me?

But I can't find it in me to care anymore.

The seconds drag as Elias stares at the bruise forming on my wrist.

"I will kill him," Elias growls, starting to rise.

"Don't."

He halts, his chest lifting and falling rapidly. His eyes sear mine as his throat works.

With a nod, he sits down and takes out his phone. Soon, "Für Elise" plays from the speakers.

My heart pounds, my gaze darts to him.

"Music can heal...at least, for someone like you."

Something in my heart breaks at the resignation in his voice.

He thinks it's too late for him.

Elias doesn't look at me as he rummages through the sewing kit. He licks the string before threading the needle, the motion practiced.

My eyes burn, remembering the boy who used to work in garment sweatshops after school to put food on the table. The boy who smelled like sewing machine oil, who had calluses on his thumbs.

His fingers are nimble as he works the thread through the delicate fabric.

"The slip stitch. Nearly invisible for silk." His words whisper across my skin. "Pull too hard, silk scars. The trick is to catch the weft, not the warp. One wrong move, the whole thing unravels."

An old ache flares in my chest as I stare at his dark hair, thick brows, the strong nose, and the divot on his chin. His fingers are steady and careful. Those hands were supposed to hold scalpels and perform sutures. They were meant to save stray dogs and cats.

They were never supposed to kill.

I cover his hand with mine. He stills, not looking up. His shoulders tremble just once.

"Kian," I whisper.

Silence pulses for a heavy beat.

"Do you know what the worst thing is?" he murmurs, lifting his head.

The ache in my chest becomes a searing pain.

Elias's eyes glitter with unshed grief. Slowly, he cradles my face, his thumb wiping my tears away.

His fingers are covered in blood, the gunshot spatter from Shkelzen.

"If I knew what would happen," he rasps, voice thick, "I wouldn't change a thing. Because I got to spend that year with you."

My heart pulverizes, and a sob wrenches from my throat.

He draws me against his chest. I listen to the reassuring thumps of his heart.

A love song, his love sonnet to me.

"Kian's gone," he whispers. "In his place is a monster. Don't hope for anything more. You'll be disappointed."

With that, he snaps the thread, his finger trailing over the nearly invisible seam.

If only hearts could forget, could mend so seamlessly.

I'm afraid he has stitched his permanent mark onto mine.

Chapter 38: LEDGER OF GHOSTS

ELIAS

"COME ON, HURRY. I don't have all day."

I sit in the dark corner of subbasement level three of Southside Crematory, which is conveniently tucked beside Chicago Memorial. During my hunt for the man in the photo, I discovered the Berishas' most valuable contribution to The Association, money notwithstanding.

They're the trash disposers.

Under layers of shell companies, they own the primary crematorium handling body disposal for the hospital and for The Association's evil deeds.

Two weeks ago, I stitched the softest silk, touched a woman I should stay away from. Today, I'm dealing death. And worse yet, I don't feel an ounce of remorse.

There's no hope for me, Lana.

I push the thought away and refocus on the man before me, who heads up this fine establishment.

Carlos Alvarez, the black sheep of the Alvarez family, was disowned decades ago. And I have a feeling I'm about to find out why.

Sweat drips down his brow despite the cold bite of the room. The stench of embalming agents suffocates the air, and I swallow to curb the acid rushing up my throat. I aim my gun straight at Carlos, who's quivering behind his office desk.

Why would the Albanians partner with the Mexicans?

Probably greed and power, the usual motivators for these assholes.

"Coast is clear. But the clock is ticking." Ren, wearing his usual black mask, materializes beside me, his gait steady and silent. *"A vat of toxic waste may have spilled in front of the elevators and the stairwell. It'll take them time to clean up."*

While an acrid chemical smell wafts through the air, in my mind, roses always try to cut through.

I nod. "I know you've got my back."

Ren smirks. *"Always."*

"Did you hear that?" I murmur to Carlos from my spot just out of sight of the cameras. "Of course not, you don't know sign language. My friend here tells me we have twenty-eight minutes to get acquainted. That's a lot of minutes."

Carlos flinches. "K-Kent, I swear I—"

"Don't know anything. Was forced to do it. I'm innocent—Stop. You were the man in the photo. Tell me who ordered the hit on the Lestes and why."

"I can't tell you because I don't know!"

"Not acceptable."

The asshole blanches. "I-I swear. The Albanian, Seely? Seelas? He handled everything. We made a deal. After this, he was getting me back into The Six's good graces."

Çela.

Fuck. The old man withheld shit before he died.

"You're making me unhappy. You don't want Elias Kent unhappy."

Carlos stammers, "I-I can find you something. Records. Bodies moved through that day were documented in the system." He starts typing, his forehead glinting with sweat.

The back door swings open. Aleksei enters, whistling a merry tune, his LED mask lit up. The neon saint is even more terrifying and unhinged in this dark space.

"You seem happy," I murmur.

"I never get to go on outings, so it's playtime."

Carlos freezes mid-keystroke.

"What are you looking at, fucker?" Aleksei says, his voice warped through his distortion machine.

Carlos jolts, his eyes blow wide. A pained gasp escapes him.

Behind him, Ren holds up a bloody knife.

He shrugs. *"Too slow. Need to speed things up."*

I glance at the camera in the corner. If I step out of my blind spot, I'll be visible.

"You're good to go. Video's looped," Aleksei says. "Damn fuckers. Closed-circuit system only accessible on site. But that's why you got me. And you're welcome."

My lips twitch. I stride to the wheezing bastard and hoist him by his collar. "I thought being in The Association gave you power and money. Why are you locked in a sublevel dealing with the dead, Carlos? What did you do?"

His eyes bulge; his face pales as he strains against my chokehold.

I whisper, "You Alvarezes wrote the book on torture. So no, that won't happen here. Instead, I'll take your hard drives. I'll plant evidence of your betrayal. Partnering with the Albanians? Stupid move. Then I'll remove your hands and tongue so you can't speak or write. All you can do is watch your own kind hunt you down and kill everyone you love. Usual punishment. How's that, Carlos?"

He quivers and shakes his head. We all know The Association—or his bloodthirsty family—won't let him off easily. A quick death at my hand is preferable.

"Are we clear? Obey, and your death will be swift, with dignity."

That's all we can hope for in my world. I have no remorse or regrets. I'm numb to it all.

"Kian," Lana whispers in my head.

He's dead. Never coming back.

Silence falls. Only the hum of the refrigeration unit fills the room.

"Shit. The hazmat team got done sooner." Aleksei eyes his laptop. "Time's up."

I jam the barrel of my pistol under Carlos's throat. "A swift death or the wrath of The Association. Your choice."

The man exhales. He types. The printer squeaks behind him.

Ren hands me the printout. His hand shakes, and he suddenly gasps.

I frown. He's clutching his chest.

"I'm fine. Heartburn." He motions to the paper.

It's a medical waste contract. The schedule starts every Tuesday at 3:28am. Twenty-eight again. This is dated February twenty-eighth, twenty years ago.

Date of the massacre.

Two adults. One baby. Their names.

My pulse blasts through my eardrums. Red veils my vision. I grit my teeth, forcing focus.

At the bottom, a signature I don't recognize, scrawled in a distinct violet ink, with a quill stamp next to it.

"Who's this?" I point.

"They call him S-Sable. That's all I know." Carlos sways, his face as pale as the paper in my hand.

Blood loss. Ren was too efficient.

"I've given you everything I know," he whispers, then clutches my arm. "I'm...I'm sorry for what happened to your family."

I freeze, papers crinkling in my fist. My gaze snaps back to him.

"Your father—different, older—you resemble him. He was a good man. I often wondered what happened to you. I added your death to the system later." He gasps, red pooling at his lip. "So they wouldn't look for you."

A lump rises in my throat. My dad was a hardworking carpenter who was a custodian at night. He told us hard work outlasted wealth. He taught me to be a good man. One with principle.

He'd be so disappointed in me. A sledgehammer clocks my chest.

"How do you know my dad?"

Carlos shakes his head. "I'm r-ready to pay my penance." He slumps in his chair, breaths slowing. "Elias Kent—you, of all people, should know there are no such things as coincidences in our world."

His eyes roll back, and he goes limp.

No coincidences in my world.

I tap his cheek. "Not so easy. What are you saying?"

He doesn't respond.

"Wake up!" I swat the other cheek. "My parents are hard-working, law-abiding people. They aren't associated with these monsters. What the fuck are you implying?"

Images of that day swirl—my dad on the floor begging, gravel digging into my kneecaps as I kneel for him to spare my family.

Her note. It's all because of her fucking note.

Footsteps pound down the stairwell.

Aleksei yanks me up. "Elias, no time. You can think later."

No coincidences. The words slam into my brain like a battering ram.

"Come on, Elias—we gotta go." Aleksei thrusts his laptop at me, lifts Carlos over his shoulder, and heads to the incinerator room.

I shove my turbulent emotions into a box. My feet follow him, but I'm not really here.

I'm drowning, trapped under a thick slab of ice. Everything happens in snippets.

The shriek of metal doors. The click of buttons. The hum of the incinerator when it turns on.

Aleksei and Ren toss the unconscious man inside and close the door. Something sparks. A flame erupts, engulfing everything inside. The sight is a gut punch, cutting off my air supply.

I'm thrown back to that day in hell.

Screams, fire, the melted chocolate in my pocket. Laughter. Smell of roses. Beatrice crying, reaching for me.

My knees aching.

The horrifying silence.

My gaze rivets on the roaring fire through the small window.

The memories continue their assault.

"Take care of the blood," Aleksei says to Ren, his voice sounding far away. "I'll get him out."

My lungs strain. Shallow breaths. Dots in my vision.

"Come on, Elias. Don't make me worry about you." Aleksei pushes me out of the room.

I can't look away from the blaze.

I can smell it. I can feel it—the heat melting everything around me. I'm trapped in that day when I was sixteen, when my life ended.

If only I'd gone home sooner.

If only...

A fist meets my cheek. Pain blunts my senses, snapping the endless loop.

I gasp, finally focusing on Aleksei, who's now in front of me.

"I've lost everyone I cared about." He pulls up his mask, revealing the same haunted eyes he had all those years ago. "I have no one left, Elias. You need to get it together."

The agony in his voice drags me back to the night we met. His parents' blood on my hands. The wretched cry from a teenage boy who had lost everything.

I spared him. I still don't understand how he can stand beside me instead of hating me.

"A life for a life," he rasps.

He grips my shoulder and shakes me. "Elias. Focus on your revenge. Keep going. Don't rest or fall apart until you kill the man who did this to you."

I nod, my chest heavy. We climb the rear stairwell. He takes back his laptop and taps a few keys.

"Done. Cameras are live again." Not looking at me, he pulls off his mask and stuffs it under his jacket. "For the vow."

"No mercy," I reply, my voice thick.

Aleksei pushes through the doors to the lobby.

We part ways like strangers.

My phone buzzes. A text from Aleksei.

Pawn Alek

I'm here if you need to talk.

I stare at the screen and the printout before sliding into the backseat of my car idling at the curb.

Thundering cracks of flames mix with her sweet voice.

The voice of my salvation. The voice of the woman who set everything in motion.

The voice of the one person I could never give up.

"Maybe you need someone to care about you," she whispers.

Clutching my head, a loud scream rips out of my throat.

The memories batter and twist, relentless.

Stop. Stop it. Stop. It hurts. Everything fucking hurts.

A bomb detonates inside my head.

My mind shatters.

Chapter 39: INTERLUDE - THE NIGHT OF KNIVES

KIAN

Past: Chicago, February Twenty-Eighth, Twenty Years Ago

OMENS.

I had never believed in them until the day my life changed.

My mom had hailed from a tiny town in Albania, and she was superstitious to the bone.

She used to say, "Keep your head down. Work hard, so the devil doesn't come to collect."

I'd laugh and tell her I didn't believe in that stuff. She'd furrow her brow, wag her finger, and say, "*Qoftë larg!*"

Don't jinx it.

Her words had echoed as I parked my bike and headed into the antique shop—the same one I was caught shoplifting from the year before and kneeled for two hours as punishment.

It was February twenty-eighth, and it should be freezing cold in Chicago, but instead, it was the opposite.

Sunlight broke through the clouds, glinting off patches of dirty snow. The world was still an endless wash of gray, but it was warm. Too warm.

And yet, nature hid. No birds. No wind. Just the world—trapped in silence.

Mom would call it an omen, a harbinger of something.

I told myself, the devil could come collect me after that day, because it was Elise's birthday.

The tiny doorbell rang as I stepped inside. The same clerk was behind the counter. He narrowed his eyes, adjusted his glasses, his lips twisting into a sneer.

"You again, pretty boy? Wanna kneel again until your knees are raw? Didn't get enough last time?"

"No, sir." I raised my hands. "I've got cash this time."

I pulled out the wad of crumpled bills from my jeans pocket. Guilt pinched my chest knowing these were all the savings I made from the sweatshop, plus the small stash I found under the bed.

It was reckless—spending all this money on something that wouldn't feed little Beatrice or fill our stomachs.

But I deserved to be selfish for once, didn't I?

I'd been working hard, taking care of my younger siblings while Mom and Dad worked double shifts. I'd scrimped and saved.

I was a "good man," as Dad would say.

I deserved to do something for myself.

That "something" being the green pendant hanging on the mannequin near the door—the same one I tried to steal the day I met her. Elise later marveled at it and said it matched the color of my eyes.

Her beloved music box was locked up tight inside a glass case. I didn't know much about jewelry or fancy stuff, but from the way those gems sparkled, I could tell there was no way I could ever afford to buy it for her. But this little green pendant—lab grown, maybe—I just might have enough.

"I want that necklace," I had told the clerk.

He eyed me, then my rolled-up, sweat-creased bills.

The clerk checked each one—fives, tens—all fruits of my labor, blood, sweat, and tears. He examined them like I ran a print shop. I snorted. If I could counterfeit, I'd never have to steal.

I swallowed my impatience as he counted. Finally, he shrugged, lifted the necklace from the mannequin, and dangled it on his fingertip.

Bubbles prickled in my chest. I imagined Elise's eyes lighting up when she saw it.

"Does it come with a box? One with a bow on top?"

The clerk sneered. "This is a clearance item. Whoever the chick is, I'm sure she'll be happy. After all, her standards can't be high—picking a guy like you."

Heat surged in my chest, but I bit my tongue.

I snatched the necklace, stuffed it into my pocket, and climbed back onto my bike.

The clerk's words bothered me more than I would admit. It was the same thing I'd been telling myself. Whenever Elise came to my rundown apartment, or when we squeezed onto that tattered twin-sized bed on the floor. Or when we'd share a slice of pizza—deep dish, my favorite—because I couldn't afford two. She'd always hug me with gratitude, and that joy carved something deep inside my heart.

It ate at me because she deserved more. A lot more than I could give.

At school, I'd look her up online—photos of her looking breathtaking at some ball at a place called The Orchid. She looked like a fairy tale princess. Her brothers, her father, all dressed in tuxes, fancy shoes, and expensive watches.

What could I ever give to the Anderson princess except a promise I couldn't keep?

And now, time was running out. She would head back to New York after the quarter.

My heart clenched. Suddenly, I couldn't breathe. I couldn't imagine a world without her, without the scent of her roses, her joyful laughter, her warmth beside me. I couldn't imagine a future where I couldn't buy her the dream house she wanted—with the music room, the library, and the indoor garden with windows big enough to see the stars.

The depressing thoughts kept me company as I entered the iron gates of Hollow Gardens. I patted my pockets, making sure the pendant and Geraldine's truffles didn't fall out.

We were supposed to meet here to celebrate her sweet sixteen.

The wind picked up out of nowhere. Smothering clouds—gray like nightmares—pressed down upon us. Looked like it'd snow again soon. I shivered and hurried to our elm tree.

But she wasn't there.

I checked my watch. Five minutes late. She couldn't have left, could she?

Something twisted inside my gut, like watching the seams unravel in a perfectly knitted sweater—all the hard work, wasted.

"I'm thinking too much," I muttered, and sat beneath the bare branches.

I traced our words on the tree, thinking about the only girl I'd ever love.

I wasn't ready to give her up. I didn't know if I ever would.

Minutes passed. Then an hour. Then two.

Worried, I paced before the tree. Cold sweat dotted my brows.

If only I had a phone, I could text her, see if she was okay. Maybe someone needed her at school.

Everything was probably fine. She probably left a message for me at the apartment.

Lead seeped through my veins as I biked home.

When my building came into view, the lead turned to anvils in my shoes.

It was quiet. Unusually so. Nothing in this neighborhood was ever quiet. It was like the Reaper came and took every soul with him.

Nonsense.

My breathing echoed in the damp stairwell as I climbed to the third floor. I turned right, moving past the apartment numbers.

Twelve...thirteen...

I stopped in front of the door that should've been number fourteen. It was sixteen now, after Dad changed it for reasons I still didn't understand. Something about fourteen being unlucky.

The doorknob burned.

The lightbulb flickered overhead, then popped. Little Beatrice cried loudly behind the door.

Panic seized me. Did someone leave the stove on? I yanked out my keys and unlocked the door.

A baseball bat slammed into my side. I crashed onto the floor.

"Kian!" Mom's muffled cries finally reached my ears.

The world swirled as I lifted my head. She was bound and gagged beside Dad by the TV. Two men in ski masks hovered, guns pointed at their heads.

Flames engulfed the drapes, bitter smoke stifling the air.

Sofia whimpered, hands clasped over her mouth. She was curled up on the sofa, little Beatrice next to her.

Dark spots swam in my vision.

I crawled toward them. "Mom," I gasped. "St-Stop this."

Slowly, I staggered to my feet, the floor tilting.

The men laughed.

"Look at him. Weak. Can barely stand," the short one sneered.

"We have nothing." I swayed and pulled out the remaining cash I had left. "This is all we have. Pl-Please let them go."

The tall man barked out a laugh. "The boy thinks we're here to rob them."

The shorter man yanked Sofia off the couch. She shrieked. "This one's a beauty. Be a shame to waste her." He eyed his partner. "Don't think The Association would mind if I take her?"

The other man shrugged.

Mom screamed through her gag, her head shaking wildly. Dad threw himself against the short man's legs.

Sofia struggled, her terrified eyes meeting mine.

"Take me! Whatever it is. Take me. I'm strong. You can use me. I'd do anything. Let my family go."

The short man studied me with interest.

"Anything, huh? You're pretty too. Maybe I could use you." He covered my sister's mouth, muffling her cries. A sadistic glint shone in his eyes. "Drop to your knees, boy. Beg us."

I kneeled, my pulse hammering inside me. Glass shards from a broken vase dug into my skin, but I barely felt them. Beatrice's cries rose to screams, her little face mottled and red.

The shorter man snarled and pointed his gun at her.

"No!" Mom cried. The man swiveled in her direction.

Bang!

Time suspended. I flinched. The sound burned into my skull.

Mom collapsed onto the floor, lifeless. Dad wailed. He threw himself over Mom.

No. No. No. I crawled toward her still body.

Beatrice's shrieking ripped into my heart.

Another gunshot thundered against the walls.

She stopped crying.

The tall man socked me across the face and white-hot pain exploded behind my eyes.

The room tilted, my limbs clumsy and slow, and smoke suffocated my lungs.

Through the haze, I still saw everything.

But nothing compared to the pain and grief shredding my insides.

Pools of crimson spread across the white tiles. Sofia kicked and flailed, her eyes bright with fear as the short man carried her out of the apartment.

Dad's mournful sobs. His body over Mom's as he begged her not to leave him. Words I didn't understand. The Association. The Six.

Bang!

Then the horrifying silence.

Black venom invaded my senses. Flames rose, a vicious monster, devouring everything in their path.

My vision flickered. Once. Twice.

Ragged breaths throttled out of me.

A sweet scent drifted to my nose—the melted chocolates in my pocket.

I heard Elise's laughter and imagined the elm tree in spring as darkness overtook me.

I woke to fire singeing my shoes, the smell of melted plastic corrosive to my nostrils.

And pain, so much pain.

Flames surrounded me, and for a moment, I thought I woke up in hell.

I staggered to my knees.

Mom. Dad. Beatrice and Sofia.

Images of what happened slammed into my mind. My family—I choked as black smoke invaded my nostrils.

But I still crawled toward where I saw them last.

Glass shards dug into my hands. More coughs wrenched out of my lungs. Too much smoke and the scorching heat—it was like my skin was melting off with each inch of forward movement.

And when I looked up, unable to get any closer with the burning furniture in the way, a sob lodged in my throat.

A fiery inferno had unleashed its wrath on everything I knew—four walls of crackling, burning hell. Charred smells reached my nose—the snapping beams and roaring flames warning me to get out.

It was too late for my parents and little Beatrice. Much too late.

Moisture clouded my eyes as I crawled toward the door. If I didn't reach it before the flames, I'd die too.

And I wanted to. But I couldn't, because Sofia was out there.

I needed to find her.

Pain scraped my legs as fire climbed my jeans. I rolled, snuffed it out, and dragged myself to the threshold, finally finding the strength to stand. A silver glint on the entryway table, which was still untouched by the flames caught my eye.

My dad's beloved lighter. I grabbed it.

Something white flapped onto the floor from the table. Feminine scrawl with one word. *Kian.*

My sweet Lana Elise.

I grabbed it and stumbled out of the building as sirens blared in the distance.

Glass and rubble crunched underfoot. I leaned against the alley wall, my lungs heaving in desperate breaths.

I unfolded the note with soot-darkened fingers.

Kian,

Dad has pneumonia, so I have to go back to New York early. Sorry I couldn't tell you in person. I'll email you when things calm down.

I miss you and love you so much.

I'll be dreaming of college in Chicago and being with you again.

Maybe I can come back during Christmas.

Love,

Your Elise

P.S. Two kind gentlemen were here looking for your family earlier. They brought presents from Albania. I knew you guys were secretive about your address, but they showed me photos of your family and said they were your uncles. So I told them to wait at the stairwell. I knocked, and your parents said they weren't expecting visitors. Anyway, the men weren't there when I went back to tell them you weren't home. They left the presents, though. I hope they're something nice for you and Sofia. You guys deserve the world.

Shock was a liver punch to the gut. I slid onto the ground, not caring about the metal scraps and glass shards stabbing my backside.

My fist crumpled the paper, my mind reeling from what Elise wrote.

What she did.

"Fire's out of control. Spreading southbound," a fireman hollered in the distance. "Need reinforcements!"

Sirens bellowed. Police arrived in swarms.

Don't trust the police. Another one of Mom's rules. Most of them were in the mob's pocket.

I staggered away, clutching the letter, my mind still refusing to accept reality.

A sharp pain speared my gut as I collided with a few box crates.

I caught my reflection in the half-boarded window. Blond hair covered in soot. Hollow eyes. Perfectly unmarred face. How was I alive, and how were they...gone?

"Pretty boy." The shopkeeper's voice. The murderer's. *"Kneel. Beg. Pretty boy."*

I fished out the pocketknife from my pocket and extended the blade.

A hiss escaped my lips as I carved a line down my left cheek.

Crimson dripped down my face.

But I barely noticed the pain.

Nothing could compare to the agony obliterating what was left of my heart.

Pretty boy no more.

The smoke thinned. My heart hardened.

And from that day on, I would *never* kneel again.

Chapter 40: OBSIDIAN PAST

LANA

Present: Chicago

LIGHTNING SEARS THE DARK room in a flash of white as the wind beats against the windows. A rare thundersnow storm descends upon us.

Cece meows and scurries out of the bedroom, no doubt to find Hannah or Ren for comfort.

Unease knots my chest as I brush my hair at the antique desk. My silk nightgown clings to my skin after my shower.

Where is he? It's midnight, and Elias is usually home by now after doing whatever he does with his shadowy business.

Ever since the Benefaction a week ago, something has shifted between us.

I'd wake up to my usual Geraldine's Chocolates on the nightstand, but now they'd be accompanied with a single, long-stemmed rose, and the lounge chair would be pulled up at my bedside.

Instead of feeling exposed, butterflies would swarm in my gut at the thought of him watching me sleep.

And a secret voice would whisper in my head.

Why doesn't he stay?

"Kian's gone... Don't hope for anything more."

Maybe he's right. The cutthroat, brutal Elias today is nothing like the sweet, gentle boy of my childhood. I saw it at the Benefaction—his viciousness as he protected my honor, the bloodlust in his eyes.

But then, there's his tender touch as he mended my dress. The way those emerald pools still stare at me like I'm his salvation.

And so, despite all the red flags he waves, I realize one truth.

If he asked—if my sweet Kian or my savage Elias asked me to give him a chance—I'd say yes. Not because it's smart or safe, but because my heart calls for it.

No one's ever made me feel the way he does. And maybe I'm still the hopeless romantic wishing for a certain music box, or the girl who'd look at her parents' wedding photos, dreaming about an enduring love—even if it ended in death.

My heart aches when I trace the carvings of the little cherubs on the desk—gold-tipped arrows and all.

That's why it looks familiar. A long time ago, when innocent Elise told gentle Kian about her dream house, she mentioned such a desk.

And he got it for me, all without ever revealing who he was.

A crash startles me. The front door slams open.

Heavy footfalls reach my ears.

My muscles tense in anticipation. I know that gait, that sound.

Elias.

I set down my brush and stand just as the door swings open.

My breath goes shallow.

Elias grips the doorframe, his dark suit jacket and shirt unbuttoned, tie hanging around his neck. His thick hair is in disarray, like he's been yanking at it.

But it's not his dishevelment, the antithesis of the calm, conniving dealer of secrets, that steals my breath.

It's his eyes.

A swirling tempest haunts those greens, like he's seen one tragedy too many.

His broad chest rises and falls, breath ragged, fingers white-knuckled around the doorframe.

I stand frozen, every nerve blooming toward him, like he's the sun I've been missing.

Thunder rattles the windows, but I barely notice.

His eyes darken as he slowly uncoils from the threshold.

A muscle tics in his sharp jaw as he advances toward me.

Something clatters onto the desk, followed by a loud thud.

My brush. The stool I was sitting on.

I back up before realizing it.

My universe narrows to the five feet of air between us.

"E-Elias," I whisper, "What's wrong?"

Something's different. I stand at the cliff's edge, seconds away from plummeting, the ground ripped away from me.

He doesn't answer me. He only swallows, his steps slow but measured. My back hits the wall by the bed.

Elias stops a foot before me, his gaze intent on mine, and slowly peels off his leather gloves.

"You know, Kian would still be alive," he rasps, his voice thick, "if it weren't for you."

He braces one hand on the wall, the other grazing my cheek, the gentleness completely at odds with the fury in his words.

"What are you talking about?" I furrow my brows. Awareness lights low in my belly, liquid heat spreading with each graze of his scarred fingers against my skin.

My body cants toward him, craving his touch, his words, anything.

He lets out a hollow laugh. "You really know nothing, do you?"

Another shiver moves through me when he trails his finger down my neck, slowly and torturously, until it rests on my racing pulse.

His question finally registers, along with his accusation. A new fire ignites in my gut.

Indignation and fury.

"I don't know what you think I did." I push at his chest, but he doesn't budge. "But I know what I went through."

Tears sting my eyes as I relive those dark months after the great Saints Hollow fire—images of death and destruction from the news scorched into my memory. I bite back the sob crawling up my throat. I refuse to cry in front of him.

"I didn't know if you were dead or alive! I called the hospitals so many times, they recognized my voice. Do you know how devastated I was when I found out your parents and little Beatrice died? How I was scared out of my mind every time I checked the casualties list, praying you and Sofia weren't there?"

I shove him again. Hard. Again and again, the bottled-up pain from all these years bursts out of me like the storm outside.

Elias takes my hits like they were nothing. He lets me use his body to vent my anger, while dark emotions swirl in his eyes as he keeps his finger on my pulse.

Like he's trying to catch me in a lie.

"Then one day out of the blue," I choke out, "I get an emerald pendant in the mail. No note, no return address."

I tug the pendant free from my neckline. His eyes flare. The gem flashes under the dim light. "I knew it was you!"

My throat burns, but I push through, because this torture, this injustice, I can no longer keep to myself.

"I sent emails. I searched for any trace of you online. Nothing!" My vision blurs and I bite my lip. "I *loved* you, Kian. I don't think I've ever stopped loving you, and you discarded me like I was nothing, like I—"

"You brought them to our door!" he bellows, his fist driving into the wall next to my head.

I jolt, stunned into silence.

A vein jumps in his temple, a wet sheen clouding his eyes.

His pained eyes.

"What?"

"The Association," he grinds out, "you led them straight to us."

No, he can't—*What?*

"I waited for you at Hollow Gardens for hours...hoping you'd show up. And during this time—" His voice cracks. "They went to my apartment, tied up my parents. They—"

"No." My mind is stuck on his earlier statement. I can't breathe. I can't think. "I didn't. You told me not to. I was careful. I never told anyone—"

I gasp, my eyes snapping up to his.

"Young lady, do you know where I can find the Lestes?" the taller gentleman asks with a smile as I descend the stairs after bidding Elias's parents goodbye and leaving my note on the entryway table.

I stop mid-step and frown, unsure how to respond.

The man motions to the shorter man by his side, who holds up two large paper bags.

"We're their cousins from Albania," he explains, his voice thick with a foreign accent, "b-but I lost their address in the cab. Silly me."

I eye their appearance—the tall one in a clean suit, the shorter one sharply dressed in a polo. They don't look like the thugs loitering around the corners, cigarettes dangling from their lips.

The tall man rubs his head like he's embarrassed. "The young lady must think we're stupid. Show her the photos."

The shorter man laughs and sets the bags on the floor. I catch brightly wrapped packages within. He fishes out his wallet and pulls out a photo.

I smile—it's a family photo of the Lestes. God, Kian was so much younger back then. The baby fat on his face, so cute.

Clearing my throat, I eye the duo again. I bite my lip and make a decision.

"Stay here," I murmur. "Let me check."

The men sigh with clear relief. "Thank you, dear."

I run back upstairs.

My vision refocuses on my cold, brutal husband staring at me with anguish.

"They were your relatives," I whisper. "Your cousins."

An icy chill slithers up my spine, up, up, up, until it wraps around my lungs.

"We don't have cousins. We don't have relatives in Albania, Lana."

No. No. No. I clamp my hands over my ears. This can't be.

The floor slants. My legs give out from under me.

Tears slide down my face. Faces flash behind my eyes—the small woman with a tired smile, his dad who'd give me a snack whenever I visited. Cute little Beatrice, with her rolls and giggles, always bringing a grin to my face. Sofia following me around, imitating the way I walk and talk, much to Kian's embarrassment.

It was me.

No wonder Elias hates me. No wonder he's avoided me like I was poison all these years. How can he *not* hate me?

Grief and guilt stab into my heart.

I led The Association straight to them. They couldn't find the apartment because his dad had switched the numbers. His parents must've known danger was coming. I saw their packed bags by the door. The two men must've followed me.

I killed them. It didn't matter whether it was ignorance or an accident. The result was the same.

Kian and Sofia became orphans overnight because of me.

"I-I'm so sorry," I sob into my knees.

Fragments of the past slam into me, not letting me go.

Kian and I carving our message in the tree.

And years later, a towering, scarred man showing up at my family's doorstep, his beautiful green eyes searing into mine.

The levers snap into place, the crisp clicking of the unsolvable puzzle finally revealing its answers.

"No, no, no," I whisper, my mind mad with grief, my heart in tatters.

Warm, rough fingers tilt my chin up. A pained sound rumbles from Elias's chest.

Then, his mouth crushes mine in a savage kiss.

Chapter 41: DESPITE EVERYTHING

LANA

I CLING TO HIM as he deepens our kiss, his mouth moving urgently against mine. He lifts and presses me against the wall, hand clutching my nape, fingers tangling in my hair. His tongue delves inside my mouth, licking, tasting, claiming me as heat unfurls low in my belly.

"Don't cry," he whispers. "Your tears hurt more than bullets."

More sobs rack me. How could he kiss me, hold me like this after what I'd done? Even if it was an accident, even if I didn't mean to. His parents and baby sister still died because of my actions.

I clutch his neck, pressing kisses over his tear-streaked face, the rough stubble on his jaw, his soft, beautiful lips, needing to tell him without words everything I'm feeling—love, guilt, regret, anger—too many emotions to name.

But I know this much.

It's always been him.

"How do you not hate me?" I ask as we break apart for air.

Elias pulls in a rough breath, the green in his eyes long eclipsed by his pupils. He brushes his thumb tenderly across my cheek, wiping away my tears.

"I tried to tell myself I hate you," he murmurs, his finger dipping to my bottom lip, slowly pressing until it trembles beneath his touch. "And sometimes I thought I had succeeded."

A whimper lodges in my throat. Keeping my eyes locked on his, I suck his thumb, my tongue dipping out and swirling, mimicking what I want to do to all parts of him.

His nostrils flare. A vein pops on his forehead as his gaze fixes on my mouth.

"The truth is," his voice is gritty like sandpaper, "it wasn't your fault. You were a kid. You didn't know any better. It was a fucking tragedy. But I wanted someone to hate—anyone. You. My parents, who were obviously involved in something they shouldn't have been...but..."

Elias groans when I bite his thumb lightly. He presses closer, singeing me with the hot brand of his chest and the throbbing hard-on digging out of his pants.

"I could never hate you, my Lana Elise," he murmurs against my lips before trailing kisses down my neck, leaving sparks in his wake. "I hated myself for not returning home sooner. For not being strong enough to stop them."

"You were a kid too—"

"I couldn't forgive myself, and hatred was all I had to keep me going. So I...I..."

He hated me. Hated himself. Self-inflicted punishment.

"Elias." Tears cloud my vision.

"Shhh." He nibbles the thin straps of my nightgown and drags them off my shoulders.

Cold air meets my skin as the fabric pools on the floor. Wetness slicks between my thighs as I rub my hard nipples against his shirt.

"Despite everything, I couldn't stay away. I couldn't let you go. I told myself my obsession with you was because of hatred. But that's a lie."

Hot, passionate kisses trail down my neck and I melt into him.

He presses his confession over my heart. "The truth is, you're the only good thing in my life. And I would've done anything to remain in yours. Sending you puzzles, the necklace—they were all because I couldn't leave you. I couldn't stand to be cut off from you."

Gripping my thigh, he bears down, dragging his groin against my soaked core, letting me feel every inch of him. "For the past twenty years, those twenty-eight minutes have been what I lived for each day."

The hiss of the zipper slices through the air, and I moan when I feel his thick cock rubbing against the seam of my underwear.

"T-Twenty-eight minutes?" I whimper when his fingers tug on the straps, ripping the delicate fabric from my body.

"Your birthday, February twenty-eighth...the day the most beautiful angel descended on earth and the day I entered hell."

Elias caresses my heavy tits, his thumb flicking one nipple while his mouth claims the other, mainlining ecstasy into my core.

My knees buckle, and he catches me easily. He hoists me up and drops me onto the bed.

A chilly draft meets my heated flesh. He hovers before me, his hands quick at work on his clothes, revealing every solid inch of him. Up close, I see the scars—slashes, burn marks, round puckered holes that must be from bullets.

Agony twists through me as I trail my fingers over each one, a testament of the pain he's endured to transform from Kian to Elias.

Then there's the scar bisecting his cheek.

I gently touch it, and he closes his eyes.

"This one I inflicted on myself," he murmurs. "A reminder that the Kian, the pretty boy, couldn't exist. Not if he wanted to avenge his family."

A lump thickens in my throat as I press a kiss on the scar. "It must've hurt."

"Don't feel sorry for me," he rasps.

He stands naked before me—glorious and breathtaking—a dark-haired demon with tattoos writhing up his arms, the vines swirling over scars. The simple Asian character stands out on his chest.

I trace the strokes with my fingertips.

He throttles out a breath and stills my hand. "*Trust. Believe.* It's the Chinese word for it."

"Because?" My gaze catches his.

His eyes soften, and he leans down, slowly pressing his hard frame against mine, burning me up with his presence.

Elias cradles my cheek the way he usually does—reverent, gentle, like I'm precious.

"I had it inked after the fire," he says quietly. "When everything I believed in...was gone."

Closing his eyes, he dips his forehead against mine. "At first, the tattoo was a reminder for me to keep going. To trust that I'd get through this. Find Sofia. Get revenge. It kept me standing while I worked my way through seedy clubs, collecting secrets, trading favors..."

"Becoming Elias Kent," I whisper, my heart cleaving in half.

His voice thickens, and he presses my hand over his heart. "But I think...secretly," he clutches my fingers tightly, "there's a voice here that still hopes Elise can find a way to love the monster within."

My breath hitches, and I pull him down and kiss him.

He still loves me. Elias, Kian, whoever he is now, this man in my arms loves me more than anything.

Our kiss turns messy. Teeth against teeth. Tongue dueling, soft suctions, sharp bites. He pins me onto the bed as he moves down my body, dragging kiss after kiss across every inch of me.

My clit throbs, my wetness leaking down my thighs. I'm aching, empty, needing him inside me, filling me up.

"Elias, please," I moan.

"Please what?"

He bites my inner thigh, and I shudder.

"Fuck me. Make love to me. Fill me up. I need you."

He lets out a masculine groan and spreads my legs. "Look at this beautiful pussy throbbing. The pretty pink. Your sweetness, all for me?"

"Yes," I cry out when he clamps his lips over my clit, tongue lashing the hard point.

Stars appear behind my eyes, and I clutch his hair, hips canting up, holding on as he devastates me with his talented mouth. Soft circles. Hard flicks, a finger teases my entrance before sliding in, then another.

The sounds of his suction and fingers join the drumming of the rain and the thundering of my heart.

Every cell in me sensitizes, pressure gathering at breakneck speed.

"So sweet," he grits out. "Fuck, you're too sweet for me. I should stay away. I'm not right for you."

No, you're exactly who I need.

Another full lick from my tight rosebud up to my clit.

"Elias, please!" My legs tremble. I feel the pinnacle barreling toward me.

"Not so fast, my beautiful Elise."

In a flash he's above me again, his cock nudging at my entrance.

His jaw tics and he braces himself on his forearms above me, holding still.

"Who am I?" he whispers, echoing the same question from the dungeon.

A flurried pulse hammers in his neck. I don't know what he wants me to call him...Kian or Elias...but it doesn't matter, because he's one person to me.

I trace the thick scar on his cheek.

"You're my husband," I whisper. "And all your scars are beautiful to me."

Those brilliant eyes widen. He crushes his lips to mine and surges in, thrusting his cock inside me to the hilt.

I cry into our kiss as the pain ignites the overpowering pleasure, and I shatter into pieces.

He threads our fingers together, joining us body and soul as he powers his hips, thrust after thrust, dragging out my orgasm.

The sparks never abate but burgeon once more.

My mind blanks, my vision flickering, I thrash under his powerful body, my feet digging into his ass as sharp currents run through my nerves again.

A live wire sizzles from deep within my core, building, building, and building, until I can no longer bear it.

A roar rips out of him, his cock becoming impossibly harder and thicker.

"Fuck yes," he grunts, his rhythm faltering. "Come for me, wife, flood me with your cum."

My release detonates. Wetness drips out of my pussy as wave after wave of his hot cum bathes my insides.

Elias presses kisses upon kisses while he moves on top of me, eking out every ounce of ecstasy. His lips travel to the sensitive pulse point on my neck, my jaw, my eyes, then my lips again, like he can't get enough.

"My *zemër*," he whispers minutes later, cradling me, chest against chest, his semi-hard cock still lodged inside me.

My eyes flutter open. Wind howls outside. Another flash of lightning slashes the room in white.

But I don't care. The unease from earlier has long vanished.

"What does that mean, *zemër*?" I smile and brush his hair from his forehead so I can see his eyes again.

My favorite emerald eyes.

"Heart." His lips curve into a small smile. "I lost my heart years ago, but you've kept it safe for me, my *zemër*."

I give him a wobbly smile, heat prickling the backs of my eyes again.

I push him down onto the bed and straddle him. His breath hitches in surprise.

My hair forms a curtain around our faces when I lean over him.

"Kian...Elias...whoever you are," I whisper, "I will always keep your heart safe. Always."

His groan fills the room when I move on top of him, letting my body speak the rest.

Later that night, he stays, our bodies touching, connected like we've been waiting all our lives.

Two hearts reunited.

Chapter 42: TWENTY-EIGHT MINUTES

ELIAS

THE EARLY DAWN BATHES Lana in a soft blue light.

And I do what I do best.

Watch her.

But this time, instead of sitting in a chair next to her bed, or observing through monitors, I'm beside her, close enough to feel her warmth, inhale her sweet roses, and count the soft flutters of her breaths.

The useless muscle behind my sternum kicks and jolts, mocking me with a truth my mind has known for years.

"I love you, Lana," I whisper, so softly she can't hear me.

For so long, I called it obsession, delusion, hatred—anything but what it was. I told myself that hating her made it acceptable to stay by her side, even though she led the killers to our door.

But I can't lie to myself anymore.

I love her.

I'd kill for her.

I'd burn for her.

I'd die for her.

She lets out a happy moan and faces me, a curl of silky dark hair draping over her soft tits.

My groin throbs as heat surges, my heart hammering harder in my rib cage.

My phone buzzes from the timer I set.

Twenty-eight minutes.

Then thirty. Thirty-five. Forty.

I ignore the reminders and trace her cheek instead, my lips hitching up slightly when she smiles in her sleep.

Beautiful dreams, I hope. Perhaps one of the past of us goofing off in the backyard. I had no money to my name, but we were happy. Back then, I wondered what the poor Kian could give to the rich Anderson princess.

Now, I wonder what the brutal king of the underworld—his hands darkened with blood—could give to the goddess who deserves to live earth-side, with sunlight warming her skin and flowers blooming around her.

She deserves someone who can love her with his all. Someone without enemies waiting to kill him. Someone who puts her on a pedestal and worships her.

Kids. A cat or two. A beautiful farmhouse in the middle of nowhere. A man who works a boring nine-to-five or spends his time running large corporations.

The simple life. The *safe* life.

My phone buzzes again, and this time, I feel a pain I haven't felt in a long time—a visceral stab to my newly beating heart.

I stare at my wife, the only woman I've ever kissed in my lifetime, and slowly press my lips to hers, tasting her sweetness again.

She moans and snuggles into my hold, but I force myself to withdraw.

Quietly, I grab my phone and get out of bed.

The screen flashes. Another incoming message.

The date catches my eye first. January fifteenth, one and a half months until Lana turns thirty-five, when this all comes to a head.

Then I see the message.

Unknown number

If you want to be one step ahead of Sable, don't wear your heart on your sleeve.

—Always watching, your friend.

A cold line carves down my spine.

My mind flashes to the masked man at the Benefaction, the mysterious phantom who's been one step ahead, but hasn't made a move to take down my rook on the chessboard.

Who is he, and what does he want?

The questions hammer through my skull as I stride to the door, but her breathy whisper stops me.

"Elias?" she murmurs and rolls over, baring one smooth shoulder. "Stay. Don't leave me."

I pause at the threshold, another sharp pain piercing my chest again.

"Never, princess. I will never leave you."

Not today, at least.

LANA

My body is pleasantly sore when I wake up. A fire roars in the fireplace, the logs crackling a merry rhythm in the background.

I smile when I smell vetiver and smoke, this time with a tinge of mint.

Elias. Kian. My husband.

After getting out of bed, I pull on a silk robe and fasten it at my waist. Images of our lovemaking last night keep me company as I head into the bathroom to freshen up. I rode him, and then he bent me over, ass up. He took me against the shower wall and then again in front of the full-length mirror.

He was insatiable, and so was I.

My face glows pink, my lips swollen, my hair knotted at the ends.

I look gloriously fucked, and a delicious ache pulses in my pussy.

He's not Kian anymore. He's Elias, a criminal mobster, a murderer.

My mind tries to rationalize, but my heart doesn't care.

Instead, it thumps a more righteous rhythm, like this is the direction I've been searching for. Like my future is supposed to be beside this man.

And I don't want to think anymore.

I finish my business and head toward the bedroom door, eager to find the enigmatic man himself, when a small object on the nightstand stops me in my tracks.

Silver. A small chain affixed to it. Delicate carvings.

His lighter.

Curious, I pick it up and lift it to the light. It's beautiful—an antique from what I can tell—with intricate markings similar to his tattoos of vines and roses etched on the side.

I thumb the ridges—small indentations I can't make sense of. It's heavier than it looks.

Then I flip it open. A small flame sparks to life.

Why does he carry this thing if he doesn't smoke? And why does it look so familiar?

The answer perches on the tip of my tongue, a nagging, invisible itch.

I set the lighter down, step through the door—and stop.

Multicolor Christmas lights line the hallway. Classic holiday songs blare from the speakers downstairs.

It's mid-January. What is he up to?

A smile tugs at my lips as I follow the music down the steps, gaping at the explosion of Christmas greeting me in the dark marble hallways.

A twelve-foot Christmas tree, complete with sparkly garlands and mismatched ornaments—like a toddler with the help of a unicorn oversaw the decorations—sits at the corner of the foyer.

More Christmas lights twinkle along the crown moldings.

A tower of Geraldine's Chocolate boxes stacked in the shape of a Christmas tree rests beside the real one.

Everywhere I look is Christmas. Ridiculous, over-the-top Christmas.

It's absurd and gaudy and so specifically *me* that my throat goes hot for a second.

Cuckoo clocks with Santas popping out. Candles burn, wafting peppermint and vanilla. A small pear tree sits by his office. A tiny wooden drummer boy on a Roomba rams the tree like it's enemy number one.

And you've got to be kidding me, is that two white doves flapping their wings in a birdcage?

Cece scratches at the bars, clearly annoyed her new best friends are out of reach.

I ruffle her fur as I pass by, spotting more chaos.

Inflatable figures of men leaping. A TV tuned to a farm show of women milking cows.

Hannah barrels past me, hands gesturing wildly, a slew of Italian curses spilling from her lips.

Then—loud squawking filters from the kitchen.

You've got to be shitting me.

"Quiet down before I make Hannah cook you for dinner. Goose pie. That's a thing, right?" a deep voice murmurs.

"Don't you dare!" I call out. "You touch the geese, the doves unionize. I'll be their fearless leader."

I hurry into the kitchen, finding Elias with his back toward me, shirtless with a Christmas hat on his head.

He's whipping something, muscles flexing, and heat blooms in my belly because from my angle, the rapid arm motions look obscene. I want to see him doing this in another setting while he pins me with his lust-filled eyes.

"You're staring, wife," he murmurs, his hand still pumping.

"Yeah, well," I clear my throat, my voice raspy, "you make quite a sight...whatever you're doing."

Elias freezes for a second.

Low chuckles rumble out of him. He rolls his neck and resumes the rapid up and down motions. Then the asshole adds sound effects.

Low grunts, growls, quickening pumps of his hips, which look mighty fine in those gray sweatpants of his.

"Wh-What are you doing?"

He barks out a laugh and turns, his green eyes bright with humor. He's whisking chocolate cake batter.

"Indulging in your dirty fantasies." Elias winks. Heat shoots embarrassingly low. "Although...they don't need to stay fantasies. I'm more than happy to give you a live demonstration later."

His gaze turns molten. My core throbs.

"Don't always think with your dick," I mutter and sit on the other side of the counter.

"I'm thinking with my hands. The dick's just enthusiastic."

Cece prances in and winds her lithe body around Elias's ankles, tail flicking like she owns the place.

"Stay away from the devil, Cece. He's annoying your mom."

Elias chuckles as the cat leaps onto the counter and purrs against his chest.

"Traitor," I mutter. "I treat you better than him."

"Technically," he says, looking up, amusement sparking in his eyes, "I saved her life."

"What do you mean?" I squint then gasp. "The café! Cece *is* the same cat from the café! I knew it!"

He turns his back to the counter and grabs another bowl. "That morning, I saw you making moon eyes at the cat. You wanted to take it home." His jaw tics. "After I dealt with those assholes and lit the place up, she was there."

A shiver slides down my spine. Of course that café fire was him. A small part of me still flinches at the bloodshed, but the rest of me knows the violence is part of his reality.

"You saved her," I whisper.

"Figured you'd want the little menace alive," he says, his lips quirked in a half-smile. "She'd make you happy."

Our gazes hold, and for a moment, I'm transported to our teenage years when we talked about dreams of the future.

Something very different from the present.

Swallowing the lump in my throat, I motion to the chaos. "So what is this? The live version of 'The Twelve Days of Christmas'? A little too late, don't you think? It's January."

"A girl once said she wanted to see why anyone would give their true love all that stuff for Christmas." He chuckles.

My breath snags. I'd almost forgotten my offhand teenage rant.

But he hasn't.

"So you're saying you're my true love then?" Butterflies flap in my stomach.

"You tell me."

Those brilliant green eyes smolder, then he looks away, pours the batter into a pan, and slides it into the oven with his hip.

A man who cooks with confidence is so sexy.

"Christmas is your favorite holiday," he adds. "I missed too many of them with you. Figured I'd redo our first one together as adults to make it more memorable."

The ridiculous decorations blur for a second as my eyes sting.

He's been carrying a torch for me all these years.

When he turns back, he accidentally knocks his spatula to the ground. It slides under the counter.

"Let me get it." I get on my knees and reach for it.

"Damn. I need to drop more stuff on the ground." He whistles low, and my skin heats.

To drive the man nuts, I arch my back like a cat, presenting him my ass. A growl churns out of him.

I snag the spatula and hold it out to him, still on my knees.

For a moment, I think he'll crouch or kneel to take it.

But he doesn't.

Instead, his jaw tightens. His throat works, his gaze flicking from my hand to the floor, and pain crosses those emerald eyes.

Something snags in my mind.

For all the things he's revealed—the scars, the fire, the losses—there's one thing he's never told me.

And one thing he never does.

Chapter 43: HONEST TRUTHS

LANA

"WHY DON'T YOU KNEEL?" I ask when I get back up.

Twenty years ago, when I met Kian, he was kneeling in the rain. And now, from the FBI clip I saw, Elias Kent would rather die than kneel.

He's a conundrum, and I want to know everything about him.

The smile slips off his face. His jaw tightens, and he glances away.

Guilt eats at me. I shouldn't have asked. It's too much, too soon.

"I-I'm sorry. Special Agent Clarke showed me a video. You said you wouldn't kneel—ignore me, I don't know why I brought it up."

"No. I want to tell you," Elias says, intertwining my fingers with his. "The night they killed my parents and Beatrice, they made me kneel before them to beg for their lives."

He presses our palms together. "It didn't work. And from then on, I vowed never to kneel again. Not for anyone."

His voice roughens on the last word, his grip tightening around my fingers. Raw pain cuts through the calm of his eyes, a flicker that vanishes before he can hide it.

The scar, the not kneeling—grief and strength forged into a sharp blade for survival.

A lump thickens my throat. "Thank you for telling me."

He smiles softly and shrugs.

"It's not a proper Christmas without your favorite drink." He slides over a red mug.

I look inside—hot chocolate with marshmallows.

"Geraldine's," he murmurs. "A girl once told me hot chocolate is overrated unless it's Geraldine's."

My heart flutters as I take a small sip.

It's divine.

I look up, not sure how to express the warmth bursting from my chest.

He ruffles his hair and grins, the expression so similar to the carefree Kian, my heart twists.

"I never got to celebrate Christmas with you that year...you mentioned it in your note..." his voice trails off, his eyes distant. "And this year, well, with the Benefaction..."

And the bloodshed. Shkelzen's tongue. The Association and its threats.

"I just want to do this for you," he finishes. "Ridiculous, I know—"

I leap up onto the counter, throw my arms around his neck, and kiss away whatever demeaning words he wanted to say.

"It's perfect."

He holds me tight, then pulls away, love shining from his gaze. "Glad you like it."

"I can't believe you arranged a live version of 'The Twelve Days of Christmas'."

The geese make a mad dash toward the living room, clearly sensing their impending demise.

Elias scowls. "It was supposed to be an elegant display. I should've let Hannah help. Motherfucking Ren disappeared the moment he saw me sign for the deliveries."

I laugh, remembering Hannah's expression and imagining Ren rearing in horror.

"Why is Ren always here anyway? He's not just a bodyguard."

Elias steps over something I don't really want to identify, takes my hand, and leads me to the living room.

He sits me down and crouches in front of me.

"Ren and I are part of The Antihero Syndicate," he says, his eyes steady. "We aren't the mafia... We're worse."

He explains his clandestine brotherhood plus Sofia, whose sole mission is to destroy The Association, and how the dungeon I found him in actually connects to their meeting place in St. Michael's.

"So you all have different reasons for doing this?"

He nods. "We don't probe each other's secrets. Sebastian never told us his reason. Aleksei blames The Association for his family's death, like I do." He shakes his head, eyes haunted. "Even though he should blame me. I killed his parents. Rafe, I think, wants to save us, but I don't know why. Ren lost someone close. And Sofia..."

A ragged exhale escapes between his clenched teeth. "I lost her for two years after the fire. She never told me what they did to her, but..."

My breath lodges in my esophagus. I think of my half sister, Taylor, the strongest woman I know, who was raped when she was sixteen at a hotel lounge during an initiation ceremony she walked into.

I squeeze his forearm. "It wasn't your fault. If anything, it was me—"

"No," his eyes flash to mine, "never say that. That's what I tried and failed to tell myself for years. It's a lie."

Elias places his hand over my heart. "The most beautiful part of you is your kind heart. And they took advantage of it."

Voice urgent, he says, "Lana, don't blame yourself. Let me shoulder it all. Promise me."

A beat passes by, and I nod, my chest heavy.

"I promise."

He exhales and lets go. I immediately miss his touch. "There's a dinner we need to attend next week. The Berishas want to know you better."

"What for?"

"Gathering intel. Lording their power over me. Your guess is as good as mine. I revealed one too many cards at the Benefaction."

My gaze darts to his.

He told them how much I meant to him by avenging me.

A muscle twitches in his jaw, and he glances away. "You'll be thirty-five in a month and a half."

His words slam down like a butcher's knife.

"You know what they want from me, don't you?" I ask.

A flash of something—fear or awareness—crosses his eyes. He nods. "It doesn't matter. I'll protect you. They can't touch you. I'll get you out of this safely."

And then what? Send me home afterward? What if I don't want to go?

Elias cradles my face, and I lean into his touch. "Trust me, I will never let anything happen to you."

Another heavy beat sits between us. "I trust you."

And I realize—it's true. Even when he held me hostage at the vault, there was a gut feeling telling me this man was safe.

He smiles. "Lunch will be ready in half an hour. Don't know if you'll like it, but I think I'm good at this."

"Let me be good at this too."

Twenty years ago, a sweet boy gave me his coat because he thought I was cold. Twenty years later, a brutal man sheltered me from the cold in front of Hollow Gardens.

He's good at it—loving me.

"I already love it."

I wrap my arms around his waist, my fingers brushing his chest.

My eyes sting when I see the bullet wounds and knife scars on his muscles there too.

How much pain has he endured?

I kiss every mark.

He shudders, gripping my fingers tightly. Slowly, he presses a searing kiss on my hand and carries me to the kitchen counter.

We don't speak with words, but with our bodies.

A hiss escapes his lips when he unties my robe, realizing I'm bare underneath. His hands drift along my skin, eliciting shivers in their wake.

I whimper and arch back as he latches his mouth onto my neck, his fingers playing with my beaded nipples, sharpening my need with each tug.

"Insatiable," he rasps before bringing his lips to one peak. "I'm insatiable for you."

My craving sharpens as he laves the tip then suckles it, sending bursts of heat straight to my clit. I curl my legs around his back and grind my wet core against the ridges of his muscles.

With a groan, he presses his pulsing dick against my clit.

A wispy exhale escapes me. I move against him, my fingers finding the waist of his sweatpants, but my position prevents me from tugging them down.

"Elias," I whine. I need his hot cock inside me more than I need to breathe. I yank his pants again.

In a flash, he tears off his bottoms and steps out of them.

"You need this, my princess?" He powers his hips forward and singes my core with his hot shaft.

Wetness slicks out of me, lubricating his length with each thrust.

"Yes, yes, yes."

The sharp pulls of pleasure build. He slides his hand between our bodies and flicks my clit in rhythm with his hips.

"Please," I beg, clawing his muscular back.

"I'm going to shove myself so deep inside your pussy, you'll feel me every fucking minute."

He slams home, the sudden intrusion ripping a cry out of my throat.

"I'm addicted. Look at you taking me so well." His breath puffs against my neck as he quickens his pace.

My eyes flutter open, my mind hazed with lust.

Elias's gaze locks on my heaving breasts. A pulse batters against his temple. Slowly, he drags his attention up my body, to my lips, my nose, and finally, my eyes.

Dark craving reflects in those dilated pupils.

He growls at whatever he sees on my face and pistons harder, deeper.

My body shakes as pressure gathers in my core.

"See that, Lana?" he grunts. "See how your pussy sucks my cock in like it can't get enough? See how you were made for me?"

Another whimper slips out of me.

"You want my cum, don't you? Greedy wife. You want me to fill you up and put a baby inside you?"

Elias's eyes widen as if his words caught him by surprise.

My pussy tightens, and he hisses. "Fuck. You want that, don't you?"

His dirty words and the image of my belly swelling send me straight to the edge.

"Give it to me." I thrash in his hold. "Give me everything."

Wetness gushes out of me, my core fluttering. I dig my heels into his back.

"Fuck. Fuck. Fuck." He reaches up, collars my throat with one hand while his fingers work my swollen clit.

Every muscle coils tight, ready to detonate. A rolling pressure spreads from deep in my core to the rest of me.

The sounds of skin slapping against skin crackle in the kitchen.

My lungs cease to work.

"Come for me, Lana. Strangle my cock," Elias commands.

He latches onto my neck and bites.

"Elias!" The pain sets me off, and I explode.

Pleasure blinds my senses as waves of ecstasy wash over me.

A guttural groan tears out of him. His motions falter, and his breath hitches.

Seconds later, his cock floods me with his cum.

"Lana, yes," he rasps, and captures my parted lips with his mouth, swallowing my cries.

Bodies slick with sweat, we ride out our orgasms, our fingers intertwined.

Christmas songs play in the background. The sweet scent of chocolate cake baking in the oven fills the air.

And when he holds me tight against him, like he can't bear to be separated from me, all I can hear is the thunderous melody of his heart.

My heart.

My *zemër.*

I cling to that sound, pretending not to feel the tension coiled in his muscles, like there's still something he isn't telling me.

Chapter 44: SHATTERED ILLUSIONS

ELIAS

Agron Berisha

> We have another assignment for you. We need more influence with the Andersons. Remember to bring your precious wife to dinner tonight. Wouldn't want her brothers getting too comfortable.

MY FIST CLENCHES MY phone as I reread the asshole's message from last night.

It's getting more and more dangerous for Lana to stay in this world.

My office chair creaks as I swipe to my surveillance feeds, watching her make her daily pilgrimage to the third floor.

Normally, I'd watch her from my monitors inside the locked room, but not today.

Not after yesterday, when she saw my scars and still gave me her love.

Because it's time to tell her the whole truth.

She deserves to know.

The sickness in my soul. The obsession. The depths I'll go for my revenge over my family's deaths.

I bite my cheek, stopping myself from pressing the kill-switch button to wipe away the damning evidence in the room.

I'm tempted. So very tempted. One little press and I can keep on pretending.

I can make every day feel like Christmas for her. I can feed her chocolate cake I don't eat because I can't deal with the sweetness reminding me of that tragic day.

I can cradle her in my arms at night like we've been doing since she learned what happened to my family.

We'll read books in the library together, watch old movies in bed until we fall asleep. I'll make sweet love to her in the middle of the night and ignore the violence and bloodshed in my real life.

I can pretend this is forever, that the monster inside me is enough.

That she'll stay with me despite who I've become.

But no. Maybe she's right. Maybe there's still a flicker of Kian inside my ruined soul.

Because she deserves a choice.

If she leaves me after this, good. Because I'm not strong enough to leave her.

Cece nuzzles Lana's arm. My *zemër* buries her nose in the calico's fur.

My heart squeezes. Useless images of an alternate reality appear behind my eyelids. Me seeing my patients at a vet clinic. Lana playing with the animals, doing whatever her heart desires because that's all I need.

For her to be happy.

But that future belongs to Kian Leste.

Elias Kent doesn't wallow in the past or live with regrets, because I'm damn good at what I do now.

I swallow the growing lump in my throat and reach for a button hidden beneath the top drawer's false bottom.

I press it.

She freezes. She's surprised.

I draw a stiff inhale and look at the screen. As expected, she heard the click of the door unlocking.

The unbreakable mystery room where all the ugliness lies.

The scar on my cheek throbs. My rib cage tightens as I watch her set the cat down and creep forward, her hand pressed to her chest.

She grips the doorknob and hesitates, as if she knows she might not like what's hiding inside.

Open it, Lana. Find out who you really married.

Tucking a lock of hair behind her ear, she straightens. My pulse kicks at the fierceness in her eyes.

That's my girl.

Then she twists the knob and takes a step inside.

She gasps.

LANA

Cece meows and digs her claws into my foot, clearly unhappy I'm ignoring her.

But I can't help it.

Earth has lost its gravity, and I can't find my balance.

My gaze snaps to the security camera on the ceiling. The familiar red light winks at me.

He's watching.

I turn back to the room, but that's too little a word for what this apartment-sized space is.

Roses fill my vision everywhere I can see—dark reds, lush oranges, soft pinks—they grow on lattices built into the walls and in pots of all sizes spread throughout the area. Gold filigree wraps around the ceiling in the shape of a lone rose, and dark green ivy climbs up the walls, interspersed with birds of paradise and peonies, flowers I didn't even know could coexist.

It's an indoor garden.

My indoor garden, the dream I shared with him all those years ago.

I strain in a breath, my eyes already filling with tears as I stagger inside and survey this secret shrine he's been hiding from me, this emblem of our past.

There are large arched windows in the far corner, wrought-iron lattice grids stretching from floor to ceiling where a skylight sits. Under it rests a lavender chaise lounge and an antique coffee table matching the desk in my room, stacked with books.

I walk over and pick up the volume.

The Unending Love of Hades and Persephone.

Greek Myths and Romance.

They're all books about my favorite story—the goddess of spring who changed the king of darkness.

A shadow crosses the floor, and I look up, finding a thousand stars smiling at me from the night sky, a stray cloud moving aside for the moonlight.

"An indoor garden," I say. "Like a greenhouse filled with roses, more books, a comfortable chair, the best hot chocolate, and big windows I can watch the stars from."

Everything. He's done it all. The wish I let go of—but he never did.

My heart bangs against my ribs, aching to find the man behind it all.

Then I spot it.

A cordoned-off space to the far right—a wall of glass and a room so different from the rest of this paradise.

Monitors—a full wall of monitors.

My chest tightens as I move toward the dark side, recognizing the images on the screens—the dungeon, my New York City apartment, my bedroom here, the library, my office inside The Orchid.

The floor sways and I grip the doorframe. A corkboard tacked with paper scraps awaits me.

Love your smile. Thanks for the extra coffee.

A busy day for you. Here's an extra tip for your troubles.

Life is full of surprises. Today's storm may be tomorrow's rainbow. Hang in there. If you ever need help, call this number.

All receipts. All from me. He's amassed stacks of them—from my coffee runs in New York to my hastily scrawled notes to a chef in Paris.

I don't know how he got them, but as I flip through the stacks, I see the dates going back years before he joined my family in New York.

Years. He's been watching me for years.

A monitor flickers, drawing my attention, and a cursor hovers over a folder, like someone is accessing the monitor remotely.

The folder name: *Anderson Strategy*

Dread tightens like a noose around my neck when the folder opens.

Inside are dossiers on my siblings, their spouses, photos of me over the years—things I'm not even surprised to see, because Elias is the dealer of secrets. Of course he'd have information on us.

But then I see the emails. The timestamps. The annotations.

And notes from one particular day ten years ago.

> *Aim the knife at a forty-five degree angle to avoid major organs.*

Medical strategies on other survivable angles.

Then, his masculine scrawl underneath.

> *Twins—alley loop, twice a week. Bodyguards peel off at the entrance. Window: five minutes.*

There are observations of my brothers—their personalities, with Elias underlining Maxwell's name, musing the oldest brother will be the most likely to help him. Notes on how to convince Maxwell to trust him, on engineering opportunities to showcase his morals—stop a bad-faith deal, fake-rescue a sex worker on the Rose floors inside The Orchid.

Every "chance" to look like a savior. Every offhand favor meticulously planned.

Strategies upon strategies on how to infiltrate my family and become one of us.

The knife in his gut when my brothers found him in the alley the day they met?

Scripted. Blocked out frame by frame like a scene.

Birthdays, weddings, which brother has what weakness—Ethan with his bucket list for his wife, Rex with his penchant for coffee pills. No stone is left unturned.

Then there's me—photos of me, files on the men who've shown interest in the past, their pictures crossed off with black marker and hasty scrawls underneath.

Interested in her money.

Secretly has a girlfriend.

Abuser. Eliminated.

Hate the face of this fucker.

The words blur. I collapse into the nearest chair, my mind spinning with the revelations.

This isn't just revenge. This is carefully crafted obsession.

Years of my life mapped out like a strategy board. Every coincidence, every conversation, every action premeditated.

I've married a man who's sold his soul to the devil to get revenge and use my family as stepping stones.

He has been telling me the truth all along.

Kian *is* dead. He's been dead for years.

The boy who kneeled in the rain and offered me his chocolates never made it into The Orchid.

My lungs strain in staccato breaths. The walls close in. I cling to the armrest for dear life.

I can't think. I can't process it all.

And most of all, I don't understand why my heart thrums stronger, why a fire travels down the length of my body, igniting every single nerve.

Why the urge to find him—*not* to run away—is stronger than ever.

Click.

Click.

My pulse jolts at the familiar sound.

Then the alluring scent of vetiver, smoke, and mint.

Then chocolate. Rich, creamy chocolate I know is from Geraldine's.

I feel his heat first, then hear him setting something in front of me.

I open my eyes, finding a cup of piping hot chocolate, because that was also part of the dream I'd told him. A magical indoor garden and a cup of hot chocolate.

He remembered every single detail.

His breath ghosts my neck, close enough to touch, and yet, he doesn't.

"You know everything now. The worst of me," he murmurs. "Meet me in the foyer tonight for the Berisha dinner if you want to stay."

His heat presses closer—almost a brand.

"Or run while you still can. I won't stop you."

Cold crashes into me when he withdraws. Two paths. One choice.

Fear wins.

I spin around and dash out of the room.

Chapter 45: KNIFE'S EDGE

LANA

TRISTAN CLARKE SLIDES INTO the seat across from me at Arcana & Bloom. His gaze pinballs around the place as Scarlett sets a cup of tea in front of him.

He frowns. "I didn't order anything."

"It's on the house."

She eyes the fed in his black suit and tie and mouths, *Do you want me to stay?*

I shake my head, and she nods and walks away.

He takes a sip, his brow cocked high. "What's this?"

"It's magic."

Tristan huffs an amused breath. "You know, for a moment there I thought you'd ghosted me."

He motions to the hydrangeas cascading from the ceiling. "This is the world you belong in. Flowers. Beauty. Safe, cozy cafés. A life with Elias Kent will never end well. Men like him don't get happy endings."

A thousand pinpricks hit my chest. Visions of him lying in a pool of his own blood at the hands of his enemies curdle my veins. I grip the cup in front of me, trying not to let my nerves show.

After seeing Elias's secret room and realizing his scrupulous plotting, panic seized me.

What kind of mind scripts a stabbing, executes it without a flicker of guilt, and turns my entire life into a puppet show with him pulling every string? "Dark" doesn't begin to cover it. This is deranged.

A smart person would run. A sane one wouldn't crave this kind of attention.

But as I sit here in front of the FBI agent—the person on the right side of the law—I can't help feeling how wrong this is.

I didn't see Elias when I dashed out, and true to his word, he didn't stop me. Ren waved from a window on the second floor and held up his phone.

Ren

Good luck, Lana. It was a pleasure.

The guards stood aside, a car already idling at the curb to take me away.

No one expected me to stay.

I should be happy. I should be thrilled. This was what I wanted—to get out of the devil's grasp. To go back to New York City and be with my family.

I should be relieved.

A dark chuckle reaches my ears, and I look up, finding Tristan staring with pensive eyes. He scratches the scruff along his jaw and gives me a soft, sad smile.

"I'm probably shooting myself in the foot, but that look on your face—it's different from when I saw you last."

I bite my lip. I have things I could tell him now. I know what The Association is, who The Six are, and Elias's endgame. I've seen him kill someone. I could be a material witness.

But instead, the next words out of my mouth are, "Can you protect my husband? Or at least make him a deal?"

"What?" His tone sharpens.

"If there was a good reason—if he really was just trapped in a dangerous position—can you protect him? Or give him immunity if I help you?"

Silence. Tristan holds my gaze, clearly weighing the cost.

"You want The Association," I say. "That's why you contacted me. That's why you were watching me, right? Your target isn't Elias Kent."

He remains silent. It's an admission.

"I can tell you everything I know. But if I do, you make sure my husband stays safe."

"Even after everything you've seen?" he asks. "Don't bother lying—I'm good at reading people. The Lana Anderson I met that day wasn't aware. But the woman sitting here knows. You know what he's capable of, what laws he's broken. And after all this, you still want to protect him."

His words rattle inside my head.

And suddenly that tight, breathless feeling finally makes sense.

"You love him," Tristan murmurs.

I hitch a sharp breath.

"Excuse me." I shoot up, grabbing my purse.

Tristan looks at me with resignation.

"I'm sorry," I add.

I glance at the clock on the wall—quarter to six. The dinner with the Berishas starts at seven. Elias should already be getting ready.

I need to run.

"Think about it," I tell Tristan. "I'll help you nail The Six. My condition is immunity for Elias. That's the only thing I want. Him safe and alive."

Without waiting for his response, I dash out of the café with Scarlett hollering after me, "Already called you a cab—it's at the curb!"

"Thank you!"

I need to find him.

Despite everything, I can't leave him behind.

ELIAS

The clock chimes six times.

I pace the foyer, clicking my lighter. Behind me, soft footsteps reach my ears.

Ren signs, *"Why are you still waiting? You let her go."*

His words dig into my chest—like he's reached inside, fisted my heart, and given it a hard twist.

"She's innocent. She deserves a good life."

"Then why are you still here?"

I don't answer because we both know the truth.

Deep down there's a kernel of hope, a selfish desire, that Lana will choose me despite everything.

"Life is too short not to go after what you want. One day," he presses a hand against his chest, *"the ticker's going to give out. And when that happens...all you'll have are regrets."*

Ren clasps my shoulder, then motions toward the door. *"I'll get the car ready."*

He walks outside.

I stare at the music box she left behind—twelve petals of glittering gems. I wind it and let our song play.

Beethoven was deaf, and he defied the world's expectations and composed masterpiece after masterpiece, like this stunning melody, "Für Elise."

I was lucky twice in my life. First, as a boy who had one unforgettable year with the girl of his dreams. Second, as a murderer who could make her dreams come true, even if it was only for a few months.

An anvil presses down on my lungs.

I snap my lighter shut, slide it into my pocket, and head for the door.

But before I can reach for the handle, it swings wide open, slamming hard against the wall.

I freeze.

A gust of frigid air blows inside. But no cold can stop the sparks racing up my spine.

Because she's standing there.

Lana.

She's still in the same outfit she wore earlier—sweatpants, sweatshirt, hair in a messy bun, jacket half-zipped.

"Lana..." My voice catches.

She's never been more beautiful.

And she came back for me. Choosing me.

Again.

"Elias. Kian. Whatever you want me to call you," she says, breathless. "I can't leave. I know you want me to. I know I should. I know it's stupid for me to stay..."

Tears shine in her eyes. The sight makes me want to rip my heart out and offer it to her as proof of my devotion.

"But I can't leave you," she whispers. "I love you, Elias. I don't think I've ever loved anyone else."

Ragged breaths rip from my lungs. My fingers tremble around my lighter, but I can't move.

I'm afraid that if I blink, she'll disappear.

"Please don't come back if you're going to walk away again," I rasp, my voice thick.

She shakes her head, her face crumbling.

Then she hurls herself at me.

I catch her and hold her tight, drowning myself in her scent and warmth.

Slowly, I brush the hair from her face. "You came back for me."

She nods, a tear-streaked smile breaking through. "Whatever it is—The Association, revenge—I'm staying. I'll be here every step of the way. Because you're my husband."

Her words echo through me. They're alive and magical. They're light—chasing away every shadow.

"My wife," I whisper. "I love you."

Then I kiss her, even as the wind howls an ominous wail outside.

Chapter 46: THE BLITZ

LANA

HIS EYES NEVER LEAVE mine during the car ride.

"Stop it." Warmth rushes to my face. I pick at the hem of the black dress I threw on.

"Never." Elias peels off his gloves and tosses them onto the seat. He laces our fingers together, thumb grazing the simple diamond wedding band.

"What are you staring at?" I try to tug free, but he growls.

"Missing a rock. A big one."

"I don't need a fancy engagement ring. I'm already married to you."

"But I do. In fact," in one swift motion, he hoists me onto his lap, "I think you should wear rings on all your fingers. So the bastards know you're taken."

His words trigger a memory—the dossiers of the men I'd dated, the ones who vanished into the ether.

"You chased them away!"

"Who?" He shrugs nonchalantly, a smug smirk on his face.

"You bastard. I thought there was something wrong with me! It gave me a freakin' complex."

"There's nothing wrong with you. You're perfect."

"I know that," I shove him and he chuckles, his green eyes warm and vibrant, "but you made me doubt myself, and for that you have to suffer!"

I straddle his thighs and dive in, fingers going for the kill.

"Shit." He laughs and squirms, full-body tremors racking his body. "This is your big revenge?"

I dig under his arms, and he lets out a very un-mobster-like squeak.

"Oh my God, the deadly dealer of secrets is ticklish!" I squeal. "You are so screwed."

Someone snorts.

"Ren, shut up." Elias bats my arms away, pinning them behind my back.

Ren shakes his head, and seconds later, the partition rises with a soft hum, giving us privacy.

Elias's breaths puff against my face, a lock of hair falling over his forehead. The air sizzles between us, and it's then I notice the hard bulge under me, which grows with each second.

Awareness thrums through my blood, my skin sensitized, breasts heavy. I gnaw my lip and his eyes snap to the motion, pupils flaring.

He slides his hands over my backside, digging his fingers into the tender flesh.

"You drive me crazy," he groans, nose dipping to my neck.

"Elias." His name escapes in a whisper as I arch to his heated kisses.

"Utterly, fucking crazy. Losing my mind." Soft suctions, hard nips, then gentle licks. "You barrel past all defenses, smash them like they're made of air."

My hips move on instinct, my mind melting in a haze. Wetness seeps out of me as I grind my pussy over his hard cock through the fabric.

"Fuck." Masculine grunts rip from his throat. He bobs me up and down his length. "I want to fill you up so you'll drip with every step you take."

I gasp. My core clenches.

"Shit. You like that. My dirty wife." He bites my ear. "And then I'm going to do it again tonight. I'll make you keep your legs up after, so none of my cum leaks out of this perfect cunt."

Elias's cock hardens even more as he thrusts against my pussy. I moan and claw at him.

"Elias." I whimper when he bites my nipple through my dress.

"Then I'll do it again. And again. And again. Breed you until I get a baby inside you."

His words push me to the edge, every cell inside me primed to detonate.

"Yes, yes, yes." I throw my head back and cling to him as my muscles tense.

"You want a baby right, Lana?"

The sudden seriousness of his tone forces my gaze back to him. There's a hint of vulnerability within the lust.

I've always loved children. Always wanted some of my own. And now, I can only see little dark-haired kids with green eyes running around.

"Yes, Elias." Tears prickle my eyes. "I want them. I want everything with you."

Eyes flaring, he grips me tighter with one hand, his other hand snaking between my dress and dipping into my panties.

"Soaked," he growls. "If we weren't minutes away from—"

Glass explodes. Blinding white light flashes from the side. Tires screech along pavement.

Bullets pelt the car, shattering windows. I scream.

Elias plows into me, pinning me to the seat.

"Down!" Ren shouts. "Incoming SUV. Shit!"

The car swerves. I'm thrown off the seat, but Elias catches me in time.

"Stay down, Lana. I got you," he rasps. "Whatever you do, don't get up."

Fear crashes into me as he cocks his gun and bolts upright.

Eyes crazed with fury, he fires off round after round out the window.

Something explodes outside. Safety glass powders my hair. I cover my ears, a high ringing sound needles my skull.

Burned rubber fills my nose. The car swerves again.

Elias swaps mags without looking, slams it home, and fires again.

I squeeze my eyes shut, afraid to look. This is what I signed up for. But it's one thing to know and another thing to go through it.

"Go, go, go!" He drops, covering me with his body again.

I clutch him tightly, unable to speak.

Ren maneuvers the car, tires screeching as we speed off.

My heart thunders, the gunshots still ringing in my skull. The car jolts, then silence, except for our ragged breathing.

"You're safe." He gathers me up, his hand brushing down my back. "Shhh, Lana. I'm here. You're safe. Nothing will ever happen to you."

The rest of the ride home was filled with tension. Elias held me against his lap while he spoke on the phone—calls to the Berishas and to others in The Syndicate.

I fell into an uneasy sleep.

When I woke up, he was carrying me up the stairs toward the bathroom.

And now, he sets me down and turns on the shower.

"Elias? What are you—"

"Shhh," he murmurs. "Let me take care of you. You're safe. Always safe."

He smooths a hand down my back when steam fogs up the room.

Only then do I realize I'm trembling.

Quietly, he undresses us and carries me into the shower, where he washes my hair with my shampoo and conditioner. Then he applies bodywash and massages my tense muscles while the hot water rinses away the bubbles.

I slowly relax. In this small space, with the sweet roses of my products perfuming the air, I feel like I'm in another world. Away from danger. Away from gunshots and deaths.

I'm with the only man I've ever loved.

Closing my eyes, I release a heavy exhale.

It's then I realize Elias has stopped moving.

Heavy breathing reaches my ears as he stills behind me, the weight of his head on my back, like he's leaning on me.

"Elias?"

I turn around.

He's dipped down, arms bracketing me against the shower wall, water sluicing over his dark hair and powerful muscles.

I tip his face up.

Reddened eyes meet mine.

"What if I can't protect you?" His voice is hoarse, full of anguish. "What if, by keeping you with me, I'm sentencing you to death?"

My eyes fill with tears, and I shake my head.

"You can't think that way."

"Yes, I can!" He slams his palm on the glass behind me. "You were safe in New York with your family. You had a good life. I took that away from you."

"Because The Association forced your hand! They would've never left me alone." I cup his cheek, grazing his stubble. "Don't you see? I'd be in danger either way. But with you, I got a shot at safety."

His throat works, but he doesn't reply.

"Because I know you, Elias. You'd protect me." Slowly getting on my tiptoes, I curl my hands around his neck and kiss him. "I trust you with my life."

With an anguished groan, he clasps my face and deepens our kiss.

Our teeth duel, our tongues clash. He drinks me in like I'm the only sustenance he needs to survive. My heart pounds as he hoists me onto the bench and spreads my legs wide.

He drags his lips over my eyes, my nose, my mouth. Then to my ears and my neck.

"I worship you." He presses his mouth over my heart.

"I adore you." He suckles my nipple before nibbling it.

Wetness slicks out of me and I pull in a strangled gasp as he continues moving down my body.

"I love every fucking part of you." He presses that talented tongue on my pussy and swipes it from my hole to my clit before inserting two fingers into my tightness.

"Elias," I moan, my hips already moving to the rhythm of his thrust.

He grunts and when I open my eyes, I see him gripping his thick, dripping cock, pumping it up and down.

An orgasm barrels in from nowhere, but before it can crest, he hauls me up and slams me onto his cock in one thrust.

"Fuck, I'm coming," I cry when the pleasure detonates into ecstasy. My eyes close as I surrender myself to the intense shockwaves.

"Yes. Let me feel you milking my cock." Slamming me against the wall, he pistons harder, wilder, his movements holding no finesse but all passion. "Become part of me, Lana. Let me be a part of you."

Then his dick thickens and throbs, bursts of cum pumping out of him as he roars my name.

The sounds of our lovemaking echo in the shower. My heart and body feel full to the brim.

I cling onto him as his movements slow, our rough, panting exhales joining the water pelting against the glass and marble.

"I'll protect you if it's the last thing I do," he says.

My eyes flutter open, my gaze finally meeting his emerald ones, and my breath catches in my throat.

Because aside from the love I see in his eyes, I also see...

Fear.

Chapter 47: THIEF OF FUTURES

LANA

FEBRUARY TWENTY-EIGHTH.

I'm locked down tighter than Fort Knox on my thirty-fifth birthday. Other than a basket of cookies from my Aria and Scarlett, who were understandably freaked out when security patted them down at the door, I haven't gone out or received visitors.

I did get on a call with my girlfriends and sisters in New York, where they updated me on things at Fleur, how their new head of PR wasn't nearly as good at her job as me. They mentioned flying here to visit and to help Rex, who begrudgingly stepped in to do some PR work, including the press junket with Chicago Memorial.

I told them I wasn't in the city most of the time, but I'd booked a flight back to New York in the summer after my exotic trip to Antarctica.

Frankly, I think my cover was blown a long time ago, but Maxwell and Rex must've said something because the girls didn't push me on it.

And then there's the motley crew downstairs.

Sofia, Elias's steel-spined sister, dressed in all black, picked at her red-manicured nails while watching the news.

Aleksei, buzz-cut and wild-grinned, promised me he had me covered with his mad hacking skills.

Another suit in a silver mask, Sebastian, known as the psychopath, sat at the dining table, aloof and cold, but there was a flicker of interest when I caught him staring earlier.

Ren said I should ignore him.

Even the priest who married us joined a video call with Elias. Rafe—that's his name.

Elias's family. The Antihero Syndicate.

After the attempt on our lives a little over a month ago, Elias spent most of his time in the house with me. He tried to distract me with romantic overtures like candlelight dinners in the backyard with him as the chef, or looking at the stars in my indoor garden until I fall asleep. There was sex, lots of mind-blowing sex, and exotic chocolates imported from all over the world.

He assured me we were safe inside his fortress, that I had nothing to worry about. But based on the hushed calls in his office—one time I even heard him yelling at the Berishas—the danger was far from over.

Worst yet, I don't think he knows who's behind it.

Now, Maxwell and Rex stare at me through the computer screen as I hold up a folded sheet of paper.

Mom's letter—a photocopy Elias made before he gave the original to the Berishas.

"No more secrets," he murmured this morning in bed. "Happy birthday, my Elise."

I pull in a deep breath, my fingers shaking.

"You don't need to read it," Maxwell says. "It doesn't matter what's inside. Your safety's most important."

"But fuck it. That's why she needs to read it," Rex mutters. "Don't you want to know what Mom's hiding and why those freaks want her?"

Part of me is afraid to find out—afraid it'll ruin the image of Mom I have in my head.

After all, she has something The Association desperately wants, and no one involved with them is ever good.

"No. I'm not running from the truth."

Mind made up, I unfold the paper, the brittle page crinkling under my fingers.

My Dearest Lana,

My darling daughter, happy thirty-fifth birthday.

I hope you never have to read this letter. Because if you do, it means I'm no longer there, and that breaks my heart because I love you so much.

But know this: I'm watching over you from above, and you and your brothers are my pride and joy.

I have no regrets other than not being there by your side.

Tears blur the looping script. My fingers trace her words.

Sometime today, you'll get a delivery, and it's important you don't tell anyone about it.

As you probably know by now, the world is a dark place. Those with old money and power will do anything to keep themselves on top.

I expect you know about The Association. I'm sure they haven't left our family alone.

> You see, the original intent when your grandfather and his friends started it wasn't to take over the world.

I gasp, my hand flying to my chest.

The *original* sixth family. That was us?

"What?" Rex asks. "What is it, Lana?"

I hold up a finger and keep reading.

> It was a beautiful vision—combining our wealth to make the world a better place. No more wars, no more starvation, pooling our funds for medical research.

> But your grandfather told me things went horribly wrong. An argument broke out among friends, and one of them was killed.

> Your grandfather was a witness. He had photos, letters, and incriminating evidence showing it was all premeditated.

> Five families against one.

> He withdrew, disappeared from the spotlight, but he kept the evidence.

Just in case. Insurance to protect us.

It was his biggest regret not stopping The Association before they grew too powerful. When I turned thirty-five, he entrusted that evidence to me.

Leverage to ensure our family remains safe.

And with regret, I do the same to you. Your brothers will be in the spotlight—they always underestimate the women in our world. My hope is you'll never have to use this evidence, only to keep it in your back pocket should our family be threatened.

I'm sorry I can't explain more. I'm sure it's shocking and terrifying.

But my Lana, from your first cry, your little fists punching the air, I knew you were the strongest of my children. You can bear the burden.

I love you forever and ever.

Mom

My mind reels. My eyes unfocused, I flip the letter to the camera so my brothers can read Mom's words.

I've always wondered why The Association stopped short of killing us when my brothers defied them in the past. It isn't their MO to let their opponents live.

And now I know why.

"Fuck," Rex mutters.

"That's it. We're pulling you out. I'm sending a security team for extraction," Maxwell says, already typing. "You're a sitting duck. They'll never let you live after they get the evidence. Them not getting it—or you—is our only shot."

"I'll call the others in," Rex adds, eyes flashing. "Can't keep them in the dark anymore." He fishes out his phone—

"No!" I shoot to my feet. The stool crashes to the floor with a loud thud.

"Lana!" Elias bursts through the door, eyes wild, gun drawn, Ren fast at his heels.

"I'm fine." I close my eyes and blow out an exhale.

His cologne wraps around me, followed by his heat at my back.

I sink into his embrace as his arms circle my waist and he presses a kiss on my hair.

When I glance back at the screen, Maxwell and Rex are frozen, staring in obvious shock.

"I'm staying," I say, my vision blurring. "I'm not leaving my husband."

Maxwell's mouth drops open. If it were any other situation, I'd laugh at my straitlaced brother rendered speechless.

"I love him," I whisper.

Elias tightens his arms and murmurs, "My *zemër*."

He tells my brothers, "I'll die before I let anything happen to Lana."

Silence.

My brothers cock their heads in near-identical expressions. I can see them working through various scenarios to arrive at how Elias won me over.

Because the man we knew for so long would never betray us, despite what happened at the vault.

Then Rex whistles and throws his head back, laughing. "Elias motherfucking Kent. I should've known. You love my sister. All that forced-marriage crap and the damn heist were bullshit. I knew it."

"I survived," Maxwell says quietly, understanding clear in his eyes. "Wouldn't have if you didn't want me to."

Elias freezes behind me. Then, a small nod.

Air rushes out of my lungs. The truth I suspected all along lands heavy, but merciful.

Elias was never our enemy.

"I'm sorry," he rasps.

Maxwell waves him off. "All I care about is what we're going to do about the situation."

"We need to lure them out." Elias straightens. "Get the evidence before they claim it."

"How do we do that?" I ask as he faces me.

He cups my face, gaze soft, thumb trailing my cheek. "A decoy."

Chapter 48: THE SURPRISE

ELIAS

LANA'S PACING AROUND THE living room when I descend the stairs.

"Sit down," Sofia exclaims. "You're making me dizzy."

"Easy for you to say," Lana mutters. "You're not the one with the target on your back."

"Maybe I've been through worse," Sofia replies quietly. Something haunted flickers in her eyes.

She flashes Lana a small, sad smile. "I've learned that in life-and-death situations, don't show fear. Don't let them get to you."

She taps her temple. "If you're strong here, you'll survive anything. Trust me."

"Boom." Aleksei whistles under his breath as he strides in. "Security cameras are all clean. No bugs. Nothing unusual."

"So we just wait?" Lana asks, pacing again, then freezes, gaze darting to Sofia. She sighs and sits. Cece jumps into her arms and purrs as if to comfort her. "Right. Mind games."

"Elias is right." Sebastian removes his mask and stares at his laptop. "Going on the offensive. That's the only logical choice."

Ren signs something, then looks at Lana and Sebastian. He rolls his eyes, clearly exasperated, and pulls out his phone.

Ren

> Plan's solid. I've got your back, Lana. Now if it were Sebastian you were relying on, I'd be worried.

"Asshole," Sebastian mutters, snapping his laptop shut. "I'm an excellent shot."

Ren smirks.

Ren

> But you have to care about the person you're protecting. You don't care about shit.

"Hm." Sebastian smirks and shrugs. "True."

My silent bodyguard winces and rubs his chest. Sebastian's eyes narrow at the motion.

I frown.

Ren catches me staring.

"Heartburn," Ren signs. *"Ignore me."*

"So when do we think something will happen?" Lana asks and gnaws her lip.

This is the wait and see part I hate.

We don't know when the package will come, only that it's meant for her.

If Lana receives it, we'll swap it before anyone else lays eyes on it. If it's a message, we'll intercept it before The Association does.

The decoy plan has to come after the swap. Since The Association knows the delivery will go to Lana, all eyes will be on her. They may trail her. They may steal the package.

So, we give them a target. Lana will go with Ren to the Navy Pier crowds while Sofia tails them. Aleksei monitors the feeds. Sebastian stays with me to hide the package and disappear the evidence.

The doorbell rings. I'm halfway down the stairs before the others move.

Lana bolts up, eyes wide.

"Stay here," I tell her.

Ren steps in front of her, gun at his side. Sebastian disappears down the hallway. Sofia's nowhere to be seen—but knowing her, she's nearby, ready to strike. Aleksei pulls on his LED mask, checks the feed, mouths *Caruso*, and slips away.

I flick off the safety of my gun and open the door.

Gabriel Caruso stands there in a perfectly tailored navy suit, holding a bouquet of pink peonies and a bottle of champagne like he's auditioning for a dating show. Behind him, the Scheduler hovers. He adjusts his horn-rimmed glasses and narrows his eyes at me.

"What are you doing here?" My hand drifts to my waist.

Gabriel's gaze flickers to the motion. Then he grins, charming and lethal all at once.

"Not very polite, Elias. It's a special day for your wife, isn't it?" He raises his gifts. "Thought we'd drop by and extend our...warmest wishes."

"Warm wishes from the Carusos? We're honored." My tone is flat.

"Invite us in, won't you?"

I pause, measuring him. The Carusos are calm and low profile. They won't risk a massacre in broad daylight. But it's odd they're visiting today, of all days.

He lifts his hands in mock surrender. "Friend, not foe. And you'll want to hear what I have to say."

"Perhaps we shouldn't be too nice to him," the Scheduler mutters.

"Not your place, Dominic." Gabriel's voice carries a steel edge. The men shift on their feet, hostility threading the air.

"My place is with your father always," Dominic says mildly, twirling an antique pen between his fingers.

Interesting.

"Fine. Come in."

Once inside, Dominic closes the door. Gabriel tosses him his coat. The Scheduler catches it and dips his head.

He's careful, deferential—too deferential—a man playing a part.

"Where's your wife?" Gabriel asks as I lead them down the hall.

"None of your business."

We settle into my office. The tension ratchets up, a powder keg waiting to explode.

I rest my hands on the desk. "If you have something to say, say it. My patience is short today."

Gabriel smiles faintly and nods at Dominic. The Scheduler moves forward, lighting a cigar for him. Smoke curls between us.

"My father sends his regards," Gabriel says. "And we have a problem. I'd like you to deal with it."

"What problem?"

"The Berishas," he replies. "Particularly Agron. Unstable oldest son. Too much bloodshed. Bad for business. And they're greedy." He swirls his hand. "Case in point. Why do you think they're after the evidence?"

Ah. I flick my lighter, understanding dawning. *An internal feud for power.*

"How does this concern me?"

"You're a dealer of secrets, Elias. When your wife receives her little delivery tonight, I want you to hand it to us, not them."

I study him. "And if I don't?"

His smile fades. "Then we find out who breaks first—you or her. Personally, I prefer to keep things civilized. I quite like Lana."

My fingers curl around the lighter. It's either that or strangle him.

Dominic steps forward, holding out a folder. "For you."

Inside are surveillance photos. New York City. A familiar SUV with Illinois plates. The same one that tailed Lana a few months ago.

My stomach drops. "It was you?"

I thought it was the damn Berishas. Not knowing this info could've killed her. Unacceptable oversight.

Gabriel chuckles. "You always think too small. The Berishas were useful once. They have clubs, hotels, and land. Real estate comes in handy when you want to move things around the globe. But their time is ending. The Andersons have what they have, but better. But that damn family is stubborn as fuck."

He leans forward, brow cocked. "They needed a good reason to join us. An inside force. You needed a little push to join The Association. I gave you that push. You're smart enough to know which family is winning this war. Join ours, and your past crimes disappear."

Check. Fucking. Mate.

If I didn't hate him so much, I'd applaud. It's not every day that I meet a worthy opponent.

His gaze grows cold. "Or find out what happens when you cross my family. Or better yet, what *will* happen to your wife."

"Touch. Her. And. Die." My jaw tics.

"A man like you should know better than to wear his heart on his sleeve."

Dominic interrupts, "You'll want to think about it, Mr. Kent. My employer's offer doesn't stay open long. Gabriel here," he smirks, "is the nice one in the family. He's offering you the best deal."

"Shut up. Not your turn to speak," Gabriel snaps. "You're our public timekeeper. But this deal is between us and Kent."

Dominic flinches, resentment flashing in his eyes. But the emotions snuff out when he bows and steps back.

Gabriel stands. "Dominic will give you my father's number. He looks forward to our partnership."

The Scheduler takes out his antique pen, scribbles on a slip of paper, then hands it to me.

I pocket the note and watch them leave.

The moment the door closes, the air decompresses.

They're playing a different game, and I don't know the rules yet. I really hate being in the dark.

The clock chimes eight. The house is silent as I sit in my chair, staring at the paper, pondering my next steps.

Suddenly, Lana bursts in, breathless, holding up her phone. "I got a message!"

"I'm on it." Aleksei barrels in from the hall, already typing on his laptop.

I take the phone from her. An anonymous email.

> `For the birthday girl: your present is located at Safe Way Storage. Locker 35. Retrieve it within the hour.`

Below it is a string of numbers—a code.

Aleksei frowns. "IP's bouncing across multiple dark-web nodes. This person's good. Probably spoofed credentials. Could take a while to trace."

"What do we do?" Sofia asks from the doorway.

Sebastian sidles up behind her. "The decoy plan. Nothing changes. It's the logical move."

"But the Carusos," Sofia says. "Won't they follow us?"

"Let me worry about them." I brush past Lana, kiss her, and whisper, "Stick to the plan. Stay safe."

Sebastian and I peel out of the mansion, heading straight for the storage facility thirty minutes away. Whoever this messenger is knows us all too well. The package isn't delivered to New York City but right at our doorstep.

Someone's mapping our every move.

"We got this," Sebastian murmurs, steering toward our destination.

Click. Click.

My fingers twirl the lighter. I flip it open. The flames burst in a staccato rhythm.

Lana and Ren should be en route to the Navy Pier now, with Sofia shadowing them. Large crowds should keep them safe.

Minutes later, Sebastian parks a block from the facility.

Safe Way Storage is dilapidated, with a lone fluorescent bulb flickering above the entrance.

It's go time.

Our breaths flee in plumes of white as we pull on our masks in case there are cameras.

Locker 35 sits in a half-empty corridor. Shadows loom tall on the walls. The air reeks of cold metal and oil. We approach with guns drawn, cameras neutralized by Aleksei's jammer.

"I'm on your six," Sebastian says.

I punch in the code from the email and yank open the locker. An ordinary paper box sits inside.

Too ordinary.

Carefully, I scan it with another of Aleksei's gadgets. No explosives, no red flags.

I tear off the lid.

Inside lies a single scrap of paper:

> One step too late again, Kian. Better luck next time. This gift I'll keep. Tell your wife happy birthday. If you want answers, meet me on parking level five, Structure B, Chicago Memorial. Ten p.m. tonight. No entourage. No funny business.

Fury tears through me. I crumple the note and slam my fist into the locker.

The package. The evidence. Our only leverage against The Association and the reason Lana is a bargaining chip instead of a loose end—it's gone. Stolen right under our noses.

The phantom from the Benefaction.

"Fuck!"

My phone buzzes. The name flashing across the screen makes my blood freeze.

He *never* calls.

"Ren, what's going on?"

Gunshots ring through the receiver. A woman shrieks.

Lana.

My heart stops. I'm already sprinting toward the exit.

"What the hell's happening? Lana, is she okay?"

"Fuck. Decoy worked. Another SUV," he rasps, his voice rough with disuse. "I just lost them. Be careful."

He hangs up.

My mind runs through the long list of suspects, my blood freezing in my veins.

Anyone could be after her. Ren's kept her safe both times. But what if our luck runs out?

Without the package, nothing's tying their hands anymore. Nothing's stopping The Association from hurting her.

What if I can't protect her?

Chapter 49: REALITY CHECK

LANA

"HERE. DRINK THIS. CALMS the nerves." Scarlett shoves a cup into my face as we huddle inside my bedroom after I almost got killed.

Again.

The gunfire still rings through my skull, the stench of charred tires burning my nose.

"What happened?" Aria rubs my back. "Breathe through your nose, out your mouth. Good. Repeat. This is what I have my trauma patients do."

Elias freaked them out half an hour ago when Aria was helping Scarlett restock the shelves at the café. He yanked the girls and deposited them here after he saw me shaking, curled up into a ball in the armchair.

His eyes were murderous, his lips peeled in a snarl, and he dashed out, saying he was going to stop it all.

"G-God, I'm so s-sorry for dragging you guys into this. You should go home. It's late."

I sip the tea, and heat slowly spreads through my body, warming my icy hands.

"Shut up. Ride or die," Aria mutters. "I don't give up on patients, and I sure as hell won't give up on you."

"You're safe now." Scarlett breathes with me. "Talking about it might help."

I nod and focus on her voice, my pulse thankfully slowing. I need to get my shit together. Panic won't save anyone. Elias brought the girls over to give me support. I trust them.

"Have you guys heard of The Association?" I ask.

Scarlett and Aria exchange glances.

Scarlett leans in and whispers, "They're hush hush but everyone in Saints Hollow has heard of them. Aria came across a few of their victims in the ER. Some mysterious organization that controls the gangs, right?"

I nod and give them a filtered-down version of what I know and don't know—namely, who's after us.

"On the way to the Navy Pier, Ren got a flat tire. Strange, because he was zealous about safety. We pulled off the freeway, and they ambushed us."

I shudder. Snippets slam into my mind again. Headlights barreling straight at us. Gunshots raining on our car. Sofia ramming her truck into their side. The screeching of metal and the white noise.

"And you guys have no idea who's behind this? It's not The Association?" Scarlett asks.

"Who *doesn't* want to kill Elias?" I whisper, my fingers trembling around the cup.

He's the dealer of secrets. This isn't the first time he's been threatened. But it's obvious from the two ambushes that with me in the crosshairs, I'm a liability to him.

He gave no one leverage before.

I'm his only weakness.

"More, please." I hand the cup to Scarlett. If I didn't need my wits about me, I'd ask for a bottle of whiskey instead.

She quickly pours more of her concoction from the teapot. "What are you going to do next?"

A rope binds around my chest, tightening as my pulse ratchets up again.

There's fear for sure—I've never had so many brushes with death before.

No PR strategies or self-defense courses ever prepared me for this.

I could leave. Elias asked me to leave when I found the secret room because he knew I wasn't born for this world. He knew it'd be safer for me to be away from him.

But is it?

When Elias told me the phantom had stolen the package, my heart dropped to the floor. That evidence was what we were banking on. It was why I was still breathing, still safe from The Association. Without it, I'm no longer useful. I'm a liability and a loose end.

Sure, Maxwell's probably negotiating with the Berishas to let me go.

But I know too much, and my brothers abide by The Association because of me. Our family will turn our backs on The Association the moment I escape.

Will a wolf ever release its prey? This isn't just the Berishas anymore. It's all of them. The whole rotten food chain.

And can I live without *him*—the dangerous man with a riveting scar, who makes my heart flutter, who has secretly loved me all these years?

"I promised him I'd stay," I whisper more to myself than to the girls.

I chose him in the dungeon. I chose him again after unlocking the secret room. But this time, it's different. This time, I've felt what he's trying to protect me from—what it's like to be this close to dying.

Yes, I'm terrified, but fear doesn't change my decision.

Mom's words flit through my mind. She said I was the strongest, the one capable of carrying the burden. Maybe this is what she meant.

"But...you could die," Scarlett says. "Is that worth it?"

Blowing out a breath, I look up, finding twin concerned expressions. They each take my hand and I squeeze them back, grateful for them.

Images crowd in—the elm tree with our carving, the music box, Elias reading, stargazing with me.

He's protected me all these years, even when he thought he hated me.

Even when he knew I had a role in his family's deaths.

It's time I do my part.

"Some melodies," I whisper, "you only need to listen once to remember forever."

"Oh, Lana." Aria squeals and hugs me tight. "So romantic."

"Just have Blake say that stuff to you. I, on the other hand, have no one," Scarlett mutters, a grin tugging her lips when she joins the group hug.

I laugh, a weight lifting off my chest.

Determination surges through me, sparring with the leftover jitters until strength wins.

After pulling back, I grip the pendant over my chest and take out my phone.

I'm not completely helpless.
I have one more card left to play.

Lana

Are you ready for a deal? Because if you are, I want to talk.

Tristan's response comes minutes later.

Geraldine's Chocolates

Paperwork's finalized. Immunity provided no additional capital offense. The best I could do. Let's meet.

I stare at the screen, my heart thrumming.
Maybe I can save Elias this time.

Chapter 50: THE MASK'S LAST GIFT

ELIAS

"SHE'S GOING TO BE fine," Sofia murmurs from the passenger seat. "Lana is tough. Anderson genes. Stubborn as hell."

I nod, knuckles white on the steering wheel as I speed toward Chicago Memorial for my meeting with the masked phantom.

Time to put an end to this cloak and dagger shit.

A text flashes across the console.

Knight Ren

> Set up on the rooftop of Structure A. Clear view. No sightings.

Bishop Seb

> Called in a favor. Note had no prints. Not that I'd expect any.

"Shit."

I swerve around a semi and gun the gas.

Five minutes to ten. I would've left earlier to scope out the place, but I had to check on Lana first.

Seeing her petrified with a vacant look in her eyes damn near killed me. She should be wrapped up in blankets, a book on her lap, laughing with friends and family.

Not hunted. *Never* hunted.

"Stop it. You're overthinking."

I snap my gaze at Sofia.

Arching her brow, she smirks. "You have micro-tells. You do this thing with your nose—never mind."

"She was fine before she married me."

"She'd be dead if she didn't marry you. Or worse. It's fate or cosmic irony. You protected her the best you could."

The exit looms ahead. I speed down the off-ramp. I'm getting my damn answers tonight.

"But I'm glad to see you like this…" Sofia's voice trails off.

"Like what?"

"Warm. Caring. *Human*," she replies, her voice bittersweet. She pulls out her gun. "I thought it'd be too late—revenge took too much from you, from us. But I'm glad I was wrong."

The hospital glows like an ember of hope in the inky darkness. But my attention is snared by the twin buildings looming like sentries beside it.

The parking structures.

"Grab your second chance," Sofia says when we swerve inside. "Lana knows what she's doing, and she chose you. Don't waste it."

My chest constricts. I drop her off on level four. Ren holds Structure A, a sniper rifle at the ready. Sofia will find a place in this building to cover me.

"Stay safe, tiger."

"Right back at you." Sofia winks and melts into the shadows.

My breaths are thready as I roll up the ramp to the fifth floor. It's mostly empty at this hour, with only a handful of cars left.

Nowhere to hide. No soul in sight.

Easing my car into a corner space, I wait, my gun loaded and ready at my side.

Fluorescent lights stutter. Fog creeps up the windshield.

Nine fifty-seven p.m. Three more minutes.

Sweat beads on my neck. I pull out my lighter and flick it. Once. Twice. Three times, watching the flames writhe.

Much like the flames on the night my parents and Beatrice died.

My eternal disease—obsession—flares, always focusing on things I should let go of for everyone's sake.

Fire. Revenge.

Lana.

The air shifts—a loud crackle and a pop. The garage plunges into darkness.

Someone slides into the backseat. I grab my gun.

"I wouldn't do that if I were you," a distorted voice warns.

Light returns. I glance in the rearview mirror.

A man sprawls across the backseat, gun aimed at me, hood over his head, facial features not visible.

He's fast and efficient. A skilled adversary.

"What do you want? Why all the theatrics?"

My voice is calm. Never show fear.

"Let's just say I'm a friend."

"A friend wouldn't steal from me."

He chuckles. "Not a friend then. An ally."

The air stills as if the world's stopped spinning. He's giving nothing away—no tells, no behavioral quirks.

"Well then, *ally,*" I say, "you stole the kill ledger at the Benefaction. You took my wife's package. You got me here. So talk. Stop wasting my time. What. Do. You. Want?"

I sense his smile even though I can't see it.

"A favor for a favor. That's your brand, isn't it, Elias? Or should I say, Kian Leste?"

My jaw twitches, but I keep my composure. Mind games.

"I don't do favors for strangers."

"We've established I'm an ally."

"Then give me something. A sign of good faith. Then we can talk."

Leather creaks and he shuffles. An envelope slides into view.

"Everything you need is inside." He opens the door and steps out. "Way more than 'good faith.' I just handed you your entire world. Remember, you owe me now."

He turns around to leave, back facing me. A silver ring flashes on his finger.

I snatch up my gun and aim it at his back. "What makes you think I won't shoot? You gave me the world after all. I have no more use for you."

He laughs. "You wouldn't. You're too damn curious."

A loud honk bellows to my left. I look away.

When I glance back, the phantom is gone. No footsteps. No shadows. Nothing left behind. Only a trace of bergamot lingers in the air.

The passenger door clicks open a few minutes later, and in slides Sofia. "The bastard's fast. Getaway car ready, plates stripped. Avoids cameras. No visuals. What did he give you?"

"The world, apparently. You do the honors."

She grins, tears into the envelope, and pulls out a stack of papers.

A gasp rips from her throat as she reads them. Wide-eyed, she hands them to me.

```
Transfer of Power: Anderson Holdings to
Lleshi Shipping Company
```

```
Cosigned: Vincenzo Caruso, Ernest Kong, Juan
Alvarez, Adam O'Callaghan, Sergei Ivanov
```

Official seals in red wax. Frayed papers. Notarized decades ago.

Then the photos—the first ones are black and white. My grandfather, in a tux, stands with five equally well-dressed gentlemen, the Statue of Liberty as the backdrop. Then, colored photos—familiar faces from childhood, family, friends.

And finally, one of a tall man with kind eyes and dark hair smiling proudly at the camera.

Our dad.

"What?" I breathe, unable to believe what I'm seeing. The papers scorch my hands. Grief, fury, and betrayal knife my chest as I put together the story I was never told before.

Grandfather's land deeds, stock purchases, bank statements with obscene zeros all under my family's name.

My parents never lied. We were rich a long time ago.

Puzzle pieces fit together—the fear in my parents' eyes, the constant moving, the different spelling of our last name, Leste, from the original Albanian version, Lleshi. Then there was Carlos Alvarez warning me there were no coincidences before he died at the crematory.

Dad always told us Grandpa had lost his fortune before the Vietnam War, but there were no records of him. No photos except one of him holding Dad as a baby.

This is why.

We were the family who took the Andersons' place in The Sixth.

We were part of them—The Association.

And somehow, we were ousted.

The same dark blood runs inside me as in these men I've sworn to destroy. A laugh tears from my throat—deranged and mocking—fate has one fucked-up sense of humor. It's a full circle, my family starting the uncontrollable monster, trying to escape its wrath, and finally me, turning into the very people I hate—remorseless, apathetic murderers—to end it.

A small slip of paper flutters onto my lap.

I lift it to the light, my vision blurring at the edges.

It's dated twenty years ago and written in the same vivid ink and script I saw in the crematory records.

Punishment: Extirpation of the Lleshi Family, Strike from The Sixth

Offenses: Betrayal of The Association, Embezzlement, and Coup.

Status: Family line eliminated except for Lestes off-branch—distant cousins.

Current Target: Family of five—two adults, one infant, one son, one daughter.

One signature. One I'm very familiar with.

Edon Berisha, incumbent member of The Sixth, executor of this task for his Rite.

A quill stamp rests next to the signature. A symbol I've seen before.

Sable. The person who signed the disposal records at the crematory had this stamp next to his signature.

Edon Berisha is fucking Sable.

I fist the copy of the kill ledger, the evidence I've sought my entire adult life. The identity of the man who ordered my family's deaths, and the reason behind it.

My parents must've known danger was upon us. Grandpa crossed The Six, and the punishment was death.

Extirpation—the elimination of the *entire* family line as punishment.

And Edon Berisha took this opportunity as his Rite to join the ranks. He sent Vasil Çela and Carlos Alvarez to wipe my family from existence.

Wrath roars up my throat.

The motherfucker.

He stepped on my family's graves to rise to power.

And he'll pay for it—with his life.

"What are you going to do?" Sofia whispers, her face pale. "They're ruthless. They'll go down fighting. It'll be a massacre. And Lana..."

My breath stalls. Edon's signature swirls in my vision.

But the images bleed into bittersweet snapshots—hearing Lana sing Christmas songs in the shower, hand-feeding her chocolates, kissing every inch of her rose-scented skin.

Then my parents tucking little Beatrice into bed, teasing Sofia about her braces, Mom ruffling my hair when I came home from school.

I can't give up my revenge.

Not just for me, but for others like me—torn apart by the Berishas' misdeeds.

I once told Lana that Kian is dead, and Elias is a monster.

I'll be the monster they all fear—just not the kind that'll snuff out her light.

There's only one option left.

With my heart in a vice, I make a call. The line connects.

"Get your sister. Tomorrow. You owe me."

The line clicks dead, and a single truth sinks like lead in my gut.

I may lose Lana.

But at least she'll stay safe, not buried six feet under. If I don't survive, let her hate me. Better she lose me than be crippled with pain.

And if I live...

I will earn her back.

Chapter 51: OMENS AND HEARTBEATS

LANA

THE SKY IS UNUSUALLY dark tonight. I stand before the floor-to-ceiling windows in the living room as the pale moonlight spills through the clouds. A lone crow settles on the nearest branch, its beady eyes fixed on me.

An omen draped in feathers.

Unease settles in my gut.

My fingers fiddle with my pendant, grazing over the imperfections.

The girls left half an hour ago. Scarlett said she was only a phone call away. Aria had a graveyard shift at the hospital but promised to check in later.

Elias's entourage had departed earlier too.

Even Sebastian, the strategic, perpetually apathetic lawyer, gave me a small smile and told me everything would be handled.

Ren called it a miracle to see him act remotely human.

Aleksei, the usually unhinged and talkative computer genius, was silent. He slipped away after saying he'd be in touch.

It's well past midnight now. Sleep won't come. My mind swirls, but mostly I'm worried about *him.*

My breath fogs the glass as I wait for Elias to come home. Perhaps the story of Hades and Persephone has infected me, because one thought keeps circling. Will I ever pull him into the light, or will the Shadow King always remain in the dark?

The air suddenly changes.

A charged stillness.

A heated presence.

He's home.

I turn.

Elias stands near the doorway, tall in a dark coat, half-hidden by shadows. His green eyes catch the dim light. The scar twisting down his face looks sharper tonight, but it doesn't frighten me. It never really did. It's a mark of his strength—proof of the will it took to climb out of the flames and survive.

"Elias," I whisper.

My feet move automatically, my dress fluttering around my ankles.

He pushes off the wall and prowls toward me, his steps measured, the gravity between us electric. But there's a softness too, a smile laced with sorrow that tells me one thing.

Something is horribly wrong.

"My Lana Elise," he murmurs, cupping my face. His thumb traces circles that make me shiver. "I was put on this earth to love you, and I'm the luckiest man to have done so."

Beautiful words—*too* beautiful. They should fill me with joy, but pain seeps through every vein instead.

"What are you saying?" I grip his shoulders. "What aren't you telling me? Did you get answers?"

He shakes his head, the sad smile still haunting his face. "All the answers I've ever needed are standing right in front of me."

He's lying. I feel it in my bones.

"Let me love you, Lana," he says quietly. "Let me worship you."

He doesn't wait for a reply. Instead, he curls his arm around my waist, pulling me against his heated flesh.

His mouth finds mine—ravenous and desperate. Yet, every second feels borrowed.

"My wife," he rasps. "You've made all my dreams come true. For the longest time, I thought I was the walking dead. But you..."

Elias pulls back, his eyes intense. "You resurrected me, made me feel human again. Even if it wasn't forever."

"Elias, what's—"

He kisses me, refusing to let me question him, even if my heart was shattering from the pain in his words.

In one swift movement, he lifts me into his arms and carries me upstairs to our bedroom.

After dropping me on the bed, he pins me with his stare, like he's mapping every inch of my body.

My heart throttles, my skin blooming before him. I reach to undo my dress.

He stops me. "Let me do it."

Wetting his lips, Elias makes a quick work of his clothes. Buttons slip free under his fingers. Fabric slithers to the floor.

Soon he's naked in his full glory, all strength and rippling muscles, his hard shaft curled against his stomach, a vein pulsing on the side. The sight steals the breath from my lungs.

My mouth waters. My core pulses. I knot my hands in the bedsheets to stop myself from climbing him.

I need him now, always and forever.

Elias stalks toward me, stopping when his legs touch mine. I widen my stance and draw him in. With reverence, he pushes me flat on the mattress. Then he tugs down the straps of my dress with his teeth, baring my heated skin to the cold air.

"You're my goddess," he breathes.

Gentle hands skim from my throat to my tits. He thumbs my nipples, and a moan slips out of me.

I arch my back, needing more. "Elias, please."

"Please what?"

"Kiss me. Touch me. Make love to me."

He groans and seals his lips over mine again, tongue sliding deep, licking, sampling, tasting like he's dying of thirst.

I whimper when he yanks off my underwear.

"You're so wet," he murmurs, his finger sweeping from my clit to my entrance.

Sparks alight. I clench his wrist, urging him on.

Low and gravelly chuckles reach my ears. "Impatient, my *zemër*."

"You're an asshole."

"Your asshole." He laughs, sliding a finger inside my entrance, curling it precisely the right way, and grazes a tender spot.

Pleasure builds sharply. My legs shake. An orgasm barrels in from nowhere.

But just as it's about to crest, he stops.

"No," I whimper.

"Not yet. This," his breath catches, "will never be enough."

The earlier ache flares behind my sternum again. He makes it sound like this is the last time, and he doesn't want it to end.

But before I can ask, he bites my nipple and gives it a hard suck.

The sensations shoot straight to my clit, drawing out a half moan, half sob.

I tremble beneath him, clutching his backside.

"Fuck. You undo me." His eyes close, features taut like he's in pain.

I flip him so he's flat on his back, needing to drag him out of whatever dark hole he's in.

With a moan, I crawl down his body until I reach his hard cock.

Wetting my lips, I cradle his length with both hands. He rumbles a guttural groan and watches me, his emerald irises nowhere to be seen.

A bead of pre-cum gathers at the tip.

His nostrils flare when I take him inside my mouth, inch by inch, tasting his addictive saltiness.

I swirl my tongue around the tip, then pull him deeper. Firm suctions. Desperate pulls.

"Shit. So good. So damn good." His eyes roll back. His cock lengthens and throbs.

With hands fondling his balls, I hum around his length, the vibrations wrenching another curse out of him.

I keep pushing until his tip hits the back of my throat.

"Fuck me," he rasps. "Look at you swallowing my cock like you were born to do this."

My eyes water as I relax my gag reflex and pump his dick deeper down my throat. I gyrate my ass against the air, my core aching to have him inside me.

Another roar. A sharp twitch. A stream of salty cum bathes my taste buds.

Before I can finish, he drags me up and tosses me back on the bed.

Elias looms before me, teeth bared, lips peeled, like he wants to devour me and leave no scraps.

And I'll let him.

"I'm going to come inside you," he growls, "but I'm dying to have a taste."

Spreading my legs apart, he groans his pleasure into my core. His tongue sweeps from my clit to my tight rosebud, licking the wetness spilling out of me.

"Oh God, please." I writhe. I grab my tits and twist my nipples.

"Look at you, Lana. You're my goddess. Elegant on the outside, filthy on the inside for me, aren't you?"

"Yes," I moan, delirious with lust and love. "Yes."

"Who's going to make you come? Stuff this pink little pussy full of his cock? Mark you with his cum?"

His dirty words pound inside my skull. I quiver as his motions quicken, two fingers stuffed tight inside my core, his pinky breaching the tight rosebud, while his tongue works hard on my clit.

The sensations become too much, too intense, too obliterating.

"Answer me, Lana. Who do you love?" He nips my neck.

I shake like I'm shocked with a live wire.

"You, Elias. I love you."

"Yes," he roars and slams inside me in one hard thrust. "Because you're my wife and I'm your husband."

My cries echo as his hips snap against mine in a harsh rhythm.

Ragged breaths wrench out of my lungs. His drives roughen, like he's branding me to his soul.

"Hold on, princess. Feel me fucking you. Remember us. Remember this."

I moan out unintelligible words, a hurricane forming in my core, swelling to the rest of me.

My lips part, a silent cry perched at the back of my throat.

I thrash as he powers his hips—sharper, harder—like he can't get enough, like we aren't close enough.

His cock reaches a spot deeper than before. Spasms rack my body, the blistering storm reaching a breaking point.

"Elias, I'm going to come!" My teeth chatter.

"Yes, grip my cock. Give me your cum. Let me just feel you." He reaches between us and pinches my clit.

The world fractures. Wetness spurts out, and I shatter, my mind blanking, vision whitening, a roar bellowing in my ears.

Ecstasy has me tight in its grasp when his rhythm falters. Hot lashes of cum bathe my core.

"Lana, I love you so, so much," he whispers, forehead kissing mine.

We clutch each other, fingers intertwined, hips still meeting thrust for thrust even as shockwaves ebb and flow. Even as my body becomes too sensitive for anything more.

I can't let him go. I'm afraid of letting him go.

When it's over, we cling to each other, bodies trembling, breaths uneven. I rest against his chest, listening to the strong, steady beats of his heart—a heart that's endured too much and still keeps going.

Seconds become minutes, which become hours.

Eventually, he reaches to the nightstand, picks up my favorite book, and begins reading, his voice deep and resonant.

"Despite the darkness swallowing him whole, he felt his heart giving, each second in her presence a borrowed heartbeat, a fragment in time."

His finger glides over the lines, and my chest aches, thinking back to all the times I've seen him read, all the books in his library.

When we strolled in Hollow Gardens as kids, he laughed at me for loving this book but promised he'd learn to read it to me one day.

"You did it," I whisper.

"I promised you," he murmurs.

"Why did you buy Hollow Gardens?" I graze the scar on his cheek.

"It's our place." Elias takes my hand and kisses it. "I want a place where Elise and Kian can live...forever."

"Elias," my eyes mist, "can you take me back to the gardens? Visit our elm tree?"

His breath hitches. A vein pulses on his forehead.

"Someday," he murmurs, "when this is all over."

He presses a tender kiss on my forehead. Then another. Like he's bestowing upon me his wishes I don't yet understand.

The fear in my heart returns with a vengeance.

This moment feels like goodbye.

His mouth finds mine again. The world narrows to heartbeats and sensations.

"Will you tell me what's wrong, Elias?" My voice trembles when we break for air. I'm afraid to ask, but I need to know. "Don't lie to me. Honesty, right?"

He doesn't answer. His arms tighten in response, his lips brushing my neck.

"Just let me love you," he whispers into my skin. "Just let me love you."

Chapter 52: BROKEN CLOCK

ELIAS

THE WIND AND SLEET knock against the windows—steady and rhythmic, a metronome counting down my last moments with her.

It's fitting. Our love story began in the rain twenty years ago, and now it ends beneath another storm.

My phone buzzes with an incoming call.

Edon Berisha. He's pissed I didn't tell him about the stolen package.

I let it ring. Anger threatens to spark, but I shove it into a box.

This isn't the time for it.

Because these are my last moments with her.

Moisture clings in the air, the early dawn light illuminating the soft rise and fall of her chest as she sleeps.

When she wakes up, I'll be gone.

I ignore the clench under my ribs and brush the silky strands off her face.

On the nightstand, the blood-red gems of the rose in the music box glint, still as beautiful as the day we found it in the antique shop as Kian and Elise. The timer on my phone ticks uselessly beside it, a habit formed from years of pain, one I'll carry as a reminder of her.

Twenty-eight minutes. February twenty-eighth—the most pivotal date of my life.

It's a blessing and a curse to know that on this date, the love of my life was born, but the very people who gave me life were cruelly stolen from me.

Months ago, the thought would've sent rage crashing through my veins until I couldn't breathe.

Tonight, something else fills the hollow.

Acceptance.

And gratitude.

I lace my fingers with hers, my nose dipping down and inhaling her sweet scent of roses.

"Don't hate me," I whisper in her ear before pressing a kiss there. "Everything I do is for you."

For years, hatred and destruction blackened my soul and obliterated my heart.

But she resurrected me.

She gave me a second chance at life.

And that's exactly why I have to let her go.

She deserves love, sunshine, and roses—a life safe and warm above the ground.

Not buried underground with me in the dark.

It isn't just revenge anymore. Not just about settling a score with Edon Berisha and The Six. It's about making the world a safer place for her, for other Kians and Elises out there, so they can have their happy endings.

Moisture blurs my vision as I reach into my pocket, pull out my last gift for her, and set it beside the music box.

Maybe one day, when the smoke clears, if I'm still breathing, I'll be worthy to chase her light again.

But until then, I give her back her life.

And I leave with her my love, my soul, my heart.

My *zemër*.

Chapter 53: CIRCLE OF STRENGTH

LANA

A SOFT KNOCK AWAKENS me.

I reach for him automatically, but the bed is cold and empty.

"Ms. Lana, your car is ready," Hannah's voice drifts through the door.

What car?

A crash of thunder rattles the windows, and I bolt upright.

My gaze snags on the music box flipped open on the nightstand. But it's the object beside it that stops my heart.

Silver. Engraved. Heavier than it looks.

His lighter.

Dread curdles low in my stomach when I spot the small white card beneath it.

My *Zemër*,

Pivotal moments demarcate my life—some joyful, some heart-wrenching.

But they all have one thing in common.

You.

Never blame yourself for what happened to my family.

You're the best thing that has happened to me.

Thrive. Be happy.

And know this.

I will always love you.

Yours forever,

Kian

P.S. My lighter is yours. Keep it with you always. A car will take you to Arcana & Bloom. It will all make sense.

Panic grips me. I grab my phone and call him.

"The number you've dialed has been disconnected—"

Tears pool under my eyes.

He signed the note as Kian, the man I knew still lived inside him all along.

I was right. Last night was a goodbye.

No. I refuse to accept this.

I snatch his lighter, throw on sweatpants and a sweater, and rush out the door.

"Where is he?"

Hannah meets me at the bottom of the stairs, the wrinkles on her forehead extra deep today.

"He didn't tell me. They left early this morning. He left strict instructions to wake you only now."

I'm running toward the basement door before she finishes. The tunnels to the dungeons—he said they connect to The Antihero Syndicate's meeting place.

The door is sealed shut.

"No, you don't get to do this," I seethe and pull out my phone, this time to text Ren.

Lana

Where is he? You tell him if he thinks I'll obey him and give up on us, he doesn't know me. At all.

Seconds pass, and just when I think Ren won't respond, a text comes through.

Ren

I'm not supposed to answer. If you won't do this for yourself, do it for him. Please.

Lana

I'm doing it for him! For us. Where is he?

Ren doesn't text back.

Ten minutes later, John drives me to Arcana & Bloom.

Rain beads my hair as I barrel through the doors, floral-scented heat enveloping me.

"Lana," Aria says, her brown eyes shining with sympathy as she pulls me close. "I got here as fast as I could."

"What's going on? No one would tell me anything." I thrust the note at her. "Why am I here?"

"Elias thought it'd be best if..."

Her voice fades when I see them.

Maxwell and Rex sit at the corner table, their faces grim, two suitcases beside them.

My suitcases.

"No." My steps falter. A packet of papers and a pen rest on the table.

I don't need to read them to know what they are.

Divorce papers.

Scarlett appears at my side and guides me forward. "Elias called us this morning. He thought it'd be easier if you were somewhere else, safe, surrounded by—"

"My family and friends." The words scrape out from my throat.

The bastard thought he could break my heart *strategically*. That he could cushion the blow if I were in my favorite café in the city with people I cared about.

"No," I bite out, fury sparking at the base of my spine. "I'm not leaving him. I'm not going back to New York. This is my home now. I'm staying."

Maxwell stands. "Elias made the right call. He's going after The Association. I don't know the details, but if he fails, the punishment is *extirpation*. They'll go after his entire family—that includes you. This is the safest decision. The smart—"

"It's *my* choice!" I scream. My brothers freeze, jaws slack. "I'm smart, capable. Just because I'm a woman, your *little* sister, doesn't mean I don't get to decide how to live my life."

"But your choice could kill the rest of us!" Maxwell slams both his hands on the table, a vein ticcing on his forehead. "Extirpation. If you stayed married, that'd include us. I don't care about myself. But the kids. Belle, Olivia, your sisters. I can't—"

The floor swirls, and I sway on my feet.

His words echo in my skull. Amid my grief and fury, I've forgotten the price if this goes south.

Aria squeezes my hand and eases me into a seat.

"I'm sorry," I whisper, heat prickling my eyes. "I just reacted. I didn't think."

Little Levi. The twins. My siblings. Their spouses. Dad.

I can't be selfish.

"I don't blame you," Rex murmurs, clasping my hand. "I'd do the same thing. Probably worse."

Scarlett slides into the booth next to me and tucks a hot drink into my hand. Aria sits across the table, her usually bright eyes solemn.

"If Olivia left you with the twins and disappeared, would you let her go?" I ask Rex.

He hesitates.

A lump constricts my throat. I turn to Maxwell. "If Belle vanished to protect you, would you just sit at home and be at peace with it?"

Then I ask Aria, "If Blake left you to face danger alone, would you be okay with his decision?"

She shakes her head, her eyes misting. "No. I wouldn't."

I take the papers, the words blurring in front of me.

Petition for Dissolution of Marriage.

Drafts prepared by his counsel, pre-filed, just needing my signature. He's thought of everything.

My fingers shake as I flip to the end and see his name scrawled in blue ink—a single period punctuating a love that's impossible to describe in words.

Memories flicker—startling green eyes, teasing smiles, gentle hands patching up my dress.

No. I won't abandon him to deal with The Association alone. I know he's doing this because he thinks he won't make it out alive. But my brothers are right. It's not only my life at stake.

Pulling in a stiff inhale, I grab the fountain pen and scrawl my name next to his.

The girls gasp.

I set the pen down and look at the people I love—my family, my friends—grim determination steeling my nerves.

I will never leave them behind.

Just like I will never leave Elias.

"No longer married," I murmur. "You should be protected. But..."

I rise, strength blasting through my veins. Mom was right. The bravery was inside me all along.

"I'm not leaving."

Admiration shines in Maxwell's eyes, and a small smile crests Rex's lips.

"Lana," Aria whispers, voice shaking. "Ride or die badass."

"She likes the scary stories too," Scarlett mutters, blinking through tears. "But I know yours will have a happy ending."

I chug down the drink she gave me, heat spreading through my chest.

Righteousness replaces fear. Purpose replaces pain.

I slam down the mug. "Now—what are we going to do about this?"

Chapter 54: THE BLACK BOOK GOODBYE

LANA

MAXWELL'S LIPS TWITCH. HE takes the divorce papers, his gaze contemplative. "Do you know what he's planning?"

I think back to the last few weeks—snippets I overheard when The Syndicate was in our home. The hushed whispers about the phantom. The stolen evidence. Gabriel Caruso's visit.

Something's there. A missing piece—a crucial one.

My scalp prickles. I shove my hand into my pocket for my phone, ready to comb through Elias's prior texts for clues.

But my fingers bump into something solid and small.

The lighter.

Gasping, I quickly pull it out, the warm café lighting reflecting the delicate engraving on it.

"Why do you have his lighter?" Rex asks, hand reaching out. "Doesn't he carry that damn thing everywhere? Let me see."

Something niggles in my chest as I hand it over.

My mind is trying to tell me something—words I don't understand, a code I haven't noticed.

What is it?

Rex flicks the lighter on. A flame bursts.

"It's heavy," he murmurs, shaking it.

"The craftsmanship is beautiful," Scarlett whispers. "The flowers, the vines. How it swirls around his name—"

My gaze snaps up. I snatch the lighter back, my heart thundering like the storm outside.

Hand trembling, I lift it toward the light, fingertips grazing the small indentations I noticed before. Like pinpricks. Almost like—

"A key," I whisper. My thumb drags over the tiny marks. "These are keyholes. They have to be."

"But where's the key?" Aria nudges closer. "Do you know?"

My mind swirls through the options. The mansion is a labyrinth, not to mention the catacombs underneath St. Michael's I haven't explored.

It could be anywhere.

But why would he give this to me if he doesn't think I can open it?

"Has he left you anything—a gift, something inconsequential?" Maxwell asks, his gray eyes sharp.

His words click.

I wrench the emerald pendant off my neck.

This and the music box are my most prized possessions from him. Both are symbols of his eternal love.

Flipping the pendant around, my breath freezes when I see small protruding marks I wrote off before.

I always thought they were handcrafted imperfections.

My vision sharpens, laser-focused on the lighter and my pendant. I hold my breath.

I snap the pendant against the marks on the lighter.

Click. A perfect match.

"Holy shit," Rex mutters. "You've had that necklace forever."

"He gave you the key years ago," Maxwell murmurs, disbelief clear in his voice. "The fucking dealer of secrets."

But I twist and shake the lighter. Nothing opens. The pendant unlocked something, but it isn't enough.

There's another missing piece.

Teeth snagging my lip, I rack my mind.

It's a puzzle, just like the ones he's sent me over the years.

My chest tightens. Tears sting my eyes again. Decades wasted, and I had no idea who he was all this time.

But I know he left this for me because he believed I could solve it.

I trace the vines, the delicate petals of the roses, his name carved on the bottom.

ELIAS KENT

My fingers still. I press down.

A small click. A shift. Just like the Japanese secret boxes he sent before.

These are levers. They shift and slide. Since it didn't budge before, the pendant key must've triggered the mechanism.

If I rearrange the letters into the right order, it'll unlock.

But what's the sequence?

Sweat beads on my upper lip. I start shifting letters.

SAINT EKE

Nothing happens.

"The motherfucker. Why can't he ever be straightforward?" Rex mutters.

I snort, the stress and absurdity of the situation finally hitting home. Aria dashes off somewhere.

"If he were an open book, he wouldn't be alive," Maxwell says.

Aria reappears with paper and pens. "Here, we can figure this out."

Tension rises, silence falls. The only sounds are pens scratching on paper and occasional curses.

"Three hundred sixty-two thousand, eight hundred eighty," Rex grumbles.

"What?" I spare him a glance.

"The number of combinations you can make with nine letters."

We gape at him.

"What? I may be a party animal, but I'm smart. A genius really—"

"Ugh." I roll my eyes, a smile twitching my lips. I miss my siblings.

"Silent Eke?" Maxwell furrows his brow. "God knows the man makes no sound."

I try it. Still nothing.

"An Elks Tie!" Aria yells.

We stare at her, and she grimaces. "I don't know. I'm a nurse, not a wordsmith."

I try that too. Nothing.

"Ink Least." Scarlett holds up her paper. "Does that mean anything?"

"No." That combo doesn't work. I slide the letters back into the original position.

ELIAS KENT

"It's something else, something—"

Then suddenly—clarity.

I slap my forehead.

"What?" That can be Rex or the girls. I don't know because my quaking pulse eclipses all sounds.

"I'm so stupid," I whisper, more for myself than for others. "He told me who he was all along."

My fingers tremble as I rearrange the letters once more.

The most obvious answer.

KIAN LESTE

"Holy shit. He's your Kian? The guy you dated in Chicago in high school?" Rex asks.

Click.

I nod, a sob wrenching out of my throat.

A tiny compartment pops open at the bottom.

A micro SD card tumbles out.

"Let me get my laptop." Scarlett scrambles off the seat.

"Elias Kent was always Kian Leste," I whisper.

It's so obvious and yet well hidden. An anagram. How did I ever miss this?

A laptop appears before me, and I glance up.

"You've got this," Maxwell says.

I slide the memory card into the slot, and a folder appears on the screen.

In it are thousands of files.

Photos. Ledgers. Videos. More folders sorted by the names of politicians, CEOs, and world leaders. There's something here on everyone.

I snap the laptop shut and yank the card free.

I won't risk them. The fewer people know about this, the better. The info will put a target on their heads.

"I have to go." I bolt out of the booth, hand fisting the items.

"Hold on. What's on the drive? Where are you going?" Maxwell hollers as I dash to the exit.

"I'll explain later. Go home. Protect your families."

Turning at the threshold, I flash them a wobbly smile. "I love you all. Stay safe."

Outside, sleet pelts from the sky. John opens the car door.

"Back to the house," I tell him. The engine roars to life.

I make a call.

"Special Agent Clarke."

"I might have what you need," I murmur. "But I need your help right now."

"I'll meet you at your place in twenty," he answers and hangs up.

My heart beats a rickety rhythm. I unfurl my fist, staring at what the Shadow King left me.

Elias gave me his black book of secrets.

His leverage against the world.

Chapter 55: WOLVES AT THE GATE

ELIAS

A LATE-WINTER SQUALL DRUMS a war cry above The Syndicate Chamber in St. Michael's catacombs.

"You sure he'll be there?" I stare at the blueprints of Chicago Memorial and the surgery schedule printed out by Aleksei.

His fingers fly across the laptop, keys tapping a furious rhythm.

"Aleksei?"

Gaze snapping up, he halts. "What?"

"Your intel. How confident are you?"

Aleksei snorts, nostrils flaring. "What do you think?"

When I purse my lips, he sighs. "One hundred ten percent, okay? If you want an audience with Edon Berisha at his weakest, it's tomorrow after lunch at one. Gallbladder surgery. He told everyone it was next week, but they did a switcheroo."

"Paranoid bastards," Sebastian mutters, twirling his penknife over his knuckles.

I scroll through the emails on my phone.

Edon has pushed all our meetings to next month, claiming he's traveling. It's consistent with Aleksei's intel.

"You aren't the only one with enemies," Sofia says as she drags one of the floor plans across the table. "I'm sure he'll be heavily protected. Powerful men always are at their weakest."

"Distraction?" Sebastian furrows his brows, staring at the diagram we drew up. Roles are assigned. We're just missing the entry plan. "Power outage is out of the question. They have backup generators. We can accost him in the room, but you'll be passing through security cameras and people. Don't even think about wearing strange masks."

"I can take out the cameras," Aleksei offers.

"Not going to work," Sebastian replies. "It's Chicago Memorial, not a hole-in-the-wall village clinic. Tons of witnesses."

The doors slam open, and Rafe strides in, hair damp, icy droplets clinging to his clerical collar.

"Honor walk," he says. Our heads swivel in his direction.

"What's that?" Sofia asks.

He rakes his fingers through his dark hair, a shadow crossing his eyes. "It's when a living donor declared brain dead is pulled off life support for organ donation. Anyone available gathers in the hallway for a send-off. I've taken part a few times after praying with the family. There's one scheduled at ten."

"You'll draw everyone in the vicinity away from where Berisha is." Sebastian cocks his brow, a smile curving his lips. "Brilliant, Rafe. Remind me, what's in this for you? You know we're killing someone tomorrow, right?" He shrugs. "Probably multiple someones."

"Seriously, Sebastian," Sofia shakes her head, "we really need to work on your reactions. A poor soul's being pulled off life support, and you're smiling like a hyena."

"Not about the patient." He levels his dead stare at her. "It's an assessment of the plan. Excellent strategy by our good priest here."

"Not a priest yet," Rafe mutters. "Transitional deacon. That's my title."

"All the same to me. Everyone calls you 'Father' anyway."

Sofia sighs. "Try to at least look sad."

Rafe turns toward the crucifix again and makes the sign of the cross, murmuring unintelligible words under his breath.

"Great. He's praying for our souls again." Sebastian snickers. Then he stiffens. "But you said the walk is at ten? Isn't Berisha's surgery at one?"

"Aleksei?" I stand and stride to the far wall, where a lone monitor sits.

CCTV of the front of the cathedral flickers on the screen.

Showing the woman I love.

My chest tightens as I trace Lana's face on the screen. She's holding a red umbrella, much like the one she had when I first met her. A frown creases between her brows as she speaks with a nun, who's shaking her head like she doesn't understand her question.

No one knows we're down here except Rafe.

"Stubborn woman," I murmur.

Lavender wafts to my nose—Sofia's calm-day scent.

"I had my doubts about her. A princess raised in a gilded cage, never experiencing poverty or hardship. So many doubts," she says, staring at the screen. "Not anymore. I like her for you. A lot."

"You really should let her in," Rafe says, joining us. "Strength is in numbers. Love is power."

"Oh please, stop with all the 'love thy neighbor' crap." Sebastian snorts in the background. "Emotions are liabilities. Pollute your mind. Make you illogical. Thank God—"

"Yes, you have no emotions, got it. Now will you shut up?" Aleksei snaps and stands. His face is blotchy, and he heaves out a heavy breath. "Sorry. Stress is getting to me. I shifted Berisha's case up by three hours and spoofed a new anesthesia log. They'll prep him early. I'll be in the server room if you need me."

He folds his laptop shut and gathers his gadgets. "Don't touch my computers." With lips flattening, he glares at Sebastian. "I'm looking at *you*."

Then he storms out of the chamber.

"What? No 'boom'? No 'I'm a genius' comment?" Sebastian hollers after him, then turns toward us. "See? Emotions are a hindrance."

"What's gotten into him?" Sofia frowns. "And where's Ren?"

"He said he's chasing something down," I reply.

"Something's going on with Ren," Sebastian muses, echoing my sixth sense. "He looks...off. And this is purely objective."

I pull out my phone.

No messages from him. My last text bounced—undelivered.

Ren didn't say much, but that's par for the course. He seemed troubled when he stopped by my Ashbourne Heights safe house this morning. When I asked him why, he only shook his head and told me to send him the final plans.

"Anything from the Carusos or the Berishas?" Rafe asks. "Do they suspect?"

I shake my head, watching Lana walk away, shoulders slumped, the red umbrella shrinking on the screen.

She turns before getting into the car, gazing straight into the camera.

For a moment, my heart stops.

It's like she can see me.

She grips the handle tightly. Even on the grainy footage, I can make out the dark circles under her eyes.

She looks too pale, too unsteady. She shivers.

I step toward the door, every atom in my body begging me to go to her, to draw her into my arms and kiss away the pain in her eyes.

But I don't. Instead, I curl my hands into fists at my sides, watching her image.

So close, yet so far away.

Lana moves her lips, whispering words I can't hear.

But I see them. I understand them.

I love you, Elias.

A pained breath scrapes out of me, invisible talons digging into my heart.

A sad smile curves her lips. She shakes her head and mouths something else.

I won't give up.

Clutching my chest, heat sharpens behind my eyes. I throttle out a deep breath, then another, until the pain eases.

Until it's bearable.

She presses her fingers to her lips, releasing a kiss into the wind and sleet. Then she gets in her car and disappears.

"She knows you're watching," Sofia murmurs.

A soft smile crests my lips. Lana knows me well.

The feed blinks, the precipitation thickening until the world becomes white and gray. My gaze drifts to the crucifix on the wall.

If there is a God, please take care of Lana. Protect her. I don't care what happens to me. I'll trade a thousand lifetimes to keep her safe.

A weight settles on my chest, and for a moment, I can't breathe. I reach for my lighter, then stop, belatedly realizing I don't have it anymore.

Because I gave it to her for protection. If I don't make it out alive, she'll have everything she needs to keep my enemies at bay.

"Easy there," Rafe murmurs, his hand at my back. "Things aren't hopeless. They never are."

Something in his voice—pain or sorrow—draws my gaze to him.

"Why *do* you help us?" I echo Sebastian's earlier question.

Decades. I've known him for decades, and he's never revealed his story. Why would he help monsters who clearly weren't destined for eternal salvation?

His gaze softens and flickers between Sofia and me. "There's always a place for you here. And there's always light even in the darkest night."

Not answering my question, he pivots toward the door.

He pauses at the threshold.

"Atonement," he says. "We all have something to atone for."

Then he disappears.

Silence lingers, thick with sorrow and regret.

Someone whistles. A chair squeaks.

"Well, that was strange." Sebastian shrugs, rises from his seat, and buttons his three-piece suit. "I'd ask you to translate, but from the look on your face, you have no clue either."

He winks, cold amusement in his eyes, no doubt from sadistic pleasure at the impending showdown. "A few doctors are on the Irish mob payroll. I called them. They'll direct stray people out of the way."

Sebastian tips his fingers in a mock salute and strides out, leaving Sofia and me in silence.

"Well?" she asks, tucking a dark lock of hair behind her ear. "You okay? You got this?"

"Always," I murmur. I glance at her and smile. "We Lestes always survive. But now..."

I stride back to the long table and stare at our options.

"We plan."

Ten a.m. tomorrow. This all ends.

Chapter 56: THE ALLIANCE

LANA

TRISTAN SHIFTS IN HIS seat and loosens his tie. He eyes the floral displays in front of him at Arcana & Bloom.

Scarlett is in the middle of swapping hydrangeas for peonies in time for spring.

The flowers smell too sweet—sickly sweet today.

"I could've chosen the place," he mutters.

"Too girly?" I smirk.

The FBI agent rolls his shoulders, his discomfort obvious.

I used to be the one smoothing PR crises in boardrooms. Now I'm in love with the king of the underworld.

As his queen, I have a few tricks up my sleeve.

My first meeting with Tristan was on his turf.

This time, it's on mine.

And in negotiations, making the other party uncomfortable gives me an edge.

Elias would be proud of me. An ache presses on my lungs. I miss him and I worry about him.

Scarlett slides a mug in front of Tristan. Her gaze drifts toward me, and I give her a subtle nod—proof I'm holding strong.

"I didn't order anything." He eyes it, brow cocked high. "Is this a thing with you guys? Free drinks?"

"You need it. Trust me." Scarlett grins and tosses her red hair over her shoulder. "And the café's closed. Consider it celebrity treatment from me."

I snicker and sip my hot toddy—lemon balm, chamomile, and a whisper of spice. "You'll get used to it."

Tristan wanted to meet after I gave him some evidence from Elias's micro SD card. I cloned parts of it onto a USB drive. There's no way I'm giving him the drive itself.

It's too valuable.

And it's leverage—protection for Elias when we get out of this situation alive.

And we will.

"You've checked the evidence?" I ask.

"Yes." Tristan leans in, fingers trailing his jaw. "Called in a few favors. It's legit." He levels his sharp gaze at me. "You have more where it came from."

"The deal is immunity. Evidence on the Berishas is a finder's freebie. I'm not giving anything more until you guarantee Elias's safety."

Tristan sits back, his head dipping in a slow nod. "I underestimated you."

"Many do."

He pulls an envelope out of his pocket and slides it across the table.

I open it and scan the pages.

"Immunity for past and future crimes as long as he cooperates. But nothing for capital offenses. I can't help him there."

Relief sweeps through me like a cool breeze in the Sahara. "Did you find anything on that Sable person?"

It was one of the documents I gave him—a crematory log with the Lestes' names on it. Tristan asked me who these people were, but I didn't tell him.

"The trail was pretty cold, but I traced the signature through our archives and consulted a handwriting specialist." Keeping his gaze firmly on me, he taps his phone and turns it to me.

On the screen are documents compared side-by-side, red circles pinpointing uniqueness in signature samples. He swipes to the next photo. A land deed filed fifteen years ago for a company, Sable Enterprises.

The signature?

Edon Berisha.

My hand flies to my mouth as the truth unravels. This is why Elias left me.

He found the man responsible for his family's deaths.

And he's going to kill him and set off a war.

That's why he gave me his black book.

The ache sharpens into a blade, twisting into my chest.

Elias really doesn't think he'll survive.

And the black book...it's his way of protecting me after he's gone.

My eyes snap up, and Tristan nods. "Your Berishas rose to power quickly. I suspect these deaths have something to do with it."

"Do you know where the Berishas are?" I haven't heard from them in ages. No press releases or PR projects. No dinners or galas.

Tristan leans forward, his voice low. "I'm not stupid. I have a feeling Edon Berisha will end up floating face down in Lake Michigan very soon. I won't lose any sleep over that, but I want to know why you're asking."

At my hesitation, he adds, "Lana, I can't help you if you don't give me all the facts. Flying in blind will get us—or Elias—killed."

My pulse quickens as I hold his gaze, searching for tells—a nose twitch, a clenched jaw—any sign he'll betray us.

The Berishas—not to mention The Association—are powerful in the city. What if this is all a trap? What if Special Agent Tristan Clarke is using me to unravel Elias's plans?

But what options do I have? I can't ask my brothers for help without risking them. I'm not a black ops specialist or anyone remotely familiar with this world.

There's only one move I can make.

"The Berishas murdered his family," I whisper, digging my nails into my palms.

Please let my gut feeling be right.

Understanding dawns in Tristan's eyes.

"The Lestes," he murmurs. "I see."

He flips his phone, knocking it on the table a few times, then straightens, apparently deciding.

"Edon Berisha is scheduled for gallbladder surgery at Chicago Memorial tomorrow at ten a.m."

I gasp, and he nods, clearly coming to the same conclusion.

"Elias Kent will make a move then," he says. "That's what I'd do."

"Can you provide backup?"

Tristan frowns, his eyes contemplative. "Like you guessed before, I'm doing this off the books. The Association's too powerful. I've bent the rules for informants in the past, but never this far. If the director finds out, I'm finished."

A vein pulses in his temple. "I'll try my best, but no guarantees. It won't be easy to get into the hospital's restricted areas, and the surgical floor is definitely one of them."

He sips his drink and nearly spits out the contents. He levels a glare at Scarlett, who's busy wiping the counters.

"If I flash my badge...someone in The Association's pocket may see it. Rumors will swirl about an FBI agent investigating something."

My palms sweat. That'll draw more attention to Elias. To whatever he's doing. It might put a target on his back.

Unless...

"What if I can get you in?"

I push out an exhale. Yes. I might pull it off.

"What do you mean?" His brown eyes sharpen.

"Chicago Memorial...we donated a billion dollars to fund their new research wing last quarter. They gave me an open invite to do a PR tour with them—full escorted behind-the-scenes access, temporary VIP badges with the right clearances. Rex was going to help with this, but as far as I know, nothing's been done yet."

Tristan's lips curve into a slow smile, and he cocks his head.

"Lana Anderson Kent," he rasps, "we *really* underestimate you."

Adrenaline churns, and I grip my mug to stop my nerves from showing.

"Will it work?"

Tristan arches a brow, his smile disappearing when he tosses back his drink. "It just might."

He leans in, his voice low. "Here's what we're going to do..."

Chapter 57: DISHONOR AND ATONEMENT

ELIAS

SOBS REACH MY EARS. Then muffled whispers. Hum of machines...*beep...beep...beep* hammers the air. The stench of antiseptic agents chokes my airway even through the surgical mask I'm wearing, like most folks on the floor.

My gaze connects with Sofia, already merged with the small crowd entering the restricted hallway of the surgical floor. Aleksei should be in the server room, ready to work his magic on the surveillance feeds. Sebastian had a last-minute call from his family to handle Irish mob business, but he assured me the doctors on his payroll would assist with crowd management. He said it'd be better if he weren't here—his apathetic face would give us away.

Ren is MIA. I frown and check the phone. No texts. Calls go to voicemail. Whatever's going on with him—it has to be an emergency. But I don't have time to dwell on that.

Unease coils around my gut, and the air around me crackles.

The calm before a storm hits.

Edon Berisha, the fucking weasel, is hiding somewhere beyond those double doors, thinking he's only getting his gallbladder removed. Right now, he's as unprotected as he'll ever be.

This is our chance.

"An honor walk will begin on Surgical Level 2 in fifteen minutes. Available staff may join outside the OR lobby," the overhead speaker announces.

Every muscle inside me clenches as I stride to the security guard standing sentry.

"He's with me," Rafe murmurs as we pass through the normally closed doors.

I flash my visitor badge to the bald security guard, whose belt strains against his gut. He looks like he couldn't catch a toddler chasing an ice cream truck.

The man barely spares me a glance.

Inside the hallway, a quiet commotion gathers. Family and friends huddle shoulder-to-shoulder along the wall. Technicians and staff in scrubs hold tissue boxes and comfort the bereaved.

A ten-ton plate presses on my rib cage. There's something about the heavy atmosphere—the slump of the weary doctors' shoulders, teary nurses putting on a brave face for families going through the unthinkable—that makes you question the path you're about to take.

They're mourning someone kind-hearted, whose last contribution to this world will be the gift of life.

I'm here to take one.

Even if it belongs to the devil incarnate.

The Kian who loved Elise would never do this. He dreamed of saving strays and stitching up the wounded in a tiny, low-cost clinic on the south side, a raven-haired goddess working beside him, her laughter infectious, her warmth spreading like sunlight.

Guilt squeezes my lungs.

The emotion has no place in my life, but that's the side effect of loving Lana, of stealing whiffs of her roses and bathing in her light—becoming partially human again.

"Father Mancini," a teary-eyed woman clutches Rafe's shoulder. "Can you pray with us?"

Rafe nods, his gaze soft, heavy with sympathy. He rolls down the sleeves of his black clerical shirt, hiding his tattoos. "I'll be right there."

As I step toward Surgical Suite 5, Rafe's voice stops me in my tracks.

"Elias," he murmurs.

I pause, meeting his eyes.

"Remember rule three. Promise me." His jaw tics.

No innocents.

I'm once again wondering why someone from the church is helping me commit a mortal sin.

"Forgiveness will set you free," he says, guilt darkening his eyes.

"If it's that simple," I whisper, "why don't you do it yourself?"

"Who says I haven't tried?"

The second stretches. I take in his tensed shoulders, the flush crawling up his neck above his clerical collar.

"Something tells me you haven't succeeded." A bitter laugh lodges in my throat. "And it's too late for me...but I promise you. No innocents."

I clasp his shoulder. "Thank you, Rafe, for everything. If anything happens, take care of Lana for me."

The priest's nostrils flare. He dips his head in a curt nod and pivots to the grieving woman.

I slip away. Keeping my head down, I pull on a doctor's white coat Sebastian's contact left for me behind the now-empty nurse's station. My footsteps are brisk but silent as I move toward the room.

Sofia, disguised in nurse scrubs, nods at the door.

We enter the room.

The hiss of oxygen pumping through machines fills the air. The EKG beeps steadily and hypnotic.

"Labs back?"

"Yep, H&H stable."

Low conversation from next door hums from the hallway.

Sofia closes the door behind us.

Edon lies on the narrow gurney, dressed in a pale-blue surgical cap and gown, IV line taped to his arm.

The asshole is scrolling on his phone, oblivious death is at his door.

"Well, well, well, Edon. The blue doesn't become you."

I pull on surgical gloves. The elastic snapping punctures the sterile quiet.

Berisha jerks, his gaze swinging in our direction, eyes wide.

"K-Kent, what are you doing here?" He scrambles back, clearly sensing danger.

Sofia pulls his gurney away from the wall and the emergency buttons.

I tsk, shaking my head. "You really don't know? A sly weasel like you suspected nothing?"

"What are you talking about? If this is about Shkelzen's behavior—"

I cross the room in three strides, my hand shackling his neck.

The tendons yield and snap. His face reddens, hands clawing at my wrist.

"I've been waiting for this," I growl, tightening my grip, "so fucking long. The only thing I dream about is watching the light leave your eyes."

Leaning in, I shove him back onto the gurney. He thrashes in my hold, completely at my mercy.

"Don't worry. I'm not letting you die this way. Too messy," I whisper, loosening my grip. I seal his lips with medical tape. His screams turn into muffled whispers. "Much better."

It'll be a nightmare in autopsy—prints around his bruised neck. Too obvious. As much as I want him to suffer just like my parents and Beatrice did, I need him dead more, and this needs to look clean.

Sofia's already prepping—hands steady and efficient, but with a rare, haunted look in her eyes.

She winks when she catches me staring and flashes five large-gauge syringes filled to the brim with one thing.

Air.

"Not a doctor. The literature's confusing." I take the first syringe and stare at the needle. "Coronary artery. Cerebral? Veins? No clue what any of that means."

Shifting closer, I hold him still as Sofia fastens his arms and legs to the gurney with bedsheets.

"Some websites say half a milliliter kills. Others say fifty. Honestly, who knows? But everyone seems to agree that a hundred milliliters of air is fatal."

I grip his chin and force the trembling man to look at me. "So this is one fifty, a little extra for the man who's changed my life."

Heat rushes to my face as I cock my head. "Not so scary anymore, Berisha? People like you only lord over the weak, like a family of five from twenty years ago. Was too much of a pussy to do it yourself. Had to send your minions."

His brows furrow, confusion obvious in his mumbling.

"What? Not ringing a bell? Here's a clue." I lean in and whisper, "The Lestes."

Berisha freezes.

Fury simmers into a boil inside my veins.

Rule one: Look them in the eyes.

"My name is Kian Leste," I rasp. "Your extirpation all those years ago wasn't thorough enough."

I slide the needle into the IV port and slowly depress the plunger. Edon thrashes, muffled screams ripping out of his throat.

Sofia slaps him hard across his face. My gaze snaps to hers, and I see tears in her eyes.

Rule two: Tell them their sins.

"You killed our parents and our sister. My grandfather...I'm sure you offed him too. For what? Power? A seat in The Six?" I fist his shirt and hand the IV to Sofia, who takes over and inserts the second syringe.

Damn hospitals for not carrying larger gauges. Not expeditious enough.

"You forged the evidence, didn't you? My grandfather's alleged wrongdoings. You wanted to take out the ruling Albanian family and become the top man."

Berisha's eyes widen in pain.

Sofia stabs in the third syringe.

"But it doesn't matter if my grandfather was guilty or not. The result is the same. You killed our family!"

Rule three: No innocents.

But there are no innocents here. Not him. Not us.

"Looks like we won't need all five syringes with you, Edon," I whisper and set his quaking body back on the bed, tucking him in like he was asleep waiting for surgery.

I glance at the clock. Five past ten. The honor walk will be over soon. Our window is shrinking.

"Rot in hell."

The syringe empties. Life slowly drains from his mottled face, his eyes rolling back in his head.

Soon, he stills. The flatline wails.

Sofia turns off the monitor, tears streaking down her face. She's trembling, her hands clutching the rails on the gurney like she's struggling to stay upright.

"I know, Sofia," I whisper.

She shakes her head and wipes her eyes, quickly gathering the syringes to get rid of the evidence.

One death won't resurrect our parents or little Beatrice, won't erase the decades of scars, turning us into shadows of our former selves.

Inhuman.

My nose burns as hollowness fills the space where rage once lived.

I feel *nothing*.

No satisfaction. No peace. No absolution.

Just empty.

I try to conjure Lana's voice, her scent of roses, but I can't. I'm not worthy.

Then the door slams open. Boots scrape on the floor.

"Elias Kent," a voice drawls, cold and satisfied. "Thank you for the help."

A gun barrel gleams, pointing straight at our faces.

Chapter 58: RAIN OF BETRAYAL

ELIAS

"YOU SAVED ME THE trouble," Agron sneers as he steps inside, his gun trained on my chest.

I arch a brow, unflinching. Of course, the bastard wanted to climb the ranks with his dad out of the way.

Sorry Rafe, but he's definitely not innocent.

"It's stupid of you," I murmur, backing until I'm pressed against the gurney. "You could've stayed home, safe with an alibi. Why show up and risk everything?"

One shift, one second, and my side holster releases my gun.

A clean shot—straight between the eyes—will take care of this trash.

He scoffs. "Have to make sure you'd do your job."

I twist. The gun clears its latch—

Agron fires a round into the cabinet beside Sofia. Glass shatters on my sister before she ducks.

Blood freezes in my veins.

Alarms wail. Red lights strobe.

Leveling his gun at her, he pivots. "One more move and your sister joins Dad in the great beyond."

Chaos from the outside bleeds through—muffled screams, harsh orders.

"What did you do, Agron?" I raise my hands, pulse hammering. "You won't escape this."

He flushes, eyes wild. "You forced this on me! I was going to take care of the old bastard months ago. Then you joined the party, hovering constantly. I couldn't do anything. You brought this upon yourself."

"What do you want then? Your dad's dead. You didn't pull the trigger. Leave. No one will know."

He laughs. "You think I'm stupid? You'll add this to your book of secrets and lord this over me forever. No." Agron's gun trembles. "You deserve to die, just like him."

My gaze flicks to Sofia, who slides something out from her sleeve—a glint of silver.

A knife or a blade. She just needs a distraction.

"You think you're so smart, Elias Kent. One step ahead of everyone," Agron spits. "But you aren't. You don't even know how much your people *hate* you—"

The door crashes open. Shrieks and shouts echo down the hall—people fleeing, code calls blaring.

"I'll get backup," a familiar male shouts from the hall. "Stay here. Don't move."

The words snag at me. I know that voice from somewhere, but I don't have time to place it.

Then suddenly, a muscular man with a shaved head and a sleeve of tattoos bursts in.

Aleksei.

"Go, Elias! I got this," he yells, gun raised.

Time slows to snippets. The ruckus dulls to a hum.

Agron turns, his attention shifting from me to Aleksei.

I move before Aleksei finishes his words.

I know what's going to happen.

Agron cocks his gun. The barrel flashes orange.

I shove Aleksei aside. Fire explodes through my chest.

"Elias," Sofia screams.

My world spins—ringing, tilting, dimming. My body hits tile. Warmth floods my shirt.

Blood. I got hit.

Loud thuds. Metal clanging. A scuffle.

Sofia cries—then a crash—her head knocks against the cabinet and she goes down.

Aleksei's fist cracks against Agron's jaw. The asshole drops like a boulder in water.

Pain spears from my chest. Crimson soaks my fingers.

Aleksei's face fills my vision, his face ghost-white, his hand gripping mine.

"E-Elias, I'm sorry."

My limbs grow cold, lips numb. I choke on air. Aleksei grips my fingers, tears gathering in his eyes.

"I'm sorry," he repeats. "I'm so fucking sorry."

"You've," I wheeze. "You've nothing to be sorry for. If anything...I'm sorry. I made you an orphan."

Images detonate.

A cold night. Fury boiling in my veins.

Gun in my hand as I accosted the couple who told Vasil Çela where my family lived. The satisfaction when the bullets pierced their skulls.

A muffled sob in the coat closet.

A teenager trembling with wide, grief-torn eyes.

Aleksei.

One moment destroyed his life—just like mine.

"I-I did it," Aleksei stammers. He presses a cloth to my wound.

"What?"

"Why do you think Agron knows you're here?" He glances away, a rough laugh tearing out of him. "Don't fall apart until you get your revenge, remember?"

I freeze, remembering what he said to me when I was spiraling in the crematorium.

My gaze refocuses on the hacker, whom I consider family. "You told him."

Of course he did. I'd laugh if it didn't hurt so much.

After all, it's peak irony. I'd built my life on revenge. Naturally, I'd raise another version of myself.

"I'm sorry," he chokes out, forehead dropping onto my chest. "I-I thought this would stop my nightmares. My parents' screams. The pain." His shoulders shake. "I regret it. I tried to stop it. Not in time—"

"Go," I whisper. "Leave before the cops come."

"What? No—"

"Go!" I squeeze his fingers, blood slick between us. "I don't blame you. Don't let them catch you. Leave. Start a new life."

A cough racks through me. Bitter iron fills my mouth.

Keeping my gaze on his, I rasp, "A life for a life. My debt's repaid."

His words. The truth. My atonement.

Slowly, he lets go of my hand. His gaze pinballs down my body, over my wounds.

"I'm sorry," he whispers. He tears himself away and runs.

Blackness devours my vision. It's so cold. Terribly cold. My eyes flutter shut.

A feminine cry cleaves the air.

"Elias!"

The scent registers first—roses, sweet roses in the rain.

No. Why is she here?

My eyes snap open.

Lana.

Chapter 59: CRIMSON VOWS

LANA

MY HEART RIPS TO shreds at the sight of Elias crumpled on the floor.

Face ashen. Red dousing his shirt. His breath a rattle.

"No," I sob, collapsing beside him, tears blurring my view of his beautiful face.

His eyes snap open, panic flashing through the haze.

"L-Lana, why are you here? Go," he whispers, voice weak. "It's too dangerous. Go, please."

I shake my head and slam my palm against the emergency button. Somewhere, alarms bloom—Code Silver, Code Red. More screams of terror.

I grab the nearest bedsheet and press it to his wound.

Warmth floods through the white fabric, relentless.

He reaches for me, fingers shaking.

I lift his hand—it's ice—to my lips and breathe warmth onto his knuckles.

"Stay strong, Elias. Tristan went to get backup and doctors. You're at a hospital. You'll be fine. Help is coming."

Elias's throat works, surprise flickering on his face.

Another sob breaks from me. "I partnered with him to save you. Got you immunity and everything. But we couldn't reach you in time."

Tears drench my face and salt my mouth. The plan had worked—until it didn't.

Our PR liaison was late, and then she took a detour to avoid the honor walk.

By the time we reached the floor, chaos erupted—shots, screams, a flood of fleeing bodies. Tristan knew we were possibly outnumbered. He went for help and to call it in.

"My *zemër*," Elias rasps, his bloody fingers trailing down my cheek. "Why would you risk yourself for me? I'm a monster. I kill. I'm not the man you remember—"

"Shut. Up." I clutch his shoulder, raining frantic kisses on his face. "I don't care if you're Kian or Elias. I love and choose both. I'd take any piece of you rather than nothing. You'll *never* get rid of me, so you listen carefully—"

Pulling back, I wipe my eyes and lace my fingers with his.

"You're going to survive this. Death didn't claim you all those years ago. It won't claim you now. Because you know why?"

I lean in, watching his pulse flutter at his temple.

"You're the Shadow King, the king of the underworld, and I'm your queen. You don't die. B-Because..."

Pressing a kiss onto his ear, I whisper, "I love you. Only you. Forever you."

Elias trembles underneath me. "My *zemër*, I love you—"

Then he jolts and stills.

A click slices through the air. A menacing heat presses on my back.

"This is touching and all," Agron rasps.

I'm yanked to my feet, a muscular arm crushing my throat.

Steel jams against my temple.

"Should've made sure I was dead. Rookie mistake."

He squeezes harder. My lungs strain for oxygen. I claw at his forearm, nails slicing skin, but he doesn't budge.

Elias struggles, cold sweat dripping over his pallid forehead. He grips the bedrail, dragging himself upright.

My throat burns. Panic claws my chest. I thrash in the bastard's hold—arms swinging, feet kicking. My vision winks. Faint grunts reach my ears.

But I don't stop fighting.

I will never stop fighting.

"How touching." Agron cackles, dragging me backward with him. "I wonder what'll happen if—"

A shot cracks through the chaos.

His grip loosens. A pained grunt rips from his throat.

I shove free, but he's too quick to snatch me against his chest like a shield before spinning us around.

Ren stands in the doorway—black-clad, half-masked. A gun smokes in his hand.

"Bastard," he rasps. He clutches his chest, sounding winded. "I got here too late. Aleksei sent me on a wild fucking goose chase around the city."

Leveling his gun at Agron, he catches my eye. "Let her go."

"No. I'm not dying today, and she's my ticket out." Agron wheezes.

I don't know where he's hit, but it's clear he's in pain.

Agron hauls me toward the corridor.

"Let her go," a faint voice calls. "Take me instead."

My heart stops, pain carving fatal wounds inside me.

Elias.

He sways on his feet, blood dripping down his clothes, eyes glazed.

"Take me. I'm more valuable. I'll tell them I did it. It was self-defense. Just let her go."

"No," I cry, shaking my head. If Agron takes him, he's dead.

Agron chuckles, his face pallid. But his grip holds strong. "The great Elias Kent never kneels for anyone."

The bastard stumbles, crashing us into a cart of alcohol wipes and machinery. A cord rips free from the wall. One fiery spark leaps from the socket, and the world catches fire.

The flames spread, overtaking the cart as heat surges.

Sprinklers burst, inferno meets storm, and the world hisses.

"Kneel, Kent. Kneel, and I just might let her live."

Elias's gaze finds mine.

Once, he swore he'd never kneel again—not after being forced to his knees in the rain, not after begging for his family's lives and watching them die, anyway.

Kneeling was the one choice the world couldn't take from him. It was his last defense.

"No," I whisper. *Don't make him kneel.*

Elias's knees buckle in front of me.

No hesitation.

They hit the floor with a thud as water sheets down from the ceiling.

In an instant, time rewinds. Strains of "Für Elise" bloom in my mind.

Young Elise shielded a shivering Kian with her bright red umbrella.

Because she'd known then, somehow, he'd matter.

Grief guts my insides as I watch Elias sway on his knees, water drenching his hair, his face, soaking through his clothes. Blood streams from him onto the floor in crimson rivers.

He's kneeling once again.

For me.

To protect me.

"Elias," I sob. "Don't. Don't do this."

His riveting green eyes, dimmed as life ekes from him, snare on mine, the intensity searing into my heart.

"I was born to love you," he breathes, "and I will die to protect you. Nothing is more important than you, Lana. Pride. Life. Revenge. *Nothing.*"

"I love you," I whisper as Agron's arm crushes my windpipe. "I love you so much."

"How poetic." Agron sneers. "The great Elias Kent down on his knees for a woman. Pathetic—"

He lunges—

A blur. A roar.

Suddenly I'm ripped free and hurled against the wall.

Ren and Agron struggle. Guns fired, rounds spray through the air. Violence baptized in rain.

A gun clangs to the ground, skittering out of view. Agron drives punches into Ren's torso, sending him flying.

Then he raises his gun—

Bang!

Agron staggers, eyes wide. A harsh groan, a half gasp. He collapses onto the floor.

I turn.

Elias sprawls on the floor, a smoking gun slipping out of his grasp. His eyes roll back.

"No!" I scream, diving to him.

Agron wheezes in the background—footsteps pound closer.

Bang! Bang!

The shots stop me in my tracks, and I look up. Tristan stands over the bastard with a grim look on his face, a gun steady in his hand.

I gather Elias's lifeless body into my arms, his blood slicking my skin.

"Don't leave me," I whisper, kissing his hair. "We haven't been to Hollow Gardens together yet."

I look up, unseeing, and scream, "Where's the doctor?"

Footsteps thunder down the hallway—SWAT teams, stretchers, people in scrubs. Someone unleashes the fire extinguisher, and the hiss of foam devours the flames.

Hands tear at me, yanking me away from the man I love.

The hall is a storm, a shipwreck caught in a tempest.

Alarms, shouts, smell of smoke and iron.

Sprinklers drench my face, streaking my skin.

Ren lies unmoving, blood pooling under him. Beside him, a familiar man in green scrubs, blond hair coated in red.

Visions flash behind my eyelids. Kind smile. Soft eyes.

Blake Amscot, Aria's fiancé. He got caught in the crossfire.

"No," I gasp.

The trauma team swarms, barking orders, wheels screeching on flooded tiles as crash carts roll in.

Gunshots still ring in my ears, drowning out the dying beats of my heart and our unending melody, "Für Elise."

"Elias," I cry, reaching for him again.

But strong arms restrain me. I thrash, kick, and scream, grief tearing through me like a hurricane.

A small prick.

Then...darkness.

Chapter 60: WHOLE HEARTS

LANA

I PACE OUTSIDE HIS ICU room as the doctors complete their exams.

"Why aren't you inside?" a quiet voice murmurs.

I glance to my right as Sofia sidles up next to me, her head wrapped in a white bandage. Thankfully, she was only knocked unconscious and wasn't otherwise injured.

A whiff of vetiver laced with lavender hits my nose. She's wearing her brother's cologne.

"I didn't want to be in the way," I murmur, motioning to the team of five inside. "There are student doctors and everything. Dr. Hayden will debrief me once he's done."

My phone buzzes again. I ignore it.

I know it's probably Scarlett or my family. After the shootout yesterday, I called them so they would hear from me before they flew down themselves.

And sweet Aria, even amid her grief—Blake didn't make it—she came up and consoled me this morning. Part of me feels guilty for being relieved about Elias when she just lost everything.

The news cycle is vicious, the headlines wild. "Anderson Princess Crossed Paths with Mobster Husband," "Is It True Love if He Doesn't Die for You?"

I don't care anymore.

My body aches—bumps and bruises from the scuffle—but none of it matters. Not when the man inside has been unconscious since they wheeled him into surgery after the SWAT team took control of the scene.

"Gunshot wound to the chest, left side. Hypovolemic shock. Through and through lung shot."

Words I remember from nurses speaking in hushed tones.

The last twenty-four hours have been the most terrifying of my life.

"But we're lucky," as Dr. Hayden, the surgeon, said.

The bullet missed his heart and the major vessels. And because we were already in the hospital, they stabilized him fast.

He should wake up soon.

God, I miss his gravelly voice and brilliant green eyes.

I miss the way he calls me his *zemër*.

His heart.

A breath whispers from me as I take the music box out of my bag and flip it open. Dazzling red gems glimmer, a splash of color against the sterile white walls. "Für Elise" tinkles in the hallway.

"He finally gave it to you, huh?" Sofia comments.

I smile. "How long did he have it?"

She frowns, thinking.

"Decades. It was the first thing he got when he cashed in on a secret he overheard while working at a nightclub. Fake ID and all. So he was eighteen, maybe. Around that time."

Almost twenty years.

He's been carrying my dream all along.

Sofia traces a petal with her finger. "He'd never let me touch it. I knew then."

"Knew what?"

Her lips curve up, the smile transforming her normally reserved face. Hints of the exuberant little girl she once was shine through.

"You were it for him. He's never dated anyone else."

My heart skips a beat. "No one?"

I look through the viewing window at the doctors hovering over him. A man like Elias Kent, with his money, dangerous good looks, and power, should have no shortage of female attention.

"No. My brother acts like a cold-hearted bastard, but he's a secret romantic. Faithful and loyal, just like our dad."

Sofia squeezes my hand. "You stole his heart twenty years ago and never gave it back. But I don't think he'd have it any other way."

A knot forms in my throat. I press my palm to the glass, my breath fogging up the window.

Deep down, I know I waited for him too.

And now, I just need him to wake up.

I want to spend more Christmases with him.

"Not dead yet, huh?" a sardonic voice drawls from behind us.

A flash of silver twirled around knuckles. A perfectly pressed shirtsleeve.

"Reactions," Sofia mutters, elbowing Sebastian, who chuckles under his breath.

"Emotions are liabilities," the man mutters. "Look at you two pining over Romeo over there. Useless pining. He either lives or dies. My bet? He's fine. Surgery was successful. Two liters of blood loss but a transfusion fixed that. The damn scar from the bullet wound would probably make him look sexier."

Sebastian sneaks a glance at me, the arrogant smirk still on his lips. "There's no reason to worry. It's illogical."

Sofia rolls her eyes. "How did you get in? You aren't family."

The Irish mobster winks. "Lawyer. Professor. More accurately, a *mob* lawyer in Chicago. I can get in anywhere."

"Not worried your family will put two and two together and think you're working with Elias to overthrow them?" I straighten when I see the doctors gathering their things.

Checkup is done.

Sebastian whistles. "Queen of the underworld, all right. Playing chess beautifully."

"I had a good teacher," I murmur.

He leans in. "I told them I wanted to see if the Albanians pointed the finger at our family. Those slippery Berishas...half fleeing, half resisting. Zero strategy."

The last I heard, the remaining Berisha brothers have gone into hiding. They're no doubt afraid of the other families.

There's probably an extirpation with their names on it.

Dr. Hayden exits, and his team disperses.

I hold my breath.

"Mrs. Kent, his vitals are good. He's responding to external stimuli. We thought we'd need to intubate him longer, but he's breathing on his own. He should wake up soon." He scribbles some notes onto his clipboard.

Should being the operative word.

"Should he wake up, we'll keep him here for two to three days and then transfer him to a regular room for monitoring." The doctor caps his pen and smiles. "All things considered, your husband's a lucky man. It could've been much worse."

A heavy exhale escapes me. "Thank you."

Dr. Hayden nods and turns to leave.

But I stop him.

"Yes?" He arches his brow.

My voice trembles. "Our friend Ren...any updates? They wouldn't tell us anything. And he doesn't have family..."

Ren's technically a John Doe—no last name, no next of kin. He doesn't even carry an ID. They rushed him into surgery at the same time as Elias.

The doctor hesitates. "I can't share details since you aren't related. They're doing the best they can, and I think it's positive."

Without saying more, he pivots and strides away.

"Ren will live," Sebastian comments.

We whirl to him.

"And how do you know that?" Sofia asks.

The man twirls his penknife. "They told me."

"And why would they tell you and not us? You're not family." I cross my arms.

Another sardonic brow lift. "Mob. Lawyer." He smirks.

"And how do you think Ren got a heart transplant," he snaps his fingers, "just like that?"

I blink. Sofia's mouth drops open.

From the bits and pieces I gathered, Ren's heart gave up during surgery. It turned out he had a congenital issue all along and was on the transplant list, which explained his pills and his strange wheezing and chest-clutching these past few months. When Blake was declared brain dead from oxygen deprivation because the bullet severed his trachea, they had to act fast.

Because he was an organ donor.

"You think they just hand out hearts like candy?" Sebastian mutters. "There's a mile-long list. Tons of red tape. Ren wasn't even remotely at the top. But the massacre helped." He smirks.

"Sebastian McEntyre," Sofia whisper-shouts, "don't smile when you say 'massacre.'"

Sebastian's smirk vanishes. "Hospital was in lockdown. I came as soon as I heard. A heart's only good for a few hours, you know? A little leverage, a small threat here and there, and *boom!*"

He stiffens. Sofia freezes, her nostrils flaring.

The reason for the sudden solemnness hits me.

Boom.

Aleksei's word.

Their friend betrayed them. He fed Ren bad information about a conspiracy within The Six to kill Elias, which sent Ren on a hunt for clues while Elias was planning the hospital siege. Our best guess was, Aleksei thought Ren could thwart his misguided revenge plans.

And now, Aleksei vanished after trying to stop the events he'd started.

No one's heard from him since.

It must be heartbreaking to lose one of their own this way.

"Will you look for him?" I ask. "Aleksei, I mean."

The duo doesn't answer me, but I can tell they're conflicted.

"I'm a psychopath. I don't have feelings," Sebastian says. "So it doesn't matter to me. Aleksei's just another person passing through."

"Liar. You feel *something*," Sofia whispers. "Or else you wouldn't convince the hospital to give Ren the heart."

She nudges Sebastian, a soft smile curving her lips.

He scoffs. "Don't think too much of it. He's just more useful to me alive than dead."

Silence falls—heavy and suffocating.

My heart clamors to be beside its partner.

"Thanks for being here," I murmur. "I'm going inside. I want to be there when he wakes up."

And he will.

I have faith in him.

In us.

Chapter 61: A NEW LIFE

ELIAS

THE INCESSANT BRAGGING WAKES me up.

"Genius. Like I said, I'm a fucking genius. I knew the motherfucker had nine lives."

Sebastian snorts. "Rex, I think you should meet someone who also thinks he's a genius. Our hacker, Alek—Ow. What's that for?"

"We don't talk about him. He's dead to us." That's Sofia.

"If Elias doesn't die from the wounds, he'll die because of you guys." A deep, stern voice.

Maxwell.

My lips twitch, pain ricocheting up my spine as my eyes open.

Bright fluorescent lights sear into my pupils, and I wince. My instinct is to shut them, but I don't.

Because Lana's hovering above me.

Her beautiful, thick hair drapes over my face. She presses a soft kiss on my forehead, her roses wrapping my heart in a hug. A faint trace of smoke clings to her dark strands, a reminder we survived.

I inhale, my fingers flexing and curling over her hand on my blanket.

Her breath catches, and she freezes.

Her luminous gray eyes, framed by tear-tipped lashes, snare mine.

"Elias," she lets out a tremulous smile, the first rays of sun breaking through twilight, "you're awake."

"How long was I out?" I rasp, my throat aching and raw.

"Two days." Tears spill as she throws her arms around me. "Oh my God, you're finally awake. I was so scared."

"Lana, I can *never* leave you. Even if I die, I'll be haunting you the rest of your life."

She lets out a choked laugh and sob, pressing her forehead to mine, trembling against me. I shush her, smoothing her frail frame with my hand.

Too delicate—her ribs press against my fingertips.

When we get home, I'm feeding her properly. Then I'll haul her over my lap and—

I stiffen. *Home.*

Will she even want to go home with me?

Edon and Agron are dead—that much I remember. The others are probably scattered to the wind. She doesn't have the evidence that could take down The Association. And I took care of a big problem for Gabriel Caruso by taking out the Berishas.

The threat is gone.

Except for the biggest one—*me.*

"What?" Lana lifts her head, a furrow creasing her brows. "What are you thinking?"

I swallow, failing to dislodge the lump stuck in my throat. "I love you, Lana. I may be an unfeeling bastard, but I know this wasn't what you signed up for."

Her lips twitch, brow arched high.

"Fine. 'Signed up' may be stretching it." I lift my hand and trace her cheek, watching it bloom pink. "If you want to go home to your family..."

I draw in an inhale. "I won't stop you."

Her eyes flare and lips part in obvious shock. Then fury. Hurt.

Desperation surges as I press my lips to her ear. "But I'm a damn bastard, because I won't give up that easily—"

She shoves me back. A little growl rips out of her. "My home is with you! If you weren't recovering, I'd climb onto the bed and strangle you for saying that. Actually," her eyes narrow, "I might do that anyway. Because how *dare* you take the choice away from me *again*! Try that one more time and I'll chain you inside that dungeon of yours and show you what corporal punishment really means."

Warmth floods my veins, waking up all parts of me. I fail to bite back my smile.

My fierce, merciless queen.

"Really now," I rasp, gaze trailing over her soft skin, her pouty lips, the delectable swells of her chest straining against her thin shirt. "I won't mind."

"Oh, hell no!" Rex hollers, bolting out of his chair. "Not here for this. Definitely no sexy shit in front of me."

My gaze flicks to the audience at the foot of the bed.

Fuck.

Totally forgot they're here.

Ignoring them, I train my gaze back at Lana. "I'm sorry. I should've known better. You're the strongest person I know, and I love you and respect you. Will you continue being my wife?"

My *zemër* smiles, a devious glint in her eyes.

She drags her finger down my cheek, lingering on my scar like she's claiming it.

"Only if," she whispers, leaning close, "you let me climb you later."

"That's it." Rex mock scowls. "I'm texting the others that you are all fine and well..." He glares at me. "*...apparently*." He storms out, muttering obscenities.

Lana laughs.

Maxwell steps forward and clasps my shoulder. "Glad to see you're alive, my friend."

I freeze. "Am I...still?"

His throat works, gaze softening. "Definitely."

He nods at Sofia and Sebastian standing in the corner. Rafe pokes his head in.

"I'll leave you to reunite with your friends. They were worried," Maxwell murmurs, and leaves the room.

Rafe pulls up a chair, fingers tangled in his rosary. "I prayed for you."

My lips curve up. "I expect nothing less. Although I'm surprised it worked on me."

He rakes his fingers through his dark hair and smiles. "Prayers always work...even if not in the way you hoped for."

"Bloody hell, I'm not here for a sermon," Sebastian mutters. "Although with what happened in Sri Lanka—"

"We don't talk about Sri Lanka," Sofia smirks, "and you love Rafe for it."

"What's love?" The psychopath shrugs. "I don't want to kill him. I suppose that's a win."

Lana settles on my bed, her fingers lacing mine.

I shift closer, ignoring the pain spearing between my ribs. I need her to feel her warmth, her vitality—proof she's real, alive, and finally...mine.

"See what I had to deal with when you were out? Now that you're awake, they're yours. I need a nice long bath and a good book. Maybe one of Scarlett's magical drinks with chocolate."

I move to the side and pull her down next to me, savoring the perfect way she fits in my arms.

My *zemër.*

"I love you," I murmur, eyes feeling heavy.

The antiseptic air burns. The hum of the overhead lights reminds me of the sprinklers and smoke when I was bleeding out.

I thought I'd die. I thought Kian would never get to love his Elise again.

"I love you," I repeat, clutching her tighter, afraid I'll lose this feeling.

"We've lost the rook," Sebastian declares, shaking his head. "He's overcome with these...'emotions.' Tragic." He lifts his hand and walks out. "I'm checking on Ren. Be back later."

My chest tightens, gaze snapping to my sister's.

She gives me a sad smile. "He's in recovery. Agron shot him too. Long story, but he had a heart transplant after his ticker gave out. Surgery's successful, but we need to wait and see."

I nod, flashes of that day barreling into my mind, finishing the puzzle I was putting together before the blood loss rendered me unconscious.

Aleksei's betrayal. His attempt to stop Agron. Me taking the bullet meant for him. Him fleeing because I forgive him. Perhaps that's Lana's impact on my life.

Empathy.

Then I remember Ren storming in to save my life.

He must've discovered Aleksei's motives. That's why he was MIA.

"He'll recover," I murmur, voice thick. I can't lose anyone again. "He has to."

"Aria's fiancé." Lana's lips tremble, and she brushes the hair off my forehead. "Blake wasn't so lucky. He wrapped up a surgery and walked into a gunfight. He didn't make it. To think that could be you..."

"I'm here," I reassure her.

Someone knocks on the door, snaring our attention.

Navy suit. Perfectly combed hair. Brown eyes.

Tristan Clarke.

"You're alive and well," he murmurs, his gaze inscrutable.

Lana stands, fists clenched, ready to defend me with her bare hands. *My queen.*

"What are you doing here, Special Agent *Clarke*?" Sofia spits out and blocks the man from entering, her hand on his chest.

The FBI agent stiffens, gaze turning icy, and stares at my sister. "A little too familiar, aren't we? I could arrest you for assaulting a federal officer." He swipes her hand off his body.

"I'd like to see you try."

The tension crackles. The two eye each other with clear disdain and distrust.

"How can we help you, Tristan?" Lana plasters a smile on her face—ever the PR professional. "It's not the best time, as you can see—"

Another suit appears in the doorway—an older man with salt and pepper hair and a grim face. "Special Agent Clarke mentioned a confession," the man begins. "This better be good because you buried us in paperwork, Kent."

I arch my brow, my mind roving through the faces I've met over the years.

And it clicks.

"Deputy Director Ferguson," I murmur, "coming out of retirement? I thought you were above all of this...'noise.'"

The man scowls. We've had a few run-ins in the past. It didn't end well for him.

"I'm here to witness your downfall, Kent. Murder in broad daylight. Risky even for you."

Lana stiffens, her hands on her hips. "If this is *that* type of visit, you'll talk to our attorneys—"

"I just need a statement," Tristan cuts in, holding up a recorder. His jaw tics.

"Mr. Kent, why were you in the hospital to begin with?"

Lana starts to answer.

Tristan stops her. "The question's for Mr. Kent."

I growl, "Don't you disrespect my wife."

He ignores me. "Were Edon Berisha and his son responsible for the ambush?"

I freeze, gaze colliding with his cold ones and glance at Lana, who's frowning with obvious confusion.

"I shouldn't speak ill of the dead," I say. Where is he going with this?

"The cameras were blown, tapes destroyed. Three men died." Tristan moves toward me, his strides measured. "Deacon Rafe Mancini testified there was an honor walk, and you were there to pay respects. But the Berishas were also there, armed and ready. Was this an ambush?"

The room falls silent except for the beeping and hissing from the machinery. My gaze sweeps over the fed, taking in the stiffness in his frame, the hard glare in his eyes.

His fingers twitch. A tell. A sign of guilt.

"Yes," I murmur, "it was a well-coordinated ambush. Self-defense. Barely escaped with our lives."

"Hm." He clicks his recorder off and turns to his boss. "Consistent with Mancini's testimony."

Deputy Director Ferguson's gaze pinballs between the two of us. "This won't be our last visit."

He storms out.

Tristan lingers at the doorway, back facing us. "Get well soon, Kent."

He disappears.

I exhale, confusion swirling. Why did he help me?

It doesn't matter. It's all minuscule.

All that matters is I'm alive, and she's here with me.

Glancing at Lana, I find her looking at me, her eyes wide and trusting.

I lift our intertwined hands and press a soft kiss on her fingertips.

"I wouldn't change a thing," I whisper, "if it meant I get to keep you."

Moisture glistens in her eyes, and she stretches up and kisses me softly on my lips.

"You've never lost me, Elias," she breathes, "not for one second."

I smile, my heart thudding a slow and steady rhythm.

Underneath the pain, there's happiness.

Because with her...

I'm finally alive.

Epilogue: UMBRELLA KEPT

LANA

Three Months Later

THE COFFEE MACHINE AT Arcana & Bloom sputters, joining the soft rain tapping the awning outside.

Cece meows as she sits atop a cat perch overlooking the street. She's become a shared pet—staying in the shop for most of the week and coming home with me on the weekends. At first, I thought she'd hate it, but surprisingly—or not—she enjoys ruling over another territory.

"Ah, shit," Scarlett mutters, a frown creasing her forehead. She shakes the machine like it insulted her mother. Her thick red hair is twisted into a messy bun. "Why doesn't the instruction manual ever tell you what to do when this happens?"

"You know my answer." I smile into my cup containing her latest concoction.

The Blooming Heart.

Rose petals drift along the scarlet surface, the sweet floral scent mixing with the tart pomegranate juice and a hint of rich chocolate.

Whack!

The machine purrs back to life.

"Seriously? Really?" Scarlett snorts and shakes her head.

"Works every time," I tease, glancing at the cuckoo clock hammered to the wall—her newest prized treasure, a rare find, according to her.

Five minutes to ten.

My pulse flutters. Ren will pick me up soon to meet Elias for our date to celebrate our second marriage. We skipped the ceremony and went straight to the courthouse last week to re-register.

My overbearing husband still insists on a Syndicate escort anytime he's tied up with business.

"That smile on your face, ugh." Scarlett leans over the counter, laughter shining in her green eyes. "And to think how sad you looked when you first walked in. Married to a mobster, scared—"

"I told you the scary ones have the best stories."

Aria slides onto the stool next to me.

My heart squeezes painfully.

She looks like she's lost half her body weight. Dark circles rim her eyes. Her dark hair resembles a bird's nest. Her blue scrubs are wrinkled and stained.

She hasn't been sleeping. Or eating.

She hasn't been taking care of herself.

Blake would be crushed if he saw her like this.

"Aria," I wrap her in my arms, "I'm worried about you. You can't keep pulling these hours at the hospital. You need to rest—"

"I'll go crazy if I rest!"

She jerks back too fast, swiping at her wet cheeks.

Her bloodshot eyes meet mine, a ragged exhale escaping her lips. "I-I'm sorry. A tough day at work. Lost a patient. I shouldn't have—"

"No." I squeeze her hands. "Don't apologize. Grief takes time. All forms of it."

Scarlett and I exchange a look. She gently hands Aria a mug—something fragrant and soothing, I'm sure.

"If you need to talk—" Scarlett begins.

"I'm fine." Aria strains a smile. She rummages through her purse. "I'm a medical professional. Trust me, I know when to get help."

The bell over the door rings.

Ren strides in, footsteps silent and lethal.

Black half-mask. Black leather jacket. Black gloves. Black hair draped over his eyes. He's recovering well, although he's quieter than usual.

Ren's steps falter when he spots Aria.

She looks up.

For a moment, time stands still.

Pain crosses his dark eyes. A sharp hitch of breath. His hand trembles, slowly rising to his chest, over his sternum.

He curls his other hand into a fist at his side.

Aria slides off the stool, seemingly oblivious to the strange tension crackling through the air. She barely seems aware of her surroundings lately, a raft lost at sea after Blake died.

"I can't find my badge," she mutters. "Must've left it at work. I have to go back for it. Or report it missing."

Without waiting for a response, she brushes past a shell-shocked Ren—straight into the early summer rain.

She doesn't even have an umbrella or a jacket. Only grief.

"I'm going after her—" I tell Scarlett, grabbing my trusty red umbrella.

But when I turn back—

Ren's gone.

A black blur darts past the window, sprinting into the rain with a dark umbrella in hand.

And sitting on the counter near where he just stood—

Aria's hospital badge.

My chest twists as I glance out the windows, their shadows long gone.

He's been looking after her. The silent assassin.

Sometime later, the door swings open again.

"Can't rely on anyone anymore," Elias grumbles.

I turn.

He's dressed in his Shadow King attire—dark coat, three-piece gray suit completed with a green handkerchief tucked in the pocket. He rolls his silver lighter across his knuckles.

"Everything okay?" I ask, gathering my things, and wave to Scarlett, who's helping another customer.

Elias scowls at his cell phone.

"Ren had an emergency. He was supposed to pick you up. New heart. Completely unreliable."

My mind flickers back to the strange interaction—the pain and heartbreak in his eyes—and shake my head.

Unreliable or finding someone to care for?

I'm thinking too much.

"Shall we?" Elias asks, his eyes soft.

"Yes."

Fifteen minutes later, we share my red umbrella and walk through the wrought-iron gates to a place I haven't entered in years. But it's been waiting for us, waiting for the right time.

Hollow Gardens.

The rain softens into a silver mist, cleansing the world of soot and grime. Sunlight peeks out from the clouds, gilding the greenery and flowers in gold.

Elias peels off his leather gloves and stuffs them into his pocket. He laces his fingers with mine and stops us in front of our elm tree.

Piano notes drift in the air, and I look at him in surprise.

Beethoven's "Für Elise."

He smiles, holding up his phone. A lock of dark hair grazes his forehead, making him look younger.

Slowly, he drops to his knees.

A gasp tumbles out of me as I watch him pull out a small navy box.

He flips it open. Nestled in a bed of black velvet is a large emerald and ruby engagement ring.

A rose—just like our music box. But the emeralds? Just like the pendant around my neck.

"I was late in giving you this," he murmurs and takes my hand. "I thought I'd never have the chance."

"Elias," I breathe.

A soft smile ghosts his lips. Those brilliant eyes train on me. "Twenty years ago, I met a girl I knew I'd love for the rest of my life. I made a vow—only to kiss her in this lifetime. And the next."

My lips tremble as he slides the ring onto my finger above my wedding band.

"Thank you for making that wish come true." He presses a soft kiss on my fingertips, the heat searing deep into my soul. "You're the only person I'll ever kneel for."

"Elias," I launch myself at him, "I love you."

Deep chuckles reach my ears. He pulls us up, brushes the tears off my face and turns us to face the tree.

A cool breeze flutters its stately branches. A lark sings a beautiful melody nearby as orange butterflies cascade from the leaves.

"It's still here," I whisper, tracing the deep carvings we made as teenagers.

The letters are worn with age, but the bark still holds them protectively, like a witness that refuses to forget.

Our tree stood tall while life happened—tragedies, heartbreak, resurrection, and second chances—waiting for us to find each other again.

The sentiment we carved that day remains the same.

"Even if it wasn't," Elias murmurs, turning me to face him. "It'll always live here."

He takes my hand and presses it against his chest, letting me feel the steady, loyal beats of his heart.

Then, he takes out something small wrapped in foil from his pocket and hands it to me.

Geraldine's Chocolates. He's always given me a piece every time we visited the gardens.

"You remember the ritual," I whisper.

"I remember everything about you."

With my heart full, I unwrap the chocolate and plop it into my mouth.

Their champagne special edition flavor—the same flavor he gave me when we first arrived in Chicago after we got married.

"I should've known it was you then," I mutter.

Elias chuckles and cups my face reverently.

I think of the young girl at boarding school with dreams of a bright future with the boy from the wrong side of the tracks.

I think of the gentle boy with a kind heart who vowed to love her forever.

I think about my parents' photos—how they looked at each other like they were the answer they'd been searching for their entire lives.

The same way the man before me is looking at me now.

Elias Kent is and isn't Kian Leste.

He's still the king of the underworld, the dealer of secrets.

He's still in The Antihero Syndicate.

He's stepped away from The Association in a rare exception—something The Fifth weren't happy about.

But my husband's too dangerous to cross.

"The Carusos know what I did for them," Elias had said last month when I asked about The Association. "They owe me."

His phone buzzes. Elias takes it out, scans the screen, then frowns.

"Everything okay?" I ask.

"Gabriel Caruso wants a meeting. My guess is he wants to keep tabs on me."

"But I thought you were out."

Sliding his phone back into his pocket, he shakes his head. "There's no such thing as getting out of The Association. Unless you're in a body bag. Anything they say otherwise is BS."

"What are you going to do? The Berishas aren't a threat anymore, but the rest of them..."

His lips were set in a grim line. "They'll go down. That was The Syndicate oath. We won't rest until The Association is destroyed." A soft smile crests his lips. "Don't worry, Lana. It'll all be fine. We'll be fine."

The mysterious phantom has vanished, but my gut tells me this isn't the last we've heard from him. My family is safe. We're flying up to New York City to visit everyone tonight. The girls scheduled our much-postponed spa night. Rex mentioned a surprise with glee in his voice, and I must admit—dread mixes with excitement.

We are safe...

For now.

And that's the life I've accepted.

Safety is an illusion when you love someone like Elias.

Any moment may be our last.

But it's okay. There are no guarantees in life.

I'd rather have tiny moments with him than none at all.

Elias reaches into his coat pocket and pulls out an envelope. "For you. Something I've been holding onto for a long time. Read it on the flight to New York."

I grin, snatch the envelope from him, and hold it up toward the sky. A letter? Did he write me a love letter?

"No cheating." Elias chuckles. "Open it later."

"So mysterious."

"I love you, my Lana Elise," he murmurs, tipping my chin up. "You're my melody, my 'Für Elise.'"

A soft rainbow crystallizes in the pale-blue sky as the clouds yield to the sun.

"And you," I whisper, pulling him down by his lapels, "you're the music I've been searching for my entire life."

He kisses me, steadfast and eternal.

My heart blooms.

ALERT: Lots of Freebies and Bonus Scenes Below. Make sure to keep reading.

- **ONE LAST SECRET:** Want to know what Kian and Elise **carved into their tree**? Piece together the letters with a dot below them from the chapter titles for your answer.

- **UP NEXT: REN & ARIA.** Their forbidden masked-antihero bodyguard romance is next. Click here for **GUARDED IN DARKNESS:** https://geni.us/guardedindarkness

- **BONUS EPILOGUES (2 CHAPTERS):** Want to know what happens when Elias and Lana arrive in New York...and what Rex has up his sleeve? Click here and grab the **SWORN IN DECEIT BONUS EPILOGUE CHAPTERS**: https://www.victorialum.com/bonus

- **PAPERBACK-EXCLUSIVE BONUS EPILOGUE:** The letter Elias handed Lana—what's in it, and why didn't he give it to her back then? This angsty and heartrending exclusive epilogue is included in **all paperback editions.** For an extra-special printed letter of Lana's response (plus Elias's love notes back to her), those goodies are **only** included in the **SIGNED PAPERBACKS** here: https://www.victorialum.com/shop/p/swornindeceitsigned

- **PREQUEL SHORT STORY:** If you haven't already read it, there's a prequel short story of when Elias and Lana first met as adults a decade ago. Click here and grab the **SWORN IN DECEIT PREQUEL SHORT STORY**: https://www.victorialum.com/bonus

- **CURIOUS ABOUT MAXWELL?** Lana's older brother has an epic arranged marriage of his own. You can read the book here:

https://geni.us/whenheartssurrender

PAPERBACK EXCLUSIVE BONUS EPILOGUE

THE UNSENT LETTER

LANA

Present: On the jet en route to New York City after the epilogue

THE LETTER WEIGHS HEAVILY in my pocket.

"Can I open it now?" I ask.

"Yes." Elias's lips hitch up in a smile.

After taking out the letter, I smooth out the wrinkles on the envelope.

My too hot for his own good husband gets up from his seat, leans down, and presses as oft kiss on my cheek.

"I'll bein the back after you're done," he says.

Without another word, he disappears into the bedroom at the back of the jet.

Puzzled, I carefully open the envelope, pull out the carefully folded cream-colored sheet, and begin reading.

ELIAS

Past: February 28th, 5 Years Ago

She's so beautiful.

That's my first thought as I start the timer on my phone and stare at the screen in the dead center of my wall of monitors.

Whiskey in hand—I've given up on the tumbler and am drinking straight from the bottle—my gaze pins on Lana, who's grinning at Rex and Ethan as she stumbles inside The Orchid. Her hair piles high on her head, her luscious body clad in a slinky silver minidress, showcasing her curves.

She throws her head back in laughter, and I wish for the millionth time I had audio installed in my cameras.

That way, I can hear what she's saying. Why she's laughing. So I can hear the soft cadence of her breaths.

Instead, I set the whiskey down, grip my fountain pen, and finish scribbling down thoughts in a letter I'll never send. A letter to accompany the newest puzzle box I acquired on a trip to Tunisia last month.

"Happy birthday, *zemër*," I whisper to no one, my finger grazing the screen.

My vision doubles, and I reach for the bottle, finding it empty.

"F-Fuck."

Frustrated, I carefully fold the letter in half before sliding it into the envelope. She'll never read it, but still, it's for her, and my princess deserves the best, including a perfectly pressed letter.

I stumble upright, stuff the puzzle box and the letter into my jacket pocket, and curse myself for drinking so much.

Alcohol doesn't solve problems. It's a coward's way out.

But it was that or relive the flames from the night that took my parents and little Beatrice's lives.

Beatrice would've been a sophomore in high school this year if she hadn't died. I wonder what she'd be like. Happy and giggly, like the cute baby she was? Would I be fending off boys fawning over her?

The thoughts batter my mind, joining the drunken haze.

My gaze snaps back to the screen, taking in Lana, now sitting by herself inside The Menagerie, a cocktail lounge tucked away in the corner of a floor inside The Orchid. She plops a maraschino cherry into her mouth, a dreamy smile curving her lips.

Flames hit my body—I don't know if it's from the memories of the fire, the anger, the lust, and God forbid...love.

You hate her. You have to hate her.

I shove those thoughts away. My timer hasn't rung yet. Time's not up. I won't waste these precious minutes of what remains of my freedom.

Lana's gray eyes meet mine now, as if she can see me. My heart skitters, my lungs failing to work.

I fiddle with my lighter, a strange heat rushing up my body, spreading to my hands and fingers, overtaking every ounce of my brittle self-control.

And then—because I'm weak, because grief and yearning make cowards out of monsters—

By nightfall, a jet ride from Chicago to New York City later, I'm standing in front of The Orchid, the doorman opening the door. My hand fists my cell phone, the screen still showing the security feed of Lana, who's returned to The Menagerie after partying it up with her siblings and friends.

Like this morning, she's sitting at the bar table by herself.

Who is she waiting for? Why is she alone?

Is she waiting for me?

Ludicrous.

But like a weak man, I stagger inside, moving on autopilot, and soon I find myself inside the quaint little lounge.

Soft jazz music muffles the pounding of my heart and the scuffing of my shoes against the floor. Silverware clinks when I accidentally stumble into a table, my head pounding from the beginnings of a hangover.

But nothing matters.

Because ten steps in front of me is my *zemër*, looking ethereal with the warm shards of light glinting off her silver dress.

So close. A few steps closer and I can smell her sweet roses.

I can feel her soft skin through my gloves.

And maybe, if I'm lucky, she'll smile at me instead of her usual death glare because I'm the asshole Elias Kent she knows, not the sweet Kian Leste from her past.

As if she senses me approaching her, her head snaps my way. Her eyes widen, and those plush red lips part.

Blood shoots straight to my cock. I imagine those lips around it, sucking the life out of me.

And I hate myself for it.

I stifle a growl.

"Elias," she whispers. "What are you doing here?"

"Not your business now, is it?"

The glare is back, stronger than ever.

"Why are you always such an ass—and you smell like you showered with alcohol? Dude, are you drunk?"

"What, you've imagined me in the shower?" I chuckle, watching with fascination as her pulse hammers in her delicate neck. "Is the prim and proper Ms. Anderson even capable of such dirty thoughts?"

She blanches, and I lean closer, my eyes snagged on her lips. "What do I look like in your imagination?"

"Y-You asshole. I don't even know why I try—"

"Wet? Muscular?" My voice shakes as I sneak in a whiff. Sweet roses rush down my veins like a drug. "Are you imagining me with my hand around my cock?"

Her eyes dilate, but she slides off her chair. "I don't have to sit here and listen to this shit—"

I grab her wrist before she can flee.

"Don't," I murmur.

"Don't what?"

"Go."

A few beats of tense silence follow, and her gaze softens. "Is everything okay, Elias? Are *you* okay?"

I want to kiss you. I want to hold you in my arms. I want to worship you.

I want to whisk you away to somewhere we can forget who Lana Anderson and Elias Kent are. Somewhere happy and safe where Elise and Kian can exist.

But instead, I straighten and let go of her wrist, her heat still burning my leather-glove-clad fingertips.

"Happy birthday, Ms. Anderson," I say, watching her eyes widen in surprise. "Someone left this at the reception for you."

I reach inside my jacket pocket, my fingers brushing my letter, and pause for a second.

Then I push it aside to take out the puzzle box.

"No return address." I place the box in her hand and wrap her fingers around it.

Her throat works, confusion clear on her mesmerizing features.

"Don't drink too much." I step back, my fingers clenching into a fist. "The next asshole you encounter might not have as much self-control as me."

Without waiting for her response, I spin around and walk away, the letter burning a hole in my pocket.

LANA

Present: On the jet en route to New York City after the epilogue

Tears prickle my eyes as I reread the letter.

My Dear Elise,

I've often wondered why your favorite story is that of Hades and Persephone.

Was it fate? Was it an omen?

Should I have known then, on that rainy day when you shielded me with an umbrella, when every instinct told me we were doomed from the start, that I should've stayed away? Because I was tempting fate?

I don't know what I'm saying, but since you'll never read this, it doesn't matter anyway.

Today is your birthday, a day that has brought me so much happiness and also agonizing pain.

Today is the day I lost everything, the day my life became a living hell.

But it was also the day you were born, the day I got to steal some of the love I didn't deserve.

The day I tempted fate and lost.

I wish I could tell you who I am, that in these precious twenty-eight minutes each day, I'd relive every single second of our memories together, that those minutes were what I breathed for.

I wish I could tell you that a part of my soul died each time I became a bastard in front of you, each time I saw hurt in your eyes because you didn't understand why Elias Kent hated you.

I wish I could tell you I still collected Geraldine's chocolates every time I passed by a store, because it felt like something Kian would do. That when I bought the chocolates, only to throw them away later, I felt like I was still alive.

I wish I were strong enough to leave you. To stay away.

It's agony. It's torture. This feeling in my chest, this nightmare in my mind. It's a prison I can never escape.

And yet, if being in this prison meant I could still be by your side…

I don't think I'd ever leave, even if my jailer tossed me the key.

On this day, your birthday, in this letter, with a small shred of honesty I allow myself,

I wish you all the luck I have inside me.
All the joys, all the love.

I wish for you to have everything good.

And I wish you knew…I still love you.

Yours forever,

Kian

Swiping the tears away from my cheeks, I ask the flight attendant for a sheet of paper and a pen. Then I quickly scribble down my response and stuff it into the envelope along with his letter.

A tremor moves through me as I stride to the bedroom where Elias is, my feet not quick enough for my mind.

I need him, my husband.

I need to show him how much I love him. I need to tell him he's not alone. Never again.

Pushing open the door, I find him sitting on the bed, his head buried in his hands.

"Elias," I whisper, my voice thick.

He looks up, those brilliant green eyes brimming with unshed tears and so much love.

"I wish I had known back then. I wish I could take away all your pain." I kneel in front of him and cup his face.

"It doesn't matter. Everything in the past led me to you."

"But you shouldn't have been alone in all of this. God, you must've been so lonely—"

"Never." He grips my hand, his eyes fervent. "Because you were there. You didn't know who I really was, but you were there. You existed."

Slowly, he leans down and presses his next words directly onto my lips. "You gave Hades his happily ever after simply by existing."

"I love you, Elias. So, so much."

He groans and hauls me onto his lap. "I love you."

I put the envelope on the nightstand and kiss him back with everything I have.

Because from this day on, Elias will never be lonely.

Ever again.

Lana's *printed* written response to Elias's letter and his scribbles back to her are ***signed*** paperback exclusives available in my store: https://www.victorialum.com/shop/p/swornindeceitsigned

Thank You

I CAN'T BELIEVE THIS is book number eleven and the start of my third series, *The Antihero Syndicate.* Elias Kent's story is finally here, and I hope it is everything you were hoping for.

For those new to my world, Elias Kent first appeared off-page in *The Coldest Passion*, which is the second book of my debut series, *LA Hearts*. Then, he appeared on-page in *When Hearts Ignite*, the first book of *The Orchid* series. So, he's been living in my mind for a long time. And considering the many emails and messages I've received from you about him every time he's appeared (which is every single book in *The Orchid* series), I think it's safe to say he's captivated you as much as he captivated me.

Back when I first had the idea for his story—and for the ultimate bad guys, The Association—the world felt a little less chaotic. These days, I find myself craving heroes who, despite their antihero tendencies, have a strong moral backbone. They know right from wrong. They go after the monsters, no matter the odds.

I hope you enjoy seeing Elias, and later on his crew, kick ass.

As always, thank you to everyone who has supported me, in no particular order:

My family: I love you all so, so much. Without you, nothing I do has meaning.

My editors: Theresa Leigh and Amy Briggs, thank you for making me a better writer.

My proofreader: Thank you to Virginia Tesi Carey for being so flexible with my chaotic timelines and for being so diligent in your work.

My PAs: Thank you to Nikki Johnson, Christina, and Bre for keeping me on track. I know I'd be lost without you all.

My cover designer: LK Farlow of Y'All That Graphic, you always bring my visions to life. Thank you.

Ren Saliba: That cover photo. Whew! It's Elias come alive.

My beta readers: My huge beta team for Sworn in Deceit (Briana, Elsa, Brittni, Jessica, June, Malia, Jenn C., Sarah, Jess, Erin, Denny, and Alicia), and my beta team for the Sworn in Deceit Prequel Short Story (June, Jenn S., Angela, Kyla, Sherrece, and Jennifer)—thank you so much for beta reading, providing your insights, and being there to answer my follow up questions (which I always have many haha). Elias's book became even better because of you. I love you guys.

My ilLUMinati girls, ARC team, and street team: I'm eternally grateful for your friendship, support, and for all the fun messages, DMs, comments, and shares. Thank you for spreading the word about my stories. And Nesta the calico cat, thank you for being the inspiration for Cece. I'm requesting a paw print autograph, please.

My agent: Nikki Groom, thank you for reading the pages and loving them. I'm so glad I found you through Elias's story!

My fellow authors: Writing books is like raising children. It takes a tribe, and I'm glad to have so many of you in my corner.

PR firms: Thank you to The Author Agency, Lunar Literary Management, and Smuthood PR for your promotional efforts and for helping me get the word out!

My fellow readers: I love you all. Thank you for reading my stories and being on this wild journey with me. I appreciate each and every one of you.

With love,
Victoria

Also by Victoria Lum

CATCH UP ON VICTORIA'S backlist! Don't miss these swoony, romantic stories with all the sizzling spice and angst. All stories are standalones and can be read out of order.

LA Hearts:
The Sweetest Agony (James and Jess)
The Coldest Passion (Parker and Liz)
The Harshest Hope (Adrian and Emily)
The Brightest Spark (Jack and Sarah)

The Orchid:
When Hearts Ignite (Steven and Grace)
When Hearts Collide (Ryland and Millie)
When Hearts Surrender (Maxwell and Belle)
When Hearts Awaken (Charles and Taylor)
When Hearts Remember (Ethan and Alexis)
When Hearts Unravel (Rex and Olivia)

The Antihero Syndicate:
Sworn in Deceit (Elias and Lana)
Guarded in Darkness (Ren and Aria)

About the Author

Victoria Lum writes angsty, emotional romances that dive deep into the complexities of love and the human heart. She's the author of *The Antihero Syndicate*, *The Orchid*, and the *LA Hearts* series, which follow characters through love's twists and turns, secrets, and second chances. A true romantic at heart, Victoria loves crafting stories that resonate with readers who crave a mix of passion, tension, and genuine connection. When she's not writing, you can find her curled up with a caramel latte and a good book or spending time with her family in sunny California.

Keep in touch!
Sign up for her newsletter below:
Newsletter
Follow Victoria on social media:
Victoria Lum's Luminaries Facebook Group
Facebook Page
Instagram
Tiktok
Bookbub
Amazon
Goodreads
Scan the QR code below for all the links!